Goodbye Nightbird

Karen Diaz

authorHOUSE®

AuthorHouse™
1663 Liberty Drive
Bloomington, IN 47403
www.authorhouse.com
Phone: 1-800-839-8640

First published by AuthorHouse 10/27/2009

ISBN: 978-1-4490-0086-8 (e)
ISBN: 978-1-4490-0085-1 (sc)

Library of Congress Control Number: 2009908196

Printed in the United States of America
Bloomington, Indiana

This book is printed on acid-free paper.

Cover art illustration by Elmo. Graphic Design Layout by Lisa Galeazzi

Note from the Author

The characters in this book are fictional. Any resemblance to appearance, names or circumstances are merely coincidental, except for the band Vagrant Justice who are friends I intentionally honored by having them in my book. There are real cities and towns mentioned in this book, but most of the locations used are fragments of my crazy mind.

Within the vines of life there lies an immortal evil.
The Blood is the life and the game;
The Vampire waits, its agony will consume you.
And Angel is its name.

Thank You

Whit, Aida, Jimmy, Mamaw, Aunt Lorene and Aunt Mary, though you're gone, your memory still lives in my heart. Jes, Jackie and Tara, you are my light. My mother, Della for everything you've done over the years. For believing in me when no one else did. Angie McKaig and Pathway to Darkness, without you none of this would be possible. To Guttervamp, (aka Matt R. Jones, thanks for all the support my fellow weirdo. Tracey, who taught me how to plant corn. Bobby and Lisa Galeazzi for help with the cover and being great friends. Lottie, Kayla, Lisa, Janice, Robin and Debbie, some of the best bitches I've ever known. Everyone on the LA Guns message board. My Ink Link family. Torch and Single Cell for all the fun and opportunities. Shane, I couldn't have asked for a better Baby Daddy. Finally to Phil Lewis, the most beautiful vampire I've ever known.

FOREWORD

Vampira, eat your heart out.

If you're looking for the standard, cookie-cutter fanged female with long black hair, matching dress, and dreary outlook, you're in the wrong place. Solange is, in many ways, the quintessential vampiress, but in other ways, she stands in defiance of the archetype. She is the victim, but she's also the aggressor. She's an immoral monster, yet upholds her own code of honor. She's the heroine, but she's often the villain as well. She is her own worst enemy, and is also the person she can depend on the most. Sometimes you loathe her, sometimes you pity her. While she may be a living paradox, one thing that cannot be denied is that she's a survivor, much like her creator, one Karen Diaz.

I had the pleasure of meeting Karen through the now-defunct (but much-beloved in its day) L.A. Guns e-zine, *Electronic Gypsy* several years back, after she'd read a piece of my fiction posted within the virtual pages of the 'zine, and we hit it off extremely well, as we knew kindred spirits when we saw them. It didn't take long before we were exchanging e-mails, chatting online, and trading drafts and ideas back and forth as though we'd been friends for years instead of months. We dreamed together, bitched together, and laughed together, and it was many a time we both helped pick one another up when the going got tough . . . it was one of those friendships that was just a natural from the word go. She also served as an unending source of inspiration for me, and I can safely say that if she hadn't been there to encourage me a few times when I needed it the most, I'd probably be slaving away in some cubicle nowadays, wondering what might have been.

You see, when we made our acquaintance, I was still a very young pup in the game (still am, but I'm not quite as clumsy as I used to be), and Karen was an old dog (no offense!), salty and seasoned, trying to make her dreams become reality, despite the fact that life seemed to be making holding her back its personal mission. I got discouraged now and again, and there were times if I wondered I wasn't just chasing a chimera that I'd never catch, but every time I pondered if maybe I should just leave the writing thing as a hobby, I thought of Karen. She got rejected time and again, and she just gave them the finger and kept trying. People told her she'd never make anything of her writing, and she told them where to stick it. Her writing ability was insulted, "experienced" writers called her a hack, and they took every opportunity to tear her writing apart . . . she laughed at them and kept putting the pen to the paper, often with a good dose of venom and determination. No matter what happened, she never gave up . . . at times, she wondered if she'd ever get published, and even then she wouldn't stop. She was one of those types that would charge an entire army with a half-empty six-shooter and a pocketknife and never once flinch or back down . . . damn the torpedoes and full speed ahead. She was (and is) someone I looked up to a great deal, and her dogged stubbornness inspired me countless times . . . she refused to give up on her dreams; could I do anything less and still sleep at night? Not a chance.

Karen is living proof that if you try hard enough, love it enough, and *want* it bad enough, you can accomplish anything, no matter what anybody says or does to slow you down . . . surrender is for the weak, boys and girls, and the heroes never say die. The book you now hold in your hands is the result of her complete and utter refusal to give up no matter what, and it's a testament to the woman who created it. It may not be the fanciest, the prettiest, or the smartest vampire book ever written, but it's a strong, honest, heartfelt story shot from the hip, and if it's not dainty enough for you, go hang, because that's how it's gonna be. And if you don't like it, learn to live with it, because if Karen has her way, this will be far from the last time you hear from her!

Seems like it was just yesterday that Karen and I were joking back and forth over the electronic ether of the internet, telling one another that if we ever got published, she'd write the foreword for my book, and I'd write the one for hers . . . and as I write these words, I'm grinning, because we've both kept up our ends of that bargain. And it makes me wonder about what the future holds, because we've joked about getting together and making complete asses of ourselves at a stuffy awards ceremony held in our honor . . . who knows? But that's for later . . . what's important now is today, when Karen, after many frustrations, obstacles, and heartache, has finally made it to the dance and is standing tall, ready to show what she can do. Congratulations, my fellow weirdo, you did good.

Matt R. Jones

CHAPTER ONE

Goodbye, Nightbird

Opening night. The vampire stood next to a marble pillar, her auburn hair, brushed to a perfect sheen, veiled the left side of her angular face. Blue eyes glittered dangerously above the wine glass raised to her red lips. The burgundy wine tasted bland on her tongue despite its rich, full-bodied flavor, as was the case when she ate or drank things other than blood, but one had to fit in.

This was not her first opening night and would not be her last. Most she never attended, but tonight the owner of the gallery, Trina, had insisted. With the release of more and more new work, Solange grew ever more popular. The gallery, Night Expressions, featured vampire artists; of course, only the vampires knew that. So many of their kind had gathered in L.A. and many had found their way to Trina. She had created a haven for them and Solange had been among those lucky ones.

Trina stood talking with some aging businessmen, her blonde hair soft and alluring, even in the fluorescent light. Intoxicated by every movement of her svelte body, or her vampire eyes, the entranced men would leave tonight with a painting, minus a great deal of money. She never fed on customers, though they would have gladly offered.

Solange watched the crowd gathering in the gallery. Every weekend more and more people came to see her work. The actual variance in the people amazed her, and their reactions amused her.

Thoughts hurtled at her from their minds: awestruck and excited thoughts from young girls; critical analysis of shapes, colors and perspective from yuppie art critics; the best came from the outraged pillars of the community. Screaming about evil and the carnality that should be censored, while their minds were swirling pools of filth that rarely surpassed the imagery of her paintings.

Disgusted, she moved her focus from them to the young girls, whose eyes were focused on a painting of Dereck. Many portraits of him filled the gallery; all dark, all beautiful, all signed "Angel" in red paint. On a thirty-by-forty-inch canvas, a dragon of paper, cloth and sequins embraced Dereck Cliffe, lead singer of Nightbird. The incandescence of his pale skin shone from beneath his long, coal-black tresses: the perfect vampire.

"How they adore your lover," purred Trina in her ear. "Do you think it's that vampire charm or his handsome face?"

"I think it's both," Solange answered her friend. "It scares me sometimes, we're too much in the public eye." She took another drink of the wine. "Notoriety is a dangerous thing for our kind."

"He seems to be handling it well," smirked Trina. She nodded her head toward the entrance, where the glass doors had swung forward to admit a throng of girls. At the center of their attention was Dereck, his dark head bent as he signed autographs and whispered to his unsuspecting public. "But forget him for a moment, I have some business to discuss with you."

Solange followed her to the office in a back room of the gallery. Fliers pinned to the wall above the desk showed previous shows and artists, while small lights accented Trina's own work on an opposite wall. The blonde vampire opened a small book bound in blue leather and said, "I know you don't want to sell the portrait of Dereck and the dragon." She held up a hand to ward off a comment from Solange. "But a young man in Atlanta is offering me any price I want for it. When I told him it was not for sale he became even more insistent. I wish you would reconsider," said Trina, her eyes pleading.

"That painting belongs to Dereck. It is only hanging because he wanted it here. Offer him another piece."

"He wants other pieces too." Trina threw her hands emphatically in the air. "But he also insists on that one accompanying his purchases. Angel, a fan with lots money is a good thing."

"Too bad, you know I don't care about the money. You know that I have more money than I can spend in a lifetime, even one of our lifetimes. Tell him over my dead body." Solange made it clear that this conversation was finished, and Trina knew not to push her any further, as she had a horrible temper. "Well, I think it's about time to rescue Dereck from his adoring public." With this she walked out of the office.

She found him still surrounded by his squealing fans. As she approached, a thought tickled at her mind, a threat. Solange stopped and looked around for the human it came from. The mind seemed so familiar, like one that had followed her for many years; one she should have killed already. She searched for the familiar face in the crowd, but it was no longer there. Perhaps it had been only in her mind, perhaps she had become as paranoid as Dereck and Trina made her out to be. But one did not live as long as she had without some caution.

Solange focused her mind back on Dereck. Her long legs brought her quickly to his side. The crowd of girls backed away at her approach, partially because she commanded them to step aside. A brilliant smile greeted her lover, just before she took his arm and kissed him on the cheek. Dereck smiled down at her but reprimanded her for chasing away his fans. "Are your claws showing, luv?"

"No, my dear, just my heart. Can I help it if I don't share your love of being mobbed by pubescent humans?" She shrugged and said, "Besides I have a strange feeling about tonight. I picked up a thought in the crowd, a dangerous thought. But now it's gone."

Dereck raised an eyebrow at her. "Your vampire hunter again, my Angel? I saw no one here."

"How could you see anyone? You were too busy signing autographs." Solange pulled away from him. "And don't make light of the hunter, he's out there. He's insane, but he's still capable of finding us."

"She's right, you know." Trina had joined them in the gallery. "I've picked up thoughts and vibes from him. His mind is shielded, perhaps by the insanity. Anyway, there have been murders lately in the papers, humans found with stakes through their hearts and their heads cut off. It seems our hunter can't tell the difference. Everyone is always scanning for him at night. I can't believe you of all people, Dereck, have missed him. How did you live to be five hundred or so years old?"

"Please don't feed her paranoia, Trina. She thinks he's out for her, like a personal vendetta," Dereck grimaced.

"Stop calling me paranoid! A little cautious, maybe, but I know what I'm talking about. I'm the one he wants. I need to find him and kill him before anyone else gets staked." Frustrated, she turned away from Dereck and Trina, but he caught her arm.

"You're not going hunting for him tonight, I have other plans for you, my little painter." He pulled her back toward him, despite her protests (although she did not protest too much).

"And what might that be my favorite model?" Her voice showed little of the humor of her words.

"Just an evening alone. No paintings to sell, no fans, and especially no vampire hunters. Deal?" He smiled that innocent boyish smile that she could never say no to.

"Okay, but have you fed?" Solange inquired.

"I had a bite at the bar. What about you?" When she shook her head no, he asked, "Do you want me to get you a girl?" Her look of disgust reminded him they were not to her taste. "Oh, I forgot about your penchant for criminals."

"Don't worry about me, this wine took the edge off my hunger. Besides, I can always hunt later, if I'm still thirsty." They quickly said their good-byes to Trina and left the gallery.

In the back of Dereck's limousine they rode in silence to their mansion. They lived there along with twenty other vampires, including Trina. Surviving in modern times meant sticking together, and this home, this coven, offered them the protection they needed, and security systems functioned during the day to provide them with the safety to attain the sleep they required.

Despite this, they had safe houses across the city in case sunrise came upon them too quickly, but they rarely ever used them.

In their suite, Dereck and Solange entered a world unknown to many humans or vampires, together, sharing a need most vampires shunned. Both of them had been alone for hundreds of years but vowed never to be again. Love could not explain what existed between them, rather like a filling of a vast void. Neither past nor present existed at these times, just the sharing of body, blood and mind.

Their lovemaking crossed thresholds of tenderness and pain that only one of immortality could sustain. Passion built as her blood flowed into him from her nipple pierced by his sharp fangs. Over and over her body quaked as his cold seed washed into her icy womb. They became as one when at her peak she sank her needle teeth into his neck and nursed the nectar that she found there. The strongest, sweetest blood came from her own kind, and Dereck's was the strongest of the strong.

Even though his blood fed her it only enhanced her hunger, and as they lay in each other's arms, she knew she must hunt tonight. Only a kill would satisfy. Tonight there was food waiting for her and she could not wait for another night to kill.

Dereck knew she would go out; it stood strongly in her mind. He touched her face, seeing the desire that his lovemaking had fueled, not extinguished. "Your taste for death will get you in trouble one day, my angel."

"I only bring death to those that deserve it." This had always been her rationale. Unable to control herself when feeding, she learned long ago there is far less guilt when you kill a creature more evil than yourself. "I am very careful, luv." She kissed him.

"Well, do be very careful, you may meet up with your vampire hunter." She wished she could slap the smirk off his face.

"Laugh, go ahead, but he's out there, I feel it." She stood and slipped back into her black mini-dress. "I don't know if I'll make it back before sunrise, just might make use of one of the other houses."

"That's okay, will you take the car?" Dereck asked, his concern for her showing on his face.

"No, I can fly, and don't want to leave it parked where I'm going for a whole day. Kiss me again before I go, dear." She leaned forward and pressed her lips to his still-bloody mouth. And then she was gone.

On a street that seemed like the other side of the world she touched down. She did not know the name of this street but it ran parallel to the one where the safe house stood. After a while all their streets looked the same. She stood shivering with hunger on a darkly lit corner when a young man caught her eye. A Latino; oh how she loved their blood and the passion found there, it reminded her of the old world. Why it was missing from so many now she could not say. But to find one who was so full of this passion, and evil as well, brought an ecstasy she so rarely enjoyed. Solange caught his eye soon after she saw him.

He mistook her for a junkie, and out of the goodness of his heart offered her something to make her feel better. She allowed him to guide her to an abandoned building where they discussed payment for his drugs. In his mind, Solange saw she would need no money.

His hands touched her hair: he had never seen a junkie with hair so shiny before. Slowly he worked his way down to her arms and breasts, touching her roughly. When he pulled her to him, she struck. Her blood teeth fully extended and sank into his neck.

Blood spurted from the vein, filling her mouth and running down his back. The man could only moan as his life force drained out of him and into his vampire killer. Tinged with his passions, the blood pounded in Solange's head, leaving her senses reeling. So involved in her victim's last thoughts and the taste of his blood, she almost forgot sunrise. Leaving the man leaning against the wall in the decrepit building, she flew to the safe house.

Tonight she seemed to be the only vampire in residence. Alone, she went to a room and sank into a silk-lined box to protect her from any harmful sunlight. As sleep overcame her she sent out a thought to Dereck, *I love you.*

Across town Dereck received Solange's thought as he lay in his own coffin. Preparing himself for sleep, he did not pick up in the threat that waited outside the mansion's gates, a threat that Solange had feared for a long time. The vampire hunter had found their haven.

Joel Killian stood outside the gates of Dereck Cliffe's home with several gas cans at his feet, and there were more in his car. He waited for sunrise with great anticipation. They would be helpless then; at last he would have the ultimate revenge. He knew the rock singer was a vampire, he'd known it from the moment he'd seen him with her . . . Angel, his nemesis that had driven him to insanity. For years he had waited for the perfect time to destroy her, and because of her he now took on the job of vampire-killer. Tonight he would get them all.

As soon as the sun shone brightly in the morning sky, he started to work. Years of training in electrical service had prepared him for opening the gates, so that they swung open for him easily. Once inside, he fitted a sprayer to a gas can and began dousing everything close to the house. The smell almost overpowered him as it rained in a fine mist onto the walls. When two hours had passed, everything reeked of gas; Joel had been very busy indeed. All that was left to do was to ignite the fire.

Plastic explosives at strategic points, set to go off within seconds of each other, would start the fireworks. Nothing could survive that, not humans, and especially not vampires; those that weren't killed by the fire would be neatly finished off by the sun. Joel laughed to himself. It had taken him twenty years, but now Angel would pay.

He had driven six miles before the explosions went off. Fire-truck sirens wailed in the distance as they sped to save the house and its occupants. *Too late*, thought Joel gleefully, *too late*. He headed for his apartment so he could celebrate his victory. Yes, he had finally done it: he had killed Angel. He was Joel the vampire-hunter.

In her coffin in the safe house, Solange screamed in her sleep. She dreamt she was on fire. Burning, her skin sloughing away in the heat. Dereck's beautiful face melting below hair that flamed. Pain racked her body; her lungs drew their last breath, which was as hot as the mists of Hell. Soon all the visions stopped and peaceful slumber returned to her.

At sunset, she could not rise soon enough. She propelled herself through the air toward home, to Dereck. Upon landing she discovered only ashes and a few stone columns where her home should be, where Dereck should be. It had to be a dream! She was still sleeping at the safe house, surely! But the ashes felt too hot under her feet as she walked over them, the dust in the air thick with the smell of death. This was no dream.

Distraught, she searched through the ruins of the fire but found nothing. Tears streaked her face, as she searched for some sign of her friends, her lover. In a rage she tore down the yellow police tape surrounding what remained of the house. Outside the stone fence fans had already begun leaving flowers and poems to Dereck. Someone had left a newspaper that fluttered in the wind. Solange picked it up, and the damning headline read: DERECK CLIFFE DIES IN FIRE WITH ARTIST GIRLFRIEND.

The vampire hunter, he was responsible for this, she thought. She would hunt him down for this, make him suffer, torture him. Her anger overtook her as she planned his death. Then she looked around her, and her anger was replaced by grief: everyone was gone. Her Dereck was gone. She screamed until there was no more air in her lungs. For the first time in twenty years, Solange stood alone.

CHAPTER TWO

Starting Over

The night is a timeless designer. Earth sleeps innocently in her dark apparel while the creatures that belong to her walk naked in her trappings. Solange stood on her balcony; the breezes wrapped around her body like chiffon, ruffling her hair into a silky auburn plume on her head. She not only belonged to the night, Solange was its favorite model. Forever clothed in the designers' cloak of evil, she grieved.

The breezes that played in her auburn hair also swirled through the ivy growing on the opposite bank of the stream. Solange wanted to smile as she leaned over the railing into the moving blackness below her; but her heart wouldn't let her. In myth her kind could never cross moving water, much less stand over it enjoying its bubbling noise. This was her first full night in this place and perhaps she had chosen it for the irony. She felt a little source of happiness because the tired old myth was not so, for the sound of moving water always had a soothing effect upon her. It allowed her to relax and her mind to wander, and she needed that. She needed to relax, to calm herself. Rest would not come to her because her very sleep was plagued by the nightmares of her past. Without anyone to comfort her, the torture grew until her heart longed for death.

Oblivious to all around her, Solange drank in the night. Its power filled her body and she drew her breath from it. Misery filled every pore of her skin. What was night without the dark bird that sang for her? Empty; empty of hope and love, yet full of this aching loneliness. With eyes focused on nothing around but staring just the same, she saw the black tresses that she adored. Closing her eyes she heard the sultry voice whispering in her ear. The wind seemed to carry the scent of warm spring grass and spice, a smell that had clung to his pale skin, rising above the exotic aroma of his blood. If he could only share this night with her, happiness again would return to her.

Night in the South could be so beautiful. In the spring, warm breezes swept through the Magnolia and honeysuckle and were immeasurably sweetened by them. Reminiscent of genteel decades spent in frivolity. That was a time past as surely as the spring; autumn's crisp winds blew darkly colored leaves into the stream below her. Dead, so bright, so beautiful, one hardly thought of these ghosts of spring past as dead, so like her. Adrift in dark flowing waters, moving fast in the current and often trapped in still pools, brushing against rocks to find a way to continue the journey. A journey of unknown, perhaps a final rest on a muddy bank, rotting in the silt or continue on down this unending stream. Every hope she had of ever being human again, fled from her reality. Like the leaf she could never return to the tree from whence she came. Never again could she feel the life giving sun or wear the colors of light. What remained was a dark, burning hatred and lurking sadness in her heart. Perhaps that is why she came here, to revive that same spark of humanity in her monstrous soul. Even after two hundred years she longed for these things, especially now in the depths of her grief.

The South always had this effect on her perhaps it was the culture that was similar to hers. So many of the French had settled here. It evoked a longing for her people, her country, but especially her family. Things she could never return to. In life she had thought they meant nothing, even hated them for their ways, but in death none of that mattered. Emptiness filled her, leaving her susceptible to the whims of madness. All alone, Solange had ached to be human, or just to be with them. Hunger, raging and demanding, threatened to reveal her when mingling with them.

Smelling their sweet blood, pulses pounding in her ears, it drove her to near madness. The thought of drinking from them was inconceivable to her. It drove her out of the culture-rich South to any remote area she could run to. Leaving this place had caused her deep sadness, like leaving a dear friend. Wandering place to place she often returned to its beauty in her mind. This led her to be discontent with everywhere she chose to live, staying sometimes less than a year, except in LA.

For more than thirty years Solange had been in Los Angeles. The culture there had made a perfect backdrop for her kind. A world too caught up with their own lives to notice her strange habits. Rock 'n' roll on the Sunset Strip, where the "vampire look" was the norm. Feeding made easier by many people the world didn't want to know and had passed by. A place where so many were mad, one more made no difference. There she could be the wild, carefree spirit, the innocent, loving girl, or the jaded, guilt-ridden killer drowning in a whirlpool of depression. No one noticed at all. It had attracted significant numbers of her kind.

"Her kind," not since her beginning had she encountered more than a handful, but in LA, they thrived. A coven of sorts existed in LA when outsiders like her banded together out of loneliness. Solange blended into the strange group. For the first time in centuries she was not alone, but part of a family.

One dark songbird, Dereck, an English vampire, grew very fond of Solange. With his long dark tresses, glittering black eyes, and flawless pale flesh, he was archetype of the classic vampire, and much more. There had been no evil in him; Dereck never gave in to the dark side of their existence, never killed a victim. He would drain one girl just enough to satisfy himself temporarily, then find another girl. She could not always do that because her hunger was hard to control at times. There seemed to be a darkness in her sometimes that craved the killing, at the same time as guilt for the deed.

Carefully she would stalk her victims, choosing only those that had no soul, human or otherwise. Their existence seemed far more evil than hers. She could telepathically read their minds like a book. Their stories were pages with lines written in human misery. Vivid pictures of women and children suffering under the hands of these creatures, it unleashed her hunger upon them. It was the only way she could feed and not feel the deep bondage of guilt for the act.

Dereck helped Solange with her self-control, telling her how dangerous unchecked hunting could become. Some vampires were often careless, and that could carry a very heavy price. Many had to leave the city for that reason, bringing suspicious policeman too close to their existence. Since his death she had not cared who found her. Her victims' crimes become less and less; some of them were simply in the wrong place at the wrong time when she was angry. She welcomed all who sought her, though the creature she was would never surrender. Without him at her side, all things reeked of death. Even blood with its sweet elixir, grew tainted in her mouth. No longer satisfying her needs, more of the warm nourishment became required to survive the lonely nights.

There were groups of humans that watched them. She often felt them near, read their thoughts as they watched. Within the FBI was a group watching vampires, but never had they interfered with her. They just watched. Although at one point, Dereck even helped them with the capture of a rogue in their city. Why couldn't they just kill her, she thought. And for what purpose were they watching and waiting? There had been no sign of them since Dereck's death.

Dereck, although a musician had been down-to-earth and never flashy, even on stage his music made the statement, not him. Solange let his music enchant her. She painted him over and over. Never did she grow tired of capturing his sharp features on canvas. Cheekbones curving yet still masculine, aquiline nose, but a smile like a child's, he captured her heart. Just before dawn he would sit in their bedroom, while she painted him. Then they would make love. Solange had not let herself get this close to anyone in centuries; she had not dared. After the loss of her human fiancé centuries before, Solange feared intimacy with anyone. A fear that caused her more loneliness than she could bear at times. No matter how empty her heart was, the fear kept her from taking steps to end her torture. There had been many human lovers but most had also been victims and she never felt anything. With Dereck there was a familiarity, a trust that bound them in more than passion. She had let down her walls, opened her heart, and returned the love he had given. They had needed each other.

Many of the paintings she did of him sold and Solange grew very popular as a painter. In fact, her paintings had captured a following of admirers, perhaps because it was Dereck. Few women could resist Dereck Cliffe; lead singer of Nightbird. But good portions of her following were men. For a human this would have been wonderful; for a vampire it was dangerous. One human followed her, just a little too closely, someone who was not a fan, nor a friend, not even from the FBI, but an enemy nonetheless. It was an enemy that had stalked her for twenty years. For weeks she had felt her adversary close at hand, but when the moment of destruction came, no premonition could stop him. Far too late, she tried to warn Dereck.

The sorrow of knowing she was the cause of this beautiful creature's destruction tortured her. With him gone, emptiness filled her heart as a coldness swept through her. She showed no mercy to the criminals she killed. Solange's power of reasoning faded; many found guilty and sentenced to death. Her madness ran rampant, killing as she wished but she truly sought the vampire-killer.

She would hunt down this human for what he had done. His death would not be easy, but long and painful. Hatred burned in her heart that perhaps had been there for centuries, but had needed the proper accelerant to combust. She knew that wherever she went the human would follow. The trap just needed to be baited. Victims left for all to see would surely make the newspapers and her hunter would come. The vampire hunter, hah, he was not Van Helsing and this was not a Bram Stoker novel. This human had made life in LA unbearable for her, so she fled. Everything reminded her of her precious Dereck and their love.

That had brought her to Atlanta. Here while she sought a way out of the depression that had been hiding until Dereck's death, she prepared herself. She prepared for the death that the hunter may bring or the punishments she longed to give him. In the darkest depths of her soul she wanted to succumb to him, to sit quietly while he drove a stake into her and ended her lifetime of centuries. Wait for the welcome cold of his blade as it sliced through her neck. It would be over. But the vampire she was resisted death, creating pictures of the grisly demise of the hunter with maniacal glee. Torn between these feelings, part of her just wanted to run, start over and never look back. A new life in an old city, it could become a perfect backdrop for her melancholy.

Of course Atlanta was no longer the peaceful and elegant South she had known before, progress marches across every land. In fact the violence, crime, and corruption of a city like LA had taken a hold in this southern city. Gangs and racial conflicts flourished in some of the industrial districts. The city tried to hold on to its disappearing heritage, but it seemed only for tourism. Landmarks seemed only a thing of the past as the homeless slept in Margaret Mitchell's birthplace and Rich's downtown closed its doors for the last time. Though many protested and stood up to save both, progress marches on.

Her favorite spot in the city; Twin Oaks Cemetery was still there and had grown vast since her last stay here. It was one of the more elaborate burial spots in the city, built in 1850, although there had been other burials there before it became an official public property. A vast heritage existed there. A city of death built up in the Victorian Era, when death outweighed many things on people's importance. The more important the person was, the more elaborate and larger the burial marker. Solange loved these places, markers not of death but of people whose names lived only on cold slabs of stone. What was their favorite color? What was their favorite music? Those things cannot be translated into marble, and were forever lost. She knew, oh God she knew, she had seen so many buried beneath neatly engraved slabs of marble. At night in the cemetery she tried to remember these things, imagining the lives these people had lived. No one cared about them, no one save a lonely vampire to pay tribute.

It was beautiful to her. But its obelisks and angels were guarded only by a crumbling stonewall as industry and graffiti crept closer every day. Tonight she would go there to walk through its marble sentinels, drink in its quiet serenity. Solange would also hunt in the area tonight; the filth abounded in the area surrounding. The thought of someone spraying graffiti on such splendid statues and markers infuriated her. No, Atlanta was not the city she once loved and remembered. But now she would call it home.

A slight noise from her left caught Solange's attention. She turned to find an attractive young man staring at her. A young man whose beauty made Solange catch her breath. His eyes were blue as a still pond in the darkness, in the light they would be like the sky. Short blond hair carelessly framed his handsome face, and he had a body that stood strong and arrogant. That face was very familiar to her, but it could not be, for that face had died two hundred years before. She was unaware that he had been watching her for quite sometime, very dangerous to be unaware. "Hi," he tossed a cigarette into the water below. "I'm, Greg."

"I am Solange," she felt an age old hunger beat within her, her depression fading with the reverie he had interrupted.

"Angel of the sun," he said with a smile. Solange smiled back and arched an eyebrow at him.

"How did you know that?" She asked.

"I just read that somewhere," he shrugged. "So where are you from?"

"Los Angeles," Solange did not want to socialize with him too long, she had not fed yet this evening. Also the familiarity of this man was frightening. Feelings thought long dead inside of her beat with a new rhythm, threatening to become overwhelming. This was crazy, for he could not be the man she knew.

"Why did you come here?" he asked. "It's not as exciting as LA, I'm sure."

"Personal reasons. But exciting is not all it's cracked up to be. Eventually you tire of it."

"I guess I would," he leaned on the railing of the balcony. "I'm sure it's far less exciting now that you've left." Greg looked at her with a confident smile. Did women actually fall for lines that obvious? In his eye was also the ghost of remembered past, and it flitted across his face as she watched. She tried to read his mind but couldn't. "Solange you are very beautiful."

"Thank you, but you are a bit forward, Greg," her heart was pounding and her hunger rising. Desire, hunger and fear so strong they fought for control over her. He was trying to seduce her with no idea that he flirted with danger. She had to get away from him soon and feed. "It was really nice meeting you, but I have to go now," said Solange as she turned to go inside, Greg started to say something in protest, but she cut him short. "Really, I have to go." She slipped inside and shut the door.

After closing the heavy drapes she leaned against the wall, the hunger within her raging. Greg was so familiar to her and so delicious, but she must not feed on him. He stirred longings in her, disturbing longings. His face swirled in her mind like a mist or was it the face of someone from the past. They were the same, an uncanny resemblance in the face, the smile, even the name. No, she could not feed on him; it would bring her too much pain. The guilt for slaying the other had lasted two hundred years, could she add more to that and continue to live? And what of her Dereck, was he so easily forgotten? Shame built inside her for the desire that pounded in her. This man could not be food. There was other prey to be had this night. Solange slipped out the door, shrouded in the night in search of it.

Opting not to take her car, Solange took to the air. As her body lifted into the sky, her mood lifted with it. The depression on the balcony could have very well belonged to someone else, and a different vampire flew into the darkness, giddy with anticipation. Night winds carried her over highways lighted by pairs of headlights on moving cars, moving like tiny glowing insects toward some unknown nest. She sailed over the Tom Moreland Interchange, known fondly to natives as "Spaghetti Junction," flew over malls with emptying parking lots, for it soon would be ten 'o'clock. From her view from the sky she could see the figures on Stone Mountain: Confederate soldiers carved into the sheer stone face of the mountain, a reminder of the times when the proud soldiers marched the street, the beginning of the end for the genteel and rich South. This mountain now a park, Atlanta had turned its heritage into a trap for tourism. Fireworks and Lasers over the effigy of Robert E. Lee. Somehow it seemed wrong. Her destination tonight however, took her just short of the mountain, to last stop on MARTA's (Metropolitan Atlanta Rapid Transit System) East line, Avondale station. Flight took so much energy and hers grew weaker without feeding. Unnoticed, Solange slipped into the station and boarded the westbound train.

She made her way to an empty seat in the back of the car. Solange could feel the cold of the plastic seat on the back of her thighs through her jeans when she sat down, thanks to the powerful air conditioner blowing strongly throughout the entire train. This particular car was empty except for one old man who seemed totally unaware that he was even on the train. He slumped in the seat, going constantly between sleep and hallucinations. He meant no harm to anyone. She could relax. A loud beep announced the train's departure. Quietly it moved down the track toward town, passing clumps of trees, just blurs in the dark.

As they approached her stop row upon row of two story Victorian houses flashed by her window. Once this had been the finest neighborhood in Atlanta, now overrun with crime, drugs, and inevitable decay. Windows broken, paint peeling, junkies hidden within their abandoned hearts, withered, broken spinsters forgotten by the society that built them. Some had started to refurbish the grand old dames, but so much work would be needed to save them all. Sadness came over Solange as it always did when she witnessed the shameful way the human race treated their past. Tossing it aside, destroying it's very existence, perhaps to forget that their present would be the past soon enough. The knowledge that all will die is a powerful force that drives humankind, conscientiously or not. No one escaped death, eventually even the children of the night would succumb to death, even her precious Dereck.

Soon the houses gave way to a more industrial area, brick buildings with soot covered smokestacks, broken windows and graffiti sprayed walls. How many were abandoned, she could not guess, many surrounded by piles of old tires, broken bricks and concrete, and other assorted garbage. Solange had a feeling that even in daylight this place would be dark. No doubt rat infested, this area served as a breeding ground for filth, pollution, and depression. The sight of the degeneration of humankind sickened her.

On the edge of this decadence stood Twin Oaks Cemetery, Solange could see the glimpses of marble in the dark grass as the train passed above. Excitement filled her. She longed to walk the pathways between the resting places of Atlanta's past elite. Impatiently she waited for the train to come to a halt at King Memorial Station.

When the doors opened Solange moved down the aisle past the old man. She saw no malice in his mind just a deep sadness and an inability to cope, her heart ached for at times she too felt this same despair. Quickly she folded a bill, placed it in his hand and stepped out onto the platform. The old man dreamed of an angel, like so many of his dreams, he opened his eyes to find no one, but in his hand lay a twenty-dollar bill. He thanked God for his blessing tonight; he would not go to bed hungry.

Her feet made no sound as they crossed the concrete to the stairs. The cemetery was a quick walk from the station down Grant Street. Under an overpass she observed the creeping social decline of youth sprayed on the concrete, "Space Seed". Some local gang or band no doubt. It infuriated her. Destruction, no matter who called it art. Grant Street led silently to her destination, lined by deserted buildings like a ghost town. Solange walked into the empty parking lot next to the cemetery. Asphalt cracked in many small pieces; miraculously held together tentatively by a film of tar to make a jigsaw puzzle. In some places weeds and grass crept up through the cracks to split them further apart. Their dry brown blades grew rampant until the sun withered them in the day. Up ahead she saw the arch that led into Twin Oaks Cemetery, her passage blocked by heavy wrought iron gates, chained and padlocked. It was there to keep out vandals, but it wouldn't stop her. Tenderly she ran her hand over one of the stone pillars that held the arch. Rough and cold under her touch, she reveled in the feel of it.

A faint hissing noise distracted her. Turning to her left a young man had just begun to spray graffiti on the stones in the graveyard wall. Due to her silent approach the youth had not noticed her as of yet. Solange overcome with anger, started toward him. How dare he desecrate such a place? The sleeves of his plaid shirt rolled up to free his arms for the work, crouched down, he shook the can. He was having difficulty getting it to spray. Before he could resume his "art," Solange stopped him.

The boy turned to face her, startled because he had not heard her approach, but once he saw it was a woman, he only smiled. He stood up measuring about five foot six not very tall but extremely muscular. His skin golden brown, black hair in dread locks, a very striking young man, very handsome. However beauty could not outweigh the anger she felt in the young man, emanating from every pore, but that anger could not outweigh her own. It swirled around her head like a cloud of poison gas, forcing her closer to an attack. "How dare you, this is a sacred place!" she snarled, her voice a near-scream.

The youth just laughed, "Bitch, you got some nerve," he said and laughed again. "Not bad looking though," he moved a little closer, "Why don't you calm down, okay?"

His laughter spun in her head over and over like a fun house tape, her madness contorting it into something maniacal. That lean young face turned from dark to one pasty and freckled, to the face of the hunter. "You will kill no more," Solange stated flatly. All the while her hunger drummed heavily inside her mind.

"What? Are you nuts?" He stared at her with fear. "Hey look, sorry I painted on the rocks, okay?" the boy said backing away. He made a feeble attempt at cleaning off his artwork with his shirt. "See, I'll clean it up, no problems. I'll leave and you leave, no problems." The fear made him shake with every word.

Her mind heard nothing, only saw his face as the hunter's. Within a second she was upon him. The youth cried out, something in her heart made her ease up on him. But when she did he pulled a sharp knife; it glinted in the moonlight. "You dare to try and kill me as you killed my Dereck?" At last her anger and hunger drowned out any pity she had for the youth. Her sharp nails slashed his throat from ear to ear, done before he could even begin a scream. She drank from the warm fountain spurting from the gash in his neck, lost in the euphoria of feeding. When the initial surge slowed she sucked the wounds not wanting to waste a single drop. Drinking until no life leaked from the youth any longer. Gingerly, she wiped her mouth on a dry part of his shirt, so that no blood dripped from her face. Like a human with a raging fever, her body warmed by the life force that no longer belonged to the boy.

She walked to the wall, almost dizzy from the blood. Feeding offered so much power, particularly when the human was strong, and it sometimes overcame her. More euphoric than any drug sold on the street, blood fed her wild manic side. The killing fed the hatred built up in her. As the blood oozed out of her mouth, she shivered, not from cold but from orgasmic spasms that wracked her body. She sat staring at the beautiful boy; he was not evil, yet she had killed him. Her mind had not really seen him. In her passion, he was the hunter. How many times had she killed that face that haunted her, only to find another when she was done? Her heart wrenched with agony. Why did she have to exist this way? Why must she kill, could she not just taste and set free, much as Dereck had done? Solange begged God to hear her sorrow, to do something, send her to Hell, for that was truly where she belonged. No answer from the heavens, only the sobbing of one lone vampire in the night.

Reverently, she touched her fingers to the stonewall, and found that some of the paint had actually scarred the stone, what a pity. Maybe she could clean it off; she took the plaid shirt off the boy's body. Luckily the paint had not dried completely, she scrubbed the rock until very little paint remained. Satisfied she tossed the shirt back to its owner. Ashamed she thought of his family and if he would be missed. Grief was an unbearable thing. Regrettably the boy would still serve a purpose. The police would find his corpse here, and it would also bring reporters, which would in turn bring her vampire hunter. She left the body where it lay. Solange walked away her guilt and depression forgotten, for the moment.

Having fed Solange decided to take a stroll through the cemetery to relieve her of some of the sadness she felt this night. Easily she jumped the high stonewall, landing without a sound on the stone path below. It had grown vast in the years since she had visited Atlanta. She glided past marble markers, obelisks glowing in the moonlight, and statues deathly still, some so old the inscriptions were illegible. Her fingers glided over the weather-roughened stones, over names of people long turned to dust. Often she had the feeling of belonging when visiting this holy ground, but feelings of guilt for not being dust herself. These were the worthy ones, the people who lived and died normal human lives, never tainted with the evil that carried her for hundreds of years. They were not aware of how wonderful that was. Too often Solange had seen humans beg for immortal life. She wished many times she had never succumbed to its evil embraces. Hours passed as she walked through the dead city. Those feelings of guilt washed over now, just like the breezes that caressed her skin.

Something strange in the wind caught her attention. It was nothing Solange could see, hear, or smell. A tingling, electric sensation carried to her in the night. She recognized it: one of her own kind was near. Years ago she had learned to sense their presence, not all were as friendly as her consorts in Los Angeles. Cautiously, she turned around and scanned the cemetery. Her eyes found nothing; however, that did not mean no one was there. Vampires were masters of invisibility, after all, but she was not human prey and would not succumb so easily. It took an old and very cunning vampire to hide from Solange. Following the sensations that washed over her, she was drawn toward a mausoleum.

This was its sleeping place. The structure built during the nineteenth century; contained six family vaults, sconces in each one to be lit for mourning, angelic statues guarded the inhabitants rest, and an ornate iron gate locked with padlock and chain. The other had been here but now eluded her, still close but not in view. She walked around the structure, but there was nothing but the tingling sensation.

"Who are you?" Solange whispered, knowing one of her own would hear her. "Show yourself." She paused. No sound touched her ears, no one appeared in her sight. It unnerved her; only an ancient could escape her in this way, an ancient who did not want her aware of them. That deceit worried her, an ancient could destroy her if they wished. A few of her kind posed a danger to others, sometimes completely and unexplainably evil, or insane. She wondered if they could they be as insane as herself. Reaching out with her mind, she tried to feel some emotion from the being. Nothing, with such a strong mind-screen, there was any doubt that it was an ancient now. "Why do you hide from me?" No answer. "Do you wish me harm, ancient one?" No answer. "If so, why? Why worry yourself with one so insignificant?" Solange looked around again, her telepathic mind searching, again nothing. "I'm sorry if I hunted on your territory, but he was desecrating this place of rest, I could not allow that," spoken only with her mind, still no answer. "I will go now."

Solange did not walk back to the train station but flew. In a blink of an eye, her feet touched down silently upon the marble platform. Soon she realized that the station was closed. Feeding had given her a surplus of energy so she would be able to fly all the way home.

After Solange left the graveyard, the other vampire came out of hiding. He had meant her no harm, but was unwilling to reveal himself. Part of him longed to touch her hair, to kiss her full lips, but he dared not let her see him yet. It had been two hundred years since he had touched her last. He had waited that long, a few more nights would make no difference.

He walked to the body Solange had left outside the wall. The anger and strength she had possessed when killing this young human surprised him, for she had been a gentle loving creature before he changed her. What had gone awry? He would soon know. Although she had been unable to read his thoughts, some of hers had hit him like bullets, and he felt her biting anguish after that fit of vehement anger. Often he had seen such behavior in new vampires, but for Solange to have grief for so long was unusual. Immortal life had been hard for her and it was his fault. She had been forced to discover her powers and her weaknesses on her own. Now Dereck no longer cared for her and kept her safe. *My God, Solange, I didn't leave you willingly*, he thought.

He touched an ancient finger to the stone that she had so meticulously cleaned. Her anger had made her careless, and now he disposed of the body she had so thoughtlessly left behind. It seemed she wanted to be discovered . . . but why? It could not remain this close to his resting place, doubtfully anyone would think to look in the vault for the culprit but he could take no chances. Taking to the air with the corpse in his arms, the ancient one deposited the body in East Lake Park several miles away. There would be no suspicion cast near the cemetery. Feeling assured of this he returned to his territory, safe for now from human speculation and Solange's carelessness.

He would not let any harm come to his angel, it had taken him too long to find her. He still loved her, no matter what she had become. Without Dereck, she needed him more than ever and he would protect her. The dark-haired vampire withdrew into the cemetery, into the mausoleum, to wait with the dead for the oncoming dawn.

Solange would just make it home before sun up. Caught up in the mysterious presence she had let time slip away. Thoughts ran rampant in her head. This had been an unbelievable night. First, her neighbor had been the image of a human love she once had known. Coincidence or fate to run into a man resembling the one she had married and murdered? She still reeled from the feelings that flooded her when she saw him. Secondly, there was the disturbing presence in the cemetery to consider. Had it not wanted to harm her? If it had, why did it not do so? Perhaps it did not think her judgment on the youth fair, she did not. This night was not only unbelievable, but also quite disquieting. Was it not enough that Dereck's absence tortured her every living moment, she thought, to now have to relive the very thing that put her on the road to madness in the beginning?

Solange landed softly on her balcony just before dawn. Quietly slipping into her Apartment, she raced upstairs to her waiting chamber. Rest, she could not fight it much longer. She closed the lid on her coffin. How strange to sleep alone after all this time, Solange found herself reaching for Dereck before the sleep took hold. His strong arms had kept the dark nightmares and the madness that came with them at bay. But Dereck was dead and so was she until night awakened her, and he lived on only in her dreams.

Her sleep that day was disturbed with many dreams indeed, dreams of a life gone by, dreams of two hundred years of this existence. Only her mind stirred restlessly as her body lay still in her velvet lined sleeping chamber. Did a man who so resembled a lover long since turned to ash, or were they haunting reminders that she also should be at rest stir these visions? Never the less, as her hand reached for a man no longer there, her subconscious carried her years back to a time before this dark existence.

CHAPTER THREE

Dreams of Life

France, the year was seventeen hundred sixty-four, a time of courts and nobility, pre-revolution. It was a time of extreme indulgence and pageantry. A time of great musicians and artists, kept at court to please the nobility. Louis XV was in power and due to his ambivalence and frivolity had lost many a thing to the English. Silly alliances led on by his mistress had cost France dearly. The year before had marked the end of the Seven Year War by the signing of the Treaty of Paris, giving up French control of land in India and America. But aristocratic society continued on the destructive path of decadence that was its downfall.

It was a coming-out for Solange. It was her sixteenth birthday and her parents had a ball planned. Time to take her place in society, to be courted, and to be a lady. It had been so grand, her dress sewn of the finest satin, lace, and brocade. It's entirety adorned with layers of ribbons, pearls and gems. Mother had spared no expense. Tonight Solange would meet her husband to be, planned from her birth by her parents. Her groom-to-be was a prince from Prussia, Gregory something or other, and was probably a bore. But after conflict between countries during the war, the marriage of two powerful families would strengthen a bond between the powers. She did not look forward to this meeting with anticipation. Love, what about love, did no one of noble birth marry for love? According to her mother, no, that would come later. Solange did not think so.

That evening before formal introductions, Solange took a stroll in the gardens. Pouting is what her father called it. Always a world away, wandering in the night, and was very unladylike according to her mother. Constantly she dreamed of more, adventure, romance, and things common people were allowed. She hated the pageantry, longed to be free. A high intellect was not very well respected in a woman; unless by some act of god she was put into a position of power, and that was a very rare thing indeed. Solange continued to drift through the artistically trimmed hedges and archways until she came to the rose garden.

The evening was warm, but with slight breezes blowing through the roses and the white satin of her gown. Earlier she had bathed in water littered with their petals, their sweet fragrance intermingling with her own. She stopped to pick a yellow one, which were her favorite. As she snapped its sturdy stem a voice stopped her. "I don't think the owner of this garden would appreciate you breaking his flowers."

Solange turned to face a young man with sky blue eyes. His face was quite handsome, even if insolent. Blond hair framed his face and was pulled back with ribbon into a ponytail. She noted that his strong body was clothed in a uniform; from what country she did not know. The dark blue of the uniform deepened the color of his eyes to a hue of a Nordic pond at midnight.

His pale hair glinted as if made of the same gold of the many buttons on the frock coat. Solange could only imagine how brilliant it would be in the sun. The sun, a sight very rare in Paris, and something that made him all the more intriguing had bronzed the skin of his face. How wonderful he would look next to those fops at court with their powdered skin, already pale from blood letting. He wouldn't need the jewels they wore to shine. Despite her attraction Solange tried to appear indignant by adopting an aristocratic demeanor. But a flutter in her heart betrayed her cool. "This happens to be my garden, I shall pick what I like." Her gaze narrowed and her voice haughtily dismissed him, " And since when does a mere foot soldier dare to speak to an aristocrat." With this she had turned gracefully and walked with head held high into the house, shaking all the while. The soldier merely stood with a smile on his face.

Inside she watched her mother bustling around giving orders and feigning panic, as was her custom. Her mother's name was Celeste, the most beautiful woman in France, or so she thought. Celeste without question was beautiful; too many had told her so, and it had made her very vain. Hair of the purest gold and cerulean eyes had captivated many a gentleman at court.

According to her mother, Solange would never attain that, but we should always try. Always she had played second best to her mother's beauty. Watching Celeste preen, pamper herself, and flirt with everyone, sickened her at times. For what, other than to be a man's pawn at court, the lovely wife, complimenting her rich husband. Solange knew that by being born into nobility had doomed her to this fate. And tonight, at her debut it would begin.

"Solange, do hurry. They are ready to introduce you," Celeste clucked. "You do not want to be tardy the first time Gregory will see you do you? He must think his bride is perfect in every way."

"Oh, *Ma 'mere*, this is such a bore," Solange protested, knowing it would do her no good. Carefully she adjusted the powdered wig all young ladies were forced to wear in court. Silently she cursed the hated thing. Inside her head itched and sweat soaked her beautiful hair, one day if she had the power, no woman would have to wear such ludicrous things.

Once everything was in place and correctly powdered she regarded herself in a mirror. Pale from all the powder applied to her, but mother said color from the sun bespoke of peasantry. They had even wanted to bleed her earlier, but she would have no part of leeches. She walked like a lady toward the grand entrance hall, with her mother one step behind her. Just before she entered the ballroom, a gentleman announced her as a debutante.

"*Mademoiselle Solange De Mont Mollian*, daughter of Lord and Lady Mollian, of Paris." Solange glided onto the top step that led into the ballroom and curtsied. Applause filled her ears as she descended the three circular steps into the ballroom. As she made her way across the crowded space, guests moved aside, ladies curtsying, and gentleman bowing. Solange nodded to all. At the other end of the ballroom, her mother waited. Hers was the first dance and it would be with Gregor, her future husband. He stood next to her mother, an insolent smile on his handsome face, wearing a deep blue soldiers uniform.

"Solange, I would like to introduce you to Prince Gregor of Prussia. Your fiancé." Her mother smiled that glass smile that was befitting of her.

"*Enchante, Mademoiselle.*" He bent to kiss her hand. Then he led her to the center of the dance floor by her hand and they began to dance. Her hand in his felt warm, her breasts crushed against him far too tightly. For along time he let her burn in quiet humiliation. Solange's eyes searched the room frantically, not wanting to meet his, knowing he could feel the shame echoing in their azure depths. Finally, he smiled and said, "It is a lovely evening for a walk in the garden."

"I apologize, I did not know who you were," Solange said, her cheeks aflame. "I was very rude."

"My apologies, how could I know the beautiful girl in the garden was my fiancé," he said nonchalantly. "You spoke to me as any aristocrat would to a foot soldier, I am humbled in your presence, *Mademoiselle.*" Solange looked up at him, he didn't look humble. Smiling so arrogantly, he wasn't the bore she thought he would be, and quite handsome too. Blue eyes so deep, she could drown in them if she allowed herself. Yes she could grow to like this man.

They talked for hours about his family and her own. Cultures so different, yet so alike. His mother was French by descent, aristocratic through and through, stuffy just like her own mother. Of course, the two elder women were best friends, and that came as no surprise to Solange; only someone like that could be friends with her mother. On the other hand his father was very sensible, in fact that was why Gregor wore a soldier's uniform. It had been family tradition that every male join the military.

Good leadership qualities developed from the experience. Gregor did not believe so. His father insisted on him starting at the lowest rank and he must earn his way to an officer. At a very young age he had fought many battles against Austria's armies. He would be a foot soldier for a few more years. They would not marry until he finished his tour of duty, then he could claim his rightful title.

They danced and discussed everything possible the rest of the evening. This joining of two families would not be as difficult as both had believed. They would grow very fond of each other, building a friendship that would last forever, or so they thought.

CHAPTER FOUR

One Day Too Late

"**D**amn!" The girl screamed in fury at the box, slamming it down in front of her. The metal box screeched as it bent from pressure from the screwdriver in her hand. The sound only added to the frustration of the last hour, which had entailed hammering, prying, and throwing, anything that could be done to open this box. The stale, hot air burned at her throat and the rickety old fan barely cooled her sweaty skin. Fingers went to eyes and rubbed away black smudges from the make-up on them. Turning, she looked in the mirror above the cheap dresser and saw black tear-trails streaking down sharp cheekbones. Gray eyes glittered back from the dark sockets in the angular face and she thought, *Sijn, you look like hell.*

With one hand she grabbed her shoulder-length hair and twisted it up on top of her head and secured it with a pick held in the other hand. That felt much better, but already the girl could feel damp, black tendrils of hair sticking to her neck. Fat drops of perspiration ran down the center of her back, leaving a damp spot on the back of the black panties she wore. Pressing a cold soda to her face, Sijn leaned down in front of the fan, letting the breeze wash over naked flesh.

As Sijn took a long-needed break, the phone on the dresser called to her. Someone needed to know where she was, and thoughts ran through her mind of who to call. There was no job to report to, as that had ended over a month ago when she had skipped out to meet Dereck. Good riddance, who wanted to work in the yarn mill the rest of their life, anyway? Every day the misery of lint in your hair and eyes or thread wrapping around your fingers, cutting the flesh. The piddling six dollars an hour did not compensate for that.

Her parents, she didn't want to call them, and they probably didn't even know Sijn was gone. She looked at the phone and then looked at the money left. The sad array of crumpled bills made her decision. Quickly, she dialed the number at her brother's trailer, hoping he would answer. His girlfriend never really liked Sijn and would not accept the charges.

The operator's mechanical voice announced, *"ATT, can I help you?"*

"Collect call from Sijn," the girl waited for her to get approval. Daryl's deep voice answered, *"Your dime go ahead."* Normally she would have laughed: her brother, the redneck comedian. His friends called him Red Dawg, not only for his strawberry hair and freckles but also for the beer he put away like water. He accepted the call. *"Sijn, where th' hell 'er ya?"* he yelled into the phone.

"Dawg, don't bitch okay? I'm in Cali," Sijn said, waiting for the next explosion.

"Shit! How'd ya git th' money to git out thar?" he asked. *"Damn, momma an' nyms been lookin' everyware fer ya. Found out ya' lost ya' job and they ain't happy."*

"Yeah right, look Dawg ya gotta help me okay?" Sijn pleaded, her voice wavering as tears started flowing down her face again. "I sold my car to get out here, only four hundred dollars. Most of that was spent on the bus ticket. Had to sit next to this Jehovah's Witness the whole way. Believe me there's nothing like listening to that crap and smelling body odor for four days." She felt the laughter coming up despite the tears. Obviously Dawg thought it was funny, too: his deep belly laugh rumbled in her ear.

"Won't that hippie help ya'? I mean ya' told him ya' was knocked-up right?" he asked.

Tears ran faster down her face as sobs wracked her body. "He's dead, Dawg, I got here and he was dead!" Sijn cried.

"*Dead? Calm down Sijn an' tell me what happened.*" Dawg sounded concerned and she knew he cared despite his roughness.

"Well," Sijn took a deep breath, "When I got off the bus, I hitched over as far as I could to where they lived. The streets were full of people, police cars, ambulances, and fire trucks. They had the place barricaded off and there was smoke all in the air. I pushed my way through the crowd so I could find out what was going on. Some asshole burnt his house down. Dawg, I got sick, I really did." The crying grew louder as she told her brother the story. Words poured out of her mouth, running together in frenzy. "They kept bringing out stretchers, but only with bags on them instead of people. I waited, hoping to see Dereck and know he was okay, but all I saw were those damned bags." Sijn had to stop; the grief overtook her and she wailed into the phone, hands on her face.

"*Oh shit, Sijn, stop cryin' and tell me the rest. I can't help ya if I don' know,*" he said and waited for her to continue.

"They said nobody lived, Dawg, nobody! For hours I stood there waiting. Even after people started to leave, I stood there. 'Fore it got dark I decided I wasn't leaving empty-handed. When nobody was looking I slipped under the yellow tape and started looking around. Nobody saw me at first." Sijn stopped talking, and loud, ragged sighs passed through her lips, blowing noisily into the phone.

"*Ya' got busted didn't ya?*" he asked. "*Do ya need money for bail?*"

"No, I'm in my motel room," Sijn explained. "I had just spotted this metal box when a cop spotted me. Without thinking I wrapped it in my leather jacket and ran like hell. My feet moved faster than they ever had before, and the fat bastard couldn't catch me, just yelled and turned back."

"What's in the box?" Dawg asked.

"Hell, I don't know, can't get it open, been trying for hours," she said. "Stole a screwdriver and hammer from the maintenance guy here at the motel, and I've been working on it since then."

"*So you ain't got no money?*" It sounded more of a statement than a question.

"Not enough to get home on," Sijn told him. "Do you think you and Dena can send me some? Just enough to get home. I didn't want to ask Momma."

"I don't know, she's up at her daddy's right now," Dawg sighed into the phone. "She's gonna pop any day now an' she's kinda testy." Dena was ready to pop every nine months, that's why he never had any money. "I'll see what I kin do, ware ya at in Cali anyway?"

"A little motel in Hollywood," she said. "Do they know I'm pregnant yet?"

"Naw, I figured you'd tell'm when ya' wanted to," Dawg said. *"I'll git ya the money. Shit, I won't have a guitar player if I don't."* They played in a band together back home, nothing big-time just some rock covers and a few originals. Music was something they had always shared, her only family.

"I wish I'd brought my guitar with me, but I wanted to travel light. Man, if I could play right now I'd feel much better," Sijn confessed, her voice not quivering as bad as before. With trembling fingers she reached for her Marlboros. Once lit, the cigarette helped calm her; too bad she had to quit.

"I'm taking care of ya' baby. Brought it and ya amp up from the house, don't want nobody tryin' to pawn it or nothin'," he explained.

"Thanks, Dawg, I love ya."

"Well, ain't no big deal. Jus' hurry home, Danny's fillin' in fer ya' but he can't play them Who songs like you can," Dawg told her. *"He ain't nowhere near as purty neither."*

"I'll call ya' tomorrow, let me get this box open and wait for you to wire some money, okay?"

"Be careful, ya' hear me?" he demanded. *"I'll send some money tomorrow. Bye."*

"Bye, thanks," she said and hung up the phone. The cigarette had burned down to the filter and Sijn put it out in the cheap plastic ashtray. Back to the box, screwdriver in hand. She pushed the flathead screwdriver into the opening already made and struck the end with the hammer. It moved a little bit. Her hand worked the tool back and forth hard as she could, making the gap in the front even wider. Now the end of the screwdriver could be worked into the lock mechanism. Once in place, Sijn swung the hammer with all her strength and the lock gave a loud click. One more blow and it the box flew open; its contents scattered on the bed.

Her chest heaving and breathing ragged, Sijn reached for the first item from the box. Her fingers held a thick piece of linen paper, folded and sealed with wax. How strange, how odd, did people still do that? The wax gave way, leaving a red stain on the crisp beige paper. Opened, Sijn could see it was dated the day before the fire and was written in flowing script. Dereck's handwriting; addressed to Solange, his lover before he died. Curiosity overtook her, and she read what was never meant for anyone but a dead woman to see. With Solange dead, it didn't seem to matter.

My Dearest Solange,

If you are reading this now, I am dead. For weeks I have felt the approaching time of my end. I am unsure of how it will find me but nevertheless it comes. This hunter you have feared so much, he may be the instrument of my demise. Despite what I have told you, I have felt him near but wished to shield you. The anger that beats so strongly in your heart worries me and he is the one to bring it forth.

Soon you will be alone again, my angel, and for this I am truly sorry. For years we have lived in our safe, perfect world, and I fear for you on your own. Your anger and bitterness threaten your existence more than the hunter. Promise me that you will not seek vengeance with this destroyer, start over and find happiness.

I have made arrangements for you, even though you have your own means. A key in this box opens a storage building that contains a new identity for you as well as my diary. It would reveal what we are if anyone else found it so I have entrusted it to you, luv. Take it, guard and cherish it forever.

There is a place for you to go, a friend, and though she is mortal she will help you. She knows what we are and accepts that. You met her briefly; she is the author Shana Collins. I have her promise to offer you shelter as long as you desire. Go to her, Solange.

Now as I sit here alone, waiting for your return I know that you will be too late. Our last night together was cherished more than anything in my five hundred years on this earth. I love you, never forget that. My beautiful angel of darkness, you have brought more light to my existence than any sun ever could. I bid you farewell.

Your love,
Dereck

Sijn watched the ink run as her tears fell onto the paper, leaving purple blotches. *My God, how he had loved her and I would have ruined that by showing up here,* she thought. Her guilt soon turned to intrigue as she considered Dereck's words. Hunter? The question formed in her mind followed by other words from the letter: mortal, five hundred years? Was he insane? Or something else?

And what did Shana have to do with this? The woman lived in Sijn's hometown, in that big old house on Main Street, and was a well-known writer. Then something clicked in her mind, and she remembered that Shana was not only a writer, but also a vampire writer. *She knows what we are,* the letter had stated, and those words stuck in her head.

She looked down at the box on the bed and saw papers with the address of the storage building on it and a key ring. On the ring was one big key accompanied by several smaller keys, like the ones that come with luggage or go to a desk. Sijn picked it up and stared at it. The key holds the answer, another box to open. She grabbed her jeans and started wiggling into them. Sijn damn sure couldn't go down there in her underwear.

CHAPTER FIVE

The Hunt

An inner alarm awakened Solange from her daily sleep: dusk, its approach triggering her to instinctively stir to life. As the last rays slipped over the horizon she opened the case where she slept on a bed of black velvet. Hunger raged through her on this night, and she knew that she must feed early. She rose and walked across the room to her closet. Hunting required special clothes for her, to blend in with the low-life she fed upon; she sometimes appeared as innocent and vulnerable as possible, other times extremely provocative. Tonight a strapless black mini-dress would be her choice, along with fishnet hose rolled up her legs and snapped to garters. Spiked black heels completed the ensemble.

Solange took a long look in the mirror, another myth, she thought. She needed no base make-up these days, as so many human girls had the pale look. She used lots of black eyeliner and mascara, but her crimson lips needed no enhancement. Her blue eyes still looked young and innocent despite her many years, belying what lay behind them. Only Solange knew of the carnage these eyes had seen; carnage she participated in and initiated. Shame and guilt often plagued her, but centuries had a way of hardening one to death. For Solange, dealing death was the basis of her survival. On many instances she tried not to kill, but the hunger was too strong. Vagrants, more often than not, were her victims or otherwise thieves, rapists, murderers, and others that deserved a death the law would never deal them. Her thoughts were of the many helpless who could not defend themselves, the ones the law never protected. Solange had appointed herself their defender, to use her uncontrollable hunger against the evil ones. This same hunger drove her out tonight.

She glided down the stairs of her darkened apartment, and with purse and keys in hand, Solange began her hunt. She walked toward her car looking every bit the lady of the night, but halfway there a voice stopped her. "Hi." Solange turned to see her neighbor going into his apartment. "Would you like to come in for a beer?"

"Well, I was on my way somewhere." She could smell his blood even from this distance. *Oh God, please don't let me lose control.* Her desire for him was very strong, and served to fuel her hunger. Solange could not bear to be near him now.

"I'll be around later if you change your mind. Just knock on the door when you get back," he said with a smile. Arrogant, but God, was he beautiful. She would never let him know what she was. "I like the dress, very hot."

Solange would have blushed if she could have: she had forgotten she was dressed like a hooker. "Thanks, I'll see you later, maybe." She waved and got into her car, hunger roaring in her like some fierce beast. She still smelled his blood, or perhaps her craving led her to believe so. He was so like Gregor, and it haunted her. The tires squealed as she abruptly pulled out of the parking lot, the craving forcing her to speed away, unable to control it, but she must not hunt near home.

Her car pulled into a dimly-lit street on the southeast side of town. It cruised along slowly, like a mist rolling from the sea, and through the tinted windows Solange looked for a victim.

Here the crime ran rampant, the Atlanta police unable to protect the poor that were forced to live here. Gangs roamed the streets, some of their members not more than twelve years old, and in a way they were more of a victim than the people they committed crimes against. Sympathy, however, needed to be left behind tonight, as only hatred could guide her to feed. Often there was a conflict of good and evil in some of her victims, like the boy the night before; those kills caused her great sorrow and she avoided that type of kill if possible.

She spotted several young men, but all were in groups. Her car continued to roll down the street, and after a time, she noticed a car following her. *Perhaps*, she thought, a brief smile coming to her lips, *perhaps*. Solange turned onto Moreland Avenue and felt a triumphant chill when the old Camaro turned behind her. She moved ahead faster and the Camaro kept pace, definitely intent upon her. Judging by the shadow in the car, he was alone. At the next intersection her pursuer pulled alongside. Solange partially rolled down her window and looked over.

A man in his late twenties sat in the Camaro, leering at her across the gap between cars. The malevolent look on his face made her want to rip his head off . . . and she would. His greasy, brown hair hung in long lengths around his pockmarked face. Some women would have been attracted, as he had what was called rugged looks. The man looked as rough as the life he most likely led. Solange smiled at him. "Hey baby do ya' wanna race?" he asked. His voice was as deep and rough as his looks, accented by a Southern drawl.

"No, I'd rather go for a ride," Solange purred suggestively. She cast a seductive look at him through the window. His thoughts were strong, uncomfortably loud in her mind. Rapist, the man was a rapist. Images seared her brain of women tortured, then left naked and crying. She wanted to cry for them, but could only avenge them. Tonight the man planned to make a leap to murderer. His hatred fueled her own.

"What kinda ride you lookin' for baby?" Now the disgusting bastard was rubbing his crotch and practically drooling. It was going to be so easy.

"A rough one, can you handle it?" She smiled, but not large enough to expose her lengthening blood teeth. "Where can we go?"

"Are you serious?" asked the man, now suspicious of her sincerity and intentions. "You're not a cop are you?" Not so eager now.

"Do I look like a cop?" she asked. "What's wrong, scared? Maybe you can't even give me what I want, I can look somewhere else." Solange started to roll up her window when he stopped her.

"Follow me, baby," he said out the window. The perp seemed like a beast salivating over a long-awaited meal. She read his mind clearly through telepathy, and she knew what he said to himself, *I'll give you a rough one all right. Real rough.* His car pulled ahead and Solange followed. His thoughts only made her laugh. Her hunger was growing, and she was the one salivating.

The Camaro pulled into a vacant lot behind a dirty brick building, with a rusted metal sign that used to say "Henderson's Cleaners." Solange pulled in behind him. She stepped out into the still night, the only sound the crunch of her heels on the gravel as she came around the car, the blue in her eyes completely gone as they glowed like a cat's in the dark. Inside her the hunger raged stronger than any sexual desire ever could. The closer she got to him, the brighter her eyes shone with bloodlust. He leaned on the hood of his car, hands in pockets, waiting for her. She came closer. Her hypnotic gaze locked his eyes, and their murky brown depths seemed to go blank.

Solange started caressing her breasts, working her nipples until they stood out through the thin fabric of her dress. Never did she drop her gaze. She laughed as his mouth fell open; obviously, he was shocked to have the tables turned on him. One step back and she hopped up on the hood of her own car. Breaking her gaze with the man gave him a moment to gather his wits. Solange saw the anger and lust build in his eyes, along with the bulge in his pants. Knowing she was still in control, her thighs spread to show a teasing view of her womanhood. "What about that ride?"

"Hey, it's not going to be that easy," he said as he removed his hands from his pockets. Solange could see the smugness on his face as he reached into his car for a billy stick. A homemade job, made from a broom handle, covered with black electrical tape, nails driven into the end of it. The freak had come to play. "I don't know what your game is, but I'm going to fuck you up that tight little ass." He came closer, Solange regarded him calmly, a slight smile on her face. "You really want it, don'tcha? What a pretty little whore." There was a trace of disgust in his voice, then he commanded, "Take off that dress, bitch, let me see what I came for."

Callused, dirty fingers pinched her nipple. Revulsion swept through her, almost as hard as the hunger, but she stood still. "Oh yeah, this is what I came for." He parted his lips to reveal tobacco-yellowed teeth and a tongue that ran slowly back forth over the bottom row. Harshly, he squeezed her breast and raised the stick to strike her. But now it was her turn.

Like lightening, her hand captured his raised arm. No matter how hard he pulled, he could not break her vise-like grip. "Now ain't you a strong little thing, " he said, laughing nervously. "How about letting go of my arm and putting that grip on my dick, honey."

She opened her eyes wide, giving him a good look at their glow. Then with one glance she caused the stick to burst into flames, and he quickly dropped it with a cry of surprise. She laughed; it had taken years to perfect her pyrokinetic skills, but then she had many years to spare. Most humans possessed this power, but like many other things it was simply untapped. The change that made her into a vampire enabled her to use the portion of her mind that humans ignored so easily.

Her would-be attacker now backed away in fear, babbling. She advanced on him with every backward step he took. "What's wrong, baby, don't you like it rough?" Solange purred, "Don't you want to give me that ride anymore?" She mocked him further as she saw him breaking down with fear. "Aren't you gonna fuck me up my ass, or can't you do that without your stick?" He backed up against his car, and she came ever closer. "Why are you backing away, isn't this what you came for?" Less than a six inches away now, she reached out and ran her hand down his chest to the waistband of his faded jeans.

Trailing a finger down, she felt his erection return. She smiled, the sound of his throbbing blood driving her to near-insanity with hunger. The man relaxed, thinking this was part of the game. He murmured something about the "neat trick, doll face," referring to the burnt stick. She laughed, her hand undoing his Levi's. No underwear, just body odor and probably a few lice covered his genitals. Softly, she encircled his penis with her hand, and said, "Still, want to feel my nice strong grip?"

"Oh yea, baby," he moaned. It would be the last sound he ever made. Solange gripped his penis and forcibly pulled it from his body. Knowing he would scream, she swept her long nails across his throat at the same time, slashing his vocal cords and arteries. His eyes wide with pain but unable to make a sound, the man fell backwards onto the hood of his car. Solange climbed up and knelt over the flood from his throat, quenching the lustful thirst that had brought her here.

Lost in the ebullience of feeding, she drank for long moments that seemed too short. The coppery warmth filled her mouth, the euphoria she felt akin to orgasm in human women. She drank until she felt the life dwindling in her prey. Eyes only half-open, the man's body quivered as his last ounces of life flowed into Solange. Feeling the approach of death, she jumped to the ground and flung him at her feet. He tried to open his eyes, probably for the last time. She threw his penis to the ground in front of his face, and set it ablaze. It was the last thing he ever saw.

"Hell will welcome you tonight."

Solange walked back to her car, stopping to pick up her dress. She opened the car door, found a towel, and wiped the blood from her face, neck and hands. Carefully she zipped her dress back on and placed the towel in a garbage bag. She only felt this good after killing the inherently evil. That one would rape no more, and as for his plans for killing, she supposed those had ended as well.

Tingling from the kill she threw her head back, and when she did another sensation struck her. It was the same one she had felt in the cemetery last night. Someone was watching her, and not just any someone, a vampire. A different vampire or the same? If the same, why follow her? Again she sent out telepathic signals to the unknown one, and again, he or she eluded her. Now her own eyes shown with fear. She got into her car, hoping the vampire would not follow her home, but if she had been followed here, it was likely the other vampire knew of her resting place. The thought shook her to her soul.

The black-haired vampire watched her drive away. He would not follow her; he had read the fear in her. *No need to fear me, young one,* he thought. The scene he witnessed had disturbed him. When that filth had touched her, he had to fight the urge to kill the man himself. But he knew it was her ploy in the hunt. From a distance, her act of drinking had looked like copulating, with her naked body astride the man, her head at his neck, and her moans audible in the night. The human made no sounds except for the blood gurgling out of his throat, but his body had been quivering. A passing stranger would have mistaken this for the throes of passion. His rage rose to match hers at that moment.

After she left he did not move to hide the body, as it did not pose a threat to his or her resting place. She had hunted well, even if she had killed out of control. It would be a bizarre case for the police but there would be no clues for tracing. The older vampire went his own way, into the night to feed.

Solange pulled into the parking lot of her apartment, still quite shaken from the unknown presence that stalked her. When she left the car, she thankfully felt nothing. No one had followed her. Inside her apartment, she glanced at the clock and noticed that it was twelve thirty-five, almost five and half hours until sunrise. Solange showered and slipped on new hose and her black mini dress; she had another desire to satisfy now. She had not lain with a human in many years as it had always been a danger for her, but after the kill tonight her hunger was satisfied sufficiently so she would not pose a threat to her lover.

Anxiously, she knocked on Greg's door. He opened the door with a smile and a beer in hand. "Hi, glad you decided to join me. I almost gave up on you." Solange followed him inside.

"Well, I had some things to take care of." His apartment was the same as hers floorplan-wise, but it was definitely a man's apartment. Currently he had a few tables sprayed with simulated stone paint and a large patio umbrella over a mattress for furniture. One wall was covered by a powerful, well-equipped entertainment center. A Rod Stewart poster, patio lights shaped like beer bottles, and a cheap copy of a Nagel served as art.

"Would you like a beer?" Greg asked.

"Sure," she said, though she couldn't drink much this evening; she had no desire for it. She still felt high from the pervert's blood. Greg left and came back with a cold beer in his hand. He popped the top and handed it to her.

Solange tried not to read his mind, but his thoughts were like beacons from a lighthouse, guiding ships to safety on a dark night. There was no safety in these thoughts for her, excitement maybe, but no safety. He planned to bed her. Little did he know he did not have to give her beer to get her there. Also in his mind, but covertly hidden, there lurked an intention she could not decipher.

Many humans unknowingly could screen her telepathic probes. Greg had that ability. Through that screen he projected the feelings that she felt herself, with odd familiarity. Could it be possible he was Gregor, reincarnated just to haunt her? Her attraction for him was so strong, she lost all sense of control.

"Did I tell you how much I like that dress?" His eyes moved over her appreciatively. Solange returned the favor. He sat down on the mattress and she joined him. "What kind of music do you like?"

"I'm pretty flexible, I like everything from Mozart to Mojo Nixon." Solange looked into his blue eyes, "But I especially like rock 'n' roll."

"Yeah me too. I picked out some CD's to listen to, no Mozart though." He smiled. Smooth, that's the word she would use to describe him. A lot of girls probably fell for that charm.

He got up to start the music, and as he did his hand ran down her leg. She tingled. Her gaze followed Greg across the room. His buttocks were round and firm underneath those shorts, long muscular legs led up to them. Under those clothes was a perfect body and she would have it. There was a quaking in her body she could not stop, much like one suffering from exposure to severe cold. This attraction for this human excited her, its sharp desire close to the strength of her hunger. After starting the music he returned to her side. His first selection began, Rod Stewart.

"Do you like Rod?" He waited for her answer.

"Love him, he's great live," Solange said.

"Where'd you see him live?" Oh boy, question time. Sunset Strip, nineteen seventy-seven, no couldn't say that.

"In L.A." Solange smiled and pretended to take a drink of beer.

"Are you going to tell me why you left L.A.?" Greg took another drink and started stroking her arm.

"I told you, personal reasons," Solange said. "I move around quite a bit, lived a lot of places." Idly she stroked the hand that moved on her arm.

"Where are you from originally? I detected a light accent." He moved his hand farther up her arm, sending chills up her spine. "Your skin is chilled, are you cold?"

"No, I'm fine, I'll warm up." The effects of the blood must be wearing off. "How did you pick up on my accent? Few people do. I was born in France, but I've lost most of my accent over the years."

"It's the way you pronounce certain words, and the way you phrase them," he laughed "Why did you come to the States?" Greg's fingers moved across her white shoulders, barely caressing her skin.

"It was many years ago, I was very young." His hand moved across to the tattoo on her left shoulder.

"This is interesting, what does it stand for?" A fingertip traced the outline of the design. He was driving her insane.

"It's my family crest, I had it done in L.A. about five years ago." Solange sat still as he traced the knight with its bat wings on a coat of arms. Actually it was the crest of her maker, added twenty years ago with an ink unresponsive to her vampire regeneration process. Never would she forget who made her into this creature.

Those strong fingers on her skin were maddening. At that point the hunger pounded through her and she knew to stay any longer would endanger this man. Even after feeding the smell of his blood maddened her. There also existed a guilt for being here so soon after loosing Dereck; she felt unfaithful. Solange looked through the sliding glass door, and suddenly she felt dawn creeping closer; though it was hours away, it must have been a warning. "I must go now."

"Why?" Greg grasped her arm as she stood up. Solange pulled away, but he held her firmly.

"There will be other times." She bent and kissed his beautiful mouth gently. She could not stand his presence any longer. Still he did not release her. "Please let me go, it is very important. I must go."

"What are you scared of, Solange?" His eyes met hers with question. "You've been trying to get away from me from the moment I met you." He slackened his grip on her arm slightly; she took advantage and pulled away. "I don't understand why you can't stay a little longer."

Solange sat down beside him again. She took his hand in hers and said, "Please, there are things you do not know about me. In time perhaps I will explain, but right now I am not ready to do that. You must go slowly." Leaning forward, she planted a soft kiss on his lips. He drew her closer, deepening the kiss for a few moments longer, then let her go. Solange stood up and straightened her dress. "Besides, I'm the girl next door and I'm not going anywhere." She walked to the door, turned, smiled and said, "Call me tomorrow night."

CHAPTER SIX

Sanford

Detective Morris Sanford pulled his unmarked sedan onto the lot. With a sigh, he opened the door and got out. Unwillingly, he approached the crowded scene. Two murders in one week, both fitting similar descriptions: slashed throats, extreme loss of blood. In his five long years as a detective he had seen many gruesome sights, but these were very unsettling. The first one had been a local gang member, found at East Lake Park. There was no sign of struggle or blood at the site, even though the corpse contained less than a pint. His guess was that the park could not have been the actual crime site, the body simply deposited there. He wondered if this would be the same. He approached a member of the crime lab team.

"What do we have?" Sanford asked, pulling out a notebook and pen.

"Throat slashed, penis cut off, extreme loss of blood. Examiner's with him now."

The young officer looked nauseated; he was obviously new.

"Dick cut off?" The officer nodded. "What the hell for?" Sanford didn't wait for an answer, and he walked closer to the body, the young officer following behind him.

"Also, we discovered something next to the body you'll need to take a look at, sir." The officer indicated a small chalked-off area near the face of the victim. Sanford knelt beside the area.

A small, badly charred fragment in a clump of ashes, he looked across the body to the examiner.

"Hugh, what do you make of that?" He pointed at the ashes.

Medical Examiner Hugh Whittacker looked up and sighed. "His dick, I think." Outwardly undisturbed by anything he saw, Whittacker continued taking samples. "I have to make tests back at the lab to be certain."

"Dick?" Sanford wiped his hand across a broad forehead. "Are you serious?"

"Well, the penis was forcibly removed from the body and the ashes appear to be the appropriate size," Whittacker said. "I'll have to do a chemical analysis to see what she burned it with."

"She?"

"The cuts or should I say tears on the throat were caused by nails, very long sharp nails." He paused and pulled back the dead man's jeans to reveal the wound in his groin. There were long, deep gashes that Hugh pointed to. "See these? They match the ones on the neck. If I'm right they'll match the ones from yesterday's murder as well."

"Is it possible a woman did this?" He furrowed his brow with a frown. "How could a woman be strong enough to do that kind of damage?"

"It's possible, I've met your mother," Hugh said.

"Let's not get personal, Hugh or I'll have to bring up how close to your sister you are." They always kidded each other this way when something really bothered them. A cop had to have his way of dealing with things, and he supposed so did a medical examiner. "Are you sure they're a match?"

"As sure as I can be. There are some differences, however. The extreme loss of blood is still the same, but unlike the previous murder this is definitely the crime scene. Blood splattered on the hood and windshield of the vehicle, and some blood on the ground."

"So 'she' didn't move the body this time."

"But there is not enough blood on the ground or car to account for this much blood loss, " Whittacker looked rather uneasy.

"What's she doing, drinking it?" He laughed. "I'll tell the crime lab guys to take soil samples, deep ones . . . it had to drain down." Sanford turned back to the young officer, who had been waiting quietly for him. "Any other evidence?"

"Tire tracks six feet from the body, not made by his vehicle, we're making casts now. Also, a small scrap of material found near the victim's hand, some sort of netting. No fingerprints except for the victim's and a piece of burned wood, nails in the ashes, which appears to have been a billy stick before it was burned." The officer looked up at the detective, to let him know that was all.

"What about witnesses?"

"Nobody saw the actual murder but we still have the man who found the body." He paused. "He's over with the responding officer, a Mr. Manny Patel, who owns this building."

Sanford shook his head. "Any I.D. on the guy?" he asked.

"Yeah, Wayne Thurman, 124 Atlanta Street, Marietta."

"Long way from home, was he?"

"That's not all, he also fits the description of a rapist we've been looking for. Responsible for eight rapes and four beatings in this area. The physical description and the car are a perfect match." The officer pointed toward the car. "We also found items missing from the rape victims in his trunk."

"Ol' Wayne got more than a fuck last night." To himself, he asked, *do we need a serial killer more than a rapist?* To the officer, "Good, comb the entire parking lot again. Also take soil samples, we're looking for blood, lots of blood. It may run deep, so make sure you measure how deep the seepage is." He walked toward his car, then turned to say, "Don't let as much as a stray cat cross this lot. There has to be more evidence here somewhere. Also have the responding officer question everyone who would have seen Thurman's car in this area. If you find anything send it to me. I'll be in the office and then over to the examiner's later when Hugh has some info for me. Also keep those pricks from the media out of here, give them only essentials, leave out the burnt dick stuff, and don't link this with yesterday's murder. Got it?" The officer nodded.

Sanford got into his gray sedan. He run his hand through the receding brown hair on his head. It made absolutely no sense. Throats torn with fingernails, rapist with his dick cut off. A woman. What kind of a woman? Rape victim? No, two murders couldn't be self-defense. She must have been strong. One stroke had made the tear in the victim's neck, that was not an easy task. What kind of woman cuts off dicks and burns them? All that blood, maybe she thought she was a vampire. A real sick one, and if she did it once, she would do it again. The thought made him sick. The thought of a serial killer made him feel weary beyond his thirty-three years.

CHAPTER SEVEN

Vampire Hunter

The man sat in his small but adequate Los Angeles apartment. In front of him lay a photo album full of newspaper clippings. "Musician Dies In Apartment Fire, Artist Lover By His Side.", "Police Search For Arsonists", and "Psychotic Fan Possibly Responsible For Fire", the man just laughed. The clippings brought him such pleasure, proof that he was fulfilling his destiny. For years he had stalked her and others like her. Followed her every move, then with one blow he killed not only one vampire, but a whole building full.

Vampires, he had known of their existence since his childhood. Most people would think him crazy, but he knew they existed, spreading their evil like a disease. He had vowed many a year ago to wipe out their race, especially Angel. She had killed his father.

Joel Killian had grown up in Los Angeles. His mother died when he was born, leaving his sole survival with his father. Charles Killian had not been a kind man, but he was all Joel had. There were times when the stocky man had punished his son severely, for no apparent reason. Life had made Charles an angry man. He spent his life drinking, whoring, and making Joel miserable.

One evening his father had returned to their shabby apartment with a girl, a very pretty girl. Auburn hair, glittering eyes, her face looked young and innocent; how had his father managed this one? He had watched them from behind a chair in the hall, watched his father undress her, drunkenly pawing at her. Then, Charles had struck her, Joel knew that had been coming: he always hit them.

The look in her eyes that night compared to nothing Joel had ever seen. They glowed like the eyes of a cat at night. No one in the room but the three of them, she attacked his father, unaware that Joel watched. With one blow from her hand, she had slashed his throat. With horror Joel had watched her drink his father's blood. He knew then she wasn't human, he had known she was a vampire. In many movies had he seen creatures like this, never believing they were real.

When she finished drinking the blood, she looked up, and sensing his presence, she turned, a nightmare with blood dripping from her extended teeth and pale chin. Joel had been sick. He felt her burning eyes probing him, and he had wet his pants. Certain that he would die the same way, tears flowed down his cheeks. But she had only looked at him, and he returned the gaze to find tears in her eyes. She touched a bloodied hand to his cheek. Whispering soft words of apologies, she had stroked his cheek while he cried. Then abruptly she had fled, leaving him sobbing behind the chair, his father dead on the floor.

Now it was twenty years later and he had killed her. It had brought him great happiness to know he had destroyed the destroyer. Just Joel, no one else. For years he had tracked her, watching the papers for unexplained murders, listening to scanners. One night he saw her on the Sunset Strip, and he had followed her. Of course, she knew he followed her through the streets, and Joel knew that the instant he turned a corner and found her serenely waiting for him. She remembered him even though he had aged twenty years; she had not aged at all. Still, she had not harmed him, only warned him. She tried to tell him how they were not evil. How she had only given his father what he deserved. What he deserved? To be a meal for a monster; to leave a kid behind to clog up the foster care system. The hatred he felt for her and her kind blocked out any warning she could give him. That day he had vowed to himself to wipe out her kind.

Joel took out a paper and began a letter. He would decide later who to address it to. The world needed to know they were out there.

A while later, Joel turned on his computer. First he typed out the letter he wrote to the FBI, Blood Disorder Division or FANG: Federal Anti-Nosferatu Group. He only knew about them because when he was watching vampires one night he saw them. At first he had thought that they were following him, but then realized that they were following the vampire.

Of course, when they noticed him he had to kill them. He took their wallets and I.D.s and started doing a search. With their I.D. numbers he was able to hack his way into the FBI computer system. While he was there he had picked up numerous I.D. numbers so he could go back. The information, plus the papers found in the men's car, only backed up what Joel already knew. Except now he had some names and places.

These people had documented every vampire they ever knew of and could find. It was like a connect-the-dot map for Joel. Now he could find and kill every vampire on their system. That's how he had found Angel, or Solange as they called her. Yes, the government did have their uses.

The advantage to being underprivileged is that the government wants you to have a job so they'll train you to do just about anything. First he studied to be an electrician, which brought in some good money for a while and some handy skills. He owned his own electrical repair and computer repair business, and that gave him the flexible hours he needed. When computers started getting hot he had taken classes for that. Joel had shown a natural ability with computers, soon learning all there was to know, spending hours discovering how to hack his way into any system. All the information in the world was available on computers.

Online, all sorts of information could be found. Joel found sites that instructed him on building incendiary devices, sites that sold illegal and legal weapons, and yes, there were even vampire-hunting sites. He thought most of them were kids pretending to be a character, because the sites were too silly. One guy claimed he worked for the Vatican. Frankly, he couldn't see a prissy priest doing what he did.

He ordered books under false names, so many volumes on weapons and bomb building that one would have thought he was a revolutionary cult leader. His whole living room wall was covered with books, maps, and magazines. He always wanted to be prepared.

The second thing he had to do tonight was check police files. He had designed a program that would search every police file in the country for the criteria he was looking for. He kept it set on murder, extreme blood loss, bite marks, unexplained death. Now all he had to do was hit enter and it would find and print out every police report in the country that fit those criteria. Of course he'd get a lot of crap but that was to be expected. Joel started going through the reports as they came off.

On the wall he had a bio of all the known vampires and their whereabouts according to the FANG computers. After he picked out the vampire murders from the pile he'd compare their location to those bios. It made it easier if he had a good idea of who he had to kill. There were always those that weren't on the list. FANG just couldn't keep up with all of them, they made new ones all the time. He had obliterated most in the California area according to the FANG files.

In his hand there was a new report, which had not been released to the press. Hard to believe the cops sat on this one, but somehow they had managed. The city was Atlanta and they had had two murders in a row. The report screamed vampire, so he took a closer look. He had went into the system as a high-ranking police chief and therefore all the information was there for him. It was all he needed to convince him it was time for a trip.

Joel looked at his bios and found there was not one in Atlanta that fit the traits of the killer. The killer was female and obviously very out-of-control; two nights and two murders in a row. This must be a new one, one that had to be stopped. Yes, he would make a trip and do some cleaning up along the way. He turned his attention to the bios, pulling down several and making a mark on his map. He would leave tomorrow. First, he had one last thing to take care of.

*   *   *

The night air was warm against the girl's skin. It had been over an hour since her last trick, and she was growing restless. Sweat trickled down the back of her neck from under her red wig, which itched her scalp to no end. Even in her skimpy outfit of halter top and miniskirt, she felt the heat, outdone only by the agony of the four inch patent leather pumps on her feet. If the rent payment wasn't hanging over her head she'd just go home. Another twenty minutes and she'd do just that.

Less than a block away Joel sat in his car. Avidly he watched the girl walk up and down the small section of the street. Looking for a meal, he thought. She didn't fool him, she was no hooker. Over the years he had learned to spot them. He got a sick feeling in his stomach whenever he drew near to one of them. It gnawed at his innards now with an intensity stronger than he had felt in weeks. A churning, fire of acid, eating away at him, twisting in him until it became unbearable, only subsiding when he destroyed them.

She had done this to him; Angel and her kind. Poisoned him with this gift of knowledge, of insight into their evil existence. For this he would kill them, wipe out as many of them as he could until they killed him. For eventually, he the hunter would become the hunted. Oh, the police sought him out now, but they were not smart enough to end his crusade. But soon they would come, the vampires.

He slowly pulled his eighty-seven Cavalier alongside the girl. His window already rolled down, he beckoned to her. Carefully he remembered to shield his mind. Every one of these creatures could snatch the thoughts right out of your head unless you locked down. Don't want to warn her. With a oily gracefulness she approached the car, her breasts brazenly visible when she bent over to peer in. Her flashy smiled showed nothing of the sharp fangs he knew hid in that luscious mouth. His gut raged so fiercely now, he felt acid burning the back of his throat, threatening to erupt. She truly was one of them.

"'Do you want a ride, sweetheart?" He patted his wallet which protruded from his jacket pocket.

"Yeah, do you have any money?" she asked, playing the part to the end.

"All you'll ever need," he answered showing her some of the cash in his wallet. She got in. Joel drove to the nearby motel where he had a room ready. The girl chatted constantly on the way over, *Geez, they're good actors,* he thought. Joel led her inside, and she went into the bathroom to freshen up. The hunter laughed to himself, he knew she couldn't read his thoughts, Angel never could. The vampire slut would never know that the dinner she thought waited for her, would in fact be her death. He opened a case on the dresser, inside lay his hunting equipment. A stake sharpened to a point, a mallet to drive it home with, a machete to chop off her filthy head, and garlic to stuff into her bloody mouth. Fiction lead him to these methods, but they had not failed him yet, and it caused less suspicion than burning buildings down.

Joel picked up the stake and caressed it with his big gloved hand. So carefully had he carved and sanded this piece of wood. Lovingly he had rubbed it with holy water, its essence soaked into every pore of the wood. A vampire's nightmare, that's what he was, terminator of evil. He stood by the door with stake and mallet in hand, waiting for her to come through the door. Surprise, unfortunately, was necessary; oh, how he wished he could torture them for what they did. But vampires had powers of guile. Once one of them almost convinced him to make love to her instead, but he had been too smart and had sank the stake in her chest anyway. From then on he gave them no opportunities. The bathroom door opened.

"Okay, doll, what's it gonna be?" she asked as she stepped out of the bathroom in nothing but her garter belt and stockings. Then she saw the stake and mallet raised above her in Joel's hand. Before she could scream it sank into her chest, plunging between ribs into the soft mass beneath. Joel steadily pounded the flat end with the mallet until nothing showed but a few inches above the gaping hole in her chest. "To hell with you, you evil blood-sucking bitch!" he shouted as he reached for the machete. Long before he sliced through her neck, the girl had drawn her last breath, her eyes staring hideously into space.

Quickly Joel grabbed the head by the long hair and stuffed the garlic into the open mouth, cramming it in until the entire bulb of the plant was in the cavity. He stood back and waited for her to start shriveling up. Nothing happened. Oh well, some did, some didn't; he never understood that.

*   *   *

Joel threw things into his trunk, things he knew he would need. It would be a long drive to Georgia and he knew that there would be others along the way to contend with. For this reason he packed triple what he needed in Atlanta. Until the wee morning hours his time had been spent sharpening more wooden stakes. It really wasn't important what kind of wood it was, just as long as it was hard and sharp enough to puncture hard skin and muscle. He had started last night with tomato stakes from the hardware store, then broom handles, and when those ran out, his own kitchen chairs. When he was done there were four cardboard boxes full of them. There was no time to soak them in the holy water so Joel had to hope for the best. He also had cleaned out every jewelry store, five and dime, and a few churches as well in the area to fill the next box with crosses and crucifixes. Each one a different size, material and design, but all were holy.

There were gallons upon gallons of water stacked in his apartment. To the common person it would look like drinking water. To Joel it was liquid death to those monsters. He had to go to every church and cathedral in the area to get enough water blessed by holy men. Too big to put in his car, he had rented a trailer to attach to the back to hold the water. Along with it he put several super soaker water guns and spray bottles in the trunk. Beside them, in a nest of burlap bags, lay two axes, a machete and a bowie knife, their edges sharpened, the silver on the edge brighter than the blood-splattered metal around it. Faded, brown rivulets ran down the handles of all the sharp implements.

In the trailer he added spray cans of gasoline and kerosene, a box of electronic parts and wires, and twenty pounds of plastic explosive; untraceable plastic explosive, because he had stolen it. Joel loaded all of his guns and a crate of hand grenades next. The guns wouldn't kill them but it could stun them long enough to stake them. Counting everything, he chucked some extra ammo into the box of guns for good measure. He slammed the doors shut on the trailer. He lacked only one thing in his arsenal, but he would get that later, on his way out.

Back in the house he made other arrangements for his trip. On the wall next to his computer was a map of the United States dotted with red pushpins. Each one of those pins was a vampire murder. Every time one of them killed and he found out about it in police files, he marked it. Every time he killed the offending vamp he took out the red pin and replaced it with a white one. Slowly but surely there were fewer and fewer red dots where he was living. In fact, there were no red dots in L.A. for the past couple of weeks. That's not to say that there were no vampires out there. They were just too slippery for the police to find out about; but not too slippery for Joel. There were so many white pins in and around Los Angeles that he had to start a map of just the L.A. area alone. Even if the police didn't have a report of a murder, he killed every single vampire he ran across. *Somebody had to do it,* he told himself.

Now, he looked across the map and numbered the pins in other places. These places he could not be reach by driving overnight, places on the other side of the country. In Georgia there were two pins he added last night. They needed Joel there. So he would go, picking up some kills on the way as well. In his hand was a book of maps which had maps of all the states. He took small red dot stickers and placed them on the maps in conjunction with the red pushpins on the wall map. Down came all the profiles pinned to the wall, the ones that weren't marked dead. All of his vampire location data was arranged in a neat folder. These things he put in a tote bag full of sandwiches, chips, and cookies. This would go into the front seat with his laptop and a cooler of drinks. There would be no stopping unless necessary. The laptop he would take in case he needed more information.

With everything ready, he put it in the car and closed the door on his apartment. All the rent for the year was paid up. If he didn't come back there was nothing here anyway, except his computer and a map. All the files on the computer had been copied to disk and erased in case someone came looking for him. Those were packed away in a box in his car as well. He got into his faded red Cavalier and easily backed the trailer out of the parking lot.

Joel drove until he no longer was in the city and no longer in the suburbs, but out into California's farmlands. It was mid-morning by the time he stopped at a small vegetable stand. A mom and pop sort of place, it was the kind run by a farmer selling what he couldn't sell to the stores. The farmer sat in jeans and a striped shirt behind a plywood counter. Tomatoes, green peppers, watermelons, and broccoli sat stacked in neat bins, but Joel didn't want any of them. He pretended to look at the tomatoes and he might have even bought some for the road, but it was not what he came for. "Do you have any garlic?"

The farmer lifted a handbasket full of the white bulbs from behind the counter. "Here you go," the farmer said.

"Oh that's not nearly enough," Joel said. "I'm buying for my dad's restaurant and we really need large quantities. Do you have anymore?"

The farmer looked at him skeptically for a moment then told him to wait there for a moment. The older man made a phone call and then asked Joel, "Exactly how much are you looking for young man?" His eyes got very large when Joel told him how much and relayed that over the phone. He hung up and told Joel to wait a few minutes.

Soon a blue pickup came from a long driveway that Joel assumed went to the farm. In the back there were two fifty pound bags of garlic. The gangly boy driving the truck had to be the farmer's son; he was only a younger version of the man. He lifted the bags out of the back as if they were nothing and brought them over to Joel's car. Together they loaded them in the trailer. "How much do I owe you?" Joel asked.

Instead of the fifty the farmer asked for, Joel laid a ten down on the plywood. "Oh, let me get some more out of the car." Something in his eyes must have sparked the old man's guardian angel. Something deep inside knew there would be death brought back from the car.

"Never mind, just take it. Couldn't sell that stuff anyway," the farmer said.

"Gee thanks," Joel didn't know why the old man gave it to him but he didn't argue, just got in the car and left.

As he drove off, the farmer and his son watched him until he was a speck on the horizon. The son, perplexed by his father's generosity, questioned what had happened. The old farmer just looked at him and said, "Only two kinds of people need that much garlic, son." The boy didn't understand still. "And you don't want to mess with either of them."

"What kind of people, dad?" the boy asked.

"Italians and vampire hunters, " the old man said. "He was definitely not Italian."

Out on the road Joel drove as fast as the trailer would handle. If he got over seventy it started to wobble and sway behind him. With the C4 in its belly, it was a good idea to keep it stable. He couldn't afford to blow up his stash before he got to where he was going. He wanted to put as many miles behind him as possible before having to stop to sleep. He didn't mind sleeping at night, if one came near him, his stomach would let him know.

The scenery changed with every passing hour. He found himself somewhere in Nevada by afternoon. Highway stretched out miles in front of and behind him, and there were a few cars but not many. As afternoon started to fade, fewer and fewer cars passed him on the road. In the cassette deck he played BTO; he loved the old rock 'n' roll of the sixties and seventies. He didn't want to listen to the new rock, too much vampire music. Every time he heard a Nightbird song he wanted to puke. So he stuck with the classic rock. Joel sang along with "You Ain't Seen Nothing Yet," almost as loud as the music.

Georgia waited on him. The faster he got there, the better. This one killed every night. This one was a woman. So far there had been two murders from this one vampire that the police knew about. *There are more the police just don't know about,* Joel told himself. The detective on the case was named Sanford. Young but experienced, this Sanford made a good cop, but nothing could have prepared this cop for what he had to deal with. Cops didn't believe in vampires, that he knew. Unless he stopped her, the killings would not end.

Joel thought about his adversary. Would she be as beautiful as Angel? Would she be as hard to kill? These were questions that played in his mind. Part of him couldn't believe he had finally killed her. He still saw her in his dreams. She would haunt him for all time. Sometimes in the dreams he lusted for her. Joel knew this was her evil trying to trick him still; he had been touched by it and forever changed. In sleep he welcomed her bloody kisses and his hands touched her smooth white skin. Even now, in the car, his desire built caused his speed to increase. The trailer behind him started wobbling and swerving. It brought him out of deep thought. Not wanting to lose the trailer, he slowed and pulled over.

Here in the middle of nowhere, the sun was just starting to set over the dry landscape. Joel's breathing came in hot and heavy pants, his heart raced, and his jeans grew increasingly uncomfortable. Damn her, he thought, damn that bitch for doing this to me. Only one thing to do about the situation, and he unzipped his jeans. The dry, warm air seemed cool against his feverish body. Images of Angel filled his head. Her red hair danced around her face like fire, waving, flickering, like flames in a maelstrom. Then like tentacles they drew him to her. So close that her lips touched his face. Those bloody lips, smearing the blood all over his skin. His desire grew to a feverish pitch as he touched her in his mind.

His stomach burned, as always when near her. Joel knew he must kill her, if he could only find a stake. He saw her fangs, extending as she opened her mouth. Blood and spit dripped from them onto his chest. Slowly she moved down, turning her attentions to his lower body. He could feel those soft lips embracing him fully. Then as her fangs sunk into his skin, he staked her right through the chest. Again and again he thrust the stake into her chest. How cold it was between her perfect breasts. His stomach churned in agitation and ecstasy. Her red eyes rolled back into her head, blood spewed from her lips, and smoke rose from the hole in her chest. Inside her, the heat from his stake burned and boiled her cold vampire heart. The thing that was Angel started to shake and convulse and would soon explode on his stake. Then it came with another push of the stake, the explosion. All around him Joel saw nothing but exploding blood, fires, and smoke. The explosion gave him his release from the creature. All the evil she caused within him expelled. He lay his head back, closed his eyes and sighed.

"That's some dream you're having, anyone I know?" asked a cold male voice just outside his window.

Joel's eyes flew open, and as he saw the vampire standing there, he wiped the wetness of his passion on his shirt and jumped upright in the seat. His stomach churning had not been a part of his dream. He had not realized how long he'd been distracted; the desert around him was dark. Outside his window, the creature had been watching him, reading his mind while unprotected. Without hesitation he filled his mind with static. That always threw them off, no matter what else he thought of, a static-filled TV screen stayed in his head.

The vampire laughed, showing Joel his long fangs. His skin was not quite pale but a golden color shone in the darkness. Short brown hair curled just above his collar, the top hidden under a Snap-On Tools hat. He wore faded jeans just a little threadbare at the knees, an unbuttoned plaid shirt, and a cotton white tanktop. His truck was parked behind Joel on the shoulder, its windows tinted dark, and they would be black even in the daytime. "I think you're in a bad situation here, boy," the vampire said, reaching in to grab Joel's shirt. When Joel was near its face, he could smell tobacco and something foul on its breath. "I don't take kindly to killers, especially where women are involved."

"Your kind deserves to die," Joel spat. "Evil, filthy fucking bastards!" Slowly he pulled the magnum out that he always kept in a side pocket of the door and pushed it under the vampire's chin. "Now, I think you better let me go."

The vampire laughed. "Do you actually think you can kill me that way? Haven't been doing this long have ya, boy?" He laughed again, not letting Joel go at all.

"Oh, I wouldn't say that, these are special bullets, silver," Joel told him with a smile.

"Boy, I ain't no werewolf."

"But they will sting like hell, and they may blow enough of a hole in your neck to disconnect your head, depending on how old you are." Now it was Joel that laughed. "You see, I have been doing this awhile. I know all about you bastards." He pulled the trigger. The gun sounded loudly, its boom echoed over and over through the desert night. The vampire released him and pulled back away from the car. The hole in his throat was huge; blood poured out of it in a gurgling river. Disoriented, the creature spun around and then tried to head for the truck. Joel was out of the car, stake in one hand, garlic in the other. He chased the creature to the door of the truck and struck. As hard as he could, he plunged the sharpened chair leg stake into the muscled chest. A sick ripping sound fell on his ears as it went deeper and muscles tore. The garlic was shoved into the hole made by the gun, which was already starting to close. The vampire made a choking sound and started pulling on the stake. From a holster on his shin he pulled a hunting knife, and giving the vampire no time to think, he swung. The sharp serrated edge of the knife hit the throat just above the garlic, slicing all the way through the muscle. The tip scraped paint on the other side as it cut through the vampire's neck.

Joel stepped back and watched the body and the head fall into two different directions. In a few moments the carcass started to smoke and make a sick, sucking noise. Shortly it burst into flames, burning until there were only some bones and dust on the ground beside the truck.

He got back in his car. Shaking as he started the engine, he cursed his own weakness and the evil that Angel had left in him.

Chapter Eight

FANG

Bylak walked around the truck several times while his partner looked at the body. After his third lap, he stopped where her small frame was bent over a pile of something. The something looked gray and dust-like with pieces of bone mixed in. No matter how many times he saw it, he couldn't get used to it. It made him think of fires and burning bodies, of German gas ovens found brimming with ashes, and ancient burial jars in museums. He had to stop watching public television; he had too many pictures in his brain. "Capuano, is it safe to say that this is a VH murder?" he asked.

His partner stood up and removed her rubber gloves. She had been digging in the dirt and ashes looking for clues. *Nothing bothers this woman,* though Bylak. Her black hair, cut in a short bob, was finely dusted with gray. The clothes she wore, a government-sanctioned gray business suit, was severely cut, with no feminine frills to soften the effect. The only soft thing about Capuano were her eyes. Amid her Sicilian face, harsh hair, and severe suit were soft brown eyes with thick black lashes. Most people didn't notice those eyes but he had been her partner for twelve years now. "This is our guy. The trucker's name, does that sound familiar to you?" Capuano asked, only saying what she had to in front of the local police and medical. "Walk to the car with me, there's something I want to show you."

Bylak and Capuano walked to their sedan together, one tall and one short. One was blond and the other dark, but both were going gray. As oddly matched physically as they were, mentally they were connected. They had successfully run this division of the FBI for the last twelve years. Inside with the doors and windows shut, Capuano opened a file with *FANG* stamped across the top. Inside there was a picture of an old Indian that Bylak knew very well.

"Do you want to tell him his son is dead?" She asked.

"Not really, " Bylak answered and closed the file.

"I think it's safe to say that Van Helsing is on the move now," Capuano said. "Wonder where we'll find the next one."

"My bet it will be closer to Atlanta," Bylak told her. "I think we should go that direction, the cops are getting a little warm down there anyway."

CHAPTER NINE

The Fan

Hungary

Greg stared at the door after Solange walked out, amazed he let her get away: most girls never turned him down. This girl was full of surprises. He climbed the stairs to the second-story bedroom he used for storage. On the wall hung a painting of a man, pale skin, long, black hair. He had made the purchase on a trip to California. When he had seen it in the Beverly Hills gallery, he had fell in love with the style. Brush strokes that were bold and colorful but not too heavy. The man in the portrait was embraced by a winged dragon, not fighting but almost one with it. He recognized the man in the portrait, Dereck Cliffe, lead singer for Nightbird. The painting could be worth quite a bit now, considering Dereck Cliffe was dead.

But it was the artist that had captured Greg's attention. Signed in bold red paint, *Angel*. Immediately, a feeling of want had come over him. Something told him he had to know this woman, had to have her in his life. That day he believed in deja vu, destiny, or whatever had brought him to her.

He possessed a small collection of her works, fascinated by her mystical style. These paintings were shared with no one, kept for his pleasure only. His heart broke when he heard she had died along with the rock singer. They had been lovers, him, dark and mysterious, and her with hair of fire and a sparkling smile. That had not deterred Greg in his quest for her, the quest that died the day they did.

What had ultimately drawn him to her were the dreams. He knew her before he ever saw her. The familiarity he felt when looking at the paintings were nothing compared to how he felt when he saw her face for the first time. For years he had dreamed of a girl with that face, wearing a white satin ball gown and powdered wig. In the dreams he danced with her in a fabulous palace. Also, he was a soldier, but details had been hazy. More like memories than imagination, the dreams persisted. One day they took a bad turn, and the wonderful creature of his dreams turned to a nightmare. The beautiful girl had turned to a vision of terror; eyes burning with the fires of Hell, long claws that ripped his flesh, extended teeth that sought his neck. Before his eyes a coat of arms flashed, which consisted of a knight with bat wings. He would always wake before he drew a last breath.

For years Greg had sought professional help, thinking he was mad. At last he came to Dr. Cornell. The doctor was accredited to be the best analyst and hypnotist in the Southeast, and Greg hoped so. Dr. Cornell led him through his past and into his deepest memories to help him rid himself of the nightmares. The doctor had suggested that some deep-rooted anxiety caused the dreams, related to his relationships with women. He believed that somewhere a woman had hurt Greg and his consciousness wouldn't let him admit it. He felt it was all tied to Angel.

Greg had collected every review and article he could find on her. After that first trip to L.A., he subscribed to the *Times* and many art publications. He not only fell for the painter, but for that beautiful face. He tracked her every chance he got, keeping every clipping. She did not make personal appearances at her showings too often, so Greg had never seen her in person, until now.

Solange, he knew she was Angel; he had studied the face too often not to know. Everyone believed her dead, but tonight she proved to be very much alive. According to the news, a psychotic fan had burned her and Dereck as they had slept. In fact everyone in the mansion had burned, no survivors. How was it that she survived with no damage? It was a true mystery. Perhaps, they just released her death to protect her from the crazy fan? That was possible. Certainly that could be her reason for not letting him close. *Geez,* he thought, *how stupid of me.* After making a pass at her so soon after Dereck's death, no wonder she had run out on him. He could imagine the pain she was in, and the last thing she needed was a man coming on to her too early.

Soon he would let her know that he knew her identity. He did not know how to tell her. She would be angry, thinking he had tricked her. And how did the coat of arms come into play? Greg had almost choked on his beer when he saw the tattoo on her back. Confusion settled in his mind. Tomorrow he would call Dr. Cornell again. He walked out of the room and closed the door of Angel's shrine. Perhaps he was mad.

Just on the other side of the wall Solange was preparing for sleep. She felt its approach with every fiber of her body. Black curtains drawn over boarded windows, she felt safe when she lay in her coffin. Settling into her sleeping position on the black velvet, she welcomed the dreams that would come to her. Dreams of Gregor, they would haunt her harder this evening, she knew. The situation with Greg, his look-alike, was getting out of control. She could not change him; she had never made another vampire, and swore to herself she would not. But if their relationship continued, unless she changed him, she would kill him.

A vampire's rest is very close to hibernating. The heart will almost completely, stop beating. This death-sleep was necessary for regeneration in cases of injury or loss of limb. It also reconstructed any cells damaged by the onslaught of time, replacing them continuously. During this time they are very vulnerable; however, Solange had found she would move at times to protect herself if necessary, without any knowledge of it. Although their bodies were inanimate, their minds went on, and dreams filled every sleeping hour. For Solange, she relived her past time and time again.

The rising sun slowly worked its magic. Solange's eyes fluttered shut and again she lived her past in her dreams. Frustration came with knowing the outcome, but she was unable to do anything to alter it. Solange roamed the strange castle by night, a guest of her schoolmate, Raphaela and her parents, the Baron and Baroness Noguchi. Very few Parisians ever visited this part of the world. Hungary, still in the power of Austrian empress Marie Therese, had some hard feelings toward the French for pulling their support during the war. In this she considered herself lucky. Solange being of noble birth herself was not impressed by the title, but the castle overwhelmed her. Her own family owned an extremely large home but far different from Raphaela's, which was stone, cold and damp, with hundreds of rooms just like the one she entered now.

Her sleep was disturbed by many dreams that night. Perhaps she missed her home, or Gregor. It had been difficult to say good-by, even for such a short Solange recently turned twenty. Still unmarried, simply because Gregor's father insisted he finish his tour in the military. That time would come in three weeks. The thought made her smile. She and Gregor had become such close friends since her debutante ball. Solange loved him dearly. The time apart would seem like an eternity for her.

She had found herself with a lighted candle, walking down a dark hallway. Whatever called her out of her room she will never know. Down dark corridors, she had went, and losing her way completely, she leaned on a wall in the west wing. Her leaning on the wall caused it to slide open to reveal a small dark room, lighted only with a candle much like her own. In the corner there was a chair, indignant of times over a hundred years ago. It was heavy, dark-stained oak with a tattered velvet cushion, and upon it he sat.

He was attractive, with black hair streaked by silver-gray, but by no means of an elderly age. Solange placed him to about thirty-five. He lifted his eyes as if expecting her, and she saw that they were green and virtually iridescent. A candle in the dark can do strange things to eyes; Solange knew this, so was not afraid. The man exuded a rugged handsomeness, though he had extremely pale skin. A smile lifted the corners of his lips as she gazed upon him. She stopped in her footsteps. He lifted his arm to motion to her, the full sleeve of his white tunic fell full under his arm. "Come in, please, Mademoiselle . . . ?" He faltered in French, waiting for her name.

"Solange . . ." she replied, her answer barely a whisper.

"Solange. Angel of the sun." The smile again touched his lips. "You are indeed of the sun, fire for hair, burning eyes; the sun should feel honored."

She did not know what to say, and she blushed and looked away. No one ever spoke to her so frankly, except Gregor. His soft laughter whispered in her ears. "Do not be embarrassed, young one. I meant no offense. It is just that I have not gazed upon such beauty or the sun in many years." He paused. "Please don't turn away, Solange, join me."

Solange drifted toward the chair opposite him and sat slowly. Her eyes could not leave his face, his beauty mesmerized her. How the light from the fire danced in his emerald eyes, holding her on sight, prisoner. Shyly she asked, "Who are you?"

"Forgive me, I am Leone." He smiled that seductive smile again.

"Why have I not met you earlier?" Solange questioned him.

"I have been away, my family is used to my absence. My business takes me away for long periods of time." He paused again. "My current absence has been so long, I'm afraid that my family has forgotten my existence. In fact, they are not yet aware of my return."

"I would hardly think you could be forgotten by anyone. What is your relation to Raphaela?"

"Raphaela?" Question briefly flitted across his face. "Raphaela is my niece, a lovely young girl, but not as lovely as you my angel of the sun." Again Solange blushed. "How old are you, Solange?" Her name on his lips seemed so sensuous. Without knowing why, she wondered what his lips would feel like and she blushed. "Solange . . . why do you turn away from me?"

She brought her eyes up to meet his and held his gaze for several long moments. Solange could not look away. "I'm twenty."

"Why are you not married, lovely one?" Leone continued to hold her gaze. "Surely some young man worships you."

"I am engaged," Solange said. "Gregor and I have been engaged for several years now." Why did she feel hesitant to tell this stranger that? "I really must go now." She stood quickly and straightened her gown. "Raphaela might awaken."

"If I were this Gregor, I would not let you wait so long." His smile was radiant in the semi-darkness.

"Sir, please, you must not speak to me that way," she said with much indignation.

"If you do not wish to stay," he said as he stood up, "I will not force you." He reached out and grasped her hands firmly. Towering over her by at least six inches, Leone looked down on her. "My only wish was to have companionship with you for awhile. You are a ray of sunshine in my dark existence."

Solange's breath had quickened at his touch, her heart raced at his closeness. Her hands burned in the coolness of his. She agreed to stay.

For several hours she had talked with him. With such pride and pleasure he regaled her with stories of his adventures. Solange felt surely that most of them were made up to entertain her. This man would have to be much older to have this many adventures. She listened with fascination, however far-fetched they were.

Suddenly he stopped talking and pulled her from her chair to stand against him. Treacherous pounding came from her heart. Her hands, going to his arms to push him away, seemed insignificant. His cool lips pressed against hers as he pulled her even closer to him. How wonderful those lips felt against her. So wonderful they caused her to think of Gregor and she panicked.

"I should not be here with you like this it is not proper." She stumbled for words her heart did not want her to say. Leone's burning eyes held her rooted to the spot. Her feet had a mind of their own or they would have carried her out of that room. "If I . . . we were caught here together it would not look right."

Solange was flustered. "A young woman in the room of an older man she doesn't even know. It is sinful."

"Solange, I am not afraid of sin." Leone pulled her closer. "Soon you will understand why I fear not. Please don't look away. You will not speak of tonight to anyone. I will also keep my peace to protect your virtue, but only if you return." Solange breathed deeply. "Come only after the castle sleeps, so to keep our secret, do you promise, my angel?"

"Yes, Leone." She pulled away. With candle in hand she turned and left the room to move quickly back down the corridor. Her room was still warmed by a dying fire in the hearth, but the linens were cool as she slipped under them. She felt guilty for spending time with a stranger. Poor Gregor, he must never know. As sleep engulfed her, Solange's thoughts that night had been of Leone.

The morning after their initial meeting, Solange rose to a normal day without one word of her secret rendezvous. Raphaela was to show her the castle today. When she went down to the morning meal everyone gathered around the table, everyone except Leone. Raphaela's family was charming. Her father was almost whimsical, with a childlike humor. Raphaela had his coloring of corn silk hair but emerald eyes like her mother, the Baroness, who had pale skin with ebony hair streaked slightly with silver and eyes a startling green. Where had Solange seen eyes like that before? Yet they did not have the iridescent quality of Leone's.

"Did you sleep well, Solange?" Inquired the Baroness.

"Yes quite well, thank you." Solange intently studied the array of fruits and breads arranged for breakfast, choosing strawberries and puff pastry for her plate. A serving girl rushed from person to person making sure all needs were seen to.

"I hope she slept well, today I'm taking her on a tour of the castle." Raphaela giggled. "We'll have the most fun."

"But remember not to go in the west wing." The Baroness nervously patted Raphaela's hand and explained to Solange, "It is being repaired, and could be dangerous." Raphaela nodded in agreement.

"Make sure you show Solange our galleries," the Baron beamed. "We have quite a collection." He rose up from his chair and kissed Raphaela on the head. "If you'll excuse me I have to go, I have business in town." He strode out of the dining hall, his footsteps sounding as he walked through the castle.

Breakfast passed quickly. Raphaela chatted busily as normal. As soon as they finished, they were off on the tour of the castle. Their long skirts made swishing noises as they walked across the marble floors. Raphaela guided her to a huge ballroom where massive chandeliers hung from the ceiling. Solange danced with Raphaela around and around on the floor, and reminisced with Raphaela of the balls her parents gave in Paris. Her mother had sent her there to learn proper social etiquette.

"There are so many handsome young men," Raphaela said excitedly.

"There are usually so many," Solange smiled, "that I cannot dance with them all." Raphaela looked jealous. "Of course I only dance with Gregor, after all he is my fiancé."

"That's quite alright. I usually have all the rest to myself," Raphaela said. "But none of them are as handsome as Gregor. He is simply divine, you are so lucky." She looked around the vast ballroom and sighed. "We never use this room. I only remember once vaguely, I was but a child." Her eyes appeared misty. "I remember all the beautiful people. I was only six years old." Raphaela paused. "It did not go well."

"Why do you say that?" Solange questioned.

"Mama was upset," she turned to face Solange. "It was the last party we ever had. No one from the village will come here now."

"Why?" This sounded so strange to Solange

"Solange, this is not France, there are many things you do not understand," Raphaela tried to explain. "There are many superstitious people in this country."

"What does that have to do with the Baroness' party?" Curiosity filled Solange.

"I am not sure of details, Mama tries to shelter me from so much," she rolled her eyes. "It seems that the village believes an evil spirit inhabits this castle. Something happened at the party and it was blamed on the spirit."

"What type of spirit?" Solange thought it a ridiculous thing, but intriguing

"Like I said, Mama does not tell me," Raphaela said nervously. "Let's move on, I have much to show you."

They moved out of the ballroom and continued the tour. They passed through large sitting rooms with many periods of furnishings, and went through one hall that was nothing but tapestries. Solange remained silent, astonished at the beauty around her. Their intricate patterns were mesmerizing. Some told stories while others offered florals and paisleys. In Paris they considered Hungary uncivilized, but this proved otherwise. A mixture of Europe and the Orient created a style all their own.

Another room was filled with antique fighting equipment, mostly from the Orient, according to Raphaela. They saw strange-looking metal stars, swords, and shields, along with several suits of armor from the crusades, Christian emblems emblazoned upon the breast plates. Ironically, next to these, the fighting equipment of their enemies the Saracens stood, as if to mock the Crusaders.

Solange wanted to stay for hours in the huge library. Not only were there very rare books but many hand-scribed parchments from the Carolingian Period, decorated with leaves, flowering vines, and one even depicted a lovely mermaid. She was enchanted by these works of art by long-dead monks, and Raphaela had to force her to leave them.

"There is more to see. You can come back here another time," Raphaela urged.

"They are so beautiful, I've only seen a few like this in the cathedral but not nearly as beautiful." Solange found them overwhelming.

"The church would not be happy to know they don't own all of them. Papa had these smuggled in last time he went to France." Raphaela smiled: she adored her father, especially his eccentricities. "Papa goes to France quite often and tries to bring treasures back each time. He does love his homeland and the things he brings back."

"If your father is French, how did he meet your mother?" To Solange they seemed an unlikely pair.

"They met when Mama was in boarding school, except then it was a convent." Raphaela sighed.

"Your mother was in a convent?"

"Not as a nun. Her parents died when she was three," Raphaela informed her. "She didn't have any family?" Solange asked

"There was an uncle who watched over the castle and gave money to the convent where Mama lived," Raphaela gaze held one of deep thought. "I have met him, only briefly, he looks like my grandfather, only not as old, by now my grandfather would be almost a hundred years old, but no one lives to be that old."

Solange herself was in deep thought; the uncle had to be Leone. "Does he come to visit often?" Her curiosity flamed, but she couldn't ask too much.

"Oh no, I have not seen him since I was a child." She paused. "He has not been to the castle in many years. Let's not talk about this anymore, I'm famished."

Solange had not realized they had been on their tour for quite some time now. It was time for lunch. "But what about the rest of the tour?" she asked, wanting to explore more rooms and find out more about Leone.

"The cook has made a marvelous lunch, I'm sure of it." Raphaela whispered to Solange, "That's why father brought her from France."

She allowed Raphaela to take her by the hand and pull her back to the dining hall. Roast chicken, steamed vegetables, and banquet bread awaited them. Solange ate while Raphaela talked fervently through the meal, which she was accustomed to. To tell Raphaela something was to tell everyone. They talked about all the lovely things they had seen in the castle that morning. Then Raphaela had an idea, "Let's go for a ride this afternoon, and finish the tour another day."

"A ride, that sounds wonderful!"

"We'll go into the village, and through the vineyards, it'll be so much fun! And I'm sure there is a horse you can ride in the stable, there will be so much we can see." Raphaela went on without stopping until they went to change into suitable riding dresses.

The stable housed twenty horses, most of which were used for pulling carriages or plowing. However the family did keep a few for riding, and Raphaela's bay mare snorted when they approached her stall. She lovingly patted the quivering nose and scratched the white star between the mare's eyes. "This is Contessa, isn't she beautiful?" Raphaela beamed. "Father bought her for me, she's quite a lady." She then made cooing noises to the animal and made motions for the groom to prepare the saddle. "Now let's find you one." They walked the length of the stable passing stall after stall. The second to last stall was dark when Solange peered in.

Immediately an enormous, black head pushed forward, snorting in warning. Its wary eyes went from Solange to Raphaela back to Solange, tossing its ebony mane. Not a white hair marred the satiny dark coat of the animal, it had been brushed until it shone like a black jewel. "He's beautiful, what's his name?" asked Solange.

"I don't know, he must be one of the new horses Papa brought back," Raphaela said. She approached the animal with an open palm, so not to scare him, but when she tried to touch him he pulled away. "Not very friendly is he?" Both girls laughed. The groom who had been saddling Raphaela's mare came rushing over, babbling in a tongue Solange did not understand.

"What is he saying?" Solange extremely curious as to what could upset the boy so.

"Just superstitious nonsense. Devil horse, hah, nonsense. It's just a black horse." She then said something to him in their language. The boy afraid muttered something in response and went back to saddling the Contessa. "He says he doesn't know where the horse came from. Papa must have just bought him. Come, let's find you another horse, that simp won't even think about saddling him." Solange reached out and the stallion let her rub his nose before retreating to the back of the stall again.

They came to a chestnut gelding with a flaxen mane, a magnificent animal, named Hunyadi. Raphaela told her that the name once belonged to a powerful Hungarian ruler. Unlike the black stallion two stalls down, he proved to be very friendly and gentle. Once the groom finished with the Contessa, he saddled the gelding for Solange.

Warm afternoon sun toasted their skin, rays burning bright over the fields to find them. Solange and her mount appeared as flames ablaze in the grasses where it found them. Hunyadi handled easily under her touch and together they set the day afire, two chestnut beauties parting the winds and reflecting the light as they rode. Raphaela watched with a feeling close to envy; she knew she could be considered beautiful, but Solange was more. Not only beautiful, but to Raphaela, her best friend exemplified radiance itself. The very sun chose her to dance upon and shone brighter there than on any of the flowers that drew their very life from it. Solange's name alone spoke of this quality, "angel of the sun." Her father had heard the name on a trip to the New World. Many times he had spoke of his journey there and of the kindness of a woman with that very name, many times, a favorite tale of Solange's eccentric father. At the birth of his daughter, this word alone came from his lips as the sun had streamed through a window. She had lived up to the name.

Raphaela knew her friend had a dark side as well, and at unguarded moments it threatened to rise up and block the light that emanated from her. A sadness bred from weariness of balls, aristocracy and being a debutante. Being at court and breeding children for some bore was not a life Solange would choose willingly, but it could not be avoided. Intelligence and adventure came to women of nobility very rarely. Even a queen found it unwise to openly outwit her husband or other noblemen, it could cost her life itself. The few that had dared often died horrible deaths at the stake or the guillotine. Her friend hid her disappointments well.

Solange brought her horse around beside Raphaela's, and their mounts snorted in a greeting. Happiness shone from her face, which had flushed from the exhilarating ride. *She really enjoys being away from the pretense of Paris,* thought Raphaela, *if not for Gregor it would be a task to get her to return.*

"Hunyadi is glorious! He does not miss a single command, no matter how softly I speak or touch." Solange leaned across the gap in between the animals to touch her friend's arm. "Thank you for thinking of this, I needed to be out in the air. Besides it will be time for me to leave soon. Then I'll be married and there will such rare opportunities for us to spend time with each other." A sadness filled Raphaela's eyes, and their mournful gaze touched Solange to the bone. They would cherish their time together, girlish giggling and playful antics; for they both knew that very soon they would be women. They rode on through the afternoon in a quiet camaraderie, each unwilling to speak due to emotions that may have betrayed the bitterness felt for that loss.

Late that evening they returned from their ride to join the family once again in the dining hall. Raphaela rambled enthusiastically to her parents about their day. Solange listened patiently; Raphaela left little chance for anyone to speak. Solange was also curious that again Leone did not attend the family's meal. To hide her secret she must remain silent and not ask any revealing questions. Solange found herself waiting in anticipation for the evening to end.

She looked up to find the Baroness' gaze upon her. A look of speculation lingered in those penetrating green eyes. A shiver ran down her spine, as if icy fingers touched there and in her mind. Unable to hold the eyes that probed at her Solange looked down in guilt. Did the woman know her thoughts? Was she able to pick them from her head? Impossible.

"Solange?" the Baroness questioned, "You seem to have much on your mind this evening." Solange wrung her hands together under the table. "Is there something that troubles you, child?"

Ever more suspicious of that stare, Solange simply answered, "No, the full day has tired me, and I was thinking about how I would write to Gregor about it." Satisfied that she had responded appropriately, she returned to eating. The Baroness asked nothing else, allowed her answer to suffice, but Solange felt the icy tendrils curling in her mind still throughout the remainder of the meal.

Once the evening had ended, Solange feigned sleep until the castle grew quiet. Assured that all slept in their chambers, she crept down the hall with candle in hand, her destination the west wing and Leone's small room. Quietly she pushed upon the cold, stone wall. It opened without hesitation, as though expecting her arrival. Leone was dressed much as he was the previous evening motioned for her to enter.

"Solange," her name on his tongue so smooth, "I am so pleased you returned." His sincerity touched her.

"I could not help but to return." Solange took in his beauty as she walked into the room. The fire flickering in his green eyes and light touching the black curls on his handsomely sculpted head entranced her as she chose a chair opposite him. "You intrigue me, Leone."

"How is that my angel?" he questioned, emerald gaze never leaving her face.

"Who are you?" Her eyes searched his, seeking some answer, but found only mystery.

"I have told you," Leone said. "My name is Leone Noguchi, this is my family home."

"Why have you not joined the family at any meal?" she asked pointedly. "Why does no one speak of you?"

Leone sighed. "Solange, I have been away. Constantly my business draws me from the castle, usually everyone is retired for the evening when I return. Soon you will understand." He reached out and held her hand.

"Are you the uncle?" she asked.

"Uncle? And whose uncle would that be?" Leone smiled slightly.

Solange questioned him no more and did not pull away. They sat for some time simply sharing the slight embrace. She told him of her life in Paris, what brought her to the castle, and of her engagement to Gregor.

"Do you love this Gregor?" Leone waited for her answer.

"I suppose so," Solange faltered. "He is the only boy I have ever known. My parents will be very pleased when we are married." She dropped her eyes from Leone's face. "He is very handsome and a prince, many girls would be thrilled to be his bride."

"Describe him to me." His curiosity surprised her.

"He has blond hair, blue eyes, and looks far younger than he is. Always tall and strong in his soldiers uniform, though he is very kind." Solange returned her gaze to Leone's. "He is very different from you."

"Will you marry him, then?" He gazed tenderly at her lip, which trembled uncertainly.

"I must." Solange looked away again. "I have given my word."

"Solange, look at me." She could not resist his command. Her eyes lifted to meet his. "Please reconsider. Since the moment you walked into my room, my heart was yours. I am overwhelmed by the torment of living without you." A gasp fell from her lips. "I want you with me always, please do not deny me."

Solange sat shocked by his fervent plea. They had only just met, even though there existed an immediate closeness. Flustered by his boldness, she could only blush and turn away. In her mind she felt icy probes teasing her thoughts. "I know we have only just met, young one, but I can see all about you in your mind. The person I find there fills me with emotions unfelt for many years."

One long finger touched her chin and lifted her face towards him again, and neither spoke a word. Leone leaned forward to capture her parted lips in a deep lingering kiss. No one had ever kissed her this way before, not even Gregor. Every morsel of resistance melted on her lips as his tongue probed there. Arms like vises circled her waist and crushed her bosom to him. Her heart pounded fiercely in her head, threatening to overtake her sanity. Reluctantly Leone pulled his lips from hers and stepped back. If not for his hands on her upper arms she would have fallen. His emerald gaze burned into her eyes.

"Do you feel it, Solange?" he questioned. "Do you feel the passion between us? You must decide now my love." She looked up at him in confusion.

"Decide what now?" she asked.

"Will you stay with me forever?" Leone pulled her close again. "My heart will break without you. You mustn't return to this Gregor. He is but a boy and too weak for someone as strong as you."

Solange leaned against Leone, her body quaking uncontrollably, images and thoughts swirling in her mind, moving too fast for comprehension. "Yes," her answer came as a whisper, even before she thought of what she said.

At this Leone kissed her again and let his lips trail across her cheek to the pulse in her neck. Her skin gave no resistance to the sharp teeth that invaded, it succumbed to his sucking lips. Leone did not drain her, but only sipped from her, not enough to make her change. When he finished, he lifted his head to look into her eyes. The ocean blue, clouded over like a stormy sky, had a vacant quality not there before.

He understood all too well how the first bite can affect, drowning one in a euphoria unlike anything known to humans. "You must leave now, young one." He gently pulled away from her, and Solange nearly collapsed. "My angel, you are so weak, perhaps I took too much? Can you make it back alone?"

"I think so . . ." She leaned toward him, swaying in his grasp. Her voice, far away, lost somewhere in a fog, asked, "What did you do to me?"

"Solange, you must be strong," he sighed. "If we are to be together forever, you must go through some changes. It will take a long time and it will be gradual. This is the first step." He pulled her close again. "Do not be afraid, young one, I will always be there. You will not face this alone." Solange only nodded.

When he looked down he saw her eyes closed and knew she could not make it back. Could he risk carrying her to her chamber? If he was seen, it would near the end for Leone and his angel. Only his daughter knew of his existence and what sort of creature he was. All others thought him long dead. Leone thought of the girl he held in his arms; they would have to fake a death for her. He must not let any harm come to Solange. Many would destroy her if they guessed the change she was going through. Carefully, he lifted her with his arm under her knees and her back.

No candle was needed in the dim hallway, as Leone knew darkness. Swiftly as possible, he strode down the passageway to Solange's sleeping chamber. He slid her under the linens and arranged them over her. A downy cheek, so smooth under his touch, begged his lips for a slight kiss. Then, the vampire was gone.

CHAPTER TEN

Perplexed

Nestled in darkness, the Atlanta streets held few tenants; perhaps a few of the homeless, or someone with no better sense than to be there at this hour. From his barred window in the downtown police station, Morris Sanford had watched the sun set hours ago, conscious of its slow descent as he worked. The fluorescent lighting cast a faint blue tone to the white papers piled in neat stacks around his desk. Remnants of a sandwich and chips lay atop crumpled debris in the trash can at his right, telling of a dinner he had paused only slightly for. Two case histories lay open in front of him.

Over and over he had looked for some sort of clue of a suspect, and he found none. Two things tied them together, loss of blood and they both had records. The loss of blood reminded him of the conversation he had with Hugh at the morgue earlier.

At four o'clock in the afternoon Sanford made his routine appearance in the examining room of the medical examiner. Hugh had been about his morbid task as the detective entered; standing over the latest victim's corpse. The bright light shined on the receding hairline, shadowing the lines on the short medical examiner's face and above the surgical green face mask, Hugh's cornflower eyes were hooded and intense on his work. "Don't lose anything in there Hugh," the detective said as he sat on a convenient stool. "Find anything I can use?"

"Found a lot of things, but I don't think they'll help you." Hugh placed his scalpel and clamps on a shining tray, covered the cadaver, and pulled off his gloves. Under his mask he sighed, "Let's go into my office."

Sanford followed him into an adjoining room he used for an office, meticulously clean, would be the only word to describe it. Unlike his own office, there were no papers stacked, no food in his wastebasket; the man had not even idly doodled on his blotter, and it was as clean as the examining room they had just left. Hugh sat down in his swivel chair and laid a manila file he had brought from the other room on his desk. A thin, almost feminine hand raised to scratch at a lackluster brown sideburn, a thinking habit Sanford knew well. The look of worry that accompanied it confirmed his thoughts.

"Well?"

"What I found makes things even more confusing," he stated soberly.

"More? Tell me," Sanford waited attentively.

"First I did test the pile of ashes, I was right, it is his penis. There are no traces of an accelerant. You know as well as I do that human flesh does not burn that well without some sort of accelerant. I've sent a sample off to a lab that has more in-depth testing equipment, but I don't think they'll find anything." Hugh stopped and looked back down at the file in front of him. He looked up at Sanford, an intense question lurked behind his eyes as he continued. "The loss of blood in both victims is tremendous. Less than a pint in either of them. Both have slashes at the throat; obviously that's the cause for loss of blood and death. There would have been more blood settled into the tissue, but there's not." He paused. "But what happened to the blood?"

"It drained out on the ground. Where else would it go?" Sanford asked.

"The first victim had been moved, so it was possible the blood did drain out. But no chance of that with the second, he was killed on the spot." Again, he scratched the sideburn. "I called the lab to get the results of the soil samples we took. The blood on the ground is only a half an inch deep and covered less than two feet of surface. That's not enough, he lost over eleven pints of blood! Someone took the blood." Very rarely did the examiner raise his voice, very rarely did he not have an answer. Sanford remained silent, allowing him to continue. "Also when examining the area around the gashes on the throat, I found saliva."

"Spit?" Sanford leaned forward. "Is it his spit? Could he have drooled and it ran down into the cuts?"

"No, it's not his," Hugh stated flatly. "In fact, it's not normal saliva, I tested it for a blood type, but found something bizarre. There was not one blood type, but a conglomerate of blood types, no one dominant." Hugh threw a pen down on the folder. "It beats the hell out of me."

"Is it possible that the blood is being drank? Are you saying that it's not human, maybe an animal?" Sanford's thoughts spun in his head like a kaleidoscope, frantically trying to make a pattern.

"No, not an animal." Hugh paused and stared at a spot on the wall for several long minutes like it held the answer to the universe. Abruptly he caught himself and continued. "I tested the saliva with every sample in the computer for a match. Information on every species known is stored in my database, for reasons of rabies or whatever, it never hurts to be prepared. No match found. That rules out animal, it does have strong similarities to human, but something's not normal."

"Could you be wrong, Hugh?"

"Anything's possible but I've been very thorough. It could just be contaminated, I guess." Hugh stopped and scratched his sideburn again, as if he could find the answer with that act alone.

"Whatever it is, it's found on both victims, slash-marks made by same method, with the same nails. And it is nails, not any kind of manmade instrument. No samples of nail or skin though. But definitely same killer and female."

"Are you still certain it's a woman?"

"Yes, one thing that I was able to determine from the saliva was gender, absolutely female." He shook his head. "There's something strange happening with these murders. I've done my research, now it's your turn."

After that, he'd handed Sanford a copy of the file made for the detective. Sanford had taken it reluctantly; the case was becoming more and more complicated, and it made his stomach queasy. He left the medical examiner alone with his corpses and the sterile environment he had created.

Now it was two o'clock in the morning. Sanford poured over evidence gathered in the crime lab and from Hugh. He had no answers. Would there be another one? He hoped not. If so, the FBI would have to be called in. They had specialists in serial killers, but he hated handing over any investigation to someone else.

Sanford cross-referenced these case descriptions with any across the country on his computer. He would cross-reference with bizarre murders, as these certainly were; bloodless corpses, satanic ritual killings, things of that nature. Perhaps somewhere he would get a lead. Why the hell didn't people just shoot each other anymore?

CHAPTER ELEVEN

Storage Center

Shana

Key in hand, Sijn found the large garage-like space she was looking for. It was not hard to find after telling the land-lord that it had belonged to her father. With the key and the papers from inside the metal box, there had been no prob-lem convincing him of that fact. The place was not classy by any means and surprised her that Dereck entrusted this place with his things. A turn of the key, a loud rumble and the large metal door rolled up and open. *Sijn, you have something here,* she thought to herself.

Inside was furniture, boxes, paintings, and books nearly stacked to the ceiling. Her heart dropped: to go through all of this would take forever and she didn't have forever. Before Sijn went through anything, she told the little man standing behind her that she could manage on her own. Shrugging, the owner left the girl to her own means. Now to find the safe first.

Box corners scraped her legs and sides as Sijn climbed and squeezed her way to the back. There among the boxes and behind a huge desk sat the safe. The huge relic was black and stood as high as herself. It looked old and dirty, and the grime on her fingers when she touched it confirmed that. She used the combination from the lockbox and the door creaked open, revealing its contents. Old brown paper covered something to make bundles. With a dirty hand she pulled out one of the bundles and untied the string holding the paper on. Money fell to the floor in all denominations. The safe was full of it. There had to be millions here. Her heart raced with excitement.

Also in the safe were volumes of books. Some ancient and worn, along with newer volumes stood end to end. Picking up one, she read the date September Eighteenth, Seventeen Ninety-two. With shock she held up the letter written to Solange next to the diary and realized it was written in Dereck's handwriting. Sijn read on and on, entranced by what she saw. The number of books and pages were never ending, so she picked through them, reading bits and pieces every couple of pages. Amazement and then panic crept into her heart. *Oh my God,* she kept saying over and over. Dereck Cliffe, the father of her child, was a vampire.

In all her years of reading about things of darkness, listening to gothic music, and wearing black, she had never guessed that these creatures really existed. *Had he drank from her?* she asked herself. Surely he had, yet she did not remember. She read on.

Some of the pages were so old they nearly crumbled when she turned them. The pages were yellowed with time and written in ink starting to fade. Dereck had been quite a writer, everything about his long life inscribed in these diaries. Sijn was the first human to read them. Guilt built within her for spying into his life, but it felt like the right thing for her to do. After all, she carried his child in her womb. Child, that word rang in her head like a bell. *What would her child be?* She thought. *Would it be human or some sort of monster?* Dereck's face appeared in her thoughts. That man had been no monster, no matter if he had been a vampire. The curiosity overwhelmed her and she read further.

For two hours she read nonstop until it was time for the storage center to close. Sijn informed the storage manager that she would be back tomorrow to have everything shipped out of the space. In her purse she had cash, pulled from the safe. She went back to the cheap motel only to get her things and relocate to a nicer hotel.

This one had air and a clean bathroom. There were no stains on the bed and no cigarette burns on the furniture. Tomorrow she would go and ship everything home. Then she must find Shana.

*   *   *

Two weeks later.

The curtains on her bed kept all light out. Since Dereck had died, the darkness made her feel better; but not as good as the Jack Daniels did. Shana Collins lay naked in her Victorian four-poster bed, covered in the burgundy brocade bedclothes. How many days she had lain there had been forgotten. The dirty blonde hair on her head hung limp and matted with days of neglect. Tobacco smoke clung to the dark velvet of the draperies and to her mouth. Strong liquor odor permeated from Shana's pores. Truth be known, she stank.

Depression could be a horrible thing; to Shana it seemed an old friend, something familiar and easy to stay in. Her friend's death had been so hard on her. First, death was the one thing she couldn't deal with. Second, Dereck should have been immortal. She couldn't deal with it, so she drifted back to sleep.

Dreams of Dereck filled her sleep. His face drifting in and out of the clouds in her mind. Even now when she lay half-awake on her bed his memory flooded Shana's thoughts. Dreams of times etched in her mind by their sheer magic. She had known he was the sexiest man she had ever seen. She had not known he was a vampire

It had been the night of a Nightbird concert at a local club. At that point Shana had known Dereck for several years, having interviewed him numerous times for her magazine. That night would be different, as she no longer did interviews, and she came as a friend. It had made her nervous to be there without the pretense of doing a story. She had been excited.

Late in the afternoon Shana had went and knocked on the door of the bus which sat outside the club. A roadie came to the door and told her to go away. When she explained who she was, he gave her a little more info but still didn't let her on the bus. He explained that Dereck was taking a nap and couldn't be bothered right now. Being who she was, that didn't sit with her very well; not the nap, but being barred from the bus. "Couldn't I just wait inside?" she asked. The bus door slammed in her face. Shana took that as a no.

So for at least two hours she had sat in her car reading. Of course it was comfortable, most limos were. Shana hated it. She missed driving all of the time. These days she dare not leave the house alone. One, she got mobbed by fans and two; the church nuts were always trailing along. Everywhere the writer went they followed with the picketing, it was a pain in the ass. So there she sat with her bodyguard Mike in the car, reading and generally watching the bus for signs of life.

"I hate fucking sitting here like a putz," Shana stated for the fiftieth time and inhaled on a cigarette. She straightened out the white frothy lace that spilled out of the sleeves of her purple crushed-velvet top. Mike looked back at her doubtfully but didn't say anything. "Mike, I worked hard to be famous so I wouldn't have to be a putz anymore, guess some people don't know that."

"Then why wait for him?" was his reply. He took a drink from a cup full of God-knew-what and stroked his beard. For years he had been a friend and now her bodyguard. His hair was going gray and his beard had gone almost white in the time that she knew him. Always the calm one, albeit the grumpy one, she needed that. She needed someone to tell her this Dereck Cliffe was just a man. Mike was that person.

"You know how it is with him," Shana explained, taking a sip of her own Jack Daniels, her preferred drink. "Something about him drives me crazy, its like an addiction."

"I'll take you to rehab," he said.

A snort her only reply, Shana looked out the window and noticed a van pull up to the backstage door. She knew that van. "Hey, Mike, Johnny's here," she said and pointed at the van. "He didn't tell me he was playing tonight, that shit."

Johnny Morgan was one of her dearest friends. The guitar player for a local band, Shana had met him years back when she went to a club. His playing had blown her away and his silliness won her over. She told him that she only interviewed vampire bands at the time. He said he wanted to bite her. From then on, his band Whisper became like family to her, and she was always hanging out with them when they played and sometimes even when they practiced. She left the car, with Mike in tow, to race across the parking lot toward him.

"Hey baby," she shouted, nearly flinging herself at Johnny. His arms went out to hug her tight. His long blond hair waving in the breeze, he reminded Shana of Greg Allman, especially with mustache and beard. "Why didn't you tell me you were opening for Dereck?"

"Didn't know myself until a little while ago," Johnny explained. "Hey you look good," he said close to her ear, and then sniffed, "And smell good too. Smell like a sweet apple blossom, mmm." His lips brushed the side of her neck.

"Knock it off would ya? You are so silly," Shana told him, but she was laughing. She liked flirting with Johnny, it felt safe. Unlike the man sleeping on the bus. She let go of his neck and he let her go so they could walk inside.

"Since your friend is here do you wanna sing with us tonight? Just one song, Didi won't care, would ya?" Johnny asked their powerful female lead as she walked through the door. She immediately came to Shana and hugged her.

"Hey girl, and no I don't care. I think it would be cool, which one are you gonna do?" Didi asked. The singer's body seemed so small next to Shana's, but looks were deceiving. Inside this petite woman lived a diva that was a cross between Tina Turner, Janis Joplin and a keg of dynamite.

"I didn't say I would. This is different from being at rehearsal: this is in front of people," she told them nervously, thinking, especially Dereck Cliffe. "I can't possibly sing in front of him."

"You used to do standup four nights a week, you're a pro in front of people, " Didi said.

"But that's not singing, there's a reason I tell jokes," she explained. "I don't know if I can do it."

"Ah hell, girl, just have a couple drinks and you'll be fine," Mike chimed in.

"Yeah Shana, we can do the Meatloaf cover," Johnny offered. "That way, we can share the vocals and you won't be alone. I'll be with you." He gave her the pleading puppy dog look that always won her over.

"Okay, I'll do it," she accepted.

"But I think you sounded good doing 'End of the World' the other day just goofing off," the singer told her.

"That's your song," Shana argued.

"I have lots of songs, you do that one, since your man is here tonight," Didi replied with a smile.

"Yeah, he'll probably laugh his gorgeous ass off too," she said, swallowing a nervous lump in her throat. She was relieved when one of Dereck's roadies came to get her. Once on the bus she waited for Dereck to wake up.

"Hey guys, you've got to see this crowd out here," Jeff, the guitar tech, said as he jumped on the bus. He pointed out toward the parking lot where the noise of a crowd could be heard.

Shana peeked through the curtains covering the bus window and sighed. Her nemesis strode around the parking lot with a sign in hand, chanting ridiculous rhetoric. "Oh, great," she said. "It looks like the good Reverend has arrived." Some of his goons must have followed her, but didn't they always? They were going to ruin her evening with Dereck if she didn't think of something.

Around and around they marched their signs reading: "DEATH TO PORNOGRAPHERS," "SLAY THE ANTICHRIST," and, "THE WAGES OF SIN IS DEATH." Of course Shana had seen them before, outside her own home, marching on the sidewalk. Reverend Jenkins and his crew thought her to be the evil creature of their warped imaginations; it sucked being the flavor of the month. Why couldn't some people distinguish the difference between fiction and real life? She wrote vampire books, but that didn't make her a vampire. How could she be something that didn't even exist?

"People get strange when religion is involved, luv," Dereck's sultry voice whispered in her ear. Shana jumped, she hadn't even heard him come from the back of the bus. He hadn't made a noise until he had spoken. She looked at him, serene and beautiful, comparing him to the sexy banshee he was onstage, the two images fought each other in her head. His breath upon her ear had left her all tingly, a soft sexual stirring felt down to her gut. As she looked into those dark eyes, a feeling of calm came over her. No longer did she feel as bothered by the Reverend as usual. "Don't worry, I wouldn't let him hurt you tonight, my guys will keep him away."

She did feel calm, but told him, "Oh, it isn't just tonight, it's everyday," Shana said with resignation. "There is a restraining order, they are not allowed within one hundred feet of me, but they push that as far as they can. My lawyer is trying to get that changed."

Dereck leaned closer to her, their lips almost touching, Shana wanted him to kiss her. Just when his lips touched hers, someone banged on the bus door. She jumped back, feeling the magic of those lips slip away. A loud, Southern voice yelled from the closed door, "Hey, Shana, it's me Johnny!" She groaned out loud and went to the door to let him in. Johnny stepped up into the bus, quickly shutting the door behind him. "Whew, your fan club is out in full force tonight, darlin'," he said with a stupid grin on his face.

"You know, being a smartass could get you hurt, Johnny," she told him trying to pretend she was mad.

"Ain't hurt me yet," he said and smiled. Then the guitarist turned his attention to Dereck. "Hey, Johnny Morgan, it's good to finally meet you." With that he extended his hand. The singer shook his hand and smiled. Johnny continued talking. "I had to tell you, I know she's here tonight but this here is my woman. She's a good girl so you better be treating her right."

"Damn, Johnny would you stop telling people that?" Shana rolled her eyes, because he told everybody that. "I'm not his woman," she told Dereck.

"Hey the man's got a right to know that he stole you away from me," Johnny said, looking for all the world like he was serious. "You don't love me anymore."

Dereck regarded him with amusement but said nothing.

"I still love you, goofball," she said to Johnny. "Now we have to find a way to deal with Mister Personality out there." Thoughts swirled in her head, around and around. When one struck home Shana simply smiled at the two men. "We know what a fool he looks like. The public has seen glimpses of it, like the time he claimed that purple dinosaur was the Antichrist. Let's give them a big look at the idiot."

"What are you planning?" Johnny asked.

Dereck simply sat there staring at her, and when Shana looked at his eye, they seemed to glow. She had the strangest feeling that he was in her mind, icy fingers prodding at her thoughts. He smiled, then she realized she stared back at him as intensely as he had her. The eye contact started that pull in her gut again, she smiled.

"Well, let me make some phone calls. I'm gonna need Mike to get my cell phone out of the limo, go see if you can pry him away from the bar would ya?" She asked.

"I'll go," Jeff said as he stood up from the bus driver's seat. Shana looked surprised, she had forgotten he was there. He left the bus to fight his way though the small flock of protesters.

"Okay, Dereck, are you sold out tonight?" Shana asked. He shook his head no. "Good, let's pack the house shall we? In order to publicly embarrass him we must have an audience. Besides we all could use the publicity for our own reasons." She smiled. "Johnny, go warn your guys that something big is brewing and be prepared for mobs of people. Then go over to the radio van and tell that deejay to get his ass over for the interview of a lifetime, the best one he'll ever have."

"Will do," he said, and as he went past her, Johnny stopped and hugged her tightly and kissed her on the cheek. "Give 'em hell darlin." Then he let her go and got off the bus.

"He really does love you, you know," Dereck said.

"I know, we've been friends a long time," she told him. "He's like a dog chasing cars though, if he caught it he wouldn't know what to do with it."

"I don't have that problem," he said and gave her the most wicked smile she'd ever seen on his face. How smug he looked sitting there, but how sexy also. His tight jeans so temptingly torn in certain places, showing delicious patches of pale skin. Midnight blue silk framed a v-shaped section of pale chest and abdomen that disappeared right above his waistband. Long black hair softly touched the shirt at the shoulders and framed that little boy face. That sweet face that never aged, and not a single wrinkle marred the perfection of it. Smooth, white skin surrounded those intense eyes that burned with a light unknown, a light that pulled her in toward those soft, pouty lips.

"Oh, I'm sure you don't, " she agreed, there was no way to argue with that one. To keep from being pulled in further, she changed the subject. "Are you with me on my little scheme?"

"Anything you say, luv. After all, who can argue with the Antichrist?" Dereck quipped, his lovely lips curving into a devilish smile again. She wanted to hit him, but he was so damned beautiful.

"Ha ha very funny," Shana told him. "I'm glad someone thinks so."

"Clever, clever girl, " he said.

The bus door opened, keeping them from being alone for too long. Mike came in, full of piss and vinegar, as usual. His heavy belly fighting with his pants, only the suspenders keeping them up, jiggled as he hoisted himself up the bus steps. In his hand was the cell phone. He turned and yelled from the top of the steps at the protesters, "Yeah, your mama too, you sacks of shit!"

"Mike don't provoke them," she suggested.

"Stick your sign where the sun don't shine, scumsucker," he roared and held his middle finger aloft.

"Mike! That's not helping," she pleaded.

He slammed the bus door and turned to her and said, "I'm supposed to be your bodyguard and I can't do a damn thing about those assholes!" The man sighed deeply. "The biggest threat to you and the law gets in the way. I have people I can call who don't care about the law. We can take care of that."

"So do I," added Dereck. "It could be a very easy thing to rid the world of Reverend Jenkins."

Shana looked at both of them, shocked that Dereck had jumped on the bandwagon with Mike. She'd never considered him violent or dangerous before. "Absolutely not," she told them. "As long as the world knows he's a pain in my ass, he needs to stay alive. Right now I'd be suspect number one. No, our main goal is to be a big a pain in the ass to him as he is to us. Which will begin right now."

Shana took the cell phone from Mike and began dialing. "Alan? Hi, this is Shana Collins, how are you?" Her voice, pleasant and full of Southern charm, went through to the other end. "Listen, how fast can you have a news truck over here?"

Within twenty minutes, not just one news truck, but several pulled into the parking lot. Johnny had been inside rounding up early concert-goers to march and chant, "Censorship is Un-American." And they were getting louder than Jenkins' group. When all the cameramen had set up, Mike gave her a signal. "Showtime."

"Are you ready?" she asked Dereck. He just looked at her and motioned for her to lead. They stepped off the bus into bright lights and microphones.

"Miss Collins, do you have a statement about the protest?" One reporter asked first. They all pushed the microphones at her.

"I just want to let people know that I didn't start this today," Shana told them. "I came down to spend time with my friends." Jenkins' group started shouting things at her. "It has been said that I am evil or a vampire, by certain people," she continued. "This is simply not true, and is nothing more than the misguided rantings of unnamed deranged individuals. What I am is a writer, a woman, and a mother. A member of society who has been unfairly harassed and threatened. First, let me say to the Christians that are watching today; do not let the speeches and name calling you are hearing make you prejudiced against me. I live a very normal life, raising my child, and working. My work is fiction, just fiction, like any other writer on the market. Second, I want people to know that the ones who claim to do this in the name of religion stalk me, threaten my family, and vandalize my property are not my impression of the Christian community. Real followers of God teach the Bible with love and respect, not with hatred and threats. The slanderous accusations made against me today by this sick and twisted person is a poor reflection on that community and should not be tolerated by them." This speech was followed by rounds of applause by onlookers but with hateful catcalls by Jenkins' people.

"I want to encourage all of my fans and any fan of freedom of speech to come down here tonight and peacefully show these hypocrites that we will not be threatened, we will not be bullied, and that we have the power of love on our side. Anyone that comes down for the concert tonight and brings one of my books will get it autographed. Please, this is a nonviolent event, prove there is no evil behind our intentions, but that we will be heard." Applause filled the air.

Suddenly Jenkins made his way to the forefront of the group to the microphones. Mike stepped up between him and Shana. The man was obviously mad, and his eyes looked glazed as he shouted at the reporters. "She is the devil incarnate! Don't be fooled by her lies, she is Lilith! Filth spews from her very mouth, the mouth of a blood-drinker!" he screamed, pushing toward her.

"Okay, buddy, you're not supposed to be within one hundred feet of her," Mike told him calmly as he grabbed the man and jerked him back. Then two police officers came forward and dragged the debunked reverend back.

"As you can see, the man is deranged, which is why I have a restraining order against him," she explained to the press. Shana then looked at the crowd and raised her arms and said, "We will not be censored." Dereck's and her fans went wild, yelling and applauding.

Mike came back to her side and pushed her toward the club, saying, "She has to go inside now, she is performing tonight as well. That's all the statement she can make at this time."

"Did I look stupid?" Shana whispered in his ear.

"Naw, just keep walking," he said as he kept pushing her away from the reporters.

Dereck hung back to give a brief interview to the reporters which brought more noise from the crowd that grew minute by minute.

Suddenly, blinding light entered into her dark, cozy world. The drapes had been drawn back by her friend Jan. "Okay, enough is enough," her friend told her sternly. "You've been laying up here feeling sorry for yourself for two weeks now. Yes, Dereck is dead, but life goes on." She pulled the curtains back even further, letting the sun that streamed through the paladin windows of the bedroom seep into Shana's brain. "My God, what a mess! If you keep this up we'll have roaches for sure!"

Shana looked at the nightstand. Its marble top was covered with empty cartons of Cherry Garcia, Jack Daniels bottles, dirty glasses, and cigarette butts overflowing the ashtrays. She had to admit it was pretty nasty, but didn't care. With a little work, she hoisted her body up and swung her legs over the side of the bed. Warm slippers waited for her feet and she reached for her favorite robe of burgundy and black velvet. "I need a shower."

"I'd say that's an understatement, you are rank!" Janet said with a wrinkled-up nose and a wave of hand. "The tabloid people are outside chomping at the bit for a pic like this. Do you really want them to get it?"

"I hate those parasites! What are they saying about me now?" Shana asked as she made her way toward the bathroom. "What load of crap are they making up?"

"Actually they are saying you are in the midst of a breakdown over Dereck's death. That you and he were secret lovers up until his death," Janet told her. "Unfortunately, they are not far from the truth of things, from the looks of you."

The writer shot her an angry look. She wasn't breaking down, Shana thought to herself, she just enjoyed a good depression. Pushing a button on her table, all the blinds went down on her windows, keeping prying eyes out of her bedroom. Padding over to the windows, she peeked out at the gawkers gathered around her fence. "Look at them. You'd think they'd have something better to do. They are always here, the fans, the nuts, the press; don't they have families or something?" she asked.

"Fame always carries a price," was Janet's sorrowful response. "Now let's get you up and going. First, you need to shower. I'll get the maid in here to clean up this mess." Shana had no choice but to head in that direction.

Inside her bathroom, Janet had started the shower, steam already collecting on the antique gilded mirrors. A dark marble covered the countertops and shower, its brown and black pattern shone almost like tortoise shell. Shana stepped into the hot jets of water, letting it wash her misery down upon the marble. Misery exuded from her, for the last couple of weeks that's what she had known. Dereck had been her lover only once but she had wanted him long after that. Those black eyes would haunt her the whole of her life. Even now, the mere thought of them made her stomach tingly. As her hands moved the soapy sponge over her body, she imagined his hands. Then the tears came.

Hot rivers of tears mixed with the steamy water that washed down her face and body. No one here to listen to her sorrowful wails. As the misery consumed her, Shana leaned heavily on the shower walls, sliding down to the built-in bench. She knew she had to get a grip on herself, to stop this before it killed her. There was no sharing of this pain, it would be kept in her heart like so many other things. Even Janet did not know the depths of her feelings for Dereck Cliffe; she wasn't so sure she had known herself.

As long as she had known him, the time just hadn't been right to let him know. Somewhere deep inside she knew that he knew, but was too much of a gentleman to say so. With Solange in his life, Shana could have never been more than casual. Casual sex didn't bother her, she'd had her share, but with Dereck it had not felt casual to her.

＊　　＊　　＊

Sijn sat in the back of the cab staring at the buildings rolling by. How amazing was it that the adventure brought her home? She directed the driver through the shady streets of Belmont, past the little square houses built for the mill workers and then past the mansions built for the mill owners. Textiles had built this community, like so many others in North Carolina. The mills had offered an almost singular source of income for decades, but were now in their decline. Even now some of these houses remained in their care. The house they stopped in front of had been built by mill dollars.

Yellow-ochre brick walls loomed in front of her. Topped off by green tile shingles, the house stood three stories high and dominated both streets that ran on either side of it. Paladin windows over French doors surrounded the first floor, each one giving glimpses of the champagne brocade curtains inside. Grand Porticos stood on each side of the house, one over the curved drive and one that faced the gardens. Magnolias and crepe myrtles dotted their white and fuchsia blossoms against the emerald green background of the lawn. Surrounding the triangular layout of the property was a fence constructed from the same yellow-ochre brick and wrought iron. That fence stood covered with people, fans, protesters, and security. She would never get in.

The driver stopped in front of the main gate, she got out and asked him to wait. Sijn did not think the security looked friendly at all. Confidently she approached the guard at the gate, holding her head high and acting as if she was important. His hand came up when she reached him and he asked her to step away. "I just flew in from L.A. to see her, it's very important that I speak with Shana," she told him.

"Yeah, you and every other person out here today," the guard commented. "Now just go stand with the crowd or go home." He started to turn away from her to emphasize her non-importance.

"But does every fan out here have this?" Sijn reached in her bag and pulled out a heavy, cream paper sealed with red wax. She waved it under his nose, "Do you know who this is from? It's from Dereck Cliffe before he died. If you don't believe me it has his crest pressed into the wax. Shana will know." The guard still wasn't sure but he called the house anyway.

*   *   *

Inside, Shana still thought of Dereck in the shower. The hot water mingled so well with her tears. Desperately she struggled to remember that night. The night she sang and looked down into his eyes, the night they made love. She could still feel his lips and teeth against her breast and his hands on her thighs. Hearing his words whispered in her ear, "Clever, beautiful girl," he had said while he thrust into her. It had been euphoric and never before or since had she felt that good. Longing for that made her hurt so much more.

"Ya getting pruney," Jan said as she reached in and turned the water off in the shower, leaving Shana crying in the steam. Being wakened from her dreams made her angry, and she scowled at her friend. "Mike's calling up here, says it's urgent. So you have to get dressed."

"But I don't have to like it," Shana answered. The writer walked into the bedroom, lit a cigarette and poured a Jack on the rocks. Not bothering to dress, she stood there and enjoyed those two luxuries everyone kept trying to take away from her. She was just reaching for her robe when Mike walked in.

"God Bless America!!!" Mike bellowed. "Could you have some respect for an old man and put ya damn clothes on!"

"It ain't like you haven't seen me naked before," Shana told him, tying on a clean robe of black velvet and onyx beads. A silver brush stroked her wet hair, getting caught in the snags she had let go too long. "So what have you got?"

"The guys at the gate says some chick showed up with a letter for you sealed with wax," he explained. "Red wax with a bird on it."

"A bird?" She wondered to herself for a moment. "Bring the letter up and let the girl wait in the parlor."

"Okay," he lifted the receiver of his radio and yelled into it, "Send the letter up but keep the girl in the parlor. Yeah keep an eye on her, don't want her stealing nothing." Mike shut off his radio and headed for the door. "I'm gonna go check out this one, make sure she's on the up-and-up."

"Probably checking out how she looks, right Mike?" she asked him jokingly.

"That too." And he was gone.

"Shana, part of the reason I pulled you out of bed was because you have guests coming tonight," Jan told her. "Do you remember?"

She sure as hell didn't. Her perplexed expression gave away her confusion. "Who?" Shana asked.

"The movie people," her friend explained. "You know, the people with the money you need?"

"Oh, those guests, ewww, I did forget," Shana sighed. This could be a big deal for her. The inheritance that her husband left her wouldn't last her forever, especially with the lifestyle she lived. Security did not come cheap. This house alone had cost her nearly a million. "Well, call caterers or whatever you need to and I'll pull myself together as best I can."

"Okay, but I deserve a raise," Jan said as she walked out of the room, closing the door behind her.

Alone, Shana went to her closet and searched through her clothes. Most had been custom made for her. Cursed with a full figure, she constantly fought her weight. Large breasts, narrow hips and a stomach that liked to go chubby on her, she needed all the help she could get in hiding her flaws. She had found a lovely lady who made anything she could dream of from just a sketch. First she chose a black velvet body suit with a square neckline that showed an enormous amount of cleavage. She put it on after she found a black bra in the same velvet. To go over it she picked black Capri pants, pleated just enough to help hide the small swell of her belly. The crowning effect came in the form of a jacket-skirt combo. Green gold shantung formed a shawl-necked jacket that bloomed into a formal-length skirt. It fastened at her waist with several gold, onyx, and diamond buttons, hiding her thick middle while the skirt billowed out full to give her the appearance of hips. The collar, trimmed in black velvet and gold thread embroidery revealed her cleavage in a very extravagant way. The split down the front of the skirt waved back to show the pants underneath and the lining of black velvet. It made her look like something out of a movie. The advantage of being wealthy and weird was wearing what you damn well pleased.

When she was dressed, Mike came back in carrying the letter, which he handed to Shana. Sitting on a chaise near the bed, she lit another cigarette and began to read. Tears filled her eyes as she read the sweet words of her friend's last request. She looked up at Mike and asked, "What does this girl look like? Does she have red hair?"

"Hell no, black as soot, the kind that comes out of a bottle. Why?" he asked.

"I didn't think it would be Solange, but I had to ask. I knew it couldn't be her," she said with a sigh.

"Because she's supposed to be dead?"

"Because I should never have gotten this letter during the daylight," Shana sighed and laid her head on the armrest of the chaise.

*   *   *

Downstairs, Sijn had been escorted into the one of the main parlors on the first floor. Antiques and extravagant fabrics all around her, she had been afraid to sit on anything. Sijn waited, nervous and alone. She felt strange sitting on the antique chair, so small and poor. Having grown up in the trailer park, none of the Blacks had ever seen furniture like this in their homes or in their friends. It was quite intimidating; still wearing her ripped jeans, her cheap shoes and her dime store makeup, while sitting on this furniture. She should have stopped to buy new things for herself, but felt guilty for what she already had spent. Dereck didn't exactly leave it for her, but surely he would have provided something for his baby's mother.

Sijn took note of the richness around her. The trim molding had been painted cream with rich, red, paisley fabric on the walls. Complementing champagne gold curtains hung over the French doors, their brocade fabric embroidered with strands of tri-colored gold thread, blocking out the sun and prying eyes. The majority of the furniture looked Victorian to Sijn, but she wasn't an expert on that kind of stuff. It was all upholstered in either red velvet or cream brocade like the chair she sat on now. The floors were covered with an old Oriental rug done in colors of red, gold, and black. A carved marble fireplace stood unlit at one end of the parlor, displaying its leaves and cherubs. She noticed that an identical one stood at the opposite end of the house in the other parlor. That parlor held a grand piano, covered with a tasseled, brocade runner. This parlor had a wet bar that looked too new to be in one corner of the room. Very fancy digs, she thought; a little too fancy for her taste.

Just as she leaned over to look at a tiny teacup set on an adjacent table, a deep voice harrumphed behind her. Startled, she bolted upright in her seat and turned her head to look where the noise came from. It was the same man who had shown her in. He seemed ill at ease; this likely wasn't his normal work, forced to play host to a girl. He stood about five feet two inches and his frame overwhelmed by his massive belly, which hung over his belt. Jeans, work boots, and suspenders printed with rulers made up his clothes. He looked more like a construction worker than some writer's assistant. With his pudgy hands wringing each other, he walked over to her and said, "My name is Mike, I'm Shana's head of security and personal bodyguard. She'll be down soon, she's reading the letter and getting dressed." Sijn didn't comment that it was four in the afternoon. She just nodded while he continued. "It's gonna be a bit. Can I get you something to drink?" He gestured toward the bar.

"No thanks, I can't drink right now," Sijn told him.

He went over and fixed himself some wild concoction of liquors in a tall glass. Quickly Mike turned it up and drank over half, leaving moist droplets on his wiry gray beard. "I've got soda or iced tea if ya like?" he offered. After she accepted he fixed her a tea with a slice of lemon.

The man reminded Sijn of some grumpy fairy tale character, the way he fumbled around. He handed her the glass and sat down on a love seat opposite her, his belly nearly touching the floor between his bent knees. He smiled. "So, who the hell are you?" Mike asked with no effrontery.

"A friend of Dereck's. My name is Sijn. I'm actually from here but I just came from Cali yesterday. Strange circumstance brought me back home," she told him.

"Yeah? Like what?" he questioned, his eyes squinting as he checked her out.

"I'd really only like to tell that to Shana. I hate to retell a story, its kinda long," Sijn explained. "Besides, it's not exactly a happy story. I don't want to get too emotional before she comes down here."

"Well, you can tell it, I'm here now," came a smoky, alto voice from behind her.

Sijn turned to see Shana Collins standing at the doorway of the room. Her soft velvet slippers had made little noise on the stairs, allowing her to enter the room without notice. The woman strode over to the bar, shiny skirt billowing behind her. She poured herself a whiskey over ice and turned to stare at Sijn with warm green eyes. They reminded her of leaves before they turned colors in the fall, soft olive with flecks of amber. With her flamboyant outfit, Shana made Sijn feel completely underdressed and self-conscious. Her makeup was perfect, almost covering the shadows under her eyes and her hair curled just right. The woman was not exactly beautiful but striking. Without another word Shana lit a cigarette and sat on a chair between herself and Mike. "I'm waiting," was all she said.

"My name is Sijn Black," she started.

"Sure it is, " Shana interrupted with a half-sneer and roll of the eyes.

Her name was pronounced Singe and everyone thought it fake. It pissed her off. "Do you want to see my driver's license?" Sijn shot back angrily. "I didn't have to come here. Without a backwards glance I could have taken all the money and things Dereck left behind and not given a damn about telling you anything. And if you are going to be a bitch, I can just leave and take this with me." She stood up and held a large nylon bag up in the air.

"Calm the fuck down, would ya?" Shana said with a grimace and puff of smoke, her southern accent a little more pronounced than before. "It's just a strange name, I had to ask. Now sit down and tell me just how you got that letter and whatever it is in the bag."

Sijn sat down and took a deep breath, she truly needed a cigarette. "I got the letter from a storage place Dereck had in L.A. after the fire. Can I start the story from the very beginning? It's kinda long but you'll understand why I'm here better if you know how it started," she explained.

"Okay, Sijn Black, I like stories, so have at it," the writer said with a smirk. So Sijn began.

*   *   *

Dereck Cliffe had seemed like a dream to Sijn. His jet, black hair veiling piercing black eyes. That seductive melody grinding away at her heart as his guitar played and a voice rich as velvet sang. Music that held every emotion she had ever felt, joy, sadness, anger, desire, performed with fierceness worthy of a warrior. For years the posters hung on her walls, the videos played in the recorder, and music blared in her bedroom. His pale-skinned, dark-eyed beauty called to her, taunted her, and yes, seduced her. So when the band Nightbird announced they were touring, Sijn planned on being there. She had to drive to Charlotte, North Carolina to see them play but it was only a half hour drive. Sijn couldn't wait.

The night of the show arrived, and her nerves had ate away her until her stomach was nothing but boiling acid. For three long hours she had waited in line just to get in, freezing cold in her short black skirt and thin paisley jacket. Perseverance paid off, though, and Sijn found herself on the front row, pressed against a wooden barrier. Surrounded by people, unable to move, she just let herself go with the music blaring from the speakers. Every concert, every club, always plays the same songs before a show. Somewhere there is a list of concert songs all deejays must play before a band comes out. She didn't mind, you could never hear "Highway to Hell" too many times and everybody knew the words. Just as Ozzy belted out the last lines of "Crazy Train" the music was cut and the lights went down. The crowd around her swayed and screams of excitement went up all around her, welcoming the opening band.

A local band started the show, unlike Nightbird they seemed more concerned with their pretty boy looks than their music. Fluff, all too familiar guitar riffs, drum solos, and high vocals covered with long blond hair and lipstick. They were cute and though lots of the girls threw themselves toward the stage, Sijn barely moved. For the full thirty minutes they played she simply stared passively waiting for it to end, while the pretty lead singer smiled and rocked his hips in front of her. No deep passion filled the notes, no sweet sorrow tugged at her tears, the emotion of Nightbird noticeably absent to her. But it wouldn't be long now.

In what seemed an eternity the road crew took away the local band's gear and began setting up the stage for Nightbird. Again the constant flow of old rock songs filled the air, beside of her two girls compared notes on every band they had ever met before, lewdly discussing size of many names she recognized. Sijn had never met anyone before, never really wanted to until she saw Dereck Cliffe. As time wore on she got more and more fidgety, tired of people crowding her, sick of the bimbos chattering next to her. She lit a cigarette, the thick smoke curling from between lips as red as the Marlboro box that she tucked into the bodice of her lace tanktop. She dragged heavy on the strong cigarette, allowing that warm buzz of the first hit to wash through her. Concentrating on the red-orange tip and the music, she could almost drown out everything around her, her mind in a box of her own world until five cigarettes later the lights went down again.

In the darkness her excitement grew, her heart pounding furiously in her chest as the sounds of a sitar emerged from the stage. No light, just the strange oriental sounds filling the air, slicing through the smoke to an audience that stood motionless. Then in one blazing second blue light and a sultry guitar's magic burst into existence, the crowd went insane. They screamed and moved closer to the stage. Sijn felt herself being pushed against the barrier, her feet leaving the floor, but she didn't care. For in front of her Dereck Cliffe wailed lyrics of a man drowning in modern technology and a world with no love. So poignant, standing there eyes closed, lips near the microphone and his graceful long fingers evoking stricken notes that plagued her heart from the black guitar. The blue light played on his ebony hair, giving it a gleaming sapphire halo, his pale porcelain skin a look of purest marble. For years she had stared at posters of him but never realized how truly beautiful he was. That angelic face that twisted with emotion when he sang stirred something in her that had never been felt before. Just a few feet away from her, he stood there like a god, and she just wanted to touch him. If only her hand could caress his bare chest, to feel those lean thighs covered in tattered denim, how delightful that would feel. Of its own violation her treacherous arm reached for him but found only air.

As the music played on, the crowd around her heaved and where before she felt the uncomfortable closeness, now she was hurting. The heat grew to an unbearable level and her breath became constricted until she felt suffocated. Dizziness threatened to overtake her and a dull ache in her ribs developed into sharp stabbing pains. With her arm still outstretched, Sijn teetered on the edge of blackness as the throng behind her battered her against the barricade. A cool strong hand grasped her arm, firmly pulling her out of the mass of people, and her feet left the ground seemingly with no effort at all. Swooning, Sijn had barely noticed that the music had stopped, a steady arm slipped around her waist as she gasped for breath. The new air in her lungs brought her to an fuzzy awareness and she opened her eyes. Looking at her with a mixture of concern and amusement stood Dereck Cliffe, his handsome face inches from hers as he whispered, "You wanted to touch me, dear." She couldn't speak or move, dumbfounded by his close presence. Then he handed her to a crew member who escorted her to a chair on the side of the stage. The metal chair felt mercifully cold against her hot body as she sat, a bottle of cold drinking water was pressed into her hand by a man with short blonde hair and a crew tag around his neck.

*   *   *

Sijn shook herself, realizing she had stood there slipping into her reverie like she was there at the concert again. Shana still stared at her with that smirk on her face, occasionally taking a drag on her cigarette. "What a charming groupie story and told with such flair, you really should try your hand at writing," the writer sarcastically commented.

"Fuck you, do you want to hear the rest or not?" Sijn asked, starting to not like this person at all. She protectively held the bag with the journal in it in her lap, her fingers working on the nylon straps.

"Okay, forgive me, do continue." Shana nodded for her to do so.

She explained how that night she had made love to Dereck Cliffe. How she had woken up alone the next day with her neck sore and not knowing why. At this point she looked Shana in the eye for any sign of a reaction, and there was a small flicker. She watched the woman's face carefully before she dropped the real bomb on her. "A month later, I realized I was pregnant. Pregnant with Dereck's baby."

Pain shot across Shana's face and she threw the whiskey glass on the floor in an angry gesture. "You're a goddamned liar! You might be pregnant but it can't be Dereck's, because he was a . . ." her voice trailed off. "Because he's a . . . a . . ."

"A vampire," Sijn answered softly, staring into the other woman's eyes. They both sat there staring at each other for a moment. She could see how hurt Shana was, how she had been hurting for a while now. Sijn understood how the other woman felt, the pain they both shared over loss of Dereck. She couldn't bring herself to say anything else at the moment. Somehow it bonded them, these two very different women.

Mike took this moment to jump in, "What a load of pig shit! Girlie you've been reading too many damn books. You ain't gonna come in here with ya wild damn stories and upset her anymore. There's the door, go stand outside with the other loonies!" he bellowed at her, trying to hoist himself off the low seat.

"Mike, hold on a minute," Shana interrupted him. "Let's wait to see what she has for me." She turned to address Sijn again. "Just what makes you think that Dereck was a vampire? Are you delusional like Mike says, or do you have some sort of proof for me?" She lifted her cigarette to take another draw but it was down to the filter. So threw it in an ashtray and lit another.

"I didn't know until two weeks ago. I went to Cali to tell him about the baby and it was the day of the fire," Sijn said and lowered her head, not wanting this woman to see her get emotional. "I took a box from the ashes and that's where I found a letter written to Solange. There was also the letter I brought you and a key. The key went to a storage place where Dereck kept some of his things. The letters hinted at what he was, the stuff I found inside storage proved it."

"And what was that, his coffin?" Mike asked, giving up his fight with getting up.

"No, don't be ridiculous. I was as surprised as you seem to be. There was a great deal of money, old passports, antiques, and did I mention a hell of a lotta money. But the most important thing I found, came in the form of a stack of old books. Some so old and dusty they could hardly be read. Dereck's diary for the past five hundred years!" Sijn's voice grew louder to emphasize that last sentence. She had their attention now, so she unzipped the bag while she continued. Holding the book aloft, she asked. "Care to take a look?"

Almost greedily Shana reached for the old dusty book bound in black leather. Its pages had long since turned yellow ochre, but the script written upon it definitely Dereck's flagrant scrawl. The date at the top of the page read, eighteen forty-one. With an almost holy reverence the woman turned page after page, until she couldn't read anymore. When she looked up again, tears crested her mascara-tinged lashes and she pulled the book up against her chest in a tight embrace.

"What was in the letter to Solange?" Shana asked.

"It told her to come to you, seems he thought a great deal of you," Sijn told her.

"I like to think so," Shana said. "Though I can't see Solange agreeing to come here. And good thing she was dead, for your sake. The psycho bitch would have ripped you apart."

"So you believe me now?" Sijn asked.

"Yes, I do, though I'm not sure how the pregnant thing happened," Shana announced. "Yeah that would have pissed ol' Soley off quite a bit. She's quite mad sometimes. I've only been around her once in a while, she doesn't care for me much. She's knows that Dereck and I were close, calls me one of his snacks." Shana stopped, thought for a moment and continued, "I would have let her come here though, I did promise him. I would let the devil stay here for Dereck Cliffe."

"Is she really so horrible?" Sijn wondered aloud, a tinge of fear in her voice.

"Sometimes, Dereck helped her a lot, I know much of her problem with me was jealousy. But you don't have to worry about that, she's dead and gone dear," Shana assured her.

"No, she's not," Sijn told her. She held out Dereck's letter to Shana. "She's alive and I came here to find her."

CHAPTER TWELVE

Should a Vampire Date?

Somewhere in Solange's trancelike sleep, there was a knocking. It resounded into her dreams as if underwater. Dusk had not taken hold of the sky on this evening, and she lay there, unable to rise. The night had thirty more minutes before it conquered the sun. Her mind struggled to reach through the murky fog to the noise.

Outside, Greg knocked on Solange's door. Her car sat in parking lot, giving her presence away. Greg had made plans for the evening. Reservations had been made for eight o'clock at Dante's Down The Hatch. It was one of Buckhead's finest restaurants. He knew she would like it. Soft jazz, good food, and a couple of drinks would loosen her up. The attraction he felt for this girl was so strong. Greg couldn't explain it, but like cocaine, he had to have it no matter what the consequences. Greg's disappointment rose within him as he knocked on the door one last time. A few minutes later he walked back to his apartment. Upstairs Solange was slowly waking. As the sky darkened outside she became more aware of her surroundings. Sometimes her sleep ended before the sun sank, thus the need for the heavy draperies. Even though fully awake she could not answer the door until the sun set. Instinctively, she knew Greg had been knocking on the door. She needed to see him again. The ever-present hunger did not beat as strong in her on this evening. Solange could see Greg, then feed. Quickly she checked directory assistance and called him.

The phone rang in Greg's apartment. He made no move to answer it. Lying back on his mattress staring at the beach umbrella above. It rang three times until the answering machine picked up. *"Hi, I'm not around right now, just leave your name and number. I'll get back to you."* Beep. *"Greg, this is Solange,"* Greg sat up quickly. *"I'm sorry I didn't answer when you knocked."* He reached for the phone. *"I was in the shower, come over in a few, thanks."* Greg grabbed the phone.

"Solange, Solange . . ." She was already gone. Greg stood up and straightened his clothing. As he stepped out the door, the last rays of the sun settled over the western sky. In a few long strides he stood outside Solange's door and softly knocked.

Solange was expecting him. Her door swung open to reveal her wearing a short purple satin robe. Greg consumed her beauty with a hunger that rivaled her needs. "Come in," she motioned him into her living room. He looked around in awe. The same floor plan as his own, but oh so different.

Except for the gray carpet, every thing was black. Luxurious black leather sofa and love seat, smoked glass accent tables, arranged asymmetrically in the rectangular room. Tall black lamps on each side of the sofa, stood with frosted crystal bowls atop. What fascinated Greg were the artifacts, accented with spotlighting around the room. On a marble stand was a statue of a jackal-headed creature carved in stone. A spotlight above caught every intricate carving on the greenish gray bust of the Egyptian god. Where had she found such a valuable piece? It had to be worth millions; gods of the underworld did not come cheap.

Several glass cases held ancient pages from the Carolingian Period, intricately decorated with flowing script, flowers, and song birds. One especially caught his eye, unlike the others it could not be the writing of holy men. The writing seemed faded, a reddish brown and illustrations of bones, fire, and gargoyles ran the length of the page. Amazingly beautiful, but quite unsettling, it exuded an aura of evil. Other things in the room were not as interesting as these, just vases, swords, and sculptures arranged around the room. This apartment suited her so well, mysterious, dark, and her the only ray of sunshine. The center of light in a dark world, that was his attraction for her. He turned in appreciation of her taste to face her beauty. She was so beautiful.

"Greg, could you give me a few moments to go upstairs and get dressed?" Solange asked. "You came over sooner than I thought you would."

Greg slipped his arms around her. "Not so fast." He lowered his lips to hers. His tongue probed her red lips for the softness within. It ran along her teeth, that were at the moment a normal human's. Solange sighed and leaned into him. Soft round breasts crushed into his chest, their erect nipples sending waves of excitement through him. He pulled her away to look into her iridescent eyes.

"You are too fast," Solange said and with a smile added, "And too arrogant."

"Well, just a little," he agreed. "Now you can get dressed so we can go to dinner."

"Dinner?" she asked.

"I've made reservations for us at eight," Greg eased her toward the stairs, "So go get dressed."

"Where are we going?" she asked. "I need to know what to wear."

"Something sexy," he said and patted her behind. "Now go."

Solange climbed the stairs to her bedroom. Arrogant, the man had to be the most arrogant human she had ever known. She turned to look at him, dressed in black trousers and dark print shirt, and he looked very handsome. "Arrogant," she called to him from the stairs. He smiled.

Suddenly she pictured him in a Prussian blue soldier's uniform, and her heart ached. He had been very arrogant then too. She left him standing in search of something appropriate to wear.

In her closet hung many things, most of which were black. Solange blended in the night easier if she wore its color. But this evening she chose a violet dress. Lightweight linen that clung to her curves, wide chiffon straps that wrapped around her bosom to cross around her neck. The skirt cut above her knee, giving a good view of her long legs, which she covered with soft violet hose. A little make-up, bronze disk earrings, violet pumps, and her outfit was complete. One long look in the mirror confirmed to her that no one would notice her vampire status. Downstairs Greg had been taking further inventory on her strange collection. Most of this stuff was museum quality, very interesting. One theme carried over throughout the collection, death. In some form or another it all related to death. On closer inspection the vases he had dismissed as ordinary were quite the contrary. They were Egyptian canopic jars used in burial ceremonies, and he hoped that the row along the wall no longer contained the ancient organs they were intended to. Angel certainly was morbid, of course that showed in her paintings. Oddly there were none of these anywhere in the downstairs rooms. Understandably some had been destroyed in the fire, and a few hung in tribute in a gallery in Beverly Hills. Certainly she still painted. He had no more time to ponder this, Solange came down the stairs. "Quite an interesting collection you have here," Greg stated. "Where'd you get this stuff?"

"From an ancestor, he was an avid collector and when he passed, I inherited it," she said. "This is not even half of it, the rest is in storage. It is quite interesting, some extremely beautiful. I picked a few pieces to bring with me."

"I was beginning to think you'd robbed a museum or something. I'd like to see the rest sometime," he paused. "You know what would really set this place off?" He didn't wait for an answer, but continued. "Paintings, no artwork in here just these artifacts. A painting would really set things off."

Solange flinched. She looked into his face but saw nothing, the barrier was there. *Did he know?* She thought to herself "You're probably right, I'll have to look around for some." Greg just shrugged nonchalantly, indicating nothing of his knowledge of her. But she felt again that familiarity in his mind.

"Are you ready to go?" He asked. "You look gorgeous." Greg took her hands in his and gave her a flutter of a kiss on her cheek. Waves of shudders traveled down her body.

"Ready when you are."

"Okay, let's go," he said as he ushered her to the door. He made no further comments about the paintings, it had been a test for reaction. Surprise had flitted across her face for the slightest fraction of a second. She didn't make any other comment, he would leave it there.

There was very little talk on the way to the restaurant. Both did not want to break the spell of the motion of the car and music playing. Greg pulled his car off the traffic crowded Peachtree Street into Dante's parking lot. The lot was crowded, much as he had predicted it to be. He lucked out and found an empty space not too far from the door. With the car parked he got out and walked around to Solange's side. The door swung open to let her get out, and when he noticed the long legs, he wanted to touch them. She looked up at him with those beautiful eyes that were always full of light even in the dark. As he helped her out, he commented on her lack of conversation. "You're strangely quiet tonight, my angel."

A tremor flitted across her face when he said that. "Why did you call me that?"

"Solange, 'angel of the sun', remember?" Did she pick up on his reference to her secret? Greg wondered.

"Oh," was her only reply.

"Come, let's go eat." He took her arm and guided her toward the entrance. They did not have to wait long for their reservations, only a few minutes in the covered walkway. The restaurant was modeled to look like an old ship, dark except for lighted candles and occasional conventional lighting to assist the wait staff. Dark wood paneled the walls, just as if in the ship's hold. Leading into the restaurant a gangplank stretched over a shimmering pool of water. In the water was a live crocodile, which hissed as Solange passed over. Greg laughed. "Don't worry dear, he can't reach you."

Solange had no fear of the reptile, in fact he was hissing to show his fear of her. Animals had a way of sensing her kind, they knew another predator when they saw one. They crossed the remainder of the way to be led to a booth. It was curved and set back into a recess, dark leather covered the seats, and it faced the rest of the restaurant. She noticed that a small jazz band played in the open area, their smoky music filled her ears. Once she sat down, Greg slid in beside her. Because of the curve of the booth, they were able to sit side by side and have plenty of space, not that he gave her any. Which did not bother her, for it was drafty in the old restaurant. She shivered.

"Are you cold?" Greg's hand reached out and ran up and down her arm. "My God, your skin is cold! We should have remembered a jacket or something." His hand continued to rub her arm.

"I'm fine, really." She snuggled a little closer, "You can warm me up."

"What a tempting offer," he smiled, "But let's eat first." He opened the menu left for them by the waiter dressed as a cabin boy. The menu consisted of fondue; as an entire meal it was a novelty, it had made the restaurant famous. The walls of the restaurant dotted with photographs of the rich and famous who had eaten there. Greg would start with the wine list. He chose a burgundy, Solange agreed it was a good choice. It would have a robust taste to fully complement the red meat she knew she would order. And she would eat; she could consume regular food. Although blood was the sustenance she needed to survive, at times she craved human food, but it would not curb the hunger. Her body could process food, but it used very little of it for restoration, and would quickly dispense of it. Even vampires used the ladies room, but only if she ate or drank things other than blood. It would often taste so bland; it left her feeling sad.

"Do you want to order the food now or wait and have some wine first?" Greg asked.

"Let's have some wine first." She smiled and placed her hand on his thigh under the table, "It'll give us time alone."

"Good." Greg asked the waiter to bring the wine and informed him they would order later. Solange leaning against him and the jazz flowing in his ears was enough for him at the moment. "Do you like this place?"

"I do, it's very unusual," she told him. To herself she thought about being on a real ship, such as this and how she had hated it.

"It's a very intimate atmosphere, we can enjoy the jazz and have a little privacy by the placement of the booth." He leaned away from her slightly and touched the tattoo on her shoulder. "This intrigues me. Could you tell me more about it?"

"I told you it is my family crest," she replied, hoping he wouldn't ask too many questions.

"Tell me more about your family, they seem to be intriguing, collecting artifacts of death, crest with bat wings." He held her hand tightly.

"Really there's not much to tell." She looked into his eyes, "I never really studied my family tree." She would avoid his answers as long as possible.

"What would you say if I told you I dreamed about your family crest before I met you?" He asked.

"I'd say you were nuts," she replied. He was beginning to worry her. This relationship was starting to feel like a mistake. Fortunately the wine came and he stopped while the waiter poured a glass for each of them. At that time Solange suggested they order the food, and his choice of conversation changed to her preference of talking for a while. She ordered the marinated beef, Greg the traditional cheese fondue of Swiss cheese, cheddar cheese, and wine. She wanted to keep conversation light; he was getting dangerously close to getting deeply involved with her and her past. She wouldn't let that happen.

"Have you ever dreamed about someone that you didn't know existed until you met them?" Greg asked.

"You watch too much Arthur C. Clark," she suggested.

"I'm being serious, and I don't watch that crap," he said. "I never gave much credit to supernatural occurrences, psychic powers, or reincarnation until recently. Until it happened to me."

"What happened to you? Did you get abducted by a UFO?" Solange asked, as lightheartedly as possible. She knew he was not going to be distracted. He knew something about her or about himself perhaps.

"I've been having dreams for years." He paused. "You're gonna think this is crazy. I dreamed about this girl, a girl I had never met." Greg stopped and stared into his wine glass for a long time before he spoke again. "At first they were pleasant dreams, but then they turned to nightmares."

"Let's not talk about this, it's giving me the creeps," she said, staring into her own wine. "I want to change the subject." Like a beacon of hope, the waiter came with simmering pots, to save Solange from her sinking ship. That was twice he had been wonderfully interruptive. He carefully set the smallest on the table in front of her, its contents of oil simmering. Underneath he lit a flame in the small burner underneath to keep oil cooking. In front of Greg he placed a larger pot with bubbling cheeses, repeating the ritual of lighting the burner. He left quickly, leaving Solange again to answer questions, but fortunately, he relented.

"Okay, I'll leave it tonight but it is something I need to tell you and I will continue," he stated very clearly, and she knew he would take it up again. "It's obvious that you want everything to stay light this evening."

"Every evening. Greg, we just met a few days ago, it's too soon to be heavy," she said. "Let's just have a good time now, we'll have plenty of time for this later."

"Don't you feel it?" he asked quite urgently.

"You're doing it again." Solange turned to look in eyes, and she touched her hand to his face, "Yes, I feel something. Is that what you want me to say? I can't give you anymore than that. I don't have it left in me. So let's just enjoy each other and not get serious, okay?" He kissed her gently on her lips. She wanted to cling to him, to ravage his body until she didn't hurt anymore but the waiter returned.

On one plate he brought one-inch cubes of raw, marinated steak and one empty plate. Along side he sat smaller bowls filled with Worcestershire sauce, horseradish, and teriyaki sauce. In front of Greg he placed an empty plate and a basket full of chunks of bread. Also he received a bowl of cubed apples. Each received several long skewers. The waiter proceeded to demonstrate how to cook and eat the fondue. He placed the first one in for her. He left them alone.

Solange took hers out first, barely cooking it. The blood would still ooze from it on her plate, only slightly brown on the outside. No sauce, she let it cool on her plate. Greg looked at her inquisitively. "Don't you need to cook that a little longer?"

"No, I like mine rare," she stated touching her finger to it to check if it had cooled any, but not too much. Things tasted better warm

"If that's the way you like it," he said, "I personally prefer mine well-done." He pointed to a piece of meat with his skewer, "May I?"

"You certainly may," she said, "but only if I can sample yours."

After placing a skewer in the pot of oil, he skewered a piece of French bread and twirled it in the cheese mixture. He let the excess drip from the bread, letting it cool. "Open wide," he said and he placed the morsel on her waiting tongue.

"Mmm." The sharp cheese delighted her heightened senses as it melted in her mouth. The rest of their dinner remained pleasant, the conversation avoiding Greg's dreams and her past. Greg's suave and humorous conversation delighted her. She enjoyed herself so much that she almost forgot her pain. The evening passed very quickly, both warmed by the wine, food and the other's company. The time came to go home.

Outside the restaurant, a dark-haired vampire waited. He had followed them to this place. As soon as he saw the human, he knew. His angel thought she had found her former love, it had taken her two hundred years but she had a second chance. She thought she could pretend to be a human once again. At one time he had won her heart from this Gregor, but this time he could not be sure. She was not innocent anymore. Blending in with the shadows of the building, he watched them exit the restaurant. Solange turned her head when she sensed his presence.

The prickly sensation washed over her. The other vampire was here, still stalking her, but why? She stopped in her tracks, making Greg stop with her. Searching with her mind as well, as her eyes, Solange found nothing. Explaining to Greg it was just a chill, she let him escort her to the car.

Greg opened the door so she could get in. As she slid in a thought, not her own, flashed through her mind. *"Be careful, young one, do not repeat past mistakes. You can't be human again."* The warning came from the other vampire. Now its shields were in place again and she could not find him. The foreboding voice in her head had a vaguely familiar ring to it, but she could not identify it. It must know her and her past to make such a warning.

She sent out her own telepathic message, *"Why do you follow me? Why do you hide? If you wanted to harm me you would have already, so either show yourself soon or leave me alone."* Greg closed the car door.

On the way home her thoughts were still on the vampire. She barely said anything to Greg in the car. Only her hand on his thigh reminded her he was even there. Back at the apartment Greg kissed her before they left the car. Solange responded passionately. "You are coming in aren't you?" he asked.

"Yes, of course," she answered, and kissed him softly. They locked the car and went into his apartment. The air conditioning cooled the inside of the apartment, causing her to shiver. Greg slipped his arms around her, pulling her body close. Every feature of his body molded to hers, an invisible string pulled their lips together. Passion spread through them, engulfing their bodies, minds and souls, oblivious to all except the flame in which they burned. Skin touching skin, lips touching skin, tender yet urgent sensations controlled their very being. Solange had loved Gregor centuries before, but never consummated that relationship. He had waited for hundreds of years for her and tonight he would have her. Her feelings soared until the all-too-familiar hunger crept through her body, hunger being a natural companion for desire with her kind. She would resist.

With Greg above her reaching the peak of his desire, she fought hard not to sink her lengthening teeth into his neck, only inches above her. Instead she sank her teeth into her own arm, curbing that desire until his had been satisfied. She would still need to hunt tonight.

Greg still lay on top of her, lost somewhere in his own feelings, and he buried his head in the curve of her neck, gently nuzzling the flesh he found there. There he stayed for long moments while Solange fought the hunger. Steady breathing soon revealed that her lover slept. Gently she rolled him over and got up. Dressing as quickly and quietly as possible, so her departure would not wake him. The hunger beating strong, she left him sleeping.

Outside she leaned against the brick of the building, letting the night breezes wash over her. She regarded what she did to her arm, which was already healing. She would need to feed soon, and as she readied for flight she caught a familiar sensation. The other vampire was hiding, waiting for some unknown reason. Hesitation set in, a fear for Greg if she left him unprotected with the vampire this close. But if she did not feed, Solange offered a greater danger to her lover. Hoping the other would follow, she took to the air.

Inside Greg slept, a world of dreams alive in his mind. In his dream he floated on an ocean of darkness, no ground, no sky, just darkness. The air surrounding him blew cold as any arctic breeze, and he shivered. A dark figure hovered above him, its face illuminated by some unknown source of light. Its eyes glowed an unearthly green, its features definitely male. Fear grew inside of Greg, but he could not move or run away, held in limbo by the will of the creature.

When it spoke, the voice was genteel, soothing. *"Solange does not belong to you."* The spirit paused. *"I created her, she is mine. She will only kill you again."* Then he disappeared as quickly as he had appeared. Greg sat up, awakened by the chill and the fear the dream had created. No spirit stood over him, no Solange beside him, and his balcony door stood open letting the breezes blow through.

CHAPTER THIRTEEN

Leone

He shouldn't have appeared to the human but he could not contain himself. Watching them make love through the glass door had nearly killed him. There was hope, however, when he watched her bite herself. Then he knew her restraint ran thin, and that the boy would soon die. Unless she changed the human, then all was lost. Leone had come too far for that to happen. Leone remembered making love to her, watching someone else was sheer torture.

For over two hundred years he had dreamed of her. Knowing that somewhere in the outside world his angel lived, while he wasted to nothing in his prison. It had been by pure luck and an act of war that he walked the earth now. Saved by the war that brutally killed so many.

An explosion from a battle close to the castle set him free. In fact, it had destroyed the castle he had been a prisoner of. The villagers had bricked him in over two centuries before, cemented the place bricked over, of course this was after driving a stake through him. Wooden stakes did not have the effect so often depicted in folklore stories or horror films. He did not melt and turn to dust and smoke before their very eyes. They could cause horrific damage, immobilizing for a long time, but not enough to put an aged vampire in mortal danger. At the time he had given a good performance, assuring them of his death. That had been the beginning of his imprisonment. The stakes and lack of blood made him too weak to break free of his prison, yet the creature in him held on to some form of life. His mind floated in a dream like state, while his body withered, but did not decay. It had given him many years to think about Solange and his life.

Never once did he dare to think of freedom, too carefully hidden in the stone recess. When explosions filled his ears one day, he thought it to be another trick of his deteriorating mind; until the stones of his prison began to shake. Fortunately it was evening and no deadly rays of sun penetrated to destroy him. The first breezes were shocking, hot from flames and burnt ground surrounding him. How long he lay there he could not be sure of. Soon a young man, mistaking him for dead, attempted to carry him off. Leone summoned enough strength to sink his teeth into the dirty bared neck.

After spending so long starved, the sweet nectar of the boy's blood fueled him; he drained him to a dry husk. It was the last time Leone had killed. Killing did not set well with him; leaving a victim with an erased memory prevented unwarranted suspicions. But this time it proved necessary, as he had starved too long. His clothes, worn for two centuries in his grave of mortar and hunger, were practically disintegrated. The once-white tunic now hung from his body in gray tatters, the leggings barely covering him. With repugnance he peeled the clothes from a corpse in a nearby field so that he looked like any other victim of the war.

He had fed several times that night, restoring his body so that he may flee this godforsaken land. Once it had been rich and beautiful, but now cold and dreary. War had ravaged his land and he cared not to linger there any longer. Something passed him on a road as he walked, a cart made of metal with no horses drawing it. He stared in amazement, such changes, but he had seen many over the centuries. Hiding would be necessary until he learned more of this age; an age in which his angel waited for him. Her life, like a tiny heartbeat in his head, called to him. Soon he would scour the world for her, but now he must survive. Survival came naturally to him. His kind was tenacious.

Adjusting himself to this modern world had been easier than one would think. With his mental abilities, he gleaned information from humans. Information which he used to guide him through this new world. His search had led him to France and Italy, but they had proven to be dead ends. Wealth conveniently built from vaults thought to be impenetrable helped him fake his mortality. He could slip past guards, mist through beams of light without triggering them and scale walls no human would ever attempt. By the time he reached Paris he traveled in comfort and style. Everything about him spoke culture and wealth. How people treated him with bowing kindness when they saw him, groveling at his feet due to his apparent monetary standing. It had always been so; people never change.

Through books and the amazing wonder the modern world called television he learned of the changes in the New World. Now called the United States, it was no longer a wilderness, but had grown into a vast continent of cities. Something told him to go there. Solange lived her life on that vast shore. Every night he watched what they called the news. Fascinated, Leone could barely drag himself away to feed. Channels devoted to nothing else but this news. He searched it every night drinking the knowledge like blood from a spouting vein.

Then one evening, when he waited for a dinner companion in the lobby of a hotel, he saw her. The pages of an American art magazine turned slowly in his fingers, shiny, glossy pages, full of color. Art had always been a passion for him and he often wondered what had become of his own vast collection. As he perused the vibrant photographs, one caught his eye. A young man, wrapped in a dragon of paper and fabric, looked familiar to Leone. He recognized Dereck, and thought the painting must indeed be old. Down below he saw the picture of the artist, and it was Solange!

With her arms locked with the young man from the painting, she smiled, her face pale yet glowing with beauty. Leone sat shocked. Both his changelings stood together, their happiness showing in their eyes. He must go to them. His two most beloved together, it brought a tear to his ancient eye. Forgetting his companion for the evening he strode from the hotel to make arrangements for his departure. The next evening he left for California.

CHAPTER FOURTEEN

Sleep, Blessed Sleep

Her craving had been satisfied this night by a homeless man. No acts of revenge, no crusade for good, just quenching the undying thirst. The man had lived his life as an alcoholic, drifting from place to place, no family, no job, just hopelessness. He had not even resisted as she cut his throat and drank from him. In fact, he had welcomed it. Solange had read the sadness in his thoughts, no will to live, yet too cowardly to end his pitiful life. She felt no guilt in killing him.

As she prepared for sleep in her apartment she wondered how humans actually accomplished suicide. In her life she had known sadness, tragedy, and sickness, but the vampire in her would not let her die. She had tried over and over. The years had faded some human feelings like washing faded one's favorite jeans. Yet it had intensified others, not all of them good. Immortality had made her aggressive, vengeful at times, and somewhat obsessive. She could be extremely passionate and sensitive one day, then cold and cruel the next. Human, but intensified, monster, but not. However many times she had felt like dying, nights spent begging God to end this existence, never would the creature she was welcome death.

As morbid thoughts rolled through her head, sleep pulled at her like an ebbing tide, gentle, yet persistent and sure. Sinking into the cushions of her sleeping chamber, she let it wash over her, wave after wave pulling her into the depths of slumber. Drifting in the currents of dreams, Solange sought a pleasant one, and found Leone.

The vampire slept on, still hours until sunset. As she slumbered in her dark haven, misty dreams rolled on with their story, tormenting her with pleasing memories and irreversible horror. Banished forever to the events at a castle in Hungary, events that made her the creature she now hated so.

*   *   *

Solange rose late the next morning. Sleep held fast to her, like a thick blanket in her head. Once awake she had no desire to stir from her bed, choosing to lie for a while and think. Drained was the way she could describe how she felt. Tired for no reason. What had Leone done to her?

Without thought her hand flew to her neck. It was sore to the touch and had a slight wound. Solange pulled back the bedclothes and unsteadily walked to the vanity. On her neck two small puncture wounds stood out against the whiteness of her skin. They must be hidden. A black choker with a small cameo covered the bite perfectly. Quickly she dressed in a low-cut, emerald gown that contrasted beautifully with her flame tresses. Solange considered herself in the mirror, a little puffy around the eyes, but no one would be the wiser. She closed the door behind her and joined the family downstairs.

"Good morning, Solange," the Baron greeted her. "We had given up on you. Do you feel well?"

"Quite well, thank you." She smiled. "Just a bit tired, that is all."

"I hope you're not too tired," Raphaela piped. "Today we are touring the galleries and I know how much you love paintings." She turned to the Baroness. "Solange paints very well. In Paris the other young ladies wish to be as talented as her."

The Baroness raised an eyebrow at Solange as she took her seat. "We were not aware you were so talented Solange. Perhaps you can paint our portraits during your stay here."

"I would be honored, Baroness," she answered.

"Dear, that is hardly suitable for a young lady of Solange's breeding," scolded the Baron. "As a hobby maybe, but commissioned work? I don't believe her parents would approve."

"Papa, it would only be for fun," Raphaela giggled. "It's not like she would be working for us."

"That's true Baron," Solange said. "Consider the paintings a gift." She paused to let the serving girl fill her plate. "It would be my thank you for all your hospitality."

"I suppose there would be no harm in it," the Baron conceded. Raphaela and the Baroness gave a sly wink at Solange, all three women smiled. The Baron stood up, looking handsome. "I'm afraid I'm off again, business you know." He turned to kiss Raphaela on the head.

"I will be gone for a while, to Paris." He looked at Solange. "Is there any message I can relay to your family or to Gregor?" It was his turn to wink.

"Just that I love them," she answered, her voice tinged with guilt.

"Then I'm off." He bent to kiss the Baroness. Solange found this very unusual for her parents never showed such affection to each other, or anyone for that matter. "Ladies, please take great care while I'm away." Then he strode out of the dining hall to the waiting carriage outside.

Raphaela waited patiently for Solange to finish her breakfast. She was eager to show her friend the galleries. "You will see all of Mama's family, it is impressive. Especially her father, he was so handsome!"

The Baroness turned to look at her. "Raphaela, do not go on so."

"But Mama, he was," she giggled. "That is where you get your beauty."

"Thank you, darling." The Baroness smiled at her daughter. "But my mother was very lovely also. She had green eyes but hair of fire, much like Solange."

"Baroness, will you join us on the tour?" Solange asked. "You can tell us so much about the paintings."

"Actually that would be lovely," the Baroness agreed. "I believe I can put aside some of my duties until this afternoon."

"Oh, thank you Mama," Raphaela clapped her dainty hands together. "A woman's day."

"My darling, everyday is woman's day," her mother replied. "How often do you see men around here?" She paused. "At meals and bedtime that's when."

"Mama!" she gasped.

"Now dear you are nearly eighteen, " Baroness continued, "You should know the truth about things"

Solange suppressed a giggle and watched the servants quickly carry away dirty utensils to the kitchen. "Come, let's go on the tour." Skirts rustled as the three women left the table and proceeded to the galleries.

The galleries were in the eastern portion of the castle. They had to cross the huge ballroom to reach it. Solange could not resist turning in circles while looking up at the chandeliers. Raphaela and the Baroness watched her whirling with smiles on their faces. "It is like watching my mother dance," said the older woman. "You are so like her, Solange. When I was a child I can remember her dancing with my father, myself so small I could hide under her skirts. That is one of the few memories I have of her." The Baroness looked sad and faraway.

Solange stopped dancing and they continued on into the galleries. Paintings from all over the world covered the stone walls. For several hours they talked about the art. A lot had been brought here by Raphaela's father and he continually added to the collection. But some pieces came here with the Baroness' father. There was even a Michelangelo. The Baroness told of how her father traveled to many places, bringing back treasure from faraway countries.

They entered another adjoining hall that devoted itself to family history, portraits lining the hall in chronological order. Solange listened intently while the Baroness explained how her family came from Italy and France originally. The original owners of the castle had died, leaving no heir, nearly two centuries ago. Frequently marrying from those countries was a tradition passed down through the Noguchi family. Hence, the Baroness' mother had been French, passing her culture down, so evident in her granddaughter. At last they halted in front of a portrait of a woman.

A striking redhead with green eyes, she favored Solange. The engraving on a plague below read: *Nanette Noguchi, Wife of Leone.* That was a familiar name. Solange could only stare at the beauty of the woman. "This is my mother, Nanette," said the Baroness. "As you can see she bears a striking resemblance to you, Solange. I only wish I had known her better. Childhood memories are so fleeting."

"She was very beautiful." Solange's gaze moved to the next portrait. She moved closer to look at a man with emerald green eyes, his dark hair wavy and turning gray at the temples. A slight smile played at his full lips. There could be no doubt who this was for the name plate clearly read: *Leone Noguchi.*

"Isn't he handsome?" asked Raphaela. "I told you he was!"

"Who . . . is he?" Solange's question sounded faint, even to her self.

"That is my father, Leone," said the Baroness. She looked at Solange with a narrow, suspicious eye. "Is there something wrong, Solange."

Solange clasped her hands to her temples, trying to stop the dizziness and confusion. "He is dead?" she asked.

"Yes, he died many years ago." As the Baroness put her hand on Solange's arm, a growing dread gripped her. "Are you all right? You look pale." Her voice held a note of the consternation fully evident on her face. Her eyes held a question as she looked at the too-pale girl. She looked at the painting and back to Solange realizing for the first time just how pale Solange was.

"Yes . . . just a little tired . . ." was all Solange managed to say before her mind left her, turmoil raging through it brought on the blackness she welcomed. Raphaela screamed as Solange collapsed on the floor.

Solange had awakened to darkness, and after a few moments of confusion she remembered she had fainted in the gallery. Next to her bed, a candle burned low, its wax dripping on the brass holder below it. She sat up and her hand flew to her neck, her choker no longer circled her throat. Whoever had undressed her surely saw the delicate punctures on the creamy skin. Leone, she must go to him.

Unsteady feet touched the cold marble floor beneath her, its shock sending a chill through her. Her white gown glowed faintly yellow in the candlelight, clinging to her woman's figure. Her mind whirled when she stood, spinning in a whirlpool of dark waters. She had not realized she was so weak. With great effort she made her way to the door of her bedchamber. When the Baroness passed by, she shrank back into the darkness. After a few moments Solange peered out to see if the hallway was empty. Carefully, she ventured out, clinging to the walls when possible. Her only thought was Leone, she must go to him.

When she reached the west wing, she saw the Baroness in the hall ahead of her, and she doused her candle so she wouldn't be seen. Certainly it was the Baroness who had helped undress her earlier and saw the marks. Hugging the wall, fighting dizziness, she followed the woman down the corridor. Catching her breath when the Baroness entered Leone's secret room. Her heart pounded in her chest so loudly, surely everyone in the castle heard. Closer she crept edging to the still open doorway, straining to hear their conversation.

"Father, I know what you do," the Baroness accused. "I have seen the marks on her."

"Yes, but I'm not using her for feeding," Leone's vibrant voice replied, "I care about her."

"But you have fed in the village, there is talk again," said the Baroness, her voice high-pitched and angry. "I will not let you endanger us again, or that girl. If you really care, leave her alone."

"She belongs with me." Solange could hear the torment in her lover's voice. "I have searched for years for a companion such as her. She will be taken care of."

"But she belongs to another. They are to be married in a fortnight."

"I do not care of this, he has tarried too long," Leone snapped as his anger rose, "He has let her slip away!"

"Please do not do this," the Baroness pleaded. "Father, I love you, and would die to protect you, but I will not let you destroy her. Changing her would do just that, she is so innocent. Besides the villagers are suspicious and if you turn her they will destroy both of you!" Solange heard her sigh. "Please leave, save yourself, save us all, before it is too late!" Her voice quivered with emotion stronger than anything Solange had ever heard.

"I will not leave without her," Leone answered firmly. "I will not let them hurt her or you, when I change her and make her my wife then shall I leave. Solange will go with me."

"Very well, if the girl is willing then there is nothing I can do." The Baroness, defeated in the argument, added on a more cryptic message, "Remember, Father, when the villagers drive a stake through her heart and cut off her head, remember it will be your fault, just like with my mother."

Solange knew she would be seen when the Baroness left, and she shrank back along the wall. A convenient statue stood to her left, she hid in its shadow and watched the woman pass. She then crept into Leone's room. He sat staring at the fire as it crackled and spit, sadness and guilt emanated from his every pore. Her heart went out to him.

"Do not pity me, young one," Leone spoke without looking at her. "I do not deserve it."

She stepped forward and touched her hands to his hair and urged him close to her. With a sigh he buried his face in her bosom. "My angel, I have caused much sorrow, and I do not wish to cause you any. I know you listened outside, I could hear your heart, smell your blood, and feel your thoughts. You must understand the monster that I am . . . Francesca is right I cannot ask you to stay with me, to give up life as you know it."

His full lips rubbed her breast through the gauzy cloth of her gown when he spoke. Passion surged through her, burning her heart like a hot brand. She tore herself from his embrace and untied her gown, exposing herself from neck to waist. The thin white cloth slid down and rested on her hips. In the firelight her pale skin appeared golden like a savage, native girl, her pink nipples erect and inviting. She lifted her hand to Leone's face. "A life without you would be sorrow. I wish only for you love me."

He drew her close, his face to her breast. His cold tongue licked softly at her nipple before he took it in his mouth. Solange could not help but gasp as he sucked hard on the pink pebble. The black currents swirling in her mind threatened to overtake her and she leaned heavily on him. His hands held her buttocks and worked the thin cloth of her gown off until she felt his icy touch against her skin. With a trail of kisses he moved his attention to her other breast. Gently he massaged her nipple until it was as hard as the other one. Goose bumps covered her flesh and she shivered and moaned in ecstasy. She begged for him to take her, but he continued his torture of her breast. "Not yet, young one."

Fingers trailed across her hip and over her stomach, down to the soft hair of her womanhood. Solange felt her juices start down the insides of thigh as he stroked the lush red bush, his cold fingers a shock to her hot flesh as he parted her pubic lips. Softly he pressed one into her so that she gasped. He stroked without disturbing her maidenhood, making her shake and push her hips down.

The hand at her back lifted until her feet were off the floor and she felt his breath stir the hair of her most intimate parts. His strength amazed her and she exclaimed in passion and surprise. Leone's other hand now grasped her rounded buttocks and pushed his face into her. Gasps and moans turned to screams of delight as his tongue slipped inside of her. Solange writhed in his grasp as he licked and sucked her juices. Over and over she begged him to take her, his lips on the swollen nub of her desire pure torture.

At last he lowered her, trailing lips up her body until they found her open mouth. Her own taste lingered on his lips as he kissed her deeply. Clinging to him, Solange exposed her marked neck and urged him to drink. Wet lips only kissed at the small punctures, and he whispered softly in her ear, "Young one, you will know me as a man first." He laughed softly against her skin, every breath caressing her. "But I do not wish to hurt you, my love."

"Please . . . you will not . . . I need you," she said, her voice raspy with her panting breath. Pressing down she felt his manhood stiff against her thigh. A slight movement of her hips and the tip pressed against her inner lips. A groan passed through Leone's lips. Hot human hands pressed against his cool, muscled chest worshipping the feel of the hardness. Solange felt the strong cool hands on her hips preventing her from her goal. "Patience my angel," he murmured against her chest. Deliciously he kissed and nibbled a trail to her left breast, again licking and teasing her nipple into hardness.

Slowly he lowered her until the tip of his thick shaft stretched her tight flesh. He slid carefully and easily until he felt her maidenhood and held himself there for a moment. Her hot juices flowed down his stiff flesh and her body convulsed and quivered around him until he could stand no more. Suddenly he thrust upward, tearing tender flesh, he smelled the blood that seeped out, and heard her shrill cry of pain. "I love you Solange." Her wet flesh gripped him until he could hold back no longer. With an upward thrust he plunged into her. He whispered against her, "I love you, my angel."

Pain erased by pleasure Solange called out, "Make me like you, my love, please . . ." her voice pleaded. She felt him moving inside of her, his flesh even in passion felt cool, which only added to her desire. Waves of orgasm swept over her body like ocean waves. With each thrust his lips moved along her breast until he sank his fangs into her. Euphoria took over Solange's mind and she sighed her final release. Soon after she felt his cold climax wash into her that sent another wave of sensations shuddering through her. All the while his lips sucked the rich, warm blood from her plump breast. She felt her life draining from her, every beat of her heart brought her closer to Leone and death. Just when she thought she would slip away, he guided her to his neck, where he had opened a vein. Her lips pressed against his hard flesh, the cold thick liquid oozed onto her tongue. She sucked the nectar gingerly at first, then with passion as her strength returned.

Leone groaned and pulled her away. "Now we will be together forever, my angel, we share the bond of blood, no one can ever break that bond. But now we sleep and wait for tomorrow's sunset." He laid her down on a small bed in the corner of the windowless room, covering her naked body with cool linen sheets. As he laid beside her, he whispered in her ear, "We are safe here, no sunlight will harm us."

"I can never again see the sun?" Solange asked.

"That, I'm afraid is necessary, as it will destroy us. But hush now my angel, when we wake I will teach you everything you need to survive. We have eternity." And they slept unaware that danger would come during the day. A danger that would steal every chance at eternity and that would cast Solange on the sea of uncertainty that would cause her so much pain.

CHAPTER FIFTEEN

Sijn Settles In

Several days after she had come to Shana's, Sijn decided to go to her mother's and get a few of her things. There was not much to speak of except for some sentimental items and her guitar. She knew Dawg watched over that precious piece of cargo. It didn't seem right bringing some of her things here into this house; yard sale crap in a house like this. Her room in the house out did anything she'd ever dreamed of. Antiques and a huge carved bed made her feel ill at ease at first. Shana's hospitality made her feel more than welcome.

The entire hostile attitude had dissipated completely. Together they had poured over Dereck's diary with awe. There were things in that last book that blew their minds. Especially the chapters dedicated to their relationships with the departed singer. It helped bond them together, the things written in that epic. It steeled them for the task before them.

When she told Shana she had to go to her family to get her things, the writer insisted on going with her. It made her uneasy that the woman would see how she lived. She could never imagine Shana Collins in a trailer park. Today she found out how stubborn the woman could be.

"Of course, I'll go with you," Shana had said. "You'll need help moving things and Mike will go too." Mike simply nodded his affirmation.

Sijn had given up the argument. What could she say that she was ashamed? So they had piled into the van and headed for the trailer park. On the way, Shana asked, "Why didn't you want me to come along?" Straight to the point as usual, her green gaze fixed on Sijn's face.

"I'm sure this is the first trip to the trailer park for you, " was all Sijn could think to say. Not wanting to share all the dirty details of her family with Shana just yet.

Shana burst out laughing. The woman laughed for a good five minutes. Sijn just watched her perplexed, not sure if her feelings should be hurt or not. She frowned. Her new friend leaned over and put her hand affectionately on Sijn's knee. "Oh, that is funny. Sweetie, I've not always been glamorous, rich and over indulged. In fact for a good many years I was fat, poor and weird." She laughed again. Mike interjected that she was still weird. Shana ignored him and kept talking. "I was born in Iron Station, North Carolina, with the name of Emma Jane Bullock. Poor, white trash, my parents, good people but never made more than fifty thousand a year combined. Before my first marriage I fucked and sucked half of Gaston County, and flipped off the other half. After that I was a single parent working out of a Toyota telling bad jokes in bars with chicken wire over the stage. So don't think I'm some born-with-a-spoon-in-my-mouth bitch who's gonna make fun of you because you were born in the trailer park."

Sijn sat there for a few minutes not really knowing how to respond to all of that. She watched Shana lean back and light a cigarette with a smile on her face. "In the magazines it said that your grandfather was some sort of famous comedian, worked with a lot of the old famous people?"

"Oh yeah he did, " Shana agreed. "But what it didn't tell you was that he was clinically unstable and blew all of his cash on drugs. That he died in an asylum before I was even born. His mind gone. My granny, an ex-showgirl, alcoholic dumped her kids on my great-grandmother because of her new alcoholic husband. Now my great-grandparents were good people, simple country store kinda folks raised my mom and her brother. Not a pretty story, necessarily but we turned out okay."

"Wow, now that would make a book, " Sijn told her. Thinking to her self that this was a little too much information about Shana. But it meant that the woman liked her if she opened up this much to her. She had been worried that she would still have bitter feelings about her relationship with Dereck. A wave of relief washed over her.

"Oh it will be one day, when I can deal with it," Shana informed her.

They pulled into the Sleepy Lane trailer park, the tires on the van jumping with every pothole in the gravel road. Sijn directed Mike to the third trailer on the left. The blue and white aluminum rusting, the grass uncut and an unusual amount of wind chimes on the rickety wooden porch. Her brother Dawg stood on the front porch with her guitar and her amp. No shirt, freckles and red, farmer's tan blazing against his white chest and belly; he was the quintessential redneck. She got out with a slam of a door.

"Hey girl, I've been worried shitless," he said, throwing his just emptied beer can into the grass. He stepped forward and locked her into a bear hug. After he released her, his eyes went to her two new friends getting out of the van. "Who'd ya' bring wit' ya'?"

"Dawg, this is Mike and Shana," Sijn introduced them. "I'm going to be staying with them for awhile."

He went over and shook hands with both of them. "Ain't you friends with Johnny?" he asked. She was slightly embarrassed when he belched while shaking hands with Shana. The woman only laughed and shook his hand harder.

"Yes, I am," she said.

"Thought I saw you sing with them before. Now Sijn, I brought your guitar over. But I gotta warn ya'. Mamma is in one of her moods," he said and paused. He looked at them and shook his head. "Don't be surprised at anything she says today. Your friends might not wanna to hear it. And for the record, she knows ya' pregnant. The ol' lady tol' her yesterdee."

"Remind me to thank her later," Sijn, said. She took a deep breath and turned to Shana. "Do you mind waiting out here? It could get real ugly in there and I won't subject my friends to that."

"For Chrissakes," Shana said with a shake of head. "I won't hear of letting you go in there alone if it's gonna be like that. If it gets too bad, I'm sure I can out bitch her. So let's go. Mike, put the guitar and amp in the van for her please."

Without a word, Mike did just that. Shana put her arm around Sijn's shoulders and led her up the steps. She smiled at Dawg who said, "I think I'm gonna like you."

"I think I'll like you too, Dawg. The door's always open," Shana told him before they went inside. At the door, Sijn hesitated. She could hear the TV playing inside and the dog barking. Her mother had a tiny mutt dog that was meaner than she was. Shana hugged her tight. "Don't be scared, I'm with you all the way." She opened the door.

Her mother sat on the couch, eating potato chips. Crumbs littered her massive bosom. A beer rested between the cushions next to her unshaved legs. Her hair uncombed, pulled into a ponytail made her face seem all the larger. Her small eyes narrowed when she saw her daughter. Her boyfriend Duane sat in a recliner on the other side of the brown couch. His feet raised up with no shoes, in dire need of a nail trimming. Wearing a Stone Cold t-shirt and beer in hand he was the first to speak. "Well, if it ain't the Queen of Sheba." His words were slurred and hateful. He looked at the small yapping dog in the floor and yelled. "Shut up, Sparky! Damn noisy rat."

"It's about time ya brung ya ass back here, " her mother said, depositing the potato chip bag on the cushion beside her. "Come crawlin' back, pregnant, I hope ya don't think we's gonna take care of ya."

"Wouldn't think of it," Sijn told her coldly. "I just came for my things."

"Well, ya' can't have'em," the boyfriend said. "Unless you have some back rent money." The dirty feet hit the floor when he sat up, his beer gut wrinkling over his belt. He kicked the dog out of his way. "Quit your damn job and lef' ya momma without even a howdy do. You can just march right on out that door."

"Yeah, we'd have sold that damn guitar of your, if'n yo' brutha hadn't hidden it from us," Momma told her. "Yer both a couple of ingrats. That wuz a damn good job ya' left without no word. Off chasin' some drug addict rock star like a floozy."

Sijn looked at Shana and she could tell that she was gonna blow. Her face set in that stone, cold attitude she had seen days before. She could feel her seething under that cold face. She had to get them out of there or it would be really ugly. "I'm getting my things and I'll never bother you again."

"Oh no missy," her mother argued and raised herself off the couch. "Ya' ain't gettin' shit, unless ya' git ya job back and hand over some of that money."

This was obviously more than Shana could stand. Before Sijn could stop her, she stepped forward and pushed her momma back on the couch. Hatred sparked in her olive eyes. She was staring the old woman down when Duane stood up and advanced toward them. "Wait a minute, ya' can't bring some uppity bitch in here and let'er push ya momma around like that. I won't have it."

"Shut up, Duane!" Sijn said, tears starting to well up in her eyes. Embarrassment made her face feel like fire.

Shana took a step toward him and said, "Yeah, sit down and shut the fuck up, Duane." Her voice very even and sounding deadly. Duane sat down. "You fucking people are not going to say another word. Sijn is going to get her things and leave with me. And the first one of you that says another mean thing to her will get an ass whooping like you've never had. If you don't believe that an uppity bitch can do that, just try me. Sijn get your stuff, before we catch something from these losers."

"She's my daughter and I'll talk to her any way I'd like," her mother told Shana. Mike chose that moment to come in the door and stand next to Shana, looking like a Santa's elf gone bad.

"Lady, I believe she told you to shut your fucking pie hole," he said. He pulled on his suspenders to hoist his belly for emphasis.

They both sat there looking from one another to Shana. Sijn went to her room and starting grabbing her stuff. There wasn't much, she got only the things she wanted the most. It included some cd's, an autograph book and some cheap jewelry. She stuffed them in a bag and came back into the living room.

Her mother was crying like a victim on the Jerry Springer show. "I tried to do my best by'em both," she wailed. "What am I supposed to do without her here to help me? I'm on disability."

"Why don't you make that bastard get a job?" Sijn said and pointed at Duane. "There's nothing wrong with him except Pabst's Blue Ribbon."

"Hey, I gotta bad back, fer yo' information," Duane piped in.

"Sijn is not your concern anymore, make the best way you can," Shana said. Turning to Sijn, she asked, "Are you ready to get the hell out of here?"

"Yes," Sijn answered quickly. She had had enough of the ugly life. Her mother had killed any love she had felt for her years ago. That hurt to admit that. It left her feeling empty inside.

"What am I gonna do without her?" her mother cried again. She never got off the couch.

"What do you want? What's the bottom line?" Shana asked pulling a checkbook from her purse. "How much will make you people go away?"

"Ya' can't buy me, Miss Fancy," Mrs. Black yelled out. "That's my daughter!"

"Check's probably rubber anyhows," Duane muttered.

"Okay then, so be it," Shana said putting her checkbook away. "But don't come around asking for any later. You had your chance. Bye bye now." They all walked out of the trailer. Outside Dawg stood next to the van, looking down at his feet. He was crying. Before they got to him he had wiped his eyes and made a tough front.

"I told you it was gonna be bad, " he said sadly.

"Yeah, I know," Sijn replied. She hugged him. "Call me, just don't give them the number."

"I won't, you can count on it," he said, hugging her back. The curses of their mother and Duane could be heard outside. "I

141

better get home. I don't want to be here today and my woman will be lookin' for me anyway."

"Bye, Dawg," Sijn said.

"Bye, Sis," he said and got into his truck.

They all three got into the van without looking at the trailer again. Silently they rode over the gravel road, the potholes jostling them to and fro. Shana was the first to break the silence. She turned in her seat to look Sijn in the face. "Is that why you didn't want me to come?" she asked.

"Yes," Sijn replied tears choking her voice. "I'm so sorry you had to see that." Tears spilled down her face freely now and she sobbed out loud.

Shana came back and sat on the seat next to her and put her arms around Sijn. She cried into the woman's chest like a baby. Shana rocked her and smoothed her hair. "Don't apologize for them, sweetie. No one should be talked to like that. I'll never let them hurt you again, I promise. Never." Sijn cried louder at this and hugged the woman back. "We're your family now, Sijn. You never have to come back here."

Sijn pulled back to ask, "You don't hate me at all?"

"Why would you think that?" Shana asked a look of question on her face.

"Because of Dereck, because I slept with him," Sijn answered, looking down at her feet.

"God, no!" Shana exclaimed. "Well, how could I get mad about who Dereck slept with, he was the pied piper of pussy. Sijn, if you hadn't slept with Dereck you wouldn't be carrying that baby. That baby is all that is left of him besides our memories. And the more I know you, the more I like you. I could never hate you for that."

Sijn hugged her again. "I was so worried about that. Thank you, Shana, thank you for everything."

"No sweetie, thank you, " Shana told her and held her tight. She thought to herself, it's Solange you need to worry about. Sijn was so eager to find her. She was such an innocent in this whole matter. She would see to it that no one hurt her, especially Solange.

Chapter Sixteen

Dr. Cornell

While Solange slept and dreamt her dreams of years gone by, brought on by a future so closely linked to them, across town someone else sat troubled by the thoughts of this very same future.

Light danced on Greg's face, brilliantly reflected from the car in a kaleidoscope of color. The interior of the car was warmed by the same light that illuminated his face. He had been sitting in the parking lot for over fifteen minutes, and the air inside the car grew more humid and stale with cigarette smoke with each passing minute. A part of him was reluctant to go inside, not wishing to share with anyone his new revelations, but part of him yearned to do just that. Dr. Cornell had been his psychiatrist and hypnotist for several years, since the frequency and intensity increased in his dreaming. No one could be trusted more than Dr. Cornell, and Greg finally crushed out his cigarette and opened the car door.

His apprehensions increased as he stepped inside the waiting room. The soft pastel surroundings, as well as the faint potpourri smell, did little to soothe him. The receptionist slid open the frosted glass window when he stepped forward, her lovely smile familiar but not as enticing as usual. "Good morning Greg," she said, "I'll let him know you're here."

"Thank you, Kelly." He turned away from the pretty receptionist to take a seat on a seafoam-green chair with wooden armrests. Greg looked at the magazines on the table beside him, but was far too distracted with his thoughts to read. He just sat fidgeting in the chair while his mind raced over and over the events of the past week. He felt things were getting out of control with Solange. His attempt to share with her what he thought only scared her. It definitely scared the hell out of him: he needed counseling, more than he ever had before. That had spawned his call to Dr. Cornell.

When he first started the therapy he never imagined it would lead to this. The dreams, seeing her in that magazine, and then after mourning her death, she shows up. The chances of running into someone you dreamed were impossible. But here he sat, with the woman living next door and the dreams increasing. It had been magical, her cool smooth skin and kisses fired him into a passion he had known from no other woman. Yet she remained so distant and Greg fought to appear aloof, but his feelings were so out of hand. Did she not feel the familiarity between them?

Sometimes he could feel her reading his thoughts, and it sent chills up and down his spine, and every mental capacity available to him went to block her out. Surely he imagined this power in her. He had read of people who could do that, but always remained skeptical. Yet he could feel her probing, like icy fingers touching his mind. He shivered in remembrance.

At that moment the door to the inner office swung open, Dr. Cornell's stocky form appeared at the door. His usual sunny demeanor shone on his face. "Greg," the doctor welcomed. Startled from his thoughts, Greg jumped slightly. "Come on back." He gestured for Greg to follow but he knew the way. Greg shook his hand, his lost in the firm, immense grasp of the black man. Even though Greg stood over the doctor by at least six inches, the other man made up for it in bulk. Once a football player, the now middle-aged man lingered somewhere between muscle and fat. If not for his jovial personality, he would be very intimidating. Greg held a great respect for the man and liked him as surely everyone whoever met him did.

Greg followed him into the office whose colors matched the waiting room, seafoam-green cushions, peach carpet and mahogany-stained wood, all meant to be calming, but had little effect on him this day. He sat in his usual deep-cushioned chair across from the desk. Sometimes Dr. Cornell sat in a chair identical to the one he occupied or at other times at the desk. Today he rested behind the desk, his sleeves rolled up, barely revealing the lower portion of a brand; the omega symbol, a permanent reminder of the man's days in the Que Dog fraternity.

"So, Greg what has upset you so much? I haven't seen you like this in months." He took a pen from its holder. "You sounded so urgent on the phone. Are your nightmares getting worse?" At that point Dr. Cornell leaned forward on his elbows and touched his fingers together in steeple under his roll of a chin. Expressive brown eyes peered through round wire spectacles in concern. The furrows on the wide expanse of brow did not completely take away the near-permanent smile on the man's face.

"My dreams are coming true." Greg paused, not sure if the man could believe this. Cornell nodded. "We talked about the past life thing before, after the hypnosis, remember? Just the fact that I really did have a past life, not just dreams of a lunatic."

"No one ever doubted your sanity." Cornell nodded that he should proceed again.

"My dreams are returning more frequently now and there have been some changes in my life." He stopped, knowing that he could sound crazy and that this man could put him away. He was hesitant to share his story for the sheer lunacy of it.

Cornell leaned back in his chair and scratched the rolls that stacked like hot dogs on the back of his neck. "Do you know what's caused the resurgence of dreams?"

"Yes," Greg said. "I've found her."

"You've found her?" Cornell suddenly leaned forward in interest, the furrows on his brow deepening. "You've found who?"

"Solange." Greg hesitated, knowing he just gave the first hint of his discovery or insanity, whichever it may be. "I first saw her in a magazine and I couldn't believe my eyes, there was the girl I had dreamt about. The article called her Angel. The article was about the rock star, Dereck Cliffe. How he had this artist girlfriend, and after her gallery opening, she joined him at some big concert he gave. I almost died when I saw that picture, it was her.

"I called the gallery it named and found out the artist is very shy and doesn't do very many public appearances, and the photo taken was a chance. I flew out there to see her work. Very moving, it touched me, like I had known her for ages. I could read so much emotion into them. The style reminded me of something, but I couldn't remember. So I bought one."

"How long ago was this?" Cornell asked.

"About six months ago."

"Why didn't you tell me?" Cornell looked concerned but not quite overwhelmed. "This is such a rare case. People don't find their 'dream girl' everyday."

"I wasn't sure, first of all. She just looked like the girl in the dreams. I didn't want to say anything because I couldn't be sure and I didn't want you to think I'd lost my mind."

"Greg, you came to me to learn to deal with your dreams. Anything related to them is relevant and I'm not going to think you've lost your mind. You have dealt with this well so far. Reincarnation is something most people couldn't remember or believe in. You have taken everything well in stride. But please continue, I feel there is more to this story."

"Well, about a month ago, Dereck died and from the media's point of view, so did Angel."

Cornell nodded, "I remember the news bulletin, twenty-three bodies, most of them burned completely beyond recognition. Very sad."

"Right, I grieved heavily for her; she died without my ever meeting her. I thought I had lost every chance of that. Until now." Greg stopped and pressed his hands flat on his legs, thinking he needed a cigarette. "Now, I know she didn't die in that fire and I have met her."

Again, Cornell scratched the rolls on his neck, a nervous gesture Greg was familiar with. Greg continued, "A few weeks ago, a girl moved into the apartment next to mine. Delivery men brought all her stuff in; someone else unpacked and arranged everything. She didn't arrive until a week later."

"I saw her standing on the balcony staring into the stream below, the wind blowing her hair, with the saddest look on anyone's face I had ever seen. She didn't even notice me, that's how lost in thought she had been. My heart fell, she was the most beautiful woman I had ever seen and I recognized her. It was her. The person I had dreamt about and thought dead, stood less than ten feet from me."

"What did you do?" Cornell leaned forward again, and Greg noticed that a small recorder had been running for some time.

"I said hello," Greg shrugged, "I think she knows or felt something. Her face when she saw me . . . she . . . she . . .just froze. Like she saw a ghost or something. She would hardly talk to me, almost broke her neck getting back in the apartment. Scared, that's all I could say about her, she was scared to death. She acted scared of me! I felt she knew me. How, I don't know."

"Did you do anything to scare her, to make her feel threatened?" Cornell asked. Greg shook his head no. "Perhaps you imagined her reaction? Or even imagined the resemblance?"

"No resemblance, it's her!" Greg adamantly replied. "She knows. I don't know how, but I think she really feels something. We've been dating. I know it's not the smartest thing I've ever done but I couldn't help it. If I tell her about everything, how do I tell her? What if she thinks I'm nuts?"

"I see," Cornell paused, trapped his fingers together, and leaned back again. "Have you been intimate with this girl?"

"Yes," Greg hesitated, "We have been. She just got up and left afterwards. She won't give me a chance to tell her anything. Any questions I ask she just sidesteps. She just cuts me off."

"You know this is very dangerous ground you are crossing?" Cornell's asked, though it was more a statement that a question. "She sounds as if she has been scared. Perhaps you are coming on a bit strong with her. If you tell her these things, one, she'll think you're crazy, two, you'll upset her. Just take things easy."

"That's not all. The dreams have increased, but I suppose that's because I'm seeing her everyday. Also, remember the emblem I dreamed about?" Cornell nodded. "It's tattooed on her shoulder. I asked her about it and she said it was her family crest."

"Have you ever found any reference in history about it?" Cornell questioned. "Remember my friend at Emory who specializes in family crest history?"

"No, not a trace." Greg looked at Cornell, hoping he was believing this. "Now things get even more strange. Last night after she left me, I had a dream. It was completely different from the others. I floated in darkness and a face appeared above me. Not her face; it was an extremely pale man, with striking long black hair with brilliant green eyes. They shone like lights. He said, 'Stay away from her . . . she belongs to me. She will only kill you again.' I woke up sweating, scared as hell, no one there, just the breeze blowing through the open door. What do you make of it?"

"I sense a lot of the apprehension you feel for her. Perhaps it's showing up as a warning in your dreams?" Cornell asked.

"Could be, but I know I'm scared; I think I'm in love with her. I'm confused; she's confused. I want to tell her so much but she'll think I'm nuts." Greg sighed. "I don't want to scare her away."

"That's understandable." Cornell played with his pen for a few moments and said, "You may be attracted to her because of the dreams, so be sure of your feelings before you proceed with this relationship. Greg, you need to look out for yourself, don't let this take over your life. Don't let dreams overcome reality. I want to prescribe some medication to help you relax a little. I think you need that more than anything right now."

After Greg left, Dr. Cornell sat at his desk making notes into the young man's file. Cornell was concerned about the man's obsession with this Angel. He had seemed nearly delusional, in the doctor's opinion. He had made another appointment before Greg had left. Cornell hoped it wouldn't come to committing Greg, but he would if he had to.

CHAPTER SEVENTEEN

Just Another Morning

"**S**on of a bitch!" bellowed Mike as he walked into the solarium. He walked over to the table where Sijn and Jan were eating breakfast and slammed a newspaper down on the table. Huffing and puffing he dropped his bulk into a chair beside of her.

Curiously, Sijn picked up the paper and her mouth dropped open in shock. In the headline, just above three-legged woman gives birth and Elvis sighted in Krispy Kreme, read the words: Vampire Lady Kidnapped My Daughter. Below those words was a picture of Shana at some awards show in a revealing black dress. Inset into that was a picture of her mother crying. Oh Jesus, Sijn thought. What would Shana think of her now? With shaking hands she handed the paper to Jan.

Jan pursed her lips together and shot Sijn a dirty look. "I knew letting you stay here was going to be trouble," she said acidly. Sijn had the feeling that Jan felt jealous over her newfound friendship with Shana. What could she do? The woman had not really done anything to her and she had not done anything to her. Yet there lingered an animosity between them. She really hoped Jan would warm up to her. Jan turned her face to Mike and asked, "Has Shana seen this?"

"Seen what?" Shana asked from the door. Dressed in a robe of silk and velvet, hair uncombed and cigarette hanging out of her mouth, she stepped onto the cool tile of the solarium. Generally not a morning person they were all surprised to see her coming to the breakfast table. She slipped into a chair between Sijn and Jan. Her attention turned to her best friend first. "Did I see you being mean to Sijn? Yes, I did see that. That bullshit has to stop. I love you, you know that, but I'm not fucking around with any petty jealousy with you. Now what is the problem this morning?"

Jan wrinkled her nose sourly and tossed the paper over at Shana. "This is the problem. Seems like someone's trashy family is talking shit about you." She smiled slightly.

"That's enough, it's not her fault they're assholes," Shana commented as she poured herself a cup of coffee. She drank the whole cup with one gulp, black and poured herself another. She picked up the paper and laughed. "That fat bastard Elvis should have more sense than to go buy jelly doughnuts. Wonder if he used the drive thru?"

"Not that story," Jan said with some exasperation.

"I know but that shit's funny," Shana said with a bit of laughter. "You're too fucking uptight today. Tampon uncomfortable or something? Geez. If you had gone with us last week, you'd be a little more understanding."

Jan looked down into her plate but said nothing. Sijn looked at her own, sad because she had caused this problem. Part of her wanted to laugh at Shana but she didn't dare. That would make Jan mad as hell. Her attention was focused completely on the scrambled eggs before her. She waited for Shana to read the story.

"Sijn, don't worry it's not the first time this lousy rag wrote a story about me," Shana explained. "In fact, I was feeling unloved because they hadn't printed anything in awhile." She opened the rag and turned to the page with her story. "They picked a good picture of me, at least. My boobs look good there, don't they?"

"Fuck your boobs!" yelled Mike. "Just read the story."

"We'll address your animosity to my bosom later, Mike," Shana quipped and kept looking at the page.

"Just read the story," he ordered.

"Okay, okay," she answered with a wave of her hand. "Here we go." She read out loud. "*Acclaimed, horror writer, Shana Collins, widow of producer Chris Collins has been accused of kidnapping a young girl whose age is undisclosed at this time. The girl's mother Tamara Black, says that, Collins burst into her house, took the girl's possessions and assaulted her. According to sources in the writer's hometown, Shana has been on a downward spiral since the death of alleged lover Dereck Cliffe. She has not left her house in weeks. Our sources say that she spends her days drinking and yelling at people who pass by her gates. In previous articles we reported that Shana was involved in a lurid love triangle with Dereck Cliffe and his artist, girlfriend, Angel. She is supposedly on a suicide watch since their untimely deaths.*"

"Bastards! Suicide my fucking ass," Shana interjected without looking up.

"*Mrs. Black shared with this reporter the bruises that the unstable writer left on her face and arms. "She cursed me and beat me about my person," says Black. "I was fearing for my life." Her daughter was then pulled from the house forcibly and into a van. Leaving the disabled Mrs. Black, helpless and worried.*"

"Hah," Shana exclaimed out loud. "I should have kicked that bitch's ass."

"Duane probably hit her, " Sijn added. "He does when he goes on a bender."

"He probably did it so she'd look good for the reporter, " added Jan.

Shana went back to reading. "*And to what purpose did this kidnapping serve? Why would a woman with her social standing need a young girl such as this? Interviews with local clergyman, Reverend John Jenkins has insight into the situation. "Ms. Collins is starting a cult" says Jenkins, a long-standing opponent of the writer's. He has previously protested against all of her books and movies. Preaching against the evil written in them. 'She is running a vampire cult in that house. Alcoholism, fornication and blood drinking goes on in that Sodom and Gomorrah.' Could it be true? One of America's prized celebrities a cult leader? At the time of printing no comment could be attained from Ms. Collins. Mrs. Black receiving no cooperation with local authorities, will seek retribution in small claims court."*

"Son of a bitch!" Shana said as she threw down the paper and looked up. "Nobody is drinking blood here. You know they'd have to have Jenkins in on the show. A cult, oh man he's going in deep now. And your mother, I wish she'd take me to court. My lawyers will chew her up and spit her out."

"What are you gonna do?" Sijn asked in a small voice. Her eggs were cold now. She'd lost all the appetite she'd had anyway. Nausea built in her throat.

"You notice she said nothing about the alcoholism and fornicating," Jan interjected.

"Shut up Jan. Not a god damned thing," Shana explained. "I never do. They print all kinds of shit about me. Who cares, its publicity, helps me sell more books. It's not worth suing them over it. Hell, last year, I was having sex with aliens. Next week, Elvis will be living here in the cult." She laughed long and hard. Sijn liked her a lot then. After all of that, she could laugh. Things wouldn't be so bad. She looked over at Jan who was frowning into her uneaten eggs. Well maybe just a little bad, she thought.

CHAPTER EIGHTEEN

Another Body

The phone rang. Reluctantly, the man rolled over in the bed and grasped the receiver. His low voice thick with sleep he said, "Hello."

"Detective Sanford?"

"Speaking," Sanford pulled himself up and looked at the clock. Two o'clock in the afternoon; he should have been up hours ago. He had put in so much time at night on this case it drained him during the day. Today was his day off and he had intended to sleep, but not this long.

"This is Matt down at the morgue, we've got one in you're gonna want to see." The line went quiet for a moment. "Hugh said if any strange ones come in to call you."

His mind still groggy from sleep, he barely understood what the guy meant. "Strange one?" he asked. "What do you mean, strange one?"

"No blood," the voice on the phone explained. "Hugh said you would know."

"Thanks, I'll be right down." Giving the man no time to answer, Sanford hung up. He lifted his body off the bed with only a few aches and pains. *Goddammit, can't even have a day off,* he thought. No wonder he felt so old. He walked into the bathroom to relieve himself, and afterwards turned on the shower, hoping the steaming jets off water would wash away the lingering sleep. Since he was officially off duty, he dressed himself in jeans and a pale blue oxford button-down. Before he stepped out of his apartment he grabbed his shoulder holster: he had been nowhere without that in fifteen years.

Down at the morgue, Hugh arrived the same time as Sanford. Together they walked into the office. He asked the Medical Examiner, "Do you know where this one came from?"

"Matt said he came in a couple of hours ago," Hugh explained. "He said they found him dead in the garbage. A homeless man."

"Who brought him in?" Sanford asked as he followed Hugh into the examining room. He put on the mask handed to him.

A young man with curly red hair sticking out of the back of his surgical cap stood at the examining table beside a sheet-draped corpse. "It was Detective Porter who handled the case. He said it was just another dead bum in the trash."

"Porter? That prick," Sanford snorted. "He wouldn't know a clue if it jumped up and bit him on the ass. So they didn't class this as a homicide?"

"No sir, he said they found nothing at the scene to say otherwise, it's marked as an unexplained death, probable natural causes," Matt said. "But as I told you on the phone, there's no blood."

Hugh went over, lifted the sheet and pulled it back. His fingers looked so long and pale in the rubber gloves as they started examining the body. He was searching for wounds. Nothing like the previous bodies in this case, Sanford could see that for himself. "Matt, how do you know there's no blood?" Hugh asked.

"Well, I tried to take a sample and couldn't get any. Also there's none settled in the lower limbs, back, or buttocks. The position they found him in, there would have been blood there. Also see how pale his face is, bloodless, the lips and eyelids are almost translucent," Matt pointed out.

"Any signs of a wound?" Sanford asked.

"Just these," the young man said and turned the corpse's head to the right. On the side of the neck, two bruised puncture marks stood out against the pale skin, their edges ragged and white. "But there's no way he could have lost this much blood through these small holes. I didn't even notice them until he was undressed, the other detective didn't see them at all."

"That's no surprise," grunted Sanford. "Goddamned Porter." He locked eyes with Hugh, who stood strangely quiet.

"This is your girl, Morris," he said quietly.

"But the MO is so different," Sanford argued. "No slashes, no mess, and this guy is homeless but no real criminal. The first was a gang member, could have tried to mug her or something, the second a rapist. What did this guy do, piss on her sidewalk? Doesn't make sense."

"Bet I find saliva on those wounds," Hugh countered. "Bet it matches the others."

"Shit," was all Sanford could say and walked out of the examining room, throwing his mask in the garbage.

Chapter Nineteen

A Plan

Shana's screams brought everyone running. Sijn and Jan led the pack down the garden path, past the fountain where a statue of a boy child tinkled into the water below, to the gazebo which held a hot tub. Mike lumbered behind them, panting but keeping up. They got to the gazebo where the writer stood up in the water, yelling, "Yes! Yes! Yes!"

"What . . . *pant* . . . in th' . . . *pant* . . . hell?" Mike bellowed. He stood trying to catch his breath, flushed red with the effort.

"I've got a plan!" Shana told them all, not even caring that she stood before them naked.

Sijn looked away, embarrassed for her. Jan noticed this. "Don't worry, you'll get used to her. She has no shame whatsoever," she explained.

Ignoring her friend, Shana sat back in the water, grinning to herself like a Cheshire cat. She lit a cigarette and looked at them all. "Mike can you get me a paper, preferably the *Atlanta Constitution* but the *Observer* will do if not."

"What for?" he asked angrily.

"We're looking for something," she told him. "We are going on a hunting trip."

Sijn looked at her, perplexed. Ever since she had been here the woman seemed so sad, so stoical. Even when the movie people were here, she acted the kind, gracious hostess, but sad nonetheless. Now she sat naked in the hot tub grinning like an idiot, cigarette in one hand and a drink in the other.

Sijn had learned a lot of things about Shana Collins in the short time she had been here. For one she wasn't as tough as she came across. Second, she had suffered a lot. Dereck was not the only man she had seen die. Her first husband, Eric, had died from cystic fibrosis after they had only been married a month. She had known he was going to die but had married him anyway. Her second, movie producer Chris Collins, died several years ago after a bout with cancer. This woman had seen pain, but kept on going. Maybe she was as tough as she seemed.

"Also bring me a phone," Shana yelled at the little chubby man. He went off, bitching mostly to himself about crazy women. "You two get over here and get in the tub. We have some war plans to discuss."

Jan did just that, although she stayed in bra and panties. Sijn hesitated, looking at both of them like they were crazy. Jan told her, "Might as well, she won't leave you alone until you do." She still didn't think it a good thing, but did it anyway.

"There, it'll relax you. Best thinking place I have here. Chris had it put in for me before he died. It's well hidden too, private, nobody can see us here or bother us," Shana explained. "I've given this situation a lot of thought. Solange won't come here, so we have to go to her. The question is how do we find her?"

"That's something we all had wondered about," commented Jan. "There is also the question of why?"

"What do you mean?" Sijn asked.

"Well, if memory serves me correct, last time she saw Shana she acted like she wanted to rip her head off," Jan told Sijn. "Now that I know what she is, that makes her even more on my not most wanted list."

"True there has been bad blood between us in the past," Shana agreed. "But a promise is a promise. This was the man's dying wish and dammit, we are gonna do it." She crushed her cigarette in the ashtray perched on the tub's edge. "Dereck wanted us all together for a reason, he must have thought some good would have come from it."

"Oh, you are so crazy! I can't believe you'd invite all of this into the house. As if you don't have enough troubles as it is, you'll just fix a vampire up with a room," Jan argued. "Why not give Reverend Jenkins a spare bed in the cellar while you're at it?"

"Don't even mention that motherfucker today, okay?" the writer said with exasperation. "We need to concentrate on finding Solange. Sijn, do you still want to find her?" Sijn nodded yes. "See, I'm not alone. I know you are afraid for me, Jan, but this is one dying wish I can keep."

Jan stopped talking; she knew what Shana meant. The guilt she carried around for not being where she should have been when her first two husbands died. It ate away at her friend and nothing could ever erase that. She knew that Shana saw this as her big chance to make up something to Dereck. So she gave in. "Okay, I'll go along for now. First fuck-up and I'm out. Do you understand that Shana?"

"Absolutely," she agreed with a toast of her glass. "Now, where is Mike with that paper?"

Jan poured herself a drink from the bottle sitting on the side of the hot tub. There was always one there. "Just what do you need the paper for anyhow? Do you think she's gonna run a personal? 'Lonely vampire bitch seeks companions she hates,' perhaps."

"Don't be facetious," Shana said leaning back in the tub. "Murders."

"Of course," chimed in Sijn. "Murders, there will be unexplained deaths. She will be hunting."

"If I know ol' Soley, she'll be half out of her gourd by now," the writer told them. "Dereck always held her back. That's why he wants me to help her, to be her friend. She needs one."

"Why Atlanta?" Jan asked.

"Because one, she's said she wanted to go there one day," Shana explained. "She lived there ages ago or something. Also, I thought I remember seeing something on the news about a weird murder there. Could be her."

"Oh, just run down there and find her just like that, huh?" Jan sounded disgusted with her friend's wild scheme. "Excuse me, Mr. Policeman, but I know the vampire you're hunting. You have to stop drinking."

"We'll take precautions. We'll make it a road trip," she smiled. "Just to check around. Flash some photos here and there, that's all."

"The hell you will!" Mike thundered from the path. With paper and phone in hand he wobbled up to the tub. "Now dammit, you're not going down there and look for some damn vampire murderer."

"Yes I am, we are all going," Shana stated. "Now hand me that paper." She looked through it and found what she was looking for. Reading from an article she said, "*There have been two murders, according to the police, the victims' throats were ripped out.*" She peeked from around the paper at them. "Very bloody," she read on. "*Police are baffled at the savage killing of these two criminals. Some unknown vigilante has struck twice in different areas of town, leaving these known troublemakers dead.*" She stopped reading. "This has to be her. She likes to snack on the bad element, no guilt."

"Sounds more like a feast to me," Mike commented.

"There will be more unless we get to her," Sijn added in.

Shana took the phone from Mike and started dialing. "Johnny? Shana . . . yes . . . I know, I've missed you guys, too . . . listen are you going to Atlanta soon?" she asked the guitarist. "Good, we'll be heading down, too. I haven't caught a road show in a while. Cool, where are you playing?" Shana nodded and licked her lips. "Yeah, I know where that is. We'll see you then. Bye, sweetie."

When she hung up she announced, "Road trip, we're heading down under the pretense of going with the band. Whisper is playing on the outskirts of Atlanta in two weeks. Soley never could resist the music."

"Hey, I know those guys," Sijn told them. "My band used to open for them. But we can't tell them why we are there."

"Hell no," Jan agreed.

"Mike, make a list. There are some things we'll need," Shana informed him. "First get my black garment bag out of the closet, take the hanger out, and tape the holes shut."

"What for?" he asked.

"Body bag," she told him.

They all looked at her. Perhaps she was crazy. Then again, no one knew vampires like she did.

CHAPTER TWENTY

A Leak In the Department

"**W**ho did it?" Sanford screamed at the room full of policeman. He slammed a rolled-up newspaper onto his desk. "Which one of you is the low down, dirty, publicity-grabbing piece of crap?"

His brown eyes scanned the room, narrowed into slits of burning fury. From face to face he moved, giving his fellow workers the look. They all looked at each other; a cop that leaked to the press would not be treated well among them. Finally, the look settled on one very smug detective. He grinned broadly when he met Sanford's eyes. "Porter, I should have known."

"You have no proof it was me, the paper said it was an anonymous police contact," the old detective smiled. "Seems to me, Fred, you can't keep the lid on your case. It had to blow sooner or later." Porter always called him Fred in reference to some seventies sitcom, today he let it slide. Mostly because the story had to break eventually, he knew that, but Sanford would have Porter's ass in a sling for it.

He picked up the newspaper and unrolled it, showing it to the rest of the room. "He knows so much about my case he blabs to the press. If you knew so much, Porter, why didn't you identify that body this morning as a victim? How could the reporter's expert on the inside totally screw up a murder investigation?" Sanford's voice thundered.

"It was just some old homeless guy, drunk himself to death," Porter said.

"Well from now on, even if you find a dead dog, I want it checked for puncture wounds or claw marks," Sanford bellowed. "I'm sure the Captain will agree with me." The phone on his desk rang. He sat down and answered it. "Sanford here," he said into the phone.

"Vampire Cult Terrorizes Atlanta. Nice headline, so who blabbed?" Hugh asked, his voice not amused.

"Same asshole who misjudged the homeless guy this morning," Sanford told him.

"Pencil-Dick strikes again," Hugh exclaimed in mock radio style. "You know you'll have to make a statement now, calm the public."

"I know, I'll talk to the Captain about a press conference. The damage is already done. Every crackpot who gets the paper will be down here, mucking up any witnesses or evidence." Sanford ran his fingers through his thin hair. He looked up to see an uniformed officer escorting a young man into his office. "It's started already, Hugh, let me go. I'll call you later." He hung up.

"This one wants to confess, Sanford, says he's a vampire," the officer said with a smirk. He shoved the handcuffed youth into the chair in front of Sanford's desk. "We caught him trying to break into the Red Cross bloodmobile. Stoned out of his gourd is more like what he is."

Sanford looked at the boy for a long time. His hair was dyed black with a blue stripe and light brown roots threatening at the scalp. Eyes, barely blue and dilated, glared from smudges of black makeup in a white pancake face. Red-stained lips and black-painted nails went along with the black trench coat and black jeans the boy wore. *Typical little Goth baby,* thought the detective, needing some attention. Somehow he knew there would be more of this before the day was out.

"What's your name?" he asked the boy.

"I am Lord Ravencroft, prince of all evil, child of darkness, sorcerer . . ." the youth arrogantly started spouting.

Sanford interrupted him. "Dammit this is not a joke!'" He wanted to shake the boy. "These are serious charges, being a multiple murder case. This many murders is not something you want to confess to very lightly."

After two hours of this type of interrogation he found out the kid's real name and called his parents. The rest of his day went the same way. The world was full of nuts and they were all lined up to talk to him.

CHAPTER TWENTY-ONE

The Lure of Guitar

Solange drove through the streets of downtown Atlanta in search of a victim. She was starved. It had been a week since her last kill, since her first date with Greg. She had been avoiding him for this time, not hunting either. Night after night she sat in front of a canvas in her apartment trying to paint. Nothing ever came, not since Dereck died had she been able to create anything. Finally, she left the house in search of a kill.

So far nothing had attracted her. But as she passed a small club, sweet music filled her ears. Inside the club music flowed, the fast notes reminded her of Dereck. Without thinking she turned the car around and headed for the club. She had to park a block away: the small parking lot was packed.

Inside the club the walls were black and covered with fliers of local bands. The area in front of the stage overflowed with a throng of young people. Girls in tight, skimpy clothing, guys in jeans and T-shirts, all swaying and headbanging. How many times had she seen the same at Dereck's shows? A touch of sadness lighted upon her heart. Carefully she waded through the sea of hot bodies, smelling the blood surrounding her. Closer to the stage she crept, her body drawn by the music. And then she saw him.

The guitar player, though only a mortal, cranked out a sound so like Dereck's she could close her eyes and imagine him there. When her hands reached the high stage, she did just that. As the music played on, she remembered Dereck, the way he played for her before the dawn every night. His face flashed before her closed lids, singing the lyrics written for her. She felt tears slip between her lashes and down her face. Agony ripped through her at the thought of him. She remembered how he would lean down and sing a song to her from the stage, his face inches from hers. So close their breath would mingle, the end of the song drawing their lips together in tender passion. It was more than she could bear, these memories.

The vampire opened her eyes to find the guitar player looking down at her. The music may remind her of her dead lover but the man could not have looked more different. Green eyes flashed from underneath sweat-soaked sandy tresses. The skin on his face held none of the paleness of Dereck's but was golden tanned from the sun. Sandy hair lightly covered his jaw and chin, matching the strands that hung down around his face. Where her precious one had been tall and thin, this one was shorter with a lean, muscled body. But the music carried her away so much, she reached out and ran her hand up the black legging-clad calve a foot away from her.

As her blue eyes stared into the hazel green ones above her, his thoughts slipped into her mind. *Why is she crying? But she is so beautiful when she does.* Solange closed her mind, she didn't want to read his thoughts, she wanted to find them and his emotions in the music. The rest of the evening she spent swaying in front of him, soaking up every drop of feeling pouring from his songs. Several times he bent down close to her as he played, the white poet's blouse he wore gaped open to reveal the sandy brown hair sprinkled across his chest. She longed to stir that hair with her breath, to feel it caress her face. Every chord his fingers struck she felt on her body. If only she could trade places with that white guitar, she would be in ecstasy.

Then suddenly the music was gone, the show over. The crowd dispersed, most going to the bar. Solange however stayed at the stage, her eyes still locking with the guitarist. He sat down on the edge of the stage next to where she was standing. "Hi," he said eyes never leaving her face.

"Hi, you were wonderful," she said. "Your music moved me."

"So, I noticed. I saw you crying, why?"

"The song made me remember something that's all." Solange smiled.

"Oh . . . by the way my name is Kyle and you?" his voice purred, she couldn't look away from his handsome face. A human so enigmatic, so powerful, lucky for her he wasn't a vampire.

"Solange," she said. "Don't you have to help?" The rest of the band was breaking down equipment, occasionally casting Kyle dirty looks.

"No, they'll get it. I'd rather talk to you." He smiled and then asked, "Do I know you from somewhere? I mean you look so familiar."

"I don't think so. I just moved here," she said.

"Maybe you just remind me of someone," he stated then reached out to touch her hair.

"You remind me of someone too. Not really you, but your music." She moved over closer to him so that she stood directly in front of him. "The notes are different but hauntingly like another."

"A lot of people say I play like Dereck Cliffe," he said with a shrug. "It's a compliment because he's one of my favorites. Too bad what happened to him. Man, our whole band went into mourning when he died."

"That must be it, no one cried for Dereck more than I," Solange said, the sadness echoing hollowly in her voice.

"Maybe that's why you cried tonight?" he asked.

"Perhaps," she paused, "Or perhaps your playing was so beautiful." The vampire leaned closer and kissed him on his full lips. There she tasted sweetness of cigarettes lingering, how many times had Dereck's lips been just the same when he kissed her? This close she inhaled the intoxicating aroma of his skin: a miasma of smoke, beer, and sweat. Ah, this was the smell of rock 'n roll, and beneath it the heady allure of blood. The thought of the salty, rich, slightly sweet elixir running down her throat made her mind race. This mortal appealed to her more than the prey she usually sought, for his blood was not the only thing she craved. A flutter of guilt ran through her mind because of Greg, but he would never know. This part of her life could never be shared with Greg, he wouldn't understand. This was the part of her life that belonged to Dereck, a part that hadn't died when he did. It had been buried within her since the fire, now upon hearing the succulent music of this band, it threatened to resurface. The cresting emotions made her easy prey to the charms of this musician, he aroused a passion left dormant too long. The touch of his lips and the steady pressure of his hand upon her back urged her closer. Too soon she felt her blood teeth slip down. *No,* she thought to herself, *not this one.*

"Do you want to take me home?" Kyle whispered in her ear. "The guys won't mind if I go ahead and leave."

"That is a tempting offer. How far away do you live?" Solange asked, not wanting to be too far away in case she got preoccupied until near dawn.

"Inman Park, we all live in an old mansion there, it's pretty cool." As he spoke he continued to caress her back. Solange felt the calluses on his fingertips as they moved on her skin.

"Sure," she said before she kissed his mouth one more time. Kyle slipped off the stage and put his arm around her, together they walked out the door.

In the car they spoke little, Solange drove and her victim rested while the radio played on. She almost cried when they played a Nightbird song; perhaps she made a sound, for Kyle opened his eyes and looked at her. "You knew him," he said softly.

"What makes you say that?" she asked, trying not to show too much emotion.

"Your face tells it all. In the club and now when that song came on I heard you, a small sob before you caught yourself." He put his hand on top of hers where it rested on the gear stick.

"We were lovers," Solange said. She didn't know why she told him this, it just came out. "But I have to go on. I have a long life and I can't spend it wishing Dereck was here."

"I knew I recognized you, you're the artist!" he announced excitedly. "But they said you were dead." His voice held a question, she knew she had to answer him.

"The fire was meant for me, Dereck just got in the way. So did all my friends," she explained, and tears again coursed down her face. "I wasn't even there, I let everyone think so . . . if I was dead he'd stop killing. He wanted me."

"Who wanted you?"

"The killer, he had been stalking me for years, so my death will save others." Solange wanted to believe that so desperately, but deep down she knew he would never stop. "Promise me you won't tell anyone, never tell a living soul."

"What are you going to do, hide the rest of your life?" His questions were starting to worry her. "You can't live like that, hiding from that psycho and the world forever."

"I have to; justice will catch up with him, I'll see to that. As for the world, Angel is dead. I want it that way, fame didn't suit me well." Solange stopped, why had she told this human so much? What was she gonna do next, tell him her deepest secret? What would he say when he learned a vampire was driving him home? This human posed a threat to her, but she missed Dereck terribly tonight. The music had triggered her longing for her old life and this one could fill the void. She should pull her hand away but the firm grip he had on it felt unexpectedly reassuring. Solange did not pull away.

Soon they arrived at his house; well, not a house, but like he said a mansion. She parked her car on the street in front. A crisp, cool breeze blew leaves over the cracked sidewalk as they walked. The stone steps were covered with the leaves and vines wound up the stone pillars on each side. The front entrance was markedly Victorian: stained glass set intricately into dark carved wood. Kyle opened the door and led her in. "Would you like a tour?" he asked. "It really is a great old house. It was built in the early 1900's by the owner of a soda company. When the neighborhood started going down they sold it and moved to something even more grand than this, if you can believe that." He led her up a dark massive staircase, its banister heavily, but beautifully carved. The walls were a faded gold brocade, squares of lighter fabric showed where paintings had once hung. "There are over thirty rooms here, four bathrooms, one of the first in the city to have indoor plumbing. Here let me show you one." At the top of the stairs Kyle led her into a room to the right. Its dimensions were greater than her bedroom at home. One corner was completely occupied by the largest tub Solange had ever seen. Green marble veined with black and white, its sides were flanked by deep, rich mahogany wood. Intricate gold fixtures along the wall for the water set off the beautifully done room. Solange, accustomed to elegance, fell in love with the room. She stood staring lovingly at the handcrafted beauty.

"How do you afford this?" she asked.

"Oh there are about twenty five of us who live here off and on. Band members, artists, writers, anyone who can pay a little rent," Kyle explained. "Come on, let's get to my favorite room." He still held her hand and kissed her on the cheek.

He took her back down the stairs and then to another staircase leading down to a room that had been like a cellar at one point. Now it had been redone to house the band's practice room. Kyle led her past that to a large dark room with no windows. "This is my room," he explained. The furniture was a plain bed with a black coverlet, a stereo, and a bookshelf with a television on it. Posters covered the wall, and a few of them were of her love. Dereck's face smiled at her, and he seemed to glow in the picture. Over the bed hung a red guitar, a B.C. Rich Warlock; Dereck had one of those once. It had burned in the house. "It's not as impressive as the rest of the house but I like it. No windows, I sleep during most of the day. I hate the sun in my eyes in the morning."

"Me too," Solange agreed. She felt him come up behind her, his arms circled her waist. His lips at her neck, kissing gently, then nibbling. Passion shot through her like fire. Arching her back, she threw her head back, exposing more of her neck to him. His hands went up to her breasts, alternately stroking and squeezing them through the fabric of her dress. She felt the straps of the garment slide off her shoulders, exposing them to his searching lips. Soon the black dress lay crumpled around her feet. The roughness of his hands on her smooth breasts drove her mad. Expertly those fingers pinched her nipples, evocating an intoxicating pain. "Oh, yes," she cried. Then without warning, he scooped her up and carried her over to the bed, gently setting her down on the soft mattress.

Facing him now she kissed those sweet, cigarette-laced lips once again. Softly at first, then harder as their passion increased. As her tongued probed his mouth, he sucked it until she felt it would be ripped out of her mouth. His teeth grazed it softly, then harder at her insistence. Solange lost herself completely in him, no longer a vampire, just a lover, living only to the pain and ecstasy he brought her. Her nails tore at his clothing until they lay ruined around his feet. Harshly she tore her lips away from him, trailing her lips down his throat as he leaned over her. At the pulse in Kyle's neck she had to remind herself he was human and take control. She let no anger or any other of her conflicting emotions creep into her mind as she nipped the soft skin of his neck. He moaned as she sank her teeth into his neck, crying out for her to bite him harder. Those pleas and the sweet alcohol-laced blood drove her harder.

She drank long but he did not weaken too fast, instead Solange felt him harden against her. Using all the restraint she could, she pulled away from the wound on his neck. Letting her lips trail down, they found the tip of his hardened cock. Her tongue, still coated in blood, licked at the plum-colored head, her lips kissing it until they drew him completely into her mouth. The long shaft slid past her teeth and pressed against the back of her throat. Solange tried to be so careful of her fangs, but he moved so fast that she felt them nick his skin. Kyle seemed not to care, urging her hand to his buttocks, where with her superior strength she took control of his movements. But from that one wound, blood ran down her throat as she sucked.

The passion rose in him and Solange felt him nearing climax. He suddenly pulled back, pushed her onto the bed and pushed up between her spread legs. Hot and wet, she was ready for him, his thrusts sending wave after wave of orgasm through her. Long sandy tresses covered her face as he bent his head to her breast.

Kyle's mouth sucked at her nipple with no gentleness. She loved it. Oh, thank God he was no vampire or she'd never leave him. Then as he sucked, his teeth claimed the delicate tissue caught in his mouth. Solange screamed, her body convulsing in orgasm. Soon after she felt his hot come deep inside her. Together they lay panting on the bed.

The vampire knew it was time to leave, before she drained this beautiful creature of every drop of blood. She had already taken a great deal. This one must be left alive, he carried a piece of Dereck in his heart, that music must not be stopped. Her lover had not been resurrected this night, but she had felt enough of him influencing this human. He must be left alive. As he slept, she pulled on her dress and left the house. Never noticing the wound on her breast that was already healing or the blood on Kyle's lips.

CHAPTER TWENTY-TWO

Dreams - A Nightmare Beginning

After spending the next evening with Greg, Solange said her good-byes, against his protests. It felt like things were different now. Growing more and more depressed, she had slipped away early to feed, the musician foremost in her mind.

By the dawn, despondent, Solange retired early. Her melancholy brought dreams that she so desperately wanted to forget. Forget how Leone had made her this creature. Too weak to fight the dreams, Solange succumbed to their tragic hold over her mind.

After they had made love, Leone had slept beside her on the small bed. As dawn approached, she felt the sun. Even through the thick stone walls, its radiance beat against her. How long they had slept, Solange did not know. Her waking she would never forget.

The Baroness screamed as she ran into their chamber, fear in her voice, and she urged them to wake. In dreamlike slow-motion, Solange got off the bed. The Baroness pulled her arm, dragging her from the room. She turned toward Leone, begging to stay with him. He simply kissed her and pushed her toward the woman.

"Go, my angel, be safe with Francesca," Leone told her. "I'll join you later."

Sternly, the Baroness pulled her arm and said, "Come, Solange, we have a coach waiting for us, we must hurry to be safe."

"But I can't leave him!" she cried. Tears coursed down her cheeks. "I thirst Leone, it hurts. What will I do?"

"It will pass, child," the Baroness told her and pulled the girl away from her new lover. His face was so beautiful and sad. She followed a few steps still looking at him.

"I will love you always, my angel," Leone called after her. "I will come for you."

"Leone!" she screamed, fighting against the Baroness to no avail. The woman was far too strong for a human.

Down the hall, she was taken. Just when they had went through a doorway, the Baroness put a hand over her mouth and pulled her into a small dark alcove. Men stormed up the stairs of the entrance hall and into the west wing. Long pointed sticks in their hands made their mission clear. Solange whimpered against the woman's hand.

Leone rushed out of the room, straight into the mob. He fought them savagely, eyes glowing in the near darkness. The first several ones to meet him dropped to the floor from the swing of his claws. Solange watched as the man became the monster of lore, killing to protect them.

"We must go now, he is fighting so we can go," the Baroness whispered. They moved furtively down the hall. Rushing, Solange had time to turn once and see them drive the sharpened stakes into Leone's body. She saw him fall to the floor. Not able to bear it she turned back and ran with the woman in front of her.

Down a back staircase they met Raphaela, who waited by the door. Her green eyes wide with terror, she cried softly. Outside the stable boy had the coach ready for them. Trunks had been packed and tied on the roof, and one large trunk sat on the floor. Quickly Solange stepped up through the open door, and the Baroness followed her. Raphaela was just stepping up when the coachman said they must go. The mob of villagers came around the corner of the castle.

Before the door was even shut the carriage began to move. Solange and the Baroness held Raphaela's arms, pulling her inside. Arms reached for the girl and pulled at her skirts. Raphaela screamed. Harder the women pulled, trying to bring her the rest of the way in. Solange watched in horror as her best friend fell backwards into the reaching arms. The coach did not stop.

The Baroness yelled for the coach to go back but one of the men driving told her they could not, it was too late. Solange screamed at them to go back for Raphaela. From the back window she watched them go farther away.

"Go back, go back," she cried. As she watched, a torch was held to her friend's skirt and Raphaela went up in flames, her screams piercing the night as she ran trying to put them out.

The Baroness pulled her away from the window and held her tight, her sobs muffled in Solange's hair. Amidst the horrible things happening, she smelled something intoxicating. It smelled warm and of food. The smell emanated from the Baroness. She nuzzled closer to the woman, her lips brushing against the Baroness' throat.

In fear, the woman pulled back, sensing what had went through Solange's mind. "Here, I must keep you safe, you must hide in here," she said and pointed to the large trunk.

"I'm so hungry, it hurts. Why does it hurt?" Solange asked.

"It won't hurt for long, I promise. We'll stop for something when we are out of danger," the Baroness told her. "Now get into the trunk, you have to hide."

Scared, Solange did what she was told. Inside the dark closeness of the trunk she huddled in a tight ball. She heard the Baroness slip chains and locks around the trunk. She pounded on the lid, pleading to be let out.

"Solange," the woman told her in a weeping voice. "You're all I have left. Please, be patient. I will protect you." Sobs replaced words now, sobs that went on for hours. She sank down in the box and listened to the wheels, the clatter of chains, and the weeping of this woman.

CHAPTER TWENTY-THREE

Awake

Morning came and went, but Kyle slept on. No dreams filled his mind, just an aimless drifting. It was the deepest sleep he had ever known. To Kyle it felt as if his breathing and heart had stopped altogether, like death had crept upon him in the night.

When consciousness finally came he opened his eyes to his empty bedroom. Kyle remembered Solange being here before he drifted off. He also remembered the sharp pains in his head and stomach, but she was not there then. He must have really drank too much last night, but he didn't feel hung over. In fact he was incredibly hungry.

His feet touched the carpet, and every fiber of the plush pile tickled his feet. The soles of his feet had never been that sensitive in his life. As he touched things around him it was like he'd never felt anything before. Kyle also noticed how everything appeared perfectly illuminated, but not a single light shone in the room. He walked over to the bathroom and looked in the mirror. The skin on his face looked paler than usual, but that didn't bother him as much as his eyes. They glowed! The hazel depths he knew now glowed faintly yellow like a cat. What the hell was wrong with him?

Maybe if he took a shower, he'd be okay. The guitar player turned the water on and stepped into its steaming jets. Scents of the night before rose to his nostrils as the water hit his body. Solange's sweet smell made him wish she had not left. Another scent he didn't recognize bombarded him; warm, rich, and coppery, it made him salivate. What had last night done to him? As Kyle soaped his body, every bubble caressed his wet skin, and they tickled him like champagne in the back of the throat, bursting when he attempted to touch them.

He opened the cabinet below the sink and pulled out toothpaste and toothbrush. The tri-colored paste squirted out onto the bristles. When he put it in his mouth he nearly gagged on the mint taste, so overpowering, he spit it into the sink.

"Jesus," he said. Kyle wiped his mouth on a towel and pulled out his razor to shave. Shaving just around his trim beard took a little care, and he accidentally cut himself under his chin, on his neck. One drop of blood came out, then stopped. It usually bled for awhile, so Kyle reached for a piece of toilet tissue to stick to it. He wiped the blood away, but the cut was gone. Gone, and no mark whatsoever remained.

An odd thought hit him, and in experiment, he dragged the razor across his inner arm. The blood welled up and ran down his arm, just like normal. Soon, however, he could see the skin closing up, healing within minutes. There was no sign of a wound there anymore. *Weird, very weird,* he thought. The blood that had run out of the cut had pooled in the palm of his hand. He suddenly had the most overwhelming urge to taste it. Tentatively he touched his tongue to the red liquid, and as he did he felt a slight pain in his teeth and gums. Something sharp pushed at his lips and he licked the last of the blood off his hand. Looking in the mirror again, he saw fangs jutting out of his mouth. In amazement he saw them retract back into his gums. "Oh sweet Jesus, " he said to himself.

Being into the scene, he had seen all the movies and read all the books. He knew what wanting blood and having fangs meant. *Kyle McDermott, you're a frigging vampire,* he told himself. Now exactly what that would mean, he had no way of knowing. He'd have to find Solange again. She would have the answers, or at least he hoped.

Kyle got dressed and stepped out of his room. The other guys were in the practice room, so he went in. They were pissed, he could tell just by their looks they gave him. "I'm sorry, I ran out on you guys last night," he offered.

"Yeah I bet you are. Did she wear you out Kyle?" the drummer, Sam, asked with sarcasm, his piercing black eyes fixed on Kyle with irritation. He pushed his dreadlocks out of his face. "We thought you were gonna sleep forever."

"It's seven o'clock, man, already dark outside," announced Rusty, the bass player. "That was very uncool, leaving us to pack up your shit."

"I know it was, but I couldn't help it. She had this hypnotizing thing about her that I couldn't resist," he explained. All around him he could smell their blood, hear their hearts beating. It distracted him badly, and he didn't know if he could stay there. "Listen, I have to go out. I'll explain later, when I know more myself, but now I have to go." He walked out on them, leaving them angry and confused behind him. It could not be helped. Kyle had to leave before he ripped into them with this hunger.

Outside he walked in the early darkness, absorbing the sights around him, like he had never seen them before. The wind in the leaves on the street . . . the air itself seemed alive to him. He had only gone a block when a voice called out to him. It was female and one he knew.

"Kyle, where are you going?" she asked. "I was coming over to party," Shelly, a girl who hung out with them sometimes, said as she came closer. She had always had a crush on Kyle. "I missed you last night. How did you get gone so fast after the show?"

"I had plans," Kyle told her and kept walking.

"I saw you leave with that girl," she said, a little hurt in her voice. "But she's not here now, is she?" Her hands touched his shoulders as she caught up with him. Her nails played along down his arm and she grabbed his hand.

Kyle stopped and turned to face her. Shelly put her arms around his neck and pressed herself against him. "Shelly, you don't need to be here right now." He tenderly tried to disengage himself from her.

"I want to be here, Kyle," she said petulantly. Smiling, she tried to press herself even closer to him. Sexually it did nothing for Kyle, but he felt that hunger in him again. He didn't want to hurt this girl, but he needed something. "I'll do anything for you, Kyle, just tell me."

Kyle put his hands around her and put his lips to her throat. He felt his teeth coming down again. He could feel her heart pounding blood through her veins and sank his fangs in her neck. Blood gushed into his mouth. He felt her tense up and a little cry escaped her lips. He drank the coppery warmth from her neck. Kyle could feel her weaken in his arms as she moaned against him. He pulled back.

He didn't want to hurt her, so he had stopped. Shelly appeared drugged as he tried to make her stand on her own. She slumped against him again. He licked at the wound on her neck again. The bleeding nearly stopped. His teeth had left two small punctures on her neck. He pulled her back and held her shoulders. She smiled groggily at him. "Shelly, look you have to forget this happened."

As if in a trance, she repeated, "Forget this ever happened." Obviously he had done something to her. This was a new thing for Kyle, and he didn't know what to do. Shelly said again, "Forget it ever happened."

Kyle told her, "Forget you saw me tonight, go home and get some sleep." He let go of her. She drunkenly teetered away, towards her apartment. Without saying goodbye, like he wasn't even there, she left.

What other powers did he have? The blood that now pumping through his system made him feel elated. He felt like he could fly. No sooner had he thought that, he realized he was five feet off the ground, going up into the air. *Fly*, he thought, *fly*. Without any effort, he was lifting above the trees and turning around. As he spiraled upward, he thought that he wanted to go to the mountain. He did just that, and in a flash he shot forward, wind in his face. Kyle laughed as he landed on the top of Stone Mountain. Happy with his newfound power, he spent the night exploring it.

CHAPTER TWENTY –FOUR

Just Outside Birmingham

Joel cruised along on Interstate Twenty, searching for the exit for I-459. He had passed through Tuscaloosa, Alabama about an hour and half ago. His car was straining by this point in the journey; it had been rode hard. Keeping a vigilant speed of ninety miles per hour took its toll after nearly two thousand miles.

Up ahead he saw the exit he needed. Veering off onto exit 106, he now headed Northeast on I-459. About forty miles outside of Birmingham now, he didn't want to stop. The closer he got to Atlanta the more eager he became. Of course, the steady diet of Jolt cola and Nodoz were taking its toll on Joel, just as the long miles had had their effect on his car. He debated stopping as he drove on until dawn.

Now it was about five in the morning, a seemingly perfect time for him to stop and sleep. Dawn brought safety for the hunter, and he could rest during daylight hours. He started searching for a motel sign as he drove on, reconnecting with I-20, headed toward the Georgia state line. He had to stop before then.

Up ahead he saw an exit for the Trustful motel, which sounded good to him. He swerved up the exit ramp and turned right, where he spotted a small motel and pulled in. Daylight was just peeking over the horizon as he shut his engine off. His legs were wobbly as he stepped out onto the gravel parking lot. *Way too much time in the car,* he thought.

The motel stood low to the ground, made of whitewashed cement block, with weeds creeping up and threatening to overtake the sidewalk. Joel walked up to the old screen-door to the office and stepped inside, where an older woman in an orange beehive sat behind the desk smoking a cigarette. The smell of morning coffee filled his nose and he longed for a cup. A sign told him he could have a Styrofoam cup full for fifty cents. He laid two quarters on the counter.

"You want cream and sugar with that?" she asked with a deep southern drawl. Her pancake makeup did not hide the wrinkles, only increased them, and Joel wondered why she bothered. She walked back to a table and poured him a large cup of coffee. He noticed the long orange-painted nails on her wrinkled hands when she handed it to him.

"I'll take it black," he said, accepting the cup. "I also need a room."

"For how long?" she asked him, puffing on her cigarette, her lips shriveled and dry under the orange lipstick. Flakes of the color clung to the butt of her cigarette as she pulled it away.

"Just for the day, too tired to drive anymore," he said with his best apple pie smile.

"That'll be forty five and sign here," she told him and pushed an old register book at him across the counter. No one else had signed the book in a long time. "You can stay in number two."

Joel took the keys and walked out into the early morning light, sipping the strong black coffee. He had no fear that the caffeine would keep him awake, he was too tired for that. After unlocking the door, he stepped into a room decorated in the fifties. Colors that had once been vibrant were now stained and worn to less than half their brilliance, and the burnt-orange carpet had large spots in darker colors of brown. Joel could have sworn some of them were blood. The walls had once been yellow ochre, but years of cigarette smoke had dulled them to a streaked shade of dirt. The room smelled of cigarettes, mildew, sex, and something else. Someone had died in this room; he could smell it still.

Not caring too much what the room smelled like, he flopped onto the old squeaky mattress. He pulled his Browning out of the hip holster hidden under his jacket and placed it on the bed next to him. The Derringer in his boot he left just where it was and slept with his boots on. There were knives hidden in his jacket, and his boots and jeans stayed where they were, too. He wouldn't sleep without them in a place that smelled of death. Eyelids fluttered and soon the hunter lay fast asleep.

Hours later he jumped awake, hand going to the gun on the bed next to him. He had slept longer than he expected to. The clock on the nightstand read six in the evening. Darkness was here and he needed to be on the road before now. Fingers tightened around the Browning, something was in the room and his stomach burned like fire.

Without turning on the light he checked around the room, searching every corner with his eyes. Adjusting to the light, he saw there was nothing in the dark corners of the room. Water ran in the bathroom; strange, he didn't leave the water on. With stealth, he swung his legs off the bed and crept against the wall to the small bathroom. The water stopped. Joel braced himself for an attack.

Out of the bathroom stepped a young girl. Or at least she looked like a young girl. Dressed in a short, homespun dress and tennis shoes, she smiled at him. A nice face, simple but pretty, surrounded by brown hair permed and feathered. In her hand she held a stack of towels.

"I was trying not to wake you," the girl said. "I brought you some clean towels." She held them out to him as an offering.

Joel didn't take the towels. He was not that stupid. Acid blazed in his stomach and he wished he had a stake handy. "You didn't need to come in here while I was sleeping," he told her.

"I know," she giggled coyly. "She told me you were cute. I think freckles are so sexy."

He slipped the Browning into his jeans, giving the appearance of no harm done. "Do you now?" he asked, pretending to play the game, all the while keeping his hand near a knife strapped to his hip.

"Yeah," she giggled again. "We don't get a lot of guests here, you know."

"I bet," Joel said, and without warning, he struck. One fluid motion pulled the knife from his hip and sliced her throat open with it. The girl didn't have time to even scream. The blade cut through the front of her neck, the second swing caught in her spine, and Joel sawed its serrated edge through the bone, using all of his strength until her head flopped backwards. The body fell to the floor with a thud. Quickly he broke a straight-backed chair and drove a jagged end into her chest.

Smoke started rising from the corpse. Its blood began to bubble out of the stump that used to be a neck. The skin shriveled and shrank, conforming to the bones. With an audible pop and a puff of fire, it burned to dust.

Joel stood back and watched it disintegrate. He had seen it before. He would see it again. It didn't frighten him, but made his stomach ease. Goddamn vampires were everywhere.

CHAPTER TWENTY-FIVE

Atlanta-Bound

"How are we gonna get out of here without the loonies following us?" asked Sijn, peering out the window at the crowd at the gate. It was a good question, one that Shana had thought of for awhile.

"We'll send a decoy. I'll get my driver to take the limo out. Let them follow it. Mike will then take the van. What they won't know is that we will be hiding in the floor between the seats. Its a bit much, but I'm sure it'll work," Shana explained. "We won't sit in the seats until we get to the interstate."

"Super sneaky," chimed in Sijn, her long black hair swinging wildly as she plopped down on Shana's bed.

Mike came into the room carrying bags of stuff he had picked up off her list. He threw them on the king size bed not far from Sijn. He had spent the last two weeks getting it all ready for her. "Here ya go, Ms. Double-Knot Spy, all the shit ya needed."

Shana pulled out her copy of the list and started picking through the stuff. From the pile she lifted a coil of rope, duct tape, and a handheld tape recorder. It had taken her the whole two weeks to decide what all they would need.

"What are we gonna do with all of this stuff?" Sijn asked.

"Well the rope is for anybody we might have to tie up, not Soley, though: she'd break this like dental floss, but you never know. The redneck in me has to always take duct tape, handy shit."

"What about the tape recorder?" asked Sijn. "How's that gonna help catch her?"

"It won't, but you never know, we could be writing a bestseller," Shana said with a smile. "Always on the almighty dollar, its a Shana rule. Also, I have tranquilizers from the vet that will fit my gun. I've got real bullets too."

"You carry a gun?" Sijn looked the writer up and down but saw nothing. "Where and why?"

Shana lifted her shirt to reveal a leather holster just inside her pants. "I don't always carry it. I just feel better wearing it now that I know our friend is out there." Shana reached to a pouch in the pile and pulled out something else. "Silver-plated, stainless steel center, quite deadly." She handed the knife to Sijn. "Can't be too careful. You know it might not be Solange that we find. I would hate to get there and interrupt some other vamp murdering people, not cool."

Together, they packed everything in nylon sports bags and set them beside Shana's suitcases of clothes. Now they just had to wait on Jan, who had to be the slowest person in America to get ready. Shana walked down the hall to her room to check on how many hours they had to go.

Jan stood in front of the mirror fixing her long red hair. The naturally curly ringlets fell in a riot down her back. It always looked gorgeous to Shana, but her friend always insisted otherwise. Her favorite saying from the hairdresser was that you had two choices with curly hair; long helmet or short helmet. Hair that only curled at gunpoint didn't understand that.

"About ready to go?" Shana asked her friend. "Daylight's burning."

"Just a minute, I'm almost ready," Jan said.

"You said that an hour and half ago," she reminded her.

"This time for real," the woman promised.

Not likely, thought Shana, but she didn't say so. Jan put her makeup in a small pouch. Simple makeup that would take longer than most people to put on. "Okay, Mike's loading the van right now. So this is a last call."

Shana walked back to get Sijn and they headed downstairs. They passed through the kitchen to the door to the garage. They watched the limo pull out into the drive. Its windows were tinted so dark you couldn't see in, so it made a perfect decoy. Mike made the call to security, who in turn announced rather loudly that Ms. Collins was approaching the gate. As it went out, Jenkins and his crowd scrambled for their cars to follow.

In the van everyone sat waiting on Jan. Mike grew very impatient with her and started fiddling with the windows and buttons. When she finally came down the door to the van was opened for her. She got in beside Shana on the floor, and Sijn closed the sliding door.

"Okay, everybody besides Mike stay down until we hit the interstate," Shana said as she slouched down, resting her head on the seat of the van. The windows being tinted helped some, but the front ones were normal glass. With a call to security for assurance that Jenkins had left, they rolled out of the garage and down the drive. She felt the bump of the tires as it went over the curb on its way into the street. "Easy there, Mike," she said in a loud whisper. "How much liquor did you have today?"

"Not as much as you, now shut up and let me drive," he said from the driver's seat. It was a quick jaunt to the interstate. They took I-85 South, and once they had passed McAdenville, Mike gave the okay. "Interstate, girls, you can get up now."

"No followers?" Jan asked.

"Not a one," he assured them.

Shana got up and went to the bucket seat beside of Mike. Dressed in what she considered incognito, all black, the sun warmed her up. She put her dark sunglasses on and lit a cigarette. Pressing a button, the window beside her glided down about two inches.

"I've got the air on," Mike told her.

"I know but I don't want the smoke bothering the little momma back there," she said and motioned her thumb at Sijn. "Girls, there is no reason why we can't try to have a little fun on this trip, either. There's a great club where the guys are playing and the motel is right across the street. Know what that means?"

"Yeah, we can get plastered because we don't have to drive anywhere," Jan offered.

"Hell yeah," Shana said and laughed. She slid a CD into the player and waited for the music to start.

"Like that's any different from any other day," Mike said under his breath. Shana ignored him and rode for a long time just singing along with the stereo.

Outside the van miles of trees and road signs flashed by. Through South Carolina and into Georgia, Shana kept up her singing. Oblivious to the rest of the car, she sang mostly to herself and to passing cars. Sijn found it very funny that she made up words and mumbled through a lot of songs. Her jests made Shana turn to her.

"You know my daughter gets real offended when I do that," Shana said laughingly. "Says if I don't know the words I should not offend her ears. She sings."

"Where is your daughter?" Sijn asked, very curious as to why she hadn't seen the child. She just didn't have the guts to ask before. "She's staying with my mother right now," Shana said sadly. "The nut-bags from Jenkins group bother me so much and I got worried about her. I still see her as much as possible. It has to be that way until I can get something settled about him."

"Should have let me break his kneecaps when I offered," chimed in Mike.

"We are not having this conversation again, Mike," Shana told him with a point of her cigarette. "I think its refill time." She pulled a thermos out from under the seat, and the familiar amber liquid poured into a cup. "No more talk of the good Reverend this trip, promise?"

"Promise." Mike didn't sound like he promised anything. Shana knew he wasn't happy. A man of simple taste and simple solutions, he sometimes became quite frustrated with the woman he protected. Frustrated that he couldn't solve all her problems with a baseball bat and a Glock.

He loved her, like family. When Shana had been poor Emma with no money, Mike had loved her. When she did stand-up comedy in trashy bars, getting booed off the stage, Mike loved her. He had danced with Shana at her wedding to Chris, even stayed up all night cooking the food for the reception. He had held her when Chris died. Mike was one of the few consistencies in her life, which is why she trusted him with it.

Shana leaned over and kissed him on the cheek just as they passed Jimmy Carter Boulevard. Four lanes of I-85 were crowded and fast moving. Mike wove the van in and out of the traffic with what could only be called a ferocity, swerving between cars so close sometimes to make even Shana, as drunk as she was, squeamish. Anyone with the misfortune of driving too slow in front of him when he couldn't pass got the treatment. The treatment consisted of a lot of shouting, cursing, middle-finger waving and extreme tailgating. Quite nerve-wracking for someone in the position of front-seat passenger.

"How much farther to this fucking place?" Mike yelled at Shana.

"A good bit, get off on I-285, there," Shana pointed to the next exit. "That's it, good thing we missed rush-hour traffic or we'd be sitting until dark. I want to be settled in before dark."

"That makes two of us," agreed Mike.

CHAPTER TWENTY-SIX

Searching

For two weeks Kyle had been searching for Solange with no luck. He went every place he could think of; art galleries, clubs, even strip clubs. No sign of her anywhere. It became depressing. He just might be in love with her.

The band grew more and more hostile to him, not understanding why he shirked some of his duties. He missed daytime practices, didn't go to his day job anymore, and he didn't pal around with them anymore. It had to be that way or they would figure out what he was. He knew he'd have to leave eventually.

Kyle felt his powers growing day by day. He usually fed on many of the available girls at the club. He learned a drop of his blood would heal the marks he left on their necks. He took care to arouse no suspicions; that was very important with the talk of a vampire cult in the papers. He somehow figured that Solange held the blame for those murders that now numbered more than five. He damned well didn't want to take the blame for them: he had killed no one.

He would go out to the Bombshelter tonight and party with some of the guys. Whisper and Vagrant Justice were playing, maybe Shana would be there. She had been friends with Dereck Cliffe, perhaps she could help him find Solange. Imagine she had known about this and told no one! He knew she could be trusted to tell no one about him. At this point in time, his very life could depend upon it.

CHAPTER TWENTY-SEVEN

Chance Meeting

The drink in his hand was a welcome friend. Though officially off-duty, Sanford let his eyes cruise the bar for potential suspects. This wasn't his usual bar, but after spending hours talking to nuts, screwed up teenagers and drug addicts, he really needed a drink, so why not have it in one of the places that kept coming up in the interviews? Supposedly, this club served as an outlet for up-and-coming rock bands. He'd have to keep his eyes open for clues that might help him out. When he wasn't pouring whiskey down his throat that is.

Tonight probably wouldn't be that bad, since some of the bands playing actually played music he might like. He just couldn't stomach much of that Marilyn Manson type of crap. The band onstage now had a tall, black singer with dreads doing a cover of David Allen Coe. Now that was funny. Their other selections consisted of hard rock, tinged with Southern flavor. He liked them. His foot beat time on the bar rail as he swallowed his whiskey.

He had just ordered another and lit a cigarette when a crowd of newcomers came through the door. Everyone in the bar turned to look at them. Led by a statuesque blonde in black, they made their way to a table down front, and the tall lead singer acknowledged the blonde with a surprised wave. She ran to the stage and gave him a hug as the guitar player did a solo. As she turned back to the table, Sanford got a good look at her.

The woman had to be in her early thirties, though time had not been unkind to her. Her hair was the color of sunshine and smoke, ashen tresses highlighted by strands of white blonde. Parted on the side, it curved beautifully around her face. The face had been artfully painted to accentuate the eyes beneath perfectly arched eyebrows. Her lips looked soft and coppery. It was a very attractive face. Her black velvet outfit was cut so low that over half of her large breasts spilled out of the bodice. He wondered what kept them from bursting from their constraints. As she sat down, she chatted non-stop and waved to various people in the bar.

Wow, he thought, *remember you're here to look for clues, old boy.* She was a distraction, for sure. The waitress that took their order came to the bar beside of him. The bartender took the order and added two Jack Daniels on the rocks to it. "Shana's usual," he said with a smile. The waitress returned with their drinks. Sanford watched the woman down the first drink and take the other in her hand to drink more slowly. He then watched the bartender fixing another one.

"I didn't order another drink," he told the man.

"Oh, it's not for you, she'll want another in about three minutes," the man informed him.

"Well, hell, so will I," Sanford said, not to be out-drank by a woman. "Who is she anyway? Everyone seems to know her."

"Shana Collins, the writer. She comes down here every once in a while. Hangs out with a lot of bands," the bartender said.

"Let me guess, she writes romance novels?" he asked as he laughed.

"No way, man. You've never heard of her?" bartender asked. "You've probably seen some of her movies. *Death in the Garden? Burgundy Wine?*"

"No, I don't get out much. She's an actress too?" He was very curious now.

The bartender laughed. "She used to do comedy but now they just make movies from her books. She writes vampire books."

Sanford nearly choked on his drink. Vampire books? Damn, how lucky could he be? What a coincidence that a vampire writer should be in town when he was investigating vampire murders! Or was It? He didn't believe in coincidence, not like that. His gaze drifted back to the writer's table. As if she felt his eyes on her, she turned to give him a long appraisal. Obviously not liking what she saw, she smirked and turned back to her friends. Slightly daunted, he turned back to the bartender.

"Vampire books, heh? That woman writes vampire novels? She's a looker," he said to the bartender.

"Yeah, but she's a pip. Been through two husbands and countless rock stars," he told Sanford. "And drinks more Jack Daniels than anyone I know. Trust me, man, that one is not worth the trouble."

"I like trouble," Sanford quipped as he slid off his stool and grabbed the drink the bartender had made for her. Slowly he made his way over to Shana's table, never taking his eyes off her. She raised a cigarette to her lips and he was there to light it for her. The writer took a drag and turned to face the source of the fire. At this close range he could see that her eyes were the color of oak leaves in late summer. Again he felt her appraising eyes on him. He put the drink on the table and pulled a chair from a table behind him.

"Ms. Collins," he said, "Do you mind if I join you for a moment?" His was voice almost drowned out by the loud guitar of the band. He sat down.

"Thanks for the drink and I just might," she drawled, her voice smoky and very cold. Her eyes turned away from him to look at the band again.

"You're welcome, and I just wanted to talk to you for a moment," Sanford explained. Suddenly he felt nervous. Prickly fingers played up and down his spine as he sat this close to her. He leaned closer to her so she could hear him better. The smell of Spellbound perfume and cigarettes filled his nostrils, intoxicating him further.

"I'm not signing autographs tonight," Shana said flatly, trying her best to ignore him. Purposely not looking at him, she nonchalantly inhaled on her cigarette and blew white rings of smoke.

"I wasn't asking for an autograph. I just wanted to ask you something," Sanford explained, never taking his eyes off of her.

Shana turned to face him. Coldly she searched his face then moved her eyes down over his body. "You're really not my type, so don't bother. What are you? Let me see if I can guess from the suit. Accountant?"

Angered slightly, though he wasn't sure why, he shook his head no. She continued to guess. "Used car salesman?"

"I am neither. If you'd just let me finish," he injected. He didn't like the fact that she had insulted his suit.

"Well, then, some sort of public servant. Hmm, maybe you're a cop?" The woman made a face when she said it. Like being a cop was something distasteful.

"Yes, I am, but . . ." He didn't have time to finish his sentence before she cut him off again.

"I don't go out with cops, so don't bother asking," she said then turned back to the band once more.

"Look lady, I didn't come over here for your autograph or to ask for a date," Sanford hissed angrily at her. "The bartender says you're some kind of vampire writer. So that would make you an expert on the subject. I simply had some questions for you."

His change in tone caught her attention. The smirk had returned to her pretty face. "Calm down . . . what did you say you're name was?" she asked.

"Sanford, Detective Morris Sanford, Atlanta homicide," he told her.

"Detective, what questions could you possibly need to ask me?" She exhaled as she looked at him, blowing more rings in his face.

"Have you read the papers lately? Are you familiar with the problems I'm faced with?" Sanford asked. His words were almost stutters, her close proximity throwing his usual calm off.

"Yes, vampire murders," she stated. The woman took another drink. "I write books, fiction books. The only advice I can give you, Detective, is that there are no such things as vampires. They are creations of superstition and imagination. Now if you'll excuse me, I drove all this way to spend time with my friends. Good night." She turned back to the band making it very clear she no longer wanted to be bothered.

Never one to be dismissed so easily he placed his card on the table in front of her and leaned close to her ear. "Call me if you feel like helping me any further." He got up and walked back to the bar.

The bartender looked at him with an I-told-you-so on his face. Sanford simply sat back on his stool and said, "You're right, trouble. Give me another drink." He watched the rest of the bar closely, trying like hell to keep his eyes off of Shana Collins.

CHAPTER TWENTY-EIGHT

Shana's Discovery

They arrived at the club in the middle of Vagrant Justice's set. Shana, of course ran to the stage to give her friend C.C. a big hug before settling down at a table up front. She kept her eyes open for Solange or anyone who looked like a vampire. As she downed her first drink she noticed a man at the bar in a gray suit. How out of place he looked here. Average looks, a nice build under the suit, the bulge under his jacket screamed carrying. A cop. Had to be one, too bad. As his gaze turned toward her she avoided his eyes. In fact she made a point of ignoring him. She turned to Sijn and said, "Don't turn around, but there's a cop watching us. We are going to pretend we don't see him. Nothing suspicious about us, just having fun." She smiled.

Shana almost dropped a load when he came over to talk. During their brief conversation she stuck to the coldest and bitchiest attitude she could muster; that could be very cold. Despite the fact that her heart raced and she felt an all-too-familiar pull in her body when he stood close, she practically ignored him. Finally he took the hint and went away. She breathed a sigh of relief.

"Damn, that was cold," Sijn commented. "I don't think I've ever seen someone be that rude to a cop and not get arrested before."

"Stick around," Shana advised. "I'm sure you'll hear worse. Why did he want to talk to me so bad anyway? Just because I write books? He couldn't possibly know why we are really here. They must have absolutely no clue if he's clutching at straws that narrow." She wondered if that was the only reason he came over. Looking around, she found her eyes meeting his accidentally and both turning away. Part of her had wanted him to come over to talk to her, about her. Just a little boy meeting girl action, deep down that's what she wanted.

Truthfully, he was not her type, but something about him touched her. Could have been those soulful brown eyes or the way his body moved through the tables as he walked. *For God's sake,* she thought, *just drink your whiskey and forget this cop.* Good sound advice, but had she ever been one to follow good advice? She had to force her eyes to stay away from him.

Eight drinks and a pack of cigarettes later, Whisper took the stage. Johnny in true form, rocked the house, that blazing Les Paul grinding out the blues-inspired rock that she loved, his long blonde hair billowing as his fan blew in front of him. Didi, dressed in faded jeans and sheer black silk, belted out the sound they were known for. Shana found herself singing along and making faces at Johnny. She had to get up and dance. Her body swayed to one of her favorite songs, raising her hands as she rotated her hips. She still held her Jack Daniels, but didn't spill any as she moved. Eyes closed, she just felt the music. It washed over her body in waves of pure ecstasy. She loved music.

All eyes in the bar were on her as she danced. She spun around and opened her eyes to find Morris Sanford staring at her intently. Shana smiled and danced her way back to the table, turning her back to him once more, but not before she had noticed a young man standing close to him at the bar. He stood there watching her intently. Long brown hair, slight of build, his body was clad in a long silk shirt and black jeans; it seemed his eyes glowed in the dark.

"I need another drink," Shana announced to everyone at the table. Without waiting for the waitress she walked up the bar. Trying her best to not look at Detective Sanford, she wedged herself between him and the hot stud beside him. How intense his eyes looked and how his skin glowed in the club's light . . . they didn't used to have that quality. "Jack Daniels on the rocks again," she told the bartender. With her back to Sanford she smiled at the other man. "Hello Kyle, long time no see."

He smiled without showing teeth. Very suspicious; she kept her mind veiled, a little trick Dereck had taught her. She avoided his eyes, because if he was what she thought he was, he could suck her in. Her hand reached out to twirl a bit of his hair around her finger. "So it has been, Shana," he said, "How are you?"

"The usual: drunk, bitter, and pissed off," she said as a joke. Unconsciously she let her eyes drift up to his. No charm going on other than what God gave him. Only concern showed in his eyes.

"I thought about you when I first heard that Dereck Cliffe died. I know you were close to him," Kyle said, his eyes saying more than those words. His hazel eyes seemed to ask her a question, but maybe that was her imagination.

"I'm fine. You know me," she said with a shrug, conscientiously aware that Sanford listened to every word they said. She had to keep this conversation vague until she could get Kyle alone. "Your band playing tonight?"

"Naw, but tomorrow we're up just before Whisper," he said. "Like old times, huh?"

"Not quite," she said and drank her whiskey. Shana ordered another one. She heard Sanford mutter something about drunks and she turned to give him a dirty look. "Lots of things have changed." Did her face say what it wanted to?

"I get your drift," Kyle acknowledged. "Why don't you guys come by before the show? You do remember where the house is?"

"Of course," she told him. "But is that wise? Should I be afraid of your charms, Kyle?" She sounded for all the world like she was flirting but the guitar player understood her perfectly. He kissed her hand and shook his head no. "Good, I'll see you around eight then, okay?"

"Perfect," Kyle said. "I'll see you tomorrow night." He walked away. Shana watched him make his way over to some adoring females and wondered if any of them knew what was in store for them.

She heard a grunt behind her and turned to face Detective Sanford. She looked at his face: he was more drunk than she was. His face was red and his lids were half-closed. With a sour turn to his lips he slurred, "You were really friendly with him."

"He's my type," Shana said and walked away, leaving the detective to his drinking. She tried hard to enjoy the rest of her night. Things were going to get crazy real fast.

CHAPTER TWENTY-NINE

Watching Shana

Sijn sat sipping cola, listening to the band. How she wanted to get up and play, to rip into that guitar with Johnny. She watched Shana get drunk; now that was a sight to see. The woman had to be crazy. The way she had talked to that detective made Sijn very nervous. No matter how much she tried to be cool, it was obvious that she liked the man. She agreed with her that they didn't need a cop nosing around.

After the show the band came over to hang out awhile. Johnny with his big stupid grin was his normal charming self. "How ya been Little Shredder?" he asked Sijn.

"Little Shredder?" Shana asked, with a drunken curious grin.

"Yeah, he always calls me that. It started when I used to hang around and ask him millions of guitar questions," Sijn explained. "Johnny was like a guitar god to me back then. One night he handed me his Les Paul and said play something."

"What did ya play?" Shana slurred, leaning forward on the table. It wouldn't be long before she passed out.

"Purple Haze," Sijn told them. "I was what Johnny, fourteen?"

"Yeah, she kicked my ass," he told them. "Been calling her Little Shredder ever since."

"Bullshit, you kick my ass," Sijn argued.

"Naw, I just make good faces," he said with the stupid grin.

"It wasn't until years later that I actually had a band," she told the others. "I still think this jerk was making fun of me."

"Would I do that?" he said in denial.

"Hell yes, you're a smartass," Shana accused. She leaned even further over on her elbows on the table. Jan watched her with a careful eye. Mike sat watching girls.

"I agree with Shana," Sijn agreed. She sipped her drink feeling good. Despite why they were here, she felt happiness sinking in. Surrounded by these people she knew to be her friends. It felt right. Even Jan had warmed up to her over the last few days.

"How's Dawg? Haven't seen that asshole in awhile." Johnny inquired about her brother. Sijn knew they got along well, even though they both had to have the spotlight all the time.

"He's fine. Getting ready to be a daddy again," Sijn told him.

"Again?" Sijn nodded to him. "That boy needs to wrap his weasel. Hey you remember that gig we played up in the mountains that time?"

"Yeah, I remember," Sijn laughed. "Man, we had too many teeth to be playing that place. The best part of that night was the guy following you around all night. I nearly peed my pants."

"I haven't heard this story," Shana quipped. "And I've heard lots of your stories Hammer. Over and over again."

"Well, this guy kept asking me for my autograph all night long. He was shit faced drunk," Johnny said, slipping into his best redneck story telling voice. It was truly a gift. "The only problem was he thought I was Greg Allman. All night long, 'Mr. Allman can I have your autograph?', 'Mr. Allman I've got all of your albums.'"

"Get out of here!" Shana laughed out loud and ordered another drink.

"He's not lying," chimed in Sijn. "He kept asking him to play Rambling Man all night. Johnny kept saying, I'm not Greg Allman. The guy just wouldn't give up." She fell into a fit of laughter at the memory so did Johnny. Yes it was good to have friends now, she thought.

"So finally I told him, I'll play it next set," Johnny went on with his story. "Now this guy was so drunk I figured he'd pass out before we were done. He didn't. After the show he came up and punched me in the nose." They all laughed. Johnny having everyone's attention continued to entertain them with stories, including how he was once mistaken for Jesus in the men's room at a NASCAR race.

They sat around listening to him until Shana announced she wanted to get naked. Which was Jan's cue that she had to make her leave. As they left the club, Sijn noted that the detective's eyes never left Shana and he was just as drunk as she was.

CHAPTER THIRTY

Investigating The Writer

The next morning Morris Sanford rolled out of bed, feeling every bit of his years. A hangover; how much had he drunk last night? That damned woman, it was her fault. Every time she had ordered a drink, so did he. He would be damned if she could out-drink him. She must have had a lot of practice, because at the end of the night, he couldn't drive home, and she still seemed herself. To hell with her.

Unable to walk nearly, he had staggered over to the motel across the street and got a room. Of course he had seen her entourage go to the same motel. He would just go to her room and demand to be let in. He would have, if he could have stood up that long. He hadn't, so he just went to sleep. Now it was morning.

He showered and dressed in the same suit again. He'd go over there now. That woman had to have some knowledge that would help him. Besides she made him weak in the knees. No one but his ex-wife made him feel that way, and she had been gone for five years. Couldn't take life with a cop. Always angry that he worked too many hours, always angry that he put himself into danger, and mostly angry because he didn't make a lot of money. He had come home to an empty apartment one day. He had sworn women off ever since.

Now one walks into his life and she was a bitch. *But is she really a bitch?* he thought to himself that she had started that bit when he tried to get close to her. She hid her heart away, like her secrets. There were secrets there, he was sure, but he just didn't know what they were. He had to find out. He had to see her again.

CHAPTER THIRTY-ONE

A Visit From the Police

"Shana," a voice called to her in her sleep. "Shana, get up, it's almost lunch-time."

"Fuck off," she growled and rolled back over.

"No," Jan insisted. "We are going to eat with the band. They're waiting for us."

Shana rolled back over and asked her friend, "Do you have your makeup on yet?"

"No, I don't," her friend replied.

"Then I have another thirty minutes," she said and pulled the covers over her head.

Sijn pulled the blanket back down and started shaking her. "Oh no, I'm hungry. Neither one of you are keeping me from a meal."

Grumpily, Shana responded. She swung her legs over the edge of the bed and just sat there. Naked as usual, she reached for her robe. Her hair hung in a crazy disarray around her head, and she had mascara smudged into raccoon rings around her green, bloodshot eyes. Basically, she looked and felt like shit. A noise from the door distracted her. "Do you guys hear that?"

"What?" asked Jan.

Shana hushed them and listened. It sounded like a scrape and a rattle. "That!" she exclaimed.

"I hear it too!" Sijn announced. "Maybe it's the maid coming in to clean."

"Like hell it is," Jan said with a frown. She went to the door and flung it open. There stood Johnny Morgan. Lit from behind by the sun he looked like an angel, except that this angel looked like Greg Allman and was wearing striped engineer overalls a tad too small.

"I was trying to see if my key worked in your door," he said with a goofy grin. He held aloft a plastic key card. "Sometimes they do, you know."

"You redneck shithead," Shana yelled out. "Nobody's even dressed yet."

"That's what I was hoping for," he said, still grinning from ear to ear. "You ladies look lovely in the morning time." Everyone responded by giving him the finger.

"Well, come on in," Jan said. "Don't stand there in the door." He did and Shana noted just how tight his overalls were.

"Where'd ya get those nut cutters?" she asked sardonically. "I hope you don't plan on wearing those onstage tonight." She also noticed the huge Wolverine work boots.

"Didi won't let me," he said disappointed.

"I don't blame her! You look like you're going to plow the back forty, " Shana countered.

"Hey, I saw you talking to pussy-boy last night," Johnny teased her. He could only be talking about Kyle. They had somewhat of a rivalry going. "All a-flutter over the pretty-boy. I should go kick his ass."

"You leave him alone," Shana snapped. Johnny didn't know what she did about Kyle, and she didn't want him to end up dead.

"You know I smoke him on guitar," Johnny stated. "Who do you think is better? Come on Shana, tell the truth."

Here we go again, she thought. He always needled her until she admitted he was the best, no matter who he compared his playing to. "You are the best, you're my number one, Johnny," she said with dramatic overtures.

"I kick both your asses," piped in Sijn. "Damn men think they have the corner market on guitars."

"Yeah then why ain't you and Dawg down here playin'?" he challenged, pointing his finger at the dark-haired girl.

"Because I'm here watching you, goofball," she said with a smile. "I mean it isn't everyday I get to laugh at Johnny 'The Claw Hammer' Morgan."

Johnny pulled a face and tried to pinch her on the underarm. Too fast for him, she scooted out of his reach, holding up her fist to him in a mock threat. He grinned and walked to the door. "I'm going back where I'm appreciated. You guys hurry up," he said as he walked out. The door shut behind him.

Immediately there was a knock at the door again. Sijn opened it. It was Johnny again. "One more time, Shana, who's your number-one guitar? I have to know," he asked and grinned.

"Would you get out?!" Shana yelled.

"I'm going, I'm going," he said as he backed out the door and shut it. He knocked again. Sijn opened the door. Johnny stuck his head back in the door and said, "I just need a little affirmation."

"Okay, okay, I love you, Johnny," Shana exclaimed. "Are you happy now?"

"You don't love me. You just like me a lot," he said. Shana threw a shoe at the door. Johnny closed it. They all waited for his knock again but nothing happened. So they started to get ready.

Five minutes later there was a knock at the door. "Damn him," Shana cursed. "I'm getting really fed-up with him." Sijn walked toward the door, Shana stopped her. "No, let me this time."

She removed her robe and opened the door buck-naked. Before the door opened she screamed, "Yes, you are the best!" The door swung wide open mid-sentence, and to her surprise Johnny did not stand on the other side. A very flustered Detective Sanford stood there staring at her.

"I take it you were expecting someone else?" he said with laughter threatening to erupt from his lips.

Undaunted, Shana held her head high, jutting out her chin. "Good Morning Detective," she motioned for Sijn to hand her the robe as she spoke. "Yes, I was. Surely you don't think I undressed for your sake?" Quickly she slipped into the robe.

"No, I don't, I know I'm not your type," he smirked. "Can I come in and talk to you? I'm really not wanting to see the great bitch show I got last night either."

"Well, you'll be disappointed, that's all there is," she told him. "But come in. You'll have to talk to me while I get ready." She turned her back to him and walked toward the bathroom.

Sanford nodded at Sijn and Jan, "Ladies." They both smiled and tried hard not to laugh. As he passed them he asked, "Is she always so damn difficult?" Then they both laughed.

"You have no idea," Jan said. At this Sanford smiled. He watched Shana from behind, her hips swaying beautifully under the black robe. At the bathroom door she turned and asked, "Are you coming, Detective?"

"You want me to come in there with you?" he asked incredulously.

"Yes," Shana replied. "It is the only time I have to spare for you. Besides you've already seen me naked." She started the water and disrobed before he came in. The shower curtain was pulled when he stepped into the bathroom. "Close the door and have a seat."

"Ms. Collins, I do believe this is the strangest place I've ever interrogated someone," Sanford said as he took a seat on the toilet.

"I do believe I'm the strangest person you've ever interrogated, Detective," Shana commented as she wet her hair under the hot spray.

"Not really, two days ago a Lord Ravencroft tried to rob a blood bank. This kid was really out there," he laughed.

"I've met a few like that. They take my books way too seriously," she commiserated. "You just wanna shake 'em."

"I bet," he answered. "Who is Dereck Cliffe?"

"You don't know, really?" she asked. When he didn't reply, Shana told him. "He was the singer, guitarist for the band Nightbird and a very close friend of mine. Why?"

"Oh, I overheard part of your conversation in the bar last night. I'm sorry, " he told her. "How did he die?"

Shana was betting that he heard more than part. "Some nut blew up his house," Shana said sadly while lathering up her hair.

"Can we change the conversation, I doubt my personal life can help with your investigation."

"Sorry." He asked a new question. "Do you think one of these vampire fans of yours could be who I'm looking for?"

"Could be," she answered. "Most are harmless, though; teenagers looking for an identity, rebelling against parents or society. You're probably looking for someone with a real mental problem."

"Why did you come down here, Shana?" he asked. "What brought you here, the papers?"

Rinsing her hair she answered, "I'm getting away from vampires this weekend, Detective. My friend's band was playing down here and it gave me the perfect excuse." She reached for the bath gel and her scrubber. "I just had Hollywood people leave my house, making vampire movies. I'm constantly hounded by crazies who think I'm a vampire. I needed a break." Which wasn't too much of a lie, actually.

"I understand," Sanford agreed. "But you didn't exactly get away from vampires by coming here."

"Thanks to you," she said as she peered around the shower curtain at him. "You're the one who brought it up, Detective."

"Point acknowledged," he nodded at her before she drew the curtain shut again. "Do you really think there are no vampires?"

"Yes," she lied. "Vampires are creatures of myth."

"If there were, hypothetically," Sanford asked. "Where would they live?"

"Depends on whose book you're reading," she explained. "Some sleep in coffins, in cemeteries, but mine don't. They have houses and condos."

"Well that's no help. I can't go through Atlanta searching cemeteries," he said. His voice sounded very exasperated.

"I told you I wouldn't be a lot of help," Shana answered back. Turning off the water, she asked him to hold a towel for her. He held out a large fluffy one. She stepped out, meeting his gaze, which never left her eyes. Shana moved into the outstretched towel. He wrapped it around her and didn't let go. Her heart pounded in her chest, she shivered despite the steamy air around them. She found herself crushed against his hard body. Isn't this what she wanted last night? "Is this how you end all your interrogations, Detective?" she asked looking up at his attractive face.

"Never," he said. "Tell me Shana, are you a vampire?"

"No," she whispered. "If I was I'd be cold, do I feel cold to you?" Her hands rested on his chest. Her body quaked, growing warmer by the moment.

"Not at all," he mumbled. Sanford lowered his lips to hers. His kiss was hard and Shana felt herself melting. As his tongue explored the soft, warm secret of her mouth, she leaned heavily against him. The towel slipped down, held up between the press of their bodies. His hands slid down her back and cupped her buttocks. She pulled her mouth away from his, gasping for breath.

Knowing she had to stop this, she whispered, "Is that your gun or are you just happy to see me?" He laughed. She pushed him away and wrapped the towel around herself again. Gaining control of her composure once again, her bitch mask slipped into place. "So the plan is to get me into bed and make me spill my guts, Detective?"

"What?" he gasped. "Do you think that is what this is about? You really take the cake, do you know that?"

"Get me to trust you and tell you my big secrets, isn't it? Well I don't have any!" Shana said just a little to angrily. "Get the hell out."

"Arrgh! You are the most crazy woman I've ever met!" he yelled at her. "You sure know how to ruin a moment. Just for a minute I thought we clicked, really clicked. Sure as hell didn't seem like you minded to me."

"I can't help how my body reacts to a man kissing me. Wasn't even that good of a kiss," she lied, not for the first time today.

"Fuck you. And you were right, you've been no help to me. Good day Ms. Collins." He yanked open the door and stormed out. Shana heard the motel room door slam a few seconds later. She walked out to see Jan, Sijn, and Mike staring at her.

"What?" she asked crossly. She looked at Mike. "When did you get here?"

"Oh, halfway through the heavy panting," he quipped. A big smile stretched across his face.

"We did notice that Detective Sanford was slightly damp when he came out," Sijn added in. All of them burst out laughing.

"Well, fuck ya'll too. Jan, I hope you have your damn makeup on. I want to go to breakfast," she told them as she started to get dressed, pulling out simple jeans and a T-shirt for the day. "We have to all have a serious talk. When we do you'll understand why I had to get rid of Detective Sanford."

"A talk about what?" Jan asked. Curious, her friend sat down on the bed next to her.

"Nobody talks to Kyle alone from here on out," Shana ordered them. "I found what we are looking for."

"Why? We've known Kyle for ages," her friend said, looking very concerned.

"Because Kyle is a fucking vampire. He wasn't a vampire a month ago. I'll give you three guesses as to who made him one and the first two don't count." Her face was very grave as she got dressed. No one said anything else. They went to meet the band for breakfast.

CHAPTER THIRTY-TWO

Death Comes Knocking

Solange had been seeing Greg for weeks now. Though he still was handsome and charming, she grew bored. In fact, with every passing day she spent less and less time with him. He seemed so bland and superficial next to the young guitarist she had encountered last week. If he couldn't hold her interest this long, he wouldn't last an eternity. He could never fill Dereck's space in her heart. He was not the Gregor that she had known all those years ago. Physically, Greg still turned her on, the sex hadn't gone downhill, but everything else had. It greatly annoyed her that she couldn't see into his mind. It became harder and harder not to kill him. She decided to break it off before she did just that.

She would have liked to find the guitar player and leave this place behind. Something in her wouldn't let her do that. How could she bring someone into this damnable existence for no other reason than her own loneliness? This madness had to end soon.

As she sat alone in her apartment the phone rang. It was Greg, he wanted her to come over. Now had to be the time. Accepting his offer, she planned what to say to her lover to make things easier. There never is an easy way.

In his apartment, Greg chatted on about everything that had been going on over the last week or so. Did he not notice how distracted she was? Obviously, he started to, because he asked her point-blank. "What's up with you?"

"I have a lot on my mind," Solange told him, trying not to meet his gaze.

"You've been really distant with me for awhile now. I'm starting to get the feeling that you don't like me anymore," Greg stated, looking sad and slightly petulant.

"We need to talk," was all Solange managed to say before he cut her off. He came and grabbed her hand urgently.

"Let me tell you something first. I haven't been totally honest with you," he admitted. "Give me this one chance to tell you before you cut things off between us."

"What do you mean?" she asked.

"I know who you are," he told her. "I've known from the moment I saw you, who you really were. I just didn't want to push you into telling me. Come upstairs and I'll show you."

"You know who I am?" This really started to scare her. Did he know what she was? What would she do if he did?

"Yes, you are Angel," he said. He pulled on her arm toward the stairs. "Come with me." She followed him up the stairs, her mind reeling from all of the things that he could possibly know. At the top of the stairs he opened his spare bedroom and her eyes grew wide. The walls were covered with her, newspaper clippings, photographs of her and Dereck, and her paintings. "Now do you understand? I was a fan. I've been buying your artwork for ages."

"You are a fan of my work?" she asked her eyes scanning the walls. "You knew all of these things and you didn't say?"

"Yes, I knew you had been hurt, by Dereck dying," he explained. "I couldn't just blurt it out, not knowing how you'd react."

Her mind went to the last conversation she had with Trina: a rich man in Atlanta wanted to buy her work. Greg was that man. Her gaze met his, and just a glimmer of her essence started to glow in them. "What else do you know about me?" It sounded like an accusation.

"I know you're supposed to be dead," he answered, a little unnerved by her tone. "Why you faked your own death does not matter to me, it's that you are alive. After I thought you were dead, I made one more trip out to California and bought this last piece." He motioned to a portrait of her Dereck. The picture had hung in the gallery on that night. No one was ever supposed to buy that painting.

With trembling hands she approached the portrait of her love. Her fingers traced his delicate face and the long black hair. A sob erupted from her throat and she fell onto the painting, her face pushed against the glass. She felt the pain and the anger building together. Solange felt Greg's hands on her shoulders, trying to soothe her. It only enraged her. How dare he touch her. She pushed him back with a shrug of her shoulders, sending him across the room. When she turned, her eyes glowed an ugly shade of red.

Greg's face, stricken with fear, watched the change in his lover. Her hands had lengthened to long sharp claws, tears flowed from her glowing eyes, and saliva dripped from extended fangs. "This does not belong to you!" Solange screamed at him. "That painting was for Dereck and no one else!"

"He's dead. It can't belong to him anymore," Greg pleaded. "Someone else would have bought it if I hadn't!" He backed away from her with nowhere to go but the wall as she still came forward.

"You tricked me! You seduced me and all along you are no better than a thief!" she cried. Froth dripped from her mouth as she ranted: the true picture of a beast from Hell.

"No," he begged. "It was not like that! Please don't kill me! It's just like my dreams! My God, what are you?"

"What am I? Who am I?" Solange asked, eyeing him insanely. "I am the monster you dream of. I am a curse upon this Earth! I am your judge and jury!" Without giving him any more time, she tore into him. Blindly she gashed him with her claws, tearing his flesh. "You helped kill my Dereck, didn't you? Your petty lust for

212

me made you plot against him who was so perfect!" Her voice was in sobs now. "Was it you?"

"No, no, no . . ." Greg kept saying over and over, his body now limp in her embrace. She sank her fangs into his neck and gorged herself on the sweet nectar she found there. Only when his heart stopped did she pull herself away. Her body heaving, she crawled over to where she had knocked the painting from the wall. Laying it flat on the floor, she collapsed onto it, covering the glass with blood and tears her sobs echoing in the empty room. Fingers returning to normal traced outlines in the fluids as she talked to herself in gibberish.

Suddenly she felt another presence in the room. Her eyes looked up through her blood-soaked hair to see black Italian shoes in front of her. A voice spoke, "My Angel, what have you done?" Solange knew that voice. It belonged to someone dead and gone. So this was the way of it? In the end ghosts would haunt her.

"Yes, Leone, look what I have done. I am a bringer of death to all that love me," she said, not even looking up, for she thought him only a ghost.

"I should have interrupted your life before now," he said with pain. Leone lifted her to her feet. She fell back on him, clinging to his soft shirt, sobbing. "You hurt, my young one, but this is not the way to ease your pain. Killing only makes it greater."

"I know," she whispered into his shirt. He lifted her easily into his arms to carry her out. She stopped him to say, "My painting, please don't leave my painting."

With one hand around her, he stooped and grabbed the painting with the other. He took both of them to her apartment. His words tried to soothe her, but she had fallen back into her recital of gibberish. "It's over now, young one. There will be no more death." He laid her on her bed. "I will clean up the mess for you."

Solange raised her head. "No! I want them to come for me. Let them kill me Leone." She slumped back onto the bed and into unconsciousness brought by her insanity. Leone watched. What would he do with her?

CHAPTER THIRTY-THREE

Meeting With A Vampire

Mike pulled the van up next to a hulking Victorian house near Little Five Points. They all piled out, Shana leading the way. Kyle and the rest of his band were outside loading the last of their gear into their own van. When they saw her they all came over for hugs and hellos. After talking with them a bit, Kyle told them to go on to the club and he would meet them there. He escorted them into the house. Everyone gone except for him, the house was quiet. Shana was the first to speak.

"Okay, we're in private now. Out with it," she ordered Kyle. She crossed her arms across her chest and waited for his story.

"What about them?" Kyle looked apprehensively at her compatriots.

"They know," she stated. "I'll tell you the whole story." She explained to him how she always knew Dereck was a vampire. Then she had Sijn tell her side of the story and how she came to Shana. The vampire listened intently, some shock showing on his face. Mike grunted and groaned throughout the catching up and complained that it was taking too long. Finally all fell silent and Shana said, "Now it's your turn."

"It started when we were playing the Bombshelter about two weeks ago," he said. "I was halfway through my set when I looked down and saw this chick crying. We were playing a Nightbird cover. She had the most beautiful eyes I had ever seen. Big, blue, and full of tears, it was too much for me. After the show I started talking to her and could tell she really dug me. So I brought her back here. I didn't know who she was until halfway to the house. Finally, it dawned on me where I'd seen her before."

"How and why did she turn you into a vampire?" Jan asked.

"We were getting all hot in the bed and I remember her teeth on me," he shrugged. "Being kinda kinky myself, I bit her. It was fucking awesome, or so I thought. I was really trashed. Then she got up and left me asleep on the bed. I didn't wake up until the next night. What a fucking surprise that was! You can't imagine what it's like, Shana."

"She didn't try to kill you?" asked Shana. She knew how Solange liked her meals.

"No way, she acted like she loved me. Maybe she imagined I was Dereck or something," he surmised. "I don't even think she knew what she did to me."

"You haven't seen her anymore?" Shana questioned. This story got stranger and stranger.

"Not once since that night," Kyle admitted. "And I didn't know dick about being a vampire either. Everything has been trial and error for me."

"Please tell me you haven't killed anybody," Shana asked with her eyes closed. Not even her imagination could see Kyle killing anyone, though, and the vampire simply shook his head.

"No, I haven't. It's really hard, stopping," he told her. "But I always do stop, just leaves them a little dizzy. It's really cool, to tell the truth. Though I think the guys are getting suspicious. They are treating me like I'm nuts or on drugs."

"Really cool, geez," Mike swore. "Just keep your fangs to yourself, Romeo. I'd hate to have to end your immortality." Kyle looked at the short man and nodded at the threat. He knew what the man meant.

"So what now?" asked the guitar player.

With a shrug of her shoulders Shana simply responded, "We wait and watch. Maybe she'll make an appearance at another show. Either that or we'll find a clue somewhere else. I just have to keep the cops away from me."

"Cops?" Kyle asked, confused.

"Yeah, you didn't notice the one standing next to you at the bar last night?" she fussed. "Some vampire you are. I'm changing motels, so he doesn't come calling at my door again."

"Oh, like you minded him in your shower this morning," grumped Mike.

Kyle's eyes turned toward Shana. With a smile he asked, "You had a cop in your shower this morning?"

"Sort of, but only because he barged in," she defended, her face a mask of guilt.

"Methinks the lady doth protest too much," quoted Mike. Kyle burst out laughing.

"Hey, leave me alone," Shana pointed to Kyle. "Your fucking around got you in a hell of a mess. So don't laugh at me. It was a very short shower."

"Yeah, he still had his clothes on, even though they were wet," Mike retorted.

"Was Shana naked?" Kyle asked.

"Hell yeah," Mike told him. "As soon as she opened the motel door!" He chuckled.

"That's my girl," said Kyle, laughing out loud. Everyone but Shana joined him in laughter. The writer just gave hateful looks to all of them. She wondered how this bunch of goobers going to make it through the storm that was coming?

CHAPTER THIRTY-FOUR

Serial Killer

Late in rising, Solange's thirst ran afire through her, a throbbing ache compelling her to feed early. Dreams of yesteryear sequestered her in a deep unwanted part of her mind, not allowing her to awaken. The visions played in her mind like the movies she often visited, but it was a poignant love story more tragic than Hollywood would ever portray. Trapped in the scarlet and black theater of her mind, forced to watch every event unfold, racing to the climax. Before the end, the story would turn to sheer horror, Solange feeling the terror to her bones, unable to leave or even close her eyes. Sequel after sequel, doomed forever to watch the acts that pained her the most.

Gloomily, she dressed and applied her make-up. Her stock hunting clothes of black mini dress and nylons never failed her. Tonight she would hunt the strip clubs, a guaranteed supply of evil. Solange knew that among the throng of eager young, other hunters stalked. Not vampires, but far more sinister and for that she hunted them.

She checked herself over, assured that she looked her best, or worst, depending on viewpoint. To the hunters she sought, her appearance made her a deliciously available target, to others it made her a slut. Hunger lending her a prowess that only a vampire could know, she yearned to leave the apartment. A discreet exit deemed itself necessary, as she could not afford for Leone to see her. The beast within her raged fully, her passion ripping her to shreds this evening.

After killing Greg, she felt like there could be no hope for her now. Soon Solange would cease to exist completely, leaving just a mindless killer. She thought of her young musician friend, wishing she could see him one more time. Solange knew that could never happen. He could never die like Greg did just the night before. She would be damned if she would let that happen.

She also knew that Leone had planned to take her away. Solange should have been happy, but hatred burned in her so much. So much resentment for what he had done so long ago.

Solange drove down North Druid Hills to Buford Highway, where a brilliant pink neon sign heralded a strip club. She pulled in, a perfect hunting spot. Adulterers, perverts of all types, there for her, prime for the picking. Less human, more than beast, not even sure which one was really her anymore, she headed in. The girl at the door looked at her questionably. Solange read her mind. The lady assumed that the vampire could only be a lesbian or a prostitute, and her knowing smile did not bother her at all. Let her think so. The huntress simply paid her cover charge and went in.

Stage lights flashed onto bodies moving like sinuous statues on platforms. Men sat at tables in the darkness, nursing drinks and desires. Solange read their thoughts, searching for a candidate. Lust oozed from minds in every corner of the room, but one stood out like the eyesore he was. At a small table directly in front of a platform where a chesty blonde danced, he sat in a three-piece suit, looking every bit the successful business man, lean, graying at the temples; but his mind told another story.

Above him the girl danced, white stockings and garters clung to skin tanned a rich bronze. Solange saw her through the man's mind, tied spread-eagle to a bed in those garters. Gagged, unable to scream as he cut her stockings with a surgeon's blade, purposely slicing the perfect legs underneath. Solange pulled away from his thoughts, the stench of the cesspool they rose from threatened to pull her in. It made her hungry.

She watched him rise and approach the stage. The blonde's large pink-tipped breasts swayed teasingly close to the man's face as she leaned closer to accept a tip of fifty dollars. Solange touched on the girl's thoughts as the man slid the crisp bill into her garter, and she found them as foul as her patron's. A hotel room, a drug-induced heart attack, the girl removing money from the dead man's wallet. A disgusting duo, unfortunately for them her hunger knew no limits this evening. Each one stalking the other, while neither of them even considered that they were both being stalked themselves, how delicious. The beast in her embraced the hunt, salvia formed in her mouth, and blood teeth threatened to burst from her gums, ready for the feeding. Red light shone faintly from her eyes. Anyone would think it a play of the lights, never knowing the truth.

The man turned and stopped as he caught the vampire's hungry gaze. Immediately she changed to a provocatively hungry look he could not refuse. She saw the flash of lust in eyes that stripped her naked. He sat at the table, and moving with a sensuous motion, she appeared to glide toward him. The slightly flared skirt of her dress swirled around her upper thighs, the bodice clinging to her breasts, and he showed his appreciation of these things clearly on his face as she sat next to him.

"Aren't we bold?" quipped the man as he ordered her a drink, not even bothering to ask if she wanted one. *Perhaps I look thirsty*, she thought. "What is it you want?" he asked.

"You," she replied as she edged closer.

"Or my money?" His attractive face twisted into a sneer.

"It is not your money that interests me, sir." Solange touched his hand. He stared into her almost feral eyes, which mesmerized him.

"You're not a hooker?" he asked, his brusque voice holding the surprise that read on his face. Solange shook her head no. Steel-gray eyes narrowed in suspicion and he muttered, "I'm leaving with someone else." He didn't bother to move her hand.

Solange looked at the blonde, who spat fire with her eyes at the two of them. The vampire smiled and sent a telepathic message,

I think you're beautiful. Immediately the girl softened and began to smile at her. She turned her attention back to her other victim. "She is exquisite, is she not? It seems we have similar taste." Solange cast a lustful look at the girl, then the businessman. One tapered finger stroked the hair on the back of his hand while her other hand fell to his lap. "Perhaps, we could share her." Her voice hung suggestively in the air, sweet as arsenic. Her hand and mind felt his answer at the same time, and Solange smiled and drew away. Taking a fifty from her purse Solange floated to the platform, holding the dancer's gaze as she approached. Thoroughly enchanted, the girl bent toward Solange. Softly she whispered, "You will finish this dance then meet us outside." The folded money lightly grazing the breast that hung close to her, she slid down to the garter on the girl's leg and slipped the money in.

Back at the table she told the now-excited man, "She'll meet us outside." They walked out arm-in-arm, her passion mounting moment by moment, not for the sex the two expected, but for the kill and blood she would satiate herself with. She now let her blood teeth lengthen, animal instinct blocking out all human emotion and thought. The lust built in the man to her side, his violent nature surging under the skin of the cool outer appearance. The night and its infinite darkness hid the hideous changes in his partner. He could not see the fingers that lengthened and sharpened with scythe-like talons, teeth that showed deadly against soft lips, or even the red fire of bloodlust that shone from her eyes.

"Here's my car," the businessman said as he motioned toward a rented burgundy sedan. As he unlocked the passenger door, the blonde had responded to Solange's telepathic command, and she walked toward them wrapped in a full-length leather coat, spiked heels ticking on the pavement, her face slack under the vampire's trance. Solange suggested they sit in the back seat while he drove to the motel. "It will give us time to get to know each other," she explained. She slid in the back seat beside the girl. Once the car pulled out of the parking lot, she leaned closer to the dancer. A taloned hand undid the belt on the coat exposing her to the waist. A fluttering heartbeat sounded loud in Solange's ears. The smell of blood, sweat and perfume burned in the vampire's nose, teasing drops of saliva down her fangs. The girl's mind hovered between fear and excitement, a very common thing for victims. Fear of death, fear of the unknown, at the same time something carnal attracted humans to the very thing that caused the fear. These conflicting emotions added to the kill, feeding her as much as the blood.

Still trapped in a trance-like state, the girl neither screamed nor moved, only shivered and whined quietly. Solange looked into the girl's wide, frantic eyes, they grew even wider as they gazed into red glowing orbs. *Sssh, don't make a sound, I wish to give you only what you deserve.* The vampire's lips never moved, but the girl heard every word. She pleaded silently for her life, knowing the vampire held that decision in her hands. Soothingly Solange touched the girl's face with a taloned finger, and she felt the girl calm. Razor points trailed down to a plump breast, slicing the soft skin. She leaned over, her mouth above the cut outstretched her tongue to lick the blood that welled up there, and a squeeze of the pink-tipped globe forced the flow of blood to Solange's mouth. Coppery warmth flowed past her fangs into her throat, and her lips sucked hungrily at the gash.

The vampire felt the eyes of the man upon them in the mirror, but he mistook what he saw there. The leather coat had fallen away so that the girl writhed and bucked nearly nude against Solange. He watched the ecstasy consume the girl's face as the red-haired woman sucked at her breast. From the view in the mirror he did not see the blood that ran in rivulets down the girl's stomach or the red frenzy of bloodlust in the vampire's eyes. Her moans and hisses of passion caused him to stiffen in excitement, he could not know the passion was for the blood that flowed into her. He grew inpatient for the room he had reserved.

The women's moans grew louder and he chuckled to himself. He would turn those moans to screams soon enough. Dark thoughts of the cutting utensils in his trunk, nestled in their felt-lined attaché case made him giddy, loving how the light reflected on the silver blades just before he sliced through all-too-yielding flesh. His own passions, like the vampire's focused on blood, not too drink but to draw it, urged his desire on. He thought of their skin, the dancer's bronze, the other's pale as fine marble, how beautifully they would bleed. He accelerated the car in his need to try the images in his mind.

For five years he had traveled, searching for the perfect ones. They were found easily enough, offering themselves to him. He didn't fear being caught, carefulness had became a way of life. Always a different town, never striking in the same place, never using his real name or credit cards. He thought of the case in the trunk with his souvenirs. Quite an assortment, crucifixes, rings, necklaces with names, even a pair of nipple rings, still crusted with blood where he had pulled them free, all reminders of his girls.

He glanced again in the rearview mirror. The blonde, quiet now, rested her head on the seat, her neck curved back in sleep. But the redhead still sucked and groped at her, by God she was a lusty one! What a surprise for him when she had approached. The moment he saw her, he forgot about the blonde dancer. His mind filled with images of cutting patterns in her perfect breasts while he rutted in her like a beast. Her hands tied over her head, legs tied spread eagle, she lay open in his fantasy, open and bleeding.

Then his plans had changed. She wanted the blonde. Never before had he killed two in the same town, much less the same night. As he had drove he made his plans. The man imagined tying the two of them to the bed, the blonde first, then the other. Matching patterns cut into their breasts, hips and legs, his finest accomplishment. He turned the car into the motel, and unknown to him the blonde dancer drew her last breath.

In the back seat, Solange had drained the dancer to near empty. Her life had flowed into the vampire with every drop of blood. With the precious liquid came memories flooding her senses. Seas of faces, night after night, leering, admiring, some even hating, as she looked down on them. She felt the dancer's contempt for them boiling in her heart. There was murder in that heart and in her mind. More men had fallen prey to the dancer's wiles than could be counted. Stripped of dignity, money, and their lives, she had felt no remorse for their deaths. Hence, Solange felt none for hers.

The car had come to a stop, Solange wiped her mouth and chin on the girl's coat and closed it over the bloody mess of the chest. During the ride the man's twisted fantasies had drifted through the mist of the dancer's memories. Hatred of them and their creator spurred her to a more frenzied feeding, and even with the girl's death, her bloodlust had not been satisfied. Her plan now included pain and terror.

Solange saw him walk to the trunk of the car to retrieve a black attaché case. The faint glow of the lights in the lot shone on his dark hair, creating glinting blue highlights. His handsome face, half-hidden in shadows, twisted into a grotesque mask. The back door opened to reveal Solange straightening herself.

"Did you enjoy the ride over?" His soft voice spoke none of the horror that dwelled in the mind. Gray eyes looked at Solange, noting the red tinge in her eyes, attributing it to the light, but their feral glow disturbed him. The blonde slumped against the seat, eyes closed, and he looked at her curiously. "What's with her?"

"Maybe she's tired." Her sly vampire smile hinted at sexually. "Could you carry her in so we can get started?"

"Why don't we wake her?", he suggested, not wishing to carry the girl; what was wrong with her anyway? "Is she stoned?"

"Maybe, but she'll be okay for our purposes." She knew the girl would be good for no one's purposes, but she needed to get them inside. The man argued no more, and simply lifted the girl from the car. Solange followed him to the motel room.

The man laid the girl on the double bed, her blonde hair cascading over the pillow. He wondered in amazement when she didn't wake. His attaché he put on the desk in the opposite corner, leaving it locked for now and turned to the other girl. She stood a few paces from the door, beautiful even in the bad light of the room. As he gazed at her, she approached, a sultry half smile on her lips. Her long fingers touched his chest, funny how he had not noticed how long they were before. Firm breasts pressed against him, the nipples hard enough to be felt through his shirt. Detaching himself from her, the man excused himself into the small bathroom.

Once there he stripped off his clothes. In the mirror he looked at his muscled body, knowing it was perfect. For long years he had worked to make it perfect; mother wouldn't have liked that. She had liked him weak and defenseless, easy pickings for her attentions. He remembered her cigarette-stained teeth biting his soft flesh; she would find it hard to do now. But she had taught him well. He looked at his manhood, large and hardened, even as a boy he had been blessed. Or so she had told him. How she had hurt him for it, the binding, twisting, and beating of his developing body. Now as he held himself he likened himself to the satyrs of Ancient Greece. Like them he pleasured women to their death. No matter how much they pleaded and screamed, the pain of his tortures brought them release, a final ecstasy. For the tortures and carved scars on him he did not hate her, rather it was her refusal to give him final release, that she did not kill him. For that he hated her, hated all of them.

While alone, Solange undressed the dead girl. Her skin already turned pale, the gash over her heart gaped like an obscene mouth. The attaché case, though locked, opened easily for her. Inside she found a number of interesting instruments. Handcuffs, several pairs, which she laid aside. Short lengths of rope and strips of cloth for gags, she also laid them aside. Under these things, nestled in felt, six implements of death lay hidden. When she reached to pick one up, a curved artist's knife, images hit her like stones; screams and bleeding flesh being cut over and over. Disgusted and tempted, Solange left them there. Waiting for him, she undressed herself; this would be a messy kill, he must feel the pain his victims had suffered. Once completely naked she sat suggestively on the bed and waited.

When he came out he stood arrogantly nude, skin tanned evenly, muscles rippling under it. Powerful and beautiful . . . unfortunately his was an utterly evil and sick soul underneath. The man's penis, however, was a disturbing anomaly. Large and hard, its thick shaft had thick ropy scars on it, as if carved for some tribal ceremony. Bent at an unusual angle, entry into a woman would not only be painful but would tear fragile flesh. He noticed where her gaze focused and hatred burned from his gray eyes. If she had not been in a crazed stage of hunger and revenge, pity for him would have overtook her, but she had to remember what he was. Solange looked away and stretched out on the bed, suggestively spreading her legs. The killer turned from her to his case without even looking at the dead girl.

Shock registered on his face, when he saw the case open, contents removed. He checked to see if the locks were broken: they were still intact, merely opened. He turned back toward Solange, anger darkening his face. How dare she open his case, or touch his tools! Just look at the whore, stretched out on the bed, smiling. Wasn't she afraid of him? Then he looked at the blonde and saw the gash in her chest. Then noticed she wasn't breathing. Dead, her life stolen from him, his masterpiece ruined. "You killed her." It was not a question.

Solange sat up and said, "I'm sorry, I couldn't wait for you. She was exquisite, simply delicious, are you angry with me?" She laughed.

"But she was mine! You bitch, how dare you take her from me! And how dare you touch my case!" His skin flushed red, and the nostrils on his perfect nose flared in madness. Solange merely stood and walked toward him, her eyes flashing brightly. As she neared him she held out her hands displaying her extended talons. She laughed, showing her dripping blood teeth. The man took a step back, realizing he had made a tragic error. Still laughing, Solange stepped forward.

"Did you know she had plans for you as well? A little white powder in a drink, a little tumble in the hay, and your life and your money gone, poof!" Carefully she registered his expression, and his anger turned to fascination. "Except Tanya didn't know she had hand-picked a serial killer." She noted his surprise. "Oh yes, I know her name and I know what you are, who you are, and where you came from. I've seen the faces of your victims, what you did to them. It's written in you mind and on those instruments."

"I may have killed them, but I gave them the ultimate pleasure," he arrogantly announced. Showing less fear, the man came closer. "They were weak, the pleasure too much for them; but what can be expected of a mere woman?" He excused his sickness. Then he reached out to her, and a well-manicured hand touched her arm. Revulsion swept through her at his touch, but she repressed the fear, knowing she had the upper hand. "But a woman like you, a vampire, for that's what you must be . . . now that is different story indeed!" Solange realized her mistake then: this one did not fear her. Actually, he was drawn to her. "Why, every time that I cut you it would heal, such pleasure we could find together. Even more if you were to share your power with me." His eyes had a fanatical light in them.

"You want to be a vampire?" Solange asked coyly.

"Yes and I also want you." She allowed the man to step forward and grasp her arms. "Together, we could be the perfect team. Two perfect killing machines, perfect lovers, you never dying from my caresses." He stood close enough now that she felt his turgid member against her stomach. "Night after night, cutting you, drinking your blood only to start all over. And would you do the same to me?" The vampire allowed him to continue his sick soliloquy, her flaming eyes continuously scanning his face, probing his mind, ready for any devious actions in planning.

"Is that what you want?" Deceptive arousal lingered on her lips as she spoke. Totally entranced, he stopped speaking to listen to her. Gray eyes, wide in his passion, roved over her body, followed by his hands. Not fighting him as he squeezed her breasts, pinching the nipples between thumb and forefinger, sexual arousal came raging from some hidden place within, but the vampire part of her was in full control. "Would you have me drain your blood as I drained your cock?" He sighed. "Yes, you want that. An incredible vampire you will make, so powerful, so beautiful, so deliciously evil. Together we will hunt, I will teach you tortures never dreamed about."

"Bite me now," he pleaded. "Change me."

"It's more complicated than that," she purred, playing into his fantasy, feeding his belief of being worthy of such power. "Great pain will rack your body, so great you may try to kill yourself and me. Most do at that point." She touched her hands to his chest and caressed the muscles found there. His hands kneaded her breasts harder as his breathing grew rapid. "I must be assured I won't lose you, no harm must come to either of us if we are to rule the night. We can use the handcuffs and rope, that should restrain you through the change. But first there is pleasure to be had." Solange crushed herself against the great wall of his body, his rod between them pressing into her flesh. His hands moved to her hips, pulling her up until her pubic hair pressed against the enormous member. His breath rasped loudly with the added excitement, while his touch became rougher and more violent. Taloned fingers dug into muscled shoulders while her legs came up to wrap around his waist, bringing her closer to him. He cried out at the pain, of the pleasure of his own blood running down his back. He sat on the foot of the bed, pulling her down with him. As his warped flesh pressed at her as she pushed him back on the bed and reached for the cuffs. With them she secured his hands to the bedposts, stretching him into a mocking image of the crucifixion. Swiftly, while he moaned in anticipation, she bound his feet in the same manner to the bottom corners of the bed.

The vampire sat astride him, staring hungrily into his handsome face. Having his attention she stroked her breasts, keeping them at the hardness he had worked them to. The man strained upwards yearning for the softness above him. Solange maneuvered herself over his hungry organ, his eyes widened in disbelief as she stretched herself over him without even a gasp of pain. Never before had that happened; they had always screamed in agony. "Did I not promise you pleasure?" He muttered yes, as she moved up and down on him. Because of his deformity he touched places untouched inside her, and she sighed, her hunger mounting. "I also promised you pain."

"Yes, yes give it to me!" he begged, like his kind always did. Foolishly, he believed all her deceits and would pay with his life. Immortal, hah, he need enjoy his pain with her, as they would be his last feelings. Her wet, sucking flesh squeezed him as her sharp claws opened the flesh of his jawbone from ear to ear, the hot blood flowed down his neck. He screamed, "Please don't stop, take me." How pitiful he was. She licked the blood from her fingers as he watched. Again she extended her claws to him, cutting around each of his nipples in swirling patterns. Bringing her hands to her breasts, Solange painted circles around her nipples with the scarlet fluid, mocking the wounds on him. Again she cut him, her fingers slipping inside the cut. Now she bent to lick the wounds, sucking at the precious fluid found there. Looking up, she contemplated the man's face, sensing that he would soon spew his seed inside her. Leaning further forward, she placed her breast in the cuts, covering the tips with blood as she pumped her body on his. Solange slid back, taking his pulsing cock into her to the base, pulling her claws along his skin in scarlet ribbons from shoulders to groin. He screamed at the agony. None of the cuts were deep enough to kill, but the pain surely drove him to near madness.

Blood gleamed red on her hands and torso, and hungrily she licked at her fingers, the salty taste driving her on. Beneath her the man writhed and pushed up into her, his cries now somewhere between pleasure and pain. Solange put her fingers to his lips and smeared his own blood on them. Greedily he licked them. Then feeling his body jerk in passion, she clamped her flesh down tight on him until she felt the hot fluid spray her inside. Then she got off him once he was finished. The man, nearly unconscious, asked, "Am I changed?"

"No," was her only reply.

"What else must I do?" the man, weary from loss of blood, begged of her.

"You must die." Shock registered on his face, eyes angry once more. "You will die as the many have died at your hands. How could you believe I could allow one like you to spend eternity with me?" she laughed.

"You filthy bitch . . ." was all he managed to say before talons ripped his throat. Quick as lightening, she fastened upon the gash and drank the gush of blood. His memories filled her with the blood. How he became the monster he was. Now that monster lay in his own filth, dead.

When he passed, Solange took no chances and severed his head. The blonde she left as she was. Her heart, despite all the blood she had drank, chilled her chest with its coldness. How detached she had become to doing this. What part of humanity remained? Nothing, without Dereck there was nothing.

Solange went into the bathroom and showered off the already-drying blood. Once she was dressed she flew back to the club to retrieve her car. The clock in her car showed two o'clock, enough time to paint.

Back in her apartment her brush made bold, angry strokes on the canvas. Frustration worked out in dark, brooding colors to picture a likeness of her dismal hunting prey tonight. On and on she painted, tears streaking her face until dawn forced her to stop.

Sometime in the night, Leone came in to stand by her. Completely ignoring him, she painted on. Sobbing and painting, these were all she knew. His hand reached out to touch her hair, and she jerked away. In pain, he whispered, "My Angel."

"Angel is dead," she said and slung a great wealth of red paint to the canvas. Leone left her there.

CHAPTER THIRTY-FIVE

Grisly Discovery

Sanford knocked on the motel room door. No answer. A maid wheeled her cart down the cement walkway, and she came to stop next to him, obviously heading for the room he stood outside of. When asked, she informed him that room was empty. *Dammit*, he thought, *the bitch moved out on me.*

Just as he was walking away, his cell phone rang. "Sanford, here," he answered. It was the Captain, informing that there were two more murders over on Buford Highway. Two in one night, the killer accelerating rang as a bad omen to the detective. "I'm on my way."

"How far out are you?" asked the Captain.

"I was outside the beltway checking on a lead, just off of seventy-five. I'll be there in about twenty minutes," he told the Captain.

"Did you eat yet?" the voice on the phone asked.

"No," answered Sanford. "Why?"

"You wouldn't want to see this on a full stomach," the Captain noted.

"Oh Jesus," muttered Sanford. "Have them lock the scene down until I get there." He slammed the door shut on his sedan and spun out of the parking lot. Out on the interstate he did no less than eighty the whole way, sirens blaring and blue light glaring.

Twenty minutes later he pulled on the scene. Barricades and yellow tape had been put up around the part of the parking lot.

Stepping through the crowd gathered, he ducked under the tape, flashing his I.D. to the cop guarding the barricade. The Captain strode over to him, gesturing him toward a burgundy sedan parked inside the barricade. The trunk was open and two guys from the forensics were placing things in plastic baggies. Sanford leaned in closer to examine their contents.

A suitcase lay open, and in it there were driver's licenses, credit cards, and jewelry. Some of the I.D.'s were women, some were the same man with different names. The jewelry included a pair of bloody nipple rings connected by a chain; it looked for all the world like a trophy case; a serial killer's trophy case. "Is this the murderer's car?" Sanford asked.

"No, one of the victim's," the Captain told him. "It's a rental and the name he used is fake. So no lead there." The Captain looked at Sanford and scratched his bald head. "Morris, I'm getting too old for this shit. If you don't solve this soon, the Mayor is gonna find a way to blame me. I want to retire with a clean slate, if you catch my drift."

"Yeah, I know what you're saying, " Sanford sighed. "I guess the FBI is gonna step in now. Not much we can do about it. If nothing else, the victim here is probably someone they are looking for. I hate those people, but I'm dumbfucked on this one."

"You said you were checking on a lead this morning, what was that all about?" his superior asked.

"A vampire writer," he explained. "Bumped into her the other night when I was on a semi-informal stakeout. How coincidental, I don't know. Couldn't get anything out of her, but my gut says she's here for a reason."

"A writer? What help could a writer be?" Captain asked. "Are you clutching at straws?"

"Hell yes!" swore Sanford. "Especially if they are lying straws. That one is up to something, I just can't get it out of her."

"Well, then let's go in and have look shall we?" Captain offered. "Hugh's already here. He is saying some weird shit for a ME, think the job is getting to him?"

"No way," Sanford said. "If Hugh Whittaker says something, no matter how strange it is, it's probably right on the money." With that he and the Captain went inside.

The scene in the motel room could only be classed as bloody . . . bloody awful. It was a standard room, until you saw the bodies. The first one on the floor was pale, blonde, and with a gaping hole between her breasts. He had seen worse. The second on the bed had to be one of the worst he'd ever seen. Swirling patterns had been cut into his skin, he noted it was a he because of the large male member in the groin, and the head had been severed and was not visible from where he stood. All that remained was a bloody stump of a neck where it should have been. As if on cue, Hugh raised his head from the other side of the bed and motioned for him to come over.

In front of the medical examiner lay the man's severed head, a look of utter terror frozen on his face forever. He was glad now he hadn't eaten. He may not be able to eat for quite some time. He asked the ME, "What's the deal, Hugh?"

"Our girl is getting out of hand," Hugh explained. "I think she killed the girl outright, drained her. This guy was not so lucky, seems like she played with him for a while. She even had sex with him before or while she was killing him."

"Shit," he said. "That's fucking sick. Why did she cut him up like that? What could that have been for, none of the rest were that mutilated."

"Remember the other guy, victim number two?" asked the smaller man.

"Yeah, the rapist," he answered.

"Remember what she did to him?" Hugh queried. "Well, I think if you do a little research on this guy, you'll find he did this to someone. She's hunting criminals remember?"

"Hell yeah, but what about the girl?" Sanford was confused.

"No explanation for that. Besides, you're the detective, I'm only giving my opinion," Hugh shrugged and made some more notes.

"You think that's why she cut his head off?" Sanford questioned.

"No, I think she didn't want him coming back, if you want my opinion," Hugh answered. "She didn't want this one to be a vampire."

"Oh bullshit! Now I know what the Captain meant," Sanford said. He found his hands going through his hair again.

"Well, that's my opinion. There is something going on here that is beyond us both as far as ordinary. I see it, why can't you accept it?" Hugh offered. "Not everything in this world is explainable, Morris. Some things are unexplainable."

They went back to work gathering information. The more they found, the more confused they became, and the more nervous Sanford became. He wished he could bring Shana Collins down here to see this. How could she say they didn't exist if she saw this? What lie would she tell then, faced with atrocity? She wasn't a killer, but how far would she go to protect someone?

By the time the bodies were removed and everyone got ready to leave, the Captain got a call. The FBI was here. *Shit*, thought Sanford. Now he knew he'd probably never get the answers he needed so badly.

CHAPTER THIRTY-SIX

Arrival in Atlanta

Finally in Atlanta, Joel found a cheap motel and set up a base of operation. He pinned his maps to the wall, marking the locations of the murders he had so far. Later he would go online and go into the police files and find if there were any new ones he needed to know about. He brought in all of his supplies except for a machete, some stakes, holy water, and a bag of garlic.

The supplies had been seriously depleted by his activities across the country. He had killed several of the bastard things along the way. It was his civic duty, he thought, to kill them. Rid the world of the monsters before they could take over. He still had plenty to deal with any vampires he met here, though, no matter how many there were. First he had to find them. He pulled out his laptop.

Joel tapped into the police computers and noted that there were more murders since the last time he checked. He added four new red pushpins to the map. Somewhere in that circle of pushpins slept the killer. The cops just didn't know it was a real vampire, so they wouldn't look where he would. He studied the map for a long while, sipping a Coke and eating cookies. Then he saw it.

Dead in the center of the murders there was a cemetery. Not just any cemetery, but an old historic cemetery, the kind with crypts; a perfect hiding place. No, the cops wouldn't think of looking there. What a genius he was! With plenty of daylight left, Joel armed himself and headed out for Twin Oaks Cemetery.

CHAPTER THIRTY-SEVEN

Disturbed

Leone slept in the crypt; he had been there tonight because it became obvious that Solange did not care for his company. He would take her away, but he had to make plans. Tomorrow night they would leave by plane to Italy, where he had a villa. There he could keep her safely and try to restore her mind. If not, he wasn't sure what he would do. He had to get her out of this city before she killed anyone else.

Perhaps there was nothing that would help her, and she was lost forever. The idea saddened him greatly. These were his thoughts as he lay waiting for the sun to sink so that he could leave the crypt. His age kept him from sleeping an entire night now, but he was still sensitive to the sun. As he lay there, something tickled at his mind.

Someone was in the graveyard. All day humans had passed by where he laid, but this was different: this human knew he was here. This human searched for vampires. His mind went out to find the thoughts. Their source headed straight for his crypt. He froze the mind, willing the man to stop in his tracks. Leone felt his hatred, his determination, and his fear. It poured from him. He held the man there until the sun dropped out of the sky.

After rising he left the crypt to face the man, who stood there in a plaid flannel shirt and jeans, his down-home, apple pie look deceitful. For in that chest beat the heart of a murderer. Peeling back layers of the man's mind, Leone read what was there. He saw this was the man responsible for this whole travesty. This man had killed Dereck Cliffe and many others. This is the man Solange would love to kill. But Leone was no killer.

He couldn't allow this one to continue his crusade, but he wouldn't allow Solange to kill him either. The human police could catch this one. Leone put a hypnotic suggestion into his mind that would get him caught, and that would be the end of the hunter.

"Leave this place, hunter of vampires, never to return," Leone commanded. "Your very life depends on it. You will sleep until tomorrow and you will not return to this place. If you try to return, you will give yourself away to the other humans."

In a trance, the man left the cemetery. Leone left to go to Solange, to tell her of his plans. This task was making him so weary, and he almost wished he could have stayed in Europe.

CHAPTER THIRTY-EIGHT

Busted

Officer Wright's cruiser sped along I-285 West, and all around him the cars slowed down. They didn't need to worry, he wasn't on traffic duty. After a long day, he was headed for the station. Only a flagrant abuse of the law or emergency could distract him from that.

His tall body ached from being in the cold rain all day. Winter crept closer every day, and in Atlanta that meant rain. Very seldom did it get cold enough to snow, but the southern city became cold and wet enough to make one miserable. It had rained for the last three days, but that didn't stop his work. In fact, today had been quite full. The morning started off with a bang, a domestic dispute. He hated those.

Some guy got off work early because of the rain. When he arrived home he found his wife having more than tea and cookies with the lady next door. The women managed to lock themselves in a room and call 911 before he broke the door down.

Wright arrived a few minutes later, as he had been parked two streets over when the call came through. A knock at the door brought no answer. He could hear shouting coming from a back room. So he went back to his car and called for backup and went in. The front door was unlocked. The scene on the other side reminded him of his intense dislike of domestic situations.

From the bedroom he heard the wails of the women and the husband's plans of teaching them to like men again. Wright grimaced and went through the bedroom door. The ladies were tied to the bed, both beaten and bleeding. No sooner had he yelled, "Police Officer!" the husband jumped from behind the door and tackled him. There's nothing like being wrestled to the ground by a big naked redneck at ten o'clock in the morning.

At six feet four inches, two hundred-sixty pounds, Wright's body had been perfectly tuned. An athlete at Morehouse University and now a cop, he was no wimp, but this guy gave him a run for his money. He fought hard for ten minutes before the cuffs could be put on him. Then when Wright read him his Miranda rights, the guy yelled racial obscenities at him. He thought to himself that the right to remain silent was often not taken seriously. He had thrown a blanket on the guy and escorted him halfway to the car before his backup arrived.

"Hey, Ken," the other officer had laughed, "You get all the good ones."

"No shit," Wright said. "Oh, could you go untie the ladies for me, unless you'd rather wrestle Bubba here into the car?" He put the blanket-wrapped husband into the cruiser, and the guy was booked on assault and attempted rape, along with resisting arrest and assaulting an officer. *Those women had better press charges*, he thought; he definitely would. His body still hurt from fighting that big idiot.

The rest of the day had passed fairly uneventful compared to that. A few car alarms, noise reports, shoplifters, nothing phenomenal, but in the rain it wore him down. All he could think about now was the fireplace in his house, his wife sitting next to him, and watching television. Just another thirty minutes and he'd be off the clock.

Then it happened. A car shot past him on the highway, Wright clocked him at ninety. *That guy's gonna kill somebody*, he thought, *especially in this weather*. He turned on his lights and sirens, then pulled out behind the speeder. The car didn't slow down, but sped forward dodging in and out of traffic. Wright stayed behind him. He called the station to alert them to the high-speed chase and his location. As they approached downtown the traffic grew heavier, harder for the officer and his fleeing suspect to maneuver around. The early-model Cavalier had no choice but to pull over. A check on the California plates had showed no offense or theft reports, no reason for the suspect to run. Officer Wright prepared for the worst, and slowly he approached the car. The driver had the window down, so he called for him to put his hands in the air where he could see them. The man complied. Wright moved forward until he stood beside the window, gun in hand.

"Step out of the car, sir," he ordered. The stench of garlic filled Wright's nostrils: the car reeked of it. "Sir, please step out of the car, now!"

"Just write me a ticket so I can go, okay?" the man asked, and he made no move to get out of the car.

"Sir, we've gone a little past that, step out of the car." Wright's voice never wavered.

"Look, I'm in a hurry," he said, his pale face turning red, his voice urgent.

"Sir, this is the last time I will tell you to step out of the car!" Wright felt a growing dread in the pit of his stomach. The guy opened the door and placed one foot on the ground. "Slowly," the officer ordered, never putting down his gun. Soon the guy stood on the asphalt with hands in the air. About twenty-five or so, red hair, blue eyes, slight muscular build, the guy stood at least six inches short of Wright. "Now, put your hands on top of the car, feet apart." The guy complied. "I'm reaching for your wallet, do not move," he said as he put his gun in the holster and patted down the suspect until he found the wallet. He opened it and glanced at the license inside, everything matched the plates, his name was Joel Killian.

"Mr. Killian, do you still live at this address?"

"Yes, I'm here on business," Joel's voice showed his nervousness.

"Why did you run?" Wright asked as he tried took a sniff to see if he smelled alcohol, but all he got was garlic. The guy seemed really wired, and Wright wondered if maybe he did drugs.

"I'm in a hurry, I have somewhere to go before dark. I have to go before dark," the guy pleaded, his whole body visibly shaking. "It will be dark in twenty minutes, it'll be too late!"

"Well, I'm afraid you're not gonna make it," Wright said as he slipped a cuff on Killian's right wrist and reached for the other. Before he could put the cuff on the guy's other wrist, Killian took a swing at him. *For a small man Killian packed one hell of a punch*, thought Wright dazedly as he shook off the effects of the punch. The guy then ran into the traffic. Within a second, Wright was after him, yelling for him to halt. All around him cars zipped past, and some had to slam on brakes to avoid hitting him or the idiot. Soon his powerful legs carried the officer closer to Killian, his outstretched hand inches from Killian's collar. With another burst of speed he tackled him as he started onto the side of the road. Together they toppled over a guardrail onto the grass.

Wright gave him no time to fight, and pushed Killian into the grass face down and slapped the other cuff on him. "You have the right to remain silent . . ."

Killian interrupted the Miranda recital by screaming, "You don't understand, you've gotta let me go, I've gotta get there before dark! You don't know what you're interfering with!"

"Let me start again. You have the right to remain silent . . ." Wright continued to read Killian his rights, but jerked him to his feet and propelled him forward. He held out his hand to stop traffic so he could cross safely. With great care he put Killian in the back of the cruiser, securing him well. Out of breath, he walked to the other side and got in.

What a day, he thought. The black uniform he wore clung to him where the rain had soaked through, and his cold hand reached for the microphone on his radio. "This car 3054, Officer Wright waiting on backup and tow truck. Bringing in suspect for failing to stop for blue light, resisting arrest, assault on an officer. Possible influence of unknown substances, will need bloodtest." He waited for response, and static crackled from the speaker.

"Backup and tow truck on its way. Also, background check revealed no outstanding warrants, car 3054, but may have to transport to Grady. Mr. Killian has a psychiatric background," the dispatcher explained.

"No shit, car 3054 out," Wright cut off the radio and stepped out of the car. He walked to Killian's red Cavalier, where the driver's door was still open, and he reached inside for the keys. The garlic smell made him sick to his stomach, and he looked to find its source. The source was a fifty-pound burlap sack full of the pungent off-white bulbs. *What the hell,* he thought, *is this guy carrying that much garlic for?*

When he stepped back from the car another cruiser pulled up. Officer Karl Ziegler walked over to Wright, and he took a deep breath and made a face. "What the hell is that?" he asked.

"Fifty pounds of fresh garlic," Wright announced as he shut the car door. "Let's take a look at what's in the trunk."

"Eight hundred cans of tomato paste?" Ziegler laughed.

"Real funny, Karl, but as long as it's not a dead body or a big naked redneck, I'll be happy," Wright said.

"Not a good day, Ken?" Zeigler asked as they walked to the back of the car. "Heard you got roughed up at a domestic this morning."

"Well, I've been in worse," Wright said as he put the key into the trunk lock. "Let's see where Mr. Killian has to go with all that garlic." As the lid opened, their eyes widened in surprise at the supplies in the trunk. "What the hell's he gonna do with this stuff?" Then he thought to himself, *maybe I don't want to know.* The trunk's contents consisted of a flamethrower, a box of crucifixes, a crossbow, a box of sharpened wooden stakes of various lengths, a clear drum of water, and one bloody machete.

"You know what I think?" Zeigler didn't give Wright time to respond before he continued. "Well, you know I'm a big sci-fi and horror buff, right?" Wright nodded. "And I read all those books by Anne Rice, so I'm kind of an expert, I guess . . . so I would say this fucker's vampire hunting."

"What?!" Wright exclaimed. "There's no such thing."

"I didn't say he was sane, I just told you what he's doing," Ziegler paused, scratching his head and straightening his thinning brown hair. "Wanna hear something else weird?" Wright rolled his eyes. "You know Sanford in homicide?" Wright nodded. "Well, that serial killer case he's been working on has all the ear-markings of a vampire." Ziegler raised his hand to ward off Wright's protests. "He's been searching files all over the country that are supposed vampire killings. Now we don't think it's a real vampire or nothing, just a nut like this one." Ziegler gestured toward Wright's car. "Maybe this guy got wind and decided to pull a Van Helsing."

"What's a Van Helsing?" Wright asked.

"Ain't you ever seen a Christopher Lee movie?" Ziegler's question came across as incredulous. "He's the guy who kills Dracula. We need to get on the horn to Sanford, let him know about this one." They both turned to look at Killian, where he sat in the car screaming.

CHAPTER THIRTY-NINE

Impatiently Waiting

"Goddamn, is it ever gonna stop raining?" screamed Shana. She looked out of the huge bay window of Kyle's house. They had abandoned the motel for here, to hide from the cops. Now they waited for Kyle to wake up. Everyone else had found something to do. Mysteriously, all of Kyle roommates had left for the day. Perhaps he had dropped a little hidden message in their minds, Shana wasn't sure. Why else would they all be out doing something on this god-forsaken day? She paced and drank, waiting for the vampire to wake up.

"Where would you be going anyway?" Mike pointed out, his large frame lounging on the sofa, enjoying some crazy drink he had concocted from the band's supply of alcohol. He never was too picky about what he drank, unlike Shana. She always carried her Jack Daniels with her, never letting the supply get low. Which was quite a task since she drank so much.

"Somewhere," she replied grumpily. "I'm just getting antsy, that's all. I need to be doing something. I've been through a pack and half of cigarettes since lunch time."

"Just sit tight, we have to wait on Mr. Longtooth to wake the fuck up," he said. "I don't want you trying to take on this psycho bitch without him."

"Where are the girls?" she asked. They had been missing for a while now.

"Taking a nap," Mike informed her. "Same as you should be doing. We'll have to be for up for awhile tonight. You'll need your sleep."

"I'll sleep when I'm dead," she told him flippantly.

"That'll be sooner than you think if you're not at your best," he told her.

"I can't sleep. I can't eat. I'm just too fucking wired," she said. "Something big is coming. Something bad, I just feel it. That cop is gonna find me again. He knows who I am, it shouldn't be that fucking hard. He'll be the one."

"Like you'd mind that," Mike reminded her.

"Fuck off," she replied and turned back toward the window. Her thoughts had been on Detective Morris Sanford. But they were not thoughts about being arrested. They were very personal thoughts. How good it had felt against his hard body. She hadn't been held like that in a long time. Oh sure, she had her share of lovers, but there was something special about that man. Those big brown eyes and hard lips. Yes, she wanted him. Too bad there could be no way she could be with him. He thought her guilty of something. Surely she was if she found Solange. As long as she hid the vampire, she couldn't have him in her life. A promise was a promise, but she wondered what was more important. A promise to a dead man or a living, breathing man like that in her life. She hoped she made the right choice.

CHAPTER FORTY

Downtown

oel had to think of something. He had screamed at that dick of a cop all the way to the station. He had to get out, if he didn't, he'd be a sitting duck for the vampire. It knew him, and if he waited to kill it, he'd be dead meat. He tried to tell these stupid pricks that, but they just gave him *that* look. He knew the look, he'd seen it before in foster homes, hospitals, schools . . . oh yeah, he knew the look all right. Soon they came and put him in a straitjacket and then into an isolation cell. They took his garlic and crucifix from around his neck, and they had also taken his knives and gun, leaving him with no protection. *Stupid, stupid, stupid, they were so fucking stupid*, he thought. With his legs he pushed against the wall until he was standing. His only view of the world was a slot and a window in the door. "I want my garlic! I want my fucking garlic now!" As he shouted he slammed his head into the Plexiglas covering the window. it wouldn't budge. But the guard came anyway.

"You better calm down in there," the guard told him. "Or we're gonna have to knock you out." Then walked away.

"They're coming! They're coming and you took my garlic, you stupid fucking pricks!" Joel screamed and slammed his head into the window again. He had only one chance of getting out of here. Detective Morris Sanford, he had heard them say Sanford wanted to talk to him, and Joel recognized the name from the files he had accessed. Sanford was a hunter, like him, and could be trusted.

Darkness had settled in outside by now, and Joel prayed the vampire wouldn't come. Unprepared for combat, he had been stripped of even the simplest of protection. *Damn them, they deserved to have their necks ripped out and blood drained*, he thought. And then he thought about the vampire, he was powerful. Compared to him, Solange had been nothing. Joel felt it when he got close to the cemetery, where it had probed his mind with a skill no other had ever been able to. Twin Oaks Cemetery had been central to some of the murders, so Joel had taken a chance. The old vampire slept in a mausoleum there, and Joel would make sure he slept forever. But now as he waited for who or what, he was unsure.

CHAPTER FORTY-ONE

Vampire Killer Formula

In the lab, Hugh Whittaker worked. He took some of the samples of body fluids he had found at the last murder scene and tested various chemicals and compounds. In addition to the saliva, he now had a small tissue sample and vaginal fluids. He knew they were not human.

If his friend were to come out of this alive, Hugh had to come up with some way to help Morris out. He might even need it himself. So he worked away, testing the samples. There were several that cause reactions, silver being the strongest. The silver burned and caused the samples to bubble. That should do the trick, but he would add the others for safety measure.

Some were harmless by themselves, but added together they could prove deadly to the right creature. *Maybe not too good for humans either*, he thought. One would have to be sure who or what he was dealing with before using this. As he mixed the agents together, he noted how it foamed and glowed slightly.

He filled two cases of hypodermic needles full of the liquid. One he would keep for himself, the other he would give to his friend. At least it would be some sort of defense against the vampire. Hugh stripped off his latex gloves and went over to his desk.

Stacked on his desk was an array of strange books, all containing documentary-type information on vampires. One interviewed people who thought they were vampires and researched various vampire-style murders. Another studied the forensic side of vampires, how death by various diseases spawned the vampire legends of old. Others were on Vlad Tepes, Elizabeth Bathory, and Lord Byron. All were marked with Hugh's highlighter and red pieces of paper to mark important passages. He would hand those over to Morris too. Now he picked up the only copy of fiction on his desk, *Dracula* by Bram Stoker. If he was going to read fiction for ideas and possible insight, he may as well go to one of the main sources. He began to read.

CHAPTER FORTY-TWO

Interrogation of a Killer

The FBI got on his damn nerves but they had to be brought in. Four members had shown up this week, two from their serial killer division and two from another division that investigated strange crimes. Sanford guessed that they were a real-life equivalent to that *X-Files* show. He wished he could break this case on his own; slim chance of that now.

His only leads to this point had been some physical evidence: red hair found on a victim, saliva samples, tire tracks, and blood-drained corpses, none of which did anything but confuse things further. And Shana Collins, couldn't forget her, she had to figure into this somewhere. Hugh's tests found complex DNA in the hair and saliva, which didn't appear to be even human. Of course the FBI had to run the test over again, thinking Hugh had made a mistake. Hugh had just laughed when they got the same thing. But now he had a break.

This Killian guy coming along was pure luck. Los Angeles Police had been looking for a vampire killer, and the MO matched the contents of Killian's trunk. Samples of blood on the machete also corroborated with samples from victims. Gotcha! But what had brought him to Atlanta? The murders had not been printed in the papers for more than a week, not enough time to drive from California, and surely Killian had come because of the murders. What self-appointed vampire hunter could pass up the opportunity? But how did he get the info? Sanford had to find out.

Sanford took his file folder with him when he joined the FBI team in the observation room. The vampire specialist team stood against the wall; Bylak, a tall lanky man with sandy hair had gray eyes that never wavered, and Sanford found them irritatingly on him at the moment. His partner, Capuano, stood only five feet four inches but had a stern face, and she looked like she could strangle you with her bare hands. Their counterparts from the serial killer division stepped out of the interrogation room. Sloanaker, was forty with steel-gray hair, and his military background showed in the stern countenance of his angular face. The other half of the duo, Fountain, was a pretty boy, with mocha skin and flashing eyes that would make Denzel Washington jealous. But Sanford knew his reputation as being tough, sly, and one of the most decorated in the agency. They all looked at Sanford with no happiness.

"What's up?" He tried to sound unconcerned.

"He won't talk to anyone but you," Bylak announced, his agitation with the situation very clear. He wanted to be totally in charge, and now he was losing face to a local dick. That made Sanford smile. "We'll watch from behind the glass. You need to get information about the California murders, we have something new to connect him with. Capuano," he said, and motioned to the woman, who pulled a folded sheet of paper from her pocket and handed it to Sanford. The detective unfolded it and read its contents:

DEAR MEMBERS OF FANG DIVISION,

Yes, I know who and what you are, and that we are alike. I too have devoted my life to hunting vampires, but where you study, I destroy. From the files I have seen, you are unsure of their reality. Have no doubts, they are real, an evil pestilence which must be wiped from the face of the earth.

I have become an expert in spotting them. With pale skin and long nails, you will find them working night jobs at convenience stores, nightclubs, and I've even met one that was a cop. For some reason, a lot of them are strippers and hookers; I suppose lonely men make easy prey. That was how I met the first one. I've killed hundreds since then. But it took me twenty years to kill her.

When I was seven she killed my father, and left me all alone. Her name was Angel, you know her as the artist living with Dereck Cliffe. He was one, too! Everyone who died in that house was a vampire; I killed them.

There are few ways to kill vampires and the old ones work best. First is the sun: they will sizzle like hot dogs on a grill in the light. But it takes a long time and they scream like banshees. I know: I staked one in the desert one time.

The second way is fire. You can burn them as well as blow them up; I should know, I'm a bomb specialist, also. Catch them during the day, when they can't get away. Angel and her evil family burned in their coffins while I was miles away.

But the last and best method is as follows: A stake through the heart. It has to be specially prepared: soaked in holy water and then dried, and should be cut from hardwood, preferably oak. But that alone will not kill it. You also have to cut off the head and stuff it with garlic. Garlic, holy water, and crucifixes will not kill them, but they don't like them, either.

When they die it gets real messy. Young vampires (and that's hard to tell because they don't age) just die, but the older ones turn to muck when you kill them.

I hope this letter has been of help. You will not hear from me again. This is not traceable by the way, so don't even try.

Thank you,
Van Helsing

Sanford looked up, everyone waiting for his reaction. He looked from one to another, then at the two from what he now knew as FANG. "This guy is sick. His instructions matched the MO in the California murders to a tee. Now he claims to have killed Dereck Cliffe, wow." He shook his head: it was all so unbelievable. Then he looked back at the FBI agents. "Is any of this true?"

"You are not authorized for that information," said Capuano, her voice haughty. "You are on a need-to-know basis only. The letter was provided to help you interrogate the suspect, that is all."

"The hell it is!" Sanford shouted. "Lady, this is still my investigation. And the way I see it is, the guy will only talk to me. He has information that will not only convict himself but lead me to my killer. Either fill me in or you're not getting squat. And by the way, I got a friend down at the *Constitution* that would love to put FANG's butt in a sling on the front page. So don't pull any of that 'deny everything' bullshit on me, because I've played hardball with the best of them. So I'm not scared of the FB fucking I." When he finished speaking his face held a look of unwavering determination. With arms crossed he awaited their answer.

Capuano and Bylak exchanged looks, Bylak stepped forward to address him. "Detective Sanford, Agent Capuano and I understand your frustration, but there are things that are not for the public's knowledge..." Before he could finish, Sanford interrupted.

"But I'm not the public, I'm a cop trying to solve a murder case!" Sanford shouted, then after a moment, he added more calmly, "If my killer is a real vampire, you can have it. I just want this to stop. I need to know what my people are up against. So do we have a deal?"

After shooting looks back and forth with her partner, Capuano said, "Okay, let us sit in with you and Killian. We can help with information, then we will go over files with you. Bylak and I expected this. But you absolutely cannot share info with other policeman, your wife, or anyone. Understand?"

"Understood, but are you confirming what this nut's screaming?" Sanford was dazed. Surely this could not be true, but had he not seen other evidence confirming this very thing? *Vampires are creatures of myth*, Shana's voice rang in his head.

"Somewhat, just bear with me until I can show you slides and photos. But this man is delusional; don't ever think he isn't. In the past, he clearly has not been able to distinguish the difference. A good majority of his victims were not vampires at all, but unlucky people. For the time being we play along with the fantasy," Capuano informed him. "Now let's go in and talk to him, Sloanaker and Fountain will watch through the two-way mirror, and Bylak will go in with us. Ready?" she asked, motioning to the door.

Inside, Killian sat staring at the door, nervous like a cat, and he almost sprang when the door was opened. He watched Sanford with a wary eye and grimaced when he saw the FBI agents. "I believe I'm only talking to Sanford," he said.

"Well, Mr. Killian, or can I call you Joel?" Sanford asked, and Joel nodded. "I'm Detective Sanford, These are Agents Bylak and Capuano." Sanford nodded toward them.

"They're from FANG," Joel stated calmly, like an accusation.

"Joel, how do you know about FANG?" Capuano asked.

"I have my sources," was his only reply.

"Okay Joel, let's be frank. I have ten murders, could be a vampire. You are on business in Atlanta with an arsenal suited for vampire hunting. What can you tell me?" Sanford asked as he pulled a chair up alongside Joel, the FANG agents hovering in the background.

"It is a vampire, I know. And your tests are wrong. It's a male vampire, I've seen him," Joel answered, and gave FANG a gloating look.

"How did you know we were looking for a female?" Joel started to answer but Sanford said, "Yeah, I know you have your sources, tell me about this vampire."

"Why?"

"I am looking for a vampire, remember?" Sanford reminded him. "Don't even think about holding out on me, Joel; remember that machete in your trunk? Well, the blood on it matches blood samples for over twenty murder victims. So you don't have anything to bargain with. Either you can help me catch the vampire or you can sit in jail and wait for him to come get you. It's up to you." He shrugged and made an expressive gesture with his hands, waiting for Killian to say something.

Joel sat there staring back at Sanford. Those eyes scared the hell out of the detective. In a matter of seconds he saw radical changes: first cold and calculation, then nervousness, and just a flicker of confusion. Then when he started to speak, he coughed then sputtered, "He . . . lives in Twin Oaks Cemetery. I was going back to kill him while he slept, before Officer Dickhead pulled me over. Probably not even there now. I mean, he knows he's not safe there anymore. He has one of two options: kill me or change sleeping places. My bet is both."

"How did you find this vampire?" Sanford asked, curious as to why this vampire's lair stood in the center of the majority of his crime scenes.

"Well, I gathered the files on the murders, and by the way I got them from the Atlanta Police computers," Joel said with a smugness that bothered Sanford. "You see, I'm a hacker, too. I find it necessary to access information from time to time. But back to business. I marked the locations on a map, which I'm sure you had done as well. What you didn't do was think like a vampire. Now some are spoiled and like the modern conveniences, and they're hard to find, but some stick to the basics. And central to some, but not all, murders is Twin Oaks cemetery, a very old cemetery with mausoleums. Not these new slot-in-the-wall deals, but with stone crypts.

"Now I showed up later than I should have, dusk. I wasn't scared, and brought all the weapons with me, but that was before I knew how powerful he would be. When I get near one of them my stomach acid begins to churn; that's why they never fool me. When I walked through those gates my stomach nearly blew up. Then I felt him in my head, trying to dig around. They can do that, you know: read your thoughts. Most of them can't read mine, don't really know why, but Angel never could. But this one, he went right in. He knew why I was there, but he couldn't come out of the crypt until dark. I was paralyzed while he raped my mind. He held me there until dark fell, and I could feel the anger pouring out of him. He walked out of the crypt and stopped, but something kept him from attacking, had to be the garlic. I had the stuff tied to me everywhere. Then he looked distracted, like he was listening to someone. A few minutes later he told me to leave or I would die. So I bolted." Killian sat shaking his head, and his hands vibrated with fear, but he continued on. "I had planned to be back there by noon today, but I slept until four. That son of a bitch did something in my head."

"What did he look like?" Sanford was curious what a vampire would look like.

"Well, this one was tall, about six two, black hair, gray-streaked. Looked older than most, about mid-thirties. He must have been turned at that age. And of course the pale skin and glowing emerald eyes; they showed his power."

Capuano stepped forward, and out of her briefcase she pulled some photos. She laid them on the table in front of Killian. "Recognize any of these?" she asked.

Joel looked through the stack, then said, "They're all vampires."

"How can you tell?" Sanford asked.

"They have a glow," Capuano answered. "We scan newspapers and videos from airport surveillance. For some reason they project a slight aura, but if you don't know, you couldn't tell the difference. It's something we've learned to look for now. I don't think the vampires even know, or they would be more camera-shy. But I need names, Joel, do you know them, or is the Twin Oaks vampire there?"

"Yes, this one," he said as he handed it to Sanford. "That's him, but I don't know his name."

The man was as Joel had described, but he couldn't imagine a gentleman this sophisticated sleeping in a hundred-year-old mausoleum. His clothing and baggage were impeccable and there wasn't a hair out of place, but he did have an aura. "Where was this taken?"

"Atlanta airport a month ago. He couldn't be the killer, though he did show up about the same time. There is another vampire here; the evidence is too strong," Bylak, who had been quiet up until this point, stated. "The name on the passenger list is Noguchi, Leone Noguchi. He's been in the United States for ten years now. This is the first time his appearance has coincided with killings. Either he's very good at disposing of bodies or he doesn't kill his victims. He came from Italy and before then we don't know. A trace on his name brought us nothing . . . well, nothing of use. The family died out over two hundred years ago. There is a Castle Noguchi in Hungary, which has been in ruins for over a century, but there was a Leone Noguchi who owned it, three hundred years ago."

"This is bullshit!" Sanford exclaimed. "You're trying to tell me that man is three hundred years old?" He looked from Capuano to Bylak then Killian. "You actually believe all this don't you? This is crazy. Maybe you're right, maybe, but I'm having a hard time swallowing this."

"I understand, but be patient, Detective." Capuano looked back at Killian and asked, "Any others you recognize?"

"Oh yeah. Angel and Dereck, but don't worry about them 'cause they're dead. That bitch killed my father," Joel announced and without realizing his confession. He sorted through pictures again pulling some out. "Don't worry about these either. This is Trina, she's dead too. She lived with Dereck and Angel, owned the gallery where Angel's paintings were. These others were the members of Nightbird, dead." He laughed, then stopped when he came to another picture of Angel. "I've never seen this before. She looks different, hair's shorter."

Dereck, *Nightbird*, hadn't he heard these names before? Vampires? Friends of Shana's, and they are fucking vampires. *That lying bitch,* he thought to himself. *She knew all along.*

"Joel, you sent us this didn't you?" Bylak took out the letter and handed it to Joel. "You burned down the mansion, right?"

"Yes, but you know why!" Joel answered heatedly. "You pussies never were gonna do anything about them."

"Joel, do you know why some that you kill don't turn to dust?" Capuano gave him no time to answer. "Because they were human Joel, human like us. Not monsters, not vampires, but human and you killed them."

"No, that's not true," he cried, his face looking stricken. "I would not kill people, I'm trying to protect people, don't you see?" Tears flowed down thehis face. "Oh God, no, you're wrong!"

"I'm afraid not, Joel. Over half were human. You also killed two of our agents, didn't you? You can't tell the difference and I don't think there's anything we can do for you now." Bylak had a guard come in with the straitjacket and had Joel returned to his cell. The vampire hunter screamed all the way out.

"We'll have to take him to Grady for psychiatric," Sanford said, shaking his head. "You know, if I didn't know what he'd done I'd feel sorry for the poor bastard."

"Well, we see people like him and that's why we observe only. There have been instances where we've had to eliminate one, and it's not pretty," Capuano said. "You see, Detective, they are not the evil beings Joel has painted them. Not all of them kill. Take the one at the cemetery for instance. Leone could have killed Killian if he had wanted to, but didn't. He never kills, he feeds then makes them forget." Capuano walked over to a table where she had set a box. "Are you ready to begin your vampire education?" she asked and almost smiled.

"Now or never, and you better hurry before I run out the door," Sanford laughed, but he was scared. Scared and mad, he couldn't get Shana's face out of his mind. Her words haunted his mind, *Dereck Cliffe was a close personal friend of mine.*

Bylak started. "Our division began in 1924 with J. Edgar Hoover. You see, J. Edgar had gangster problems, but what most people don't know is that Capone was a vampire. We never found out how he got that way or how long he'd been one, but he was a bitch to kill. In 1947, we took him out and cut off his head, not the syphilis story that's recorded. From the moment he discovered what Capone was, Hoover had someone keeping track of vampire sightings and killings. Over the years we've built up quite a lot of data, but not enough."

"They can virtually live forever, although very few do." Bylak paused to set up a slide projector, while Sloanaker and Fountain came in quietly. "Capuano, can you get the lights, please?" The lights went out and the first slide was an Indian medicine man. "He's called Night Bear for obvious reasons. This photo was taken in 1950 by a group of tourists in Wyoming. See the aura? Not as clear but that's due to bad equipment. Legends say he is over one thousand years old, but he doesn't look a day over twenty.

He's different from Capone and his lot, doesn't even drink human blood. He lives off of animals, never bothers anything. Now I would be here all day if I went over every vampire case on file. But I wanted to give you a good idea of how old they can live to be. So let's skip to the important ones."

"Are there that many of them?" Sanford was shocked.

"Oh yes, not as many as before, partly thanks to Mr. Killian," Bylak grimaced. "Unfortunately, he killed ones that weren't, as he said, evil. Let's start with Leone. We don't dare get too close to him, for he is one of the most powerful. We've never observed him with other vampires, however we believe he is looking for Solange, who Killian called Angel.

"According to legend and scrambled bits of history we've uncovered, he was bricked into the wall of his castle over two hundred years ago. The peasants in the village still curse that place. All of the family money and artifacts, and they were quite a few, as he was a collector, were shipped to the United States in 1820. We believe they came to Solange." Bylak moved onto the next slide. A man in his early twenties with long black hair and glittering black eyes, stood next to the most beautiful woman he had ever seen, with eyes almost the color of the ocean and flaming red hair accenting an angelic porcelain white face. Both had the glow. "The man is Dereck Cliffe, lead singer of a popular rock band called Nightbird. We've tracked Dereck since the 1960's, he was over five hundred years old."

"He's dead, right?" the detective asked.

"Yes, we have his remains in our lab in Washington. Just a burnt-out husk." Bylak paused for a moment, took a deep breath, and began again. "That brings us to Solange. We estimate her being about 220 years old. Since 1972, she has lived with Dereck in Los Angeles. Her art is still sold nationwide. Together they were a really hot couple on the club scene. It lasted for over twenty years, but they were only in the limelight for the past ten. Their notoriety was their undoing."

"She's dead too, what a shame," Sanford said. "What a looker."

"She's not dead, take a look at this," Bylak said as he brought up another slide, where the beautiful vampire exited an airplane. "This was taken a month ago at Atlanta Airport, right after Dereck's mansion burned down. And this was filmed at MARTA's MLK station the night of the first murder. Solange could be your killer."

Sanford looked at the beautiful girl with the red hair and thought, *she looks so innocent.*

"Don't be fooled by her appearance, she is a killer. We were able to question another vampire recently. He was only too willing to tell on his companions, since they had thrown him out of the haven for indiscriminate killing. Dereck helped us capture him after he killed some of our agents; he'd wanted to get even. According to him, Solange cannot control her hunger, so she must kill. He also said that she was emotionally unstable, and if something ever happened to Dereck she'd snap.

"We think that's what's happened now. Even though she kills, Solange sees herself as a vigilante, killing criminals. We have never had evidence of her killing innocent people, so we have left her alone and watched. Also, we are afraid to approach her, as she is erratic and very powerful. Which is why we are here."

"So she is pretty much unstoppable?" Sanford asked, seeing the mayor going into fits without an arrest being made.

"Unless we destroy her, and we don't want to do that," Capuano expressed, "We have considered talking to her, but it could be very dangerous."

"Talk to her? Jesus, how would you be able to stop her? I know what I saw in Killian's trunk, but does that stuff really work?" he asked.

"Well, from what we know garlic, holy water, and crosses have no effect on them, and is just superstition. Also superstition is not being able to cross running water, not having a reflection, and they don't turn into bats or wolves, although they can fly. They are not impotent as most writers accredit them and the men have reproduced but the children are always human. They also form a mist or fog to shroud themselves in..." Capuano's lecture was cut short by the detective's inquiry.

"They can have babies? You mean, hybrid babies born to human women?"

"Well, there are very few instances, but yes, although they are not born vampires. Some of them have shown ESP capabilities and high intellect, but are human. Now the women lose all capabilities to conceive, where the men are fertile, but for what reasons we do not know." Capuano shrugged.

"What about stakes through the heart?" Sanford had so many questions.

"Well, it won't kill them, but it can weaken them. Mostly it just pisses them off. Joel has been very fortunate not to have been ripped to shreds. What does kill them is cutting off the head, burning, or exposure to sunlight, just like Joel described." Bylak paused, then added, "Of course, one would be lucky to get that close. Vampires have excellent powers of the mind. They all have different aspects of ESP, such as hypnosis, telepathic capabilities, telekinetic and pyrokinetic abilities. They are very hard to sneak up on."

"Pyrokinetic meaning they can burn things, right?" Bylak nodded. "If Solange has these powers, that could explain my second victim's condition," Sanford said more to himself than anyone.

"So now you know as much as we do, more or less," announced Capuano. She flipped on the light and cut off the projector. "Now the question is what to do. Are you in, Sanford?"

Her question told him he could die if he was, but wasn't that true everyday for a cop? Vampires, who'd have ever thought it? After a few minutes, Sanford gave his answer, and he hoped he wouldn't regret it. He also secretly hoped it would make his path cross with Shana Collins again. He owed her an ass chewing.

CHAPTER FORTY-THREE

A Visit From Leone

In his cell, Joel waited to be transferred to Grady hospital, where he would be analyzed to see if he was insane. For the first time in his life he wondered about his mission. Had he really killed humans by mistake? No, they just wanted to pin this on him. Soon they would come to drug him for transport, and hopefully they chose something Joel had built an immunity to. That's how he would escape.

Plans for escape were running through his mind when he heard the guard outside his door. But when the door swung open, there stood the vampire. The dim light caught the silver glimmer in his dark hair as he arrogantly told the guard to close the door and forget he'd seen him.. The thick steel door slammed and locked behind him. "Please don't get up, Joel, and don't worry I'm not going to hurt you," the vampire said, his voice smooth and intoxicating. "My name is Leone, you don't need to tell me anything: I see it all in your mind, vampire hunter."

Leone stood before Joel looking down on him, and he appeared like a god to the human. Never before had he seen a vampire with such power, and he thought to himself, *if he wasn't an evil creature, I could love him.* "Joel, Joel, Joel, I'm not evil and neither is Solange. I admit there are those among us who practice black arts, but my kin and I are not among them." Leone stopped speaking to scan Joel's broken mind. "You have committed horrible crimes, some would say that it is you who are evil. But I am not here to judge you; the humans will do that. It is fortunate that I found you instead of Solange, she has much to be angry with you about."

"She's dead," Joel said aloud even though he didn't have to.

"Oh no, my dear vampire hunter, she is quite alive," Leone said and then laughed. "If you are going to burn down a house to kill someone, you should make sure the person you wish to burn is there. She waits for you: I have seen this in her mind. Her anger for you fuels the passion of her hunger, and that is why she kills more now. Solange wanted you to come here. But by finding me first you saved your life. No, what the humans will do to you will be far worse. That will be my punishment for you, that and making you feel the pain of your victims and the ecstasy of being a vampire, which you will never know. Your mind will be tortured for the rest of your life with what you have done and how wrong you were about us." Leone's words echoed in Joel's mind. He could do nothing as Leone came closer. He felt the sharp claws dig into his back and pull him against the vampire. *No, not this,* he thought, *not me.* Icy breath on his neck made the skin there tingle. Joel shuddered when the soft lips pressed against the throbbing pulse found there, and in an instant flash of red-hot pain, needle fangs ripped into him.

He felt his blood flowing into Leone. Then Joel's mind filled with images of Solange, before she was a vampire, her naked skin glowing in firelight, and feeling like satin. He could feel every sensation, loving her through Leone. How exquisite the pleasure he felt, and her smile, her soft sweet kiss make him wonder why he had ever hated her so.

Then he was cut off from her, and someone stacked stones before him until he saw nothing but darkness, feeling a dull ache in his chest. Joel felt Solange's hysteria and pain caused by the separation, then her immense loneliness. All the confusion and desperation of her life flooded him. As Leone drank on, tears flowed from Joel's eyes, and sobs escaped from his throat. Still Leone did not stop his assault.

Now warmth, comfort, and love surrounded him. Joel realized he felt the love of Dereck and Solange. How wonderful he had been to her, loving her eternally. Leone showed how the musician had been Solange's long-needed redemption. Then he felt heat. Not just any heat: he was on fire. Joel knew the burning pain belonged to Dereck. His clothes seared to his skin, and flames licked at his flesh as it sloughed off in ragged pieces. Unbearable, immobilizing pain wracked his body until he drew his last breath. But it was not his death it was Dereck's. Over and over he begged Leone to stop these torturous memories, but he did not.

The final assault had begun with Solange's savage sobs and building hatred, hatred for him and the painful revenge she wanted to take on him. Then he felt a sharp pain in his chest, opened his eyes as saw himself, Joel, standing over him, the face a mask of insane fervor as he pounded the wooden stake into his chest. A second later he opened his mouth to scream but a machete blade sliced through his neck. Even being dead and beheaded was not enough, and he still felt a big hand grab his long hair and a bulb of garlic choked him as it was forced into his mouth.

The images stopped when Leone pulled away and flung him against the wall. Joel watched the tall figure as he spun around, like the rest of the room was doing. Soon his dizziness subsided and he could focus again. The vampire now stood over him, those lips still red from Joel's blood. "Human, vampire hunter, remember all I've shown you. Remember the mercy which I have shown, for if our paths cross again I assure you I will not be so kind. Heed my words, leave me and mine alone," Leone warned, his voice low and forbidding. Then he was gone.

Joel slumped against the wall and screamed until someone came. The guards, then Sanford came running in, and they all stared at the screaming man with blood running down his neck.

*   *   *

Later, Sanford and the agents from FANG sat in front of a monitor screen. People could be made to forget, but cameras could not. They searched the last few hours of videotape from the entrances; lots of people coming and going, but no vampire.

But suddenly Capuano yelled, "Wait, back up . . . little more, there! See him? Right there." The video stopped on a dark-haired man in black walking through the door. "Leone."

"He walked right on in and no one stopped him!" Sanford exclaimed. "Nobody even tried. Do you think Solange could have walked in her like that?"

"Absolutely, but I knew it wouldn't be her," Bylak said. "Killian's still alive."

At that point a guard came in, out of breath. "Detective, Killian's escaped!" he gasped.

"How the hell did that happen?" Sanford couldn't believe his ears. "The man was in a straitjacket in the middle of a police station for chrissakes!"

The guard looked rather awkward and stood there like a kid in the principle's office. His fair face flushed scarlet, his eyes downcast. "Well, when he was attacked his strait jacket got torn . . . I guess he wiggled out of it," he explained sheepishly. "That guy fought us like a wild animal; he really snapped."

"Yeah, yeah, put a APB out on him," Sanford sighed and ran his hand through his hair. "He couldn't have gotten far."

CHAPTER FORTY-FOUR

Escapee

Joel hid in an alley to escape the police as he worked his way out of the straitjacket the vampire had torn. With the jacket off, he flagged down a taxi that took him back to his motel. Luckily the police had not discovered where he was staying. Once back into the room, his mind whirled. Angel still alive. That could not be possible.

Leone almost had him convinced that he had been wrong, but his higher mind could not accept that fact. He knew evil when he saw it. He would now finish this. Today he would kill the evil that was Angel.

He took out his laptop and hacked his way into the local telephone company's records. Joel wanted all the new services connected over the past month. It was a slim chance, but he had to check it anyway. There were hundreds of names in the Atlanta area alone, and he went through them alphabetically. After an hour he was just to the names beginning with C. As he scrolled down he came to the name Cliffe, Angela Cliffe. *Bingo,* he thought.

Stupid bitch should have picked a better alias than that. He wrote down the address, then put that into a map program and printed out directions to the place. Joel then took out a backpack and loaded it up with supplies: police scanner radio, C4 compound, detonation device, and a remote control went into the bag. On his person he strapped a gun and three knives.

There would be no escaping him this time. This time she would die. Hopefully the other vampire would be with her and die as well. Joel never wanted to see his face again. He took another cab, as he was sure the police would be searching the transit system.

Chapter Forty-Five

Too Close For Comfort

All throughout the night they had searched the city for Killian; mad and hurt, he was hidden in Atlanta somewhere. Just when Sanford thought he'd get a bit of rest, the clock struck noon and his pager went off. Sighing, he picked up a phone and called in. Another murder, another vampire murder, in Sandy Springs. Reluctantly he got back in his car and headed out.

The murder site was in some older apartments off of Roswell Road. Normally a very upscale and quiet complex, today it stood flooded with policeman, ambulances, and onlookers. Hugh's coroner vehicle was parked next to the building where the body had been found. FANG had also arrived.

By the small playground, Capauno stood questioning the apartment manager. Seems the young man in apartment J didn't show up for a doctor's appointment. The doctor thought the boy to be in danger due to some things brought up in their recent sessions. He had called the police, and the apartment manager had opened the apartment for them. They had found his body upstairs. Sanford listened to the woman talk about what a nice young man he was, surely one of those women had done this. Seems he was a bit of a Romeo and had them coming and going all the time.

"This is good, let's talk to some of the neighbors to see if they know any of the girls or can give us a description that may match up with Solange," Capauno said. They would call and question the good doctor later.

"But this isn't her MO, she kills criminals remember?" Sanford countered.

"Well, if that's the case, Detective, then again it could be someone else," Bylak offered, by no means reassuring Sanford. "But remember, she killed the homeless man, too, who obviously was no criminal."

"Yeah I remember. It could be the other one, though," Sanford said. As he made his way around through the tenants and over to the apartment, Bylak followed. Upon entering the building his nose was assaulted by the putrid smell of death. The body had been here for a while. He reached into his pocket for his Vicks rub and swabbed a bit under each nostril. Hugh's voice sounded from upstairs, loud and angry. They went up to find out why.

The body lay face down on the gray carpet, blood splattered on the floor and walls in wide arches. The walls were covered in artwork by Solange and newspaper clippings. *Well, there's the link,* Sanford thought. *The stiff is a fan, or was.* Hugh stood beside the body, in argument with a suit from FANG. They were gonna shut him out. He, who had known all along and Sanford wouldn't listen. Angrily he turned to his friend and yelled, "Sanford are you gonna let them kick me out of here? I'm the goddamned ME, for fuck's sake!"

Hugh Whittaker didn't get mad often, but today was a banner day. His limpid blue eyes shone and his nostrils flared wide at the end of his narrow nose. "Hugh, let me talk to some people, but for now let them have the room they need," Sanford explained to him.

"What a fucking day, that you would side with the FB god damned I. This has been our case from the start, I know more than that bastard could possibly know," he snapped.

"Hugh," Sanford said, his voice very placating, "There are things going on here, things that you could have no fucking idea are going on."

"Bullshit. Can we talk outside, alone?" the ME asked.

"Sure, let's go." He left Bylak and headed back down the stairs, then out the sliding glass doors to the balcony.

"You can't bring me in can you?" Hugh asked, seemingly knowing the answer.

"Nope," Sanford told him, though he didn't want to.

"For all of these years we have worked together, I never thought you'd cut me out. Especially on a big one like this," Hugh said, shaking his head.

"That's not the way I want it to be, but I don't have a choice," Sanford tried to explain. He felt like a genuine heel.

"So be it. Been working on a little something for ya," Hugh said. He reached into his pocket and pulled out a small box. Without opening it he handed it to Sanford.

Sanford had to look. Inside there was four hypodermics full of a glowing liquid.

"What are in these?"

"I call it VK1000. Let's just say it's a little mickey for the vampires," Hugh told him. "I'm not sure if it'll kill them, but it'll damn sure make them sick at least."

"Why are you giving this to me?" Sanford asked.

"Because you are gonna need it," Hugh said and walked away.

Feeling like shit, Sanford went back upstairs. He'd never let his friend down before but he knew it was a dangerous business, knowing about vampires. He wanted to protect Hugh, though he may not need as much protecting as Sanford thought, after the detective looked at the formula in his hands.

In the room with the body, Bylak stared at a blank wall. The detective walked up to him and asked, "So, what do you think?"

"I think she took something," the tall FBI man said. "There was a painting here. See where the wall is dirtier around this square? She took it, whatever it was."

"Maybe it wasn't hers and she didn't like it," Sanford suggested.

"Could be," Bylak agreed. "Seems a shame to get killed for your taste in art. Or maybe it was hers and she reclaimed it." Sanford didn't answer. One of the cops yelled for him then: the doctor was on the phone. He went down to question him.

"Sanford here," he said into the phone.

"*Yes, this Dr. Jarrod Cornell. I called in about Mr. Jamison, he was my patient,*" the deep voice explained.

"What kind of doctor are you, Cornell?" Sanford asked with no niceties, as he was too tired for that.

"*I'm a psychologist and a licensed hypnotherapist. I have been treating Greg for the past two years. He had dreams that troubled him,*" Cornell told him.

"What kind of dreams?" He was now writing on a small notepad pulled from his breast pocket.

"*Well, in the beginning I thought them only to be past-life dreams. So I did a regression to help him explore that,*" the doctor answered.

"So he thought he was reincarnated, is what you're telling me?" Sanford asked with a sigh. Bylak came down the stairs to stand next to him. He looked at the him and said softly, "The plot thickens, more weird shit."

"*Reincarnation could explain the dreams, Detective, but I felt that lately they were something else. He had become quite delusional, which is why I was concerned when he didn't show up.*" Sanford could hear the quiver of sadness in the man's soothing voice.

"Cornell, I want you to tell me about the dreams," he told the man on the phone. "Don't fall back on the doctor-patient thing, either. This guy is dead and it may have been by a serial killer we are tracking. It's very urgent because we need to stop this person and if you can help me at all, don't hold out."

"*I understand, detective,*" Cornell said without any anger. "*Well, the dreams started out as dreams of a woman in a white ball gown. The kind they wore two hundred years ago. In the dream he was some kind of royalty. He seemed to be in love with this woman, married to her in the dreams.*"

"Did he ever describe the woman in detail, besides the dress?" he questioned.

"*Oh yes, beautiful, flowing red hair, blue eyes, but they sometimes turned to red and she became a monster. I thought this a sign of anxiety, as stress makes monsters in our dreams,*"

Detective." Sanford just listened as Cornell gave his descriptions, closing his eyes and letting the man finish. *"Then he said he died in the dream . . . actually he said she killed him."*

"You said that lately he was delusional. What made you come to that conclusion?"

"Well, he found an artist that he said looked like the girl from his dream. He began to collect things about her, becoming obsessive. Then she died. I knew he was on the edge when he told me two weeks ago that he saw her again. Now I knew this woman had not come back from the dead. He probably was projecting onto another woman, imagining that she looked like this Angel woman."

"Dear God," was all Sanford could think to say. The doctor had just given him so much information without even realizing. "Please continue, doctor."

"Well, he said he was involved with this woman. One night after she left, he said that a man came to him in a dream and told him that she would kill him again." The doctor paused. *"I think this was the anxiety again."*

"Had either of you tried to find out who he could have been before? Could he have found out?" Sanford asked.

"We hadn't gotten that far, we had discussed it, but I don't think he ever did find out, " Cornell explained.

"Thank you, you have been a tremendous help. I'll be calling you again for testimony, if that's okay," Sanford told the man. He was looking at Bylak; he had some questions for him.

"Sure thing detective, anything to stop a murderer." Dr. Cornell hung up the phone.

"Bylak, what is Solange's history? I mean, what do you know about her life before vampirism?" He waited on the expert to answer him as patiently as he could, feeling an excited tremor in his leg, making the limb twitch and shake. It probably wanted to run, run right out of here. His leg was smarter than he was.

"We know a few things from history. Pre-Revolutionary France, as a matter of fact; it started right before she disappeared. We're not sure how she escaped the guillotine. In life she had been upper class, and her parents had arranged a marriage with a member of the Prussian monarchy for her. We know that they did marry, but she killed him. We assume that was about the time she became a vampire, and he was her first victim. Why is this so important now, Sanford?" Bylak asked him.

Sanford fidgeted with his pen and paper for a moment, then sighed and raised his gaze to Bylak's face. "I believe we have a dead prince upstairs, Bylak," he told him. "Let's go back up and I'll explain." They climbed the stairs as Sanford relayed the doctor's story, Bylak listened intently. They both realized just how much information lay dead on the floor.

Later on, outside by the playground again, they had ran out of tenants to question when Sanford noticed an old woman staring at him from behind a tree. Hoping for the best, he went over to talk to her. Dressed in traditional Hindu clothes, her bright sari emphasized the nut color of her wrinkled skin. Thick gray hair pulled back straight brought the red dot on her forehead to your attention. He asked, "Did you see a woman coming from that apartment ma'am?"

His answer was a string of garbled speech that he could not understand, along with a lot of pointing and gesturing. Immediately, several family members ran over to try and pull her away. The man, about forty, with a heavy mustache, spoke apologetically to the detective, "Forgive my mother, sir, she is old and full of much superstition and stories. She is only here soon from our country and speaks no English."

"What is she saying?" he asked the man.

"It is old stories that mean nothing," the son told him.

"I'll be the judge of that," Sanford told him. "I want to hear it, no matter how strange."

The mother looked at the son with fierce indignation and shrugged his hands from her tiny shoulders. Then, once again, she very vehemently started on that string of babble accentuated with the pointing and gesturing.

"She says that a devil killed the boy," the son explained. "She says the devil has been coming and going out of that apartment for the last several weeks." She let out some more garbled language and looked at Sanford with bright bird eyes. "She knows what it is, for it only comes at night and the black cat only comes to its door. There is a great black cat in the neighborhood, she says it is evil and it was brought by the devil."

"Ask her what this devil looks like," Sanford told him.

The son repeated the words in their language and the woman's only reply was a string of babble in her language after which she spit on the ground and made a sign in the air.

"She speaks of a myth about a woman who comes to men in their sleep and drains them. It also steals children to drain their blood or breast milk from mothers," the son relayed. Capauno walked over and joined the conversation.

"Could be blood or spirit."

Sanford pulled the picture of Solange from his pocket and pointed to it. "Is this the demon?" he asked.

The old woman started talking with blinding speed. Her hand pointed at the apartment next to the boy's as she shouted.

Sanford and Capauno looked at each other and the closed door. So close, so very close they were that it scared them.

* * *

Joel had barely gotten his bomb set up before the police got there. Damn cops, did they think they could stop her? After setting the C-4 up under the building, he had crawled along the creek bed and hid in some dumpsters at a Chinese restaurant. From here he could watch everything that went on from a hole in the dumpster, but no one could see him. A handheld police scanner kept him alert of everything going on out there. His other hand held a remote for the bomb. Some cops were gonna die today, but it couldn't be helped. *That's the way of war,* he thought. He would sit and wait patiently for just the right moment.

Angel and that bastard Leone were in that building and they must die. The police babbled away on their radios. Seems they didn't even know Solange was right under their noses. They were there to investigate a murder, a vampire murder. How laughable. These trained professionals stood outside the murderer's very door.

273

Come sunset, if still here, they could burn with the vampires. Joel waited, remote in hand.

* * *

The plans began. Swat teams arrived, not just your average team. Their dress did not reveal their identity. Sanford just knew when they came off the truck with flamethrowers attached to their backs. They surrounded the premises and evacuated as many tenants as possible.

Sanford spent his time with Bylak and Capauno, learning how to block his mind. It seemed silly to him, but if they said it worked, he'd have to take their word for it. Bylak explained, "Just imagine a wide screen television, detective. Now instead of football or women on the screen, imagine snow. Lots of the static that you get without cable." Sanford tried. "Now from here on out imagine all of your thoughts inside that television. They are behind the screen so hidden from everyone. Keep this in your mind and you will be safe."

"Oh boy, saved by bad reception, " Sanford commented.

"It'll take more than that, detective, " Capauno assured him.

CHAPTER TWENTY-THREE

End of Madness

"He's out there!" Solange nearly screamed at Leone. "I can feel him, that damn static in my head." She tore about the room pulling at her hair and screaming. Leone watched her with growing concern. Her sanity shattered, littered over the minefield of her mind or what was left of it. Somewhere deep inside was the woman he loved so dearly. At times she smiled that sweet smile that had made him want her so much, so long ago. "I have to go out there! I have to kill him!"

"No," Leone said firmly as he grabbed her arm. Furiously, she pulled against him, trying her hardest to break his grip on her. "There are people outside, Solange. People who know what we are and they have weapons. They wait for you. Do you think they will not try to stop you?" he said, his anger and frustration with her reaching the perimeter of his control. "It is this insane disregard for our safety that has brought them here. Did you not think that the boy's body would bring them? No, because you did not think!"

"I don't care, do you hear me? I don't care! I wanted them to come, I want them to kill me!" Tears ran down her face in gray mascara-tinged streaks. She continued pulling, using all her vampire strength to fight him, knowing he wouldn't let her go. "Kill me, Leone. Make it all go away. They won't kill you. Let me save you, like I couldn't save him!"

Leone pulled away from her, his own tears running down his face. Her words hurt as if a sword had ran through him. "Solange, my dearest, be reasonable. I cannot destroy you."

Her anger flamed brighter toward him, and with fury she lashed out at him, striking him in the chest with her small fists. "But you had no problem making me, did you? You had no problem putting me in pain for centuries! Damn you, damn you, damn you!" The fists striking him didn't hurt, but her words made his heart wither. She pummeled him until she collapsed, sobbing on the floor at his feet.

"My Angel." Leone's words were barely more than a whisper. His grief for her kept his voice low. "My intentions toward you were never to cause you pain. Things have gone terribly awry of my plans. If not for fate, you would have spent these past centuries by my side, safe from the torment you feel now. I love you above all things, it is I who wants to keep you safe the most. So don't ask me to destroy you."

She looked up at him, eyes watery, lips trembling and bleeding where she had bit them herself. "Torment, what do you know of my torment? I saw you die, or so I thought. Then as we ran, they took Raphaela. They set her on fire Leone. We couldn't go back, and we left her burning and screaming. Oh, don't turn your face away, Leone, it is because of you that your flesh and blood granddaughter suffered."

"An unfair accusation, young one," Leone said, though he often felt this guilt.

"My wedding night, a supposed time of joy, ruined by these hungers you gave me. After your daughter kept me locked in a trunk all the way from Hungary, I was starved. Unknowingly they held the wedding anyway, they simply thought of me as ill. Do you know how I felt after I ripped out my Gregor's heart?" Solange snarled, her voice now the pitch of a scream as she hurled these things at Leone. She saw the pain she caused him, but she wanted to hurt him. "As I hid from everyone, my parents both went to the guillotine, their heads chopped off while I did nothing. I can thank your daughter for getting me out of there with my head and your fortune, but she couldn't save her own. Leone, did you feel her die? Could you feel the pain when they cut off her head?"

She stopped and stood up, walking away from him, for she couldn't look at his face as he wept. Her tirade continued, "Do you have any idea how I felt, killing innocent people? Feeling their life extinguish in my hands? How long I stayed away from humans. For decades I hid myself away from them, but there was always one coming too near. Then there was Dereck. Dereck, my precious one, my savior, my only happiness in this misery you gave me! Gone, killed by that bastard out there!" Her hand pointed toward the door. Leone watched her, weeping for the things she said, things that had hurt her so, things that hurt him.

"Angel, dying will not bring them back, it will not change anything," he tried to explain to her.

"You are such a coward, you stand there and weep for the pain I feel but you will do nothing to end it!" she spat at him. "You won't kill me, but they will." There was a maniacal look in her eyes and she started for the door. "First he dies, then I do."

"No!" Leone shouted at her, but the door was already opening. A man stood there with fist raised as if to knock. Solange rushed past him, knocking him down.

CHAPTER FORTY-SEVEN

Anticipation

Shana paced back and forth, waiting for Kyle to wake. Right after sunset he came from his basement room, looking like a true rock 'n' roll god. Something akin to worry sat on his face, and she asked him what bothered him.

"It's weird," Kyle started. "I've been having strange dreams all day; dreams about things that I've never seen or done. Old castles, being trapped in a trunk, and blood and I think they are coming from Solange."

"Has she sent you images before?" Shana asked. Curious, she edged nearer to him.

"No, that's what's weird. It's like she's hurting and I'm feeling it," he said. "I think she may be in trouble. I keep getting feelings even now that I'm awake."

"Oh shit." Shana thought about what to do. "Do you think if you really concentrated, it would help you get a fix on her? Track her down with these feelings?"

"I could try," he said and sat in a chair. The vampire closed his eyes and tried to think about Solange. He tried to call to her with his mind. *Can you hear me Solange?* he projected. He sat for a few minutes, saying nothing.

Shana watched him. She watched his eyes flutter shut and the expressions crossing his face. *Oh please let this work,* she prayed to herself, *I cannot let Dereck down.*

Suddenly Kyle jumped and his eyes flew open. "She heard me, I'm sure of it!" he cried. "She's crying and angry. Someone is hurting her, and there is someone with her, though I can't see who it is. Her mind says danger. She says not to come to her."

"She heard you?" inquired Shana. She wondered why Solange did not answer Kyle before. Why now? Why did she tell him not to come? It must be some serious shit going down.

"I'm going anyway," he said as he jumped up. "She needs me and I'm going. This could be our only chance to help her. She's going to die, I feel it."

"Don't go," Shana told him. "We can't lose you, too." She had lost too many old friends recently. She wanted to help Solange but not at Kyle's expense. She flung her arms around the guitar player.

"I'll be back Shana," he told her as he pushed her away. "You are my friend, one of the best anyone could have. But I love her and I have to go." He kissed her on the cheek. "If I don't come back, you'll know why." He let her go and went out the door and disappeared.

She looked out the window. It had stopped raining. For some reason, that didn't make her feel any better. Would she lose another friend tonight? She hoped not. Shana lit another cigarette; that would make two packs for the day. What the hell, not even vampires lived forever anymore.

Chapter Forty-Eight

The Strike

"Okay, people here we go. Keep your minds clear and be ready for anything," Sanford said softly over the radios. He would bet that the vampires knew they were here. From what he had learned, the creatures could hear far better than humans and read minds. Despite the static they sent, they had to know. He had sent the special teams around the other side of the building, in case they went out that way. As he waited, the team leader was approaching the underside of Solange's balcony over the water. Sanford walked to the apartment door. As he started to knock, the door flew wide open and something cold and hard knocked him down and flew past him.

"What the hell?" Sanford exclaimed from the sidewalk. He looked up to see the vampire that had come into the police station standing in front of him, tears running down his face. "Leone Noguchi?"

"It is of no importance who I am, we must go after Solange," the vampire said and started to quickly walk toward the door.

Sanford panicked, fumbled for the vials in his pocket that Hugh had given him. He spilled them on the ground except for one. "Stay right where you are!" He shouted at Leone. "You are under arrest, do you hear me?" He held the hypodermic like a dagger, pointing it at the weeping creature.

"Foolish man, I have committed no crime, I want to stop her same as you," Leone said. "But I will save her from you and herself, she will not die today." He extended his hand to Sanford to help him up.

The detective didn't take his hand but stood up on his own. Soon Bylak and Capuano stood by his side as they all walked back into the apartment. "She has to die," was all that Sanford could say to him. "This has to end."

Static crackled over the radio. "San.........crackle, hiss, crackle.....this is.....hiss, screech...." Sanford slammed the handset against his palm, hoping for the best, but to no avail. "I gotta go outside to hear this, you stay here for a minute," He said as he walked out the door, radio in hand. Capuano followed him. "Okay, leader one come again, " he said into the handset.

"I'm in the creek bed directly underneath the balcony. There's a hole in the bricks under here, looks like somebody took them out. I'm gonna have a look in there."

"No need, Leader One, subject has left apartment, we need everyone up here."

"Okay, let me get out of here . . ." There was a pause then the soldier said, *"Oh shit, there's a—"* Static filled the airwaves. Then before Sanford could question what Leader One was saying, an explosion rocked the earth around him.

In reflex he grabbed Capuano and threw her to the ground beneath him. Sanford felt himself being hit by flying debris, bricks, dirt, and hot flames. His arm went over his head to protect himself the best he could. He heard the panic spreading through his teams. When he felt it was safe to stand he did, and brought the petite FBI agent with him. Flames leapt out of the apartment building, its heat nearly singing his eyebrows. He pulled both of them away. He heard her whispering Bylak's name over and over in shock. Somewhere in the distance fire engines wailed. And one heart-piercing scream sounded behind him.

He turned to see Solange standing in the middle of the parking lot, screaming, her red hair whipping in the wind around her face, which was contorted with rage. If there ever had been a time when Sanford had been scared, it was right then. She came toward them with talon-like hands outstretched, still screaming

Leone's name, accusing them. "You killed him! You will die for what you have done!"

"Solange, get back!" Sanford yelled, trembling even as he spoke. "We did not cause the explosion, we had people in there, too!" He saw her stop and lower her hands. "There was a bomb, but we didn't set it. We mean you no harm."

"Liar! You came here to kill me, but I know you didn't set the bomb. I see it in your mind," the vampire said. "The hunter did it, that is why he is here." She turned and headed for the garbage dumpsters. Sanford saw Killian jump from one of them and start running. As she got closer the man held a large silver crucifix aloft. Solange laughed in his face and took it away from him. "You! How long have I waited for you? You took my Dereck, my beautiful sweet Dereck." She stopped, tears running down her face again, Sanford could hear her sobbing. "Now you've killed Leone, too. You son of a bitch, you have caused me too much pain!"

"Pain? Pain, you talk about pain, you ruined my life you bloodsucking bitch! You put this evil in me. It makes me hunt you! You all must die, you are all evil!" Killian screamed back at her. He raised a gun and fired. The shot hit her in the chest and she didn't even flinch. "You will all die for your crimes!"

"Leone's only crime was to be too much of a coward to kill you! I assure you I won't have that problem," she told him. With lightening speed she grabbed him by both arms and pulled him closer.

Sanford didn't know which one was the most insane, but he had to do something. The fervor that was built up between the two could get someone besides them killed. He yelled out, "Solange let him go, he's going to jail, and we'll make sure he never gets out! He has to face what he did to Dereck!"

"Stay out of this, detective," she said. "Jail? Why should this filth even live when my Dereck and now Leone is dead because of him?" Solange held the man more tightly, and by the look on Killian's face, he was in growing pain.

"You cannot be judge and jury, that's for the law to do," Sanford said. He raised his pistol and fixed his sights on her and shouted a warning, "Let him go now!" She paid him little attention, so he fired.

The shot hit her in the arm. Blood gushed for only a moment and Sanford could see it already starting to heal. The pain of it infuriated her, and she grabbed Killian by the head. She slung his body back and forth. Sanford put another slug into Solange, this one went into her side. She screamed and pulled the man's head. As she pulled her long talon-like nails dug into the neck. Blood spurted out of the gashes as she tugged at him. Then with a twist the head came off. With a wet thud she dropped the grisly object to the pavement. Her face and body were splattered with his blood as she turned to Sanford.

Believing totally that he was a goner; he remembered the vials Hugh gave him. Several had been dropped on the floor of the apartment and were gone but there was one in his pocket. He grabbed it with his hand and removed the cap. He watched, prepared but terrified, as she came toward him. Sanford then saw the change in her.

No longer did her eyes glow red, but were the brilliant blue of the Caribbean. Her hands were no longer claws and her face held only sadness. Solange stopped five feet in front of him when he held up the hand with the syringe in it. With humility she dropped to her knees and lowered her head. "Do it," the vampire said with no emotion.

"You want me to kill you?" Sanford couldn't believe his ears; it had to be some sort of trick.

"Kill me, there is nothing for me," she said and looked up at him with those sparkling eyes. Her gaze told of all the sadness within her. "Do it, you know you should. What will you do, arrest me? No, no jail for such as me. Death can only stop this madness. You must do it."

He couldn't do it. He looked at those eyes and that face filled with so much pain, and all he could do was feel pity. Knowing he should do this, knowing that she wanted him to do it, yet still he couldn't. Such a beautiful, delicate creature knelt before him. Gone were those nightmarish visions of a few moments ago.

Sanford didn't want to kill Solange, he only wanted to comfort her. "I can't."

"Coward," she said. "Same as Leone, because you see me as beautiful or because I look so young, is that why you will not? I assure you I am neither, I am the monster. Do it!" She stood up and quickly took the syringe from his hand. She looked at it and asked, "Will this kill me? What is it?"

"I don't know what's in it," he answered truthfully. "It's experimental, the Medical Examiner made it. It may kill you, but at the very least it will definitely hurt and make you sick."

Without waiting for another word, she plunged it into her chest, and the glowing liquid in the syringe was gone in a flash. The hole left by the syringe closed up as soon as she removed it. The woman's eyes flew open wide, and she clutched her chest. "It burns, *it burns!*" she cried. Then she fell to her knees and vomit issued from her in a furious stream. Blood, bile, and fluorescent liquid pooled on the ground around her. Her body shook in ferocious convulsions as she gagged.

Several members of the special unit advanced to the stricken vampire. Sanford noticed the packs they carried, flame-throwers. They were going to burn her. He felt sick in his stomach but he knew it was inevitable. Capuano's hand touched his shoulder. "It's never easy," she said as she held his arm.

The flames flickered from the ends of the nozzles while the vampire continued to writhe and vomit on the ground. Surrounding her, they silently counted down, and then nodded.

Suddenly there was another one standing over Solange; a young male with long brown hair and a beard. He quickly picked her up and flung her over his shoulder and said, "Sorry, there'll be no BBQ today boys." In an instant they were gone.

"What the?" Sanford asked, blinking.

"I have no idea," Capuano said, as surprised as the detective. "I've never seen a file on him before, and believe me, we know everyone Solange knows. He must be new."

"I've seen him before," Sanford said, remembering his night at the bar. "I stood right next to that son of a bitch at a bar and didn't have a clue."

"Do you know his name?" asked Capuano.

"Just his first name. Kyle, she called him Kyle," he said.

"Who is she?" Curiously Capuano looked at him.

"Shana Collins," Sanford admitted. "The fucking vampire writer. She sat right there and told me there were no such things as vampires. And she was talking to him at the bar. Shit, shit, shit!" Sanford yelled and stomped his foot. That lying bitch, he was gonna nail her for this! "Now what do we do?"

"First we get this fire out and do clean-up," Capuano said, and a tear ran down her stern face. "Then we get our friends out of there before the press gets wind of it."

Sanford had a lot of admiration for that woman. *Tough as hell,* he thought. He knew it was killing her, losing Bylak that way. Yet she stood there barking orders and running everything like a pro. He liked her more than most people he had ever met.

The wind brought a scrap of burning material that landed on the ground at his feet. Sanford stomped it out and picked it up. It made him think of the vampire. The scrap was a piece of canvas; all that remained of her work in the house. Singed around the edges was the face of Dereck Cliff, whose death had started this whole fiasco. If this guy loved Solange, as well as the others, she couldn't be that evil. Her face would be in his memory always with those beseeching cerulean eyes and blood dripping down. Part of him was glad she didn't die today. He walked over to help Capuano.

Chapter Forty-Nine

Still Alive

In the stream, Leone crawled over the rocks and through the water, his body burnt beyond recognition. Every movement took an eternity and hurt him to his soul. He had lain under the bridge and listened to the showdown between Solange and the authorities. He knew she lived, and while he did not know this vampire who saved her, he was grateful. Now came the time to hide and wait. To let his wounds heal while he eluded the FBI. Hopefully they thought him dead as Solange did.

When the time came he would go to Sanford. Sanford was a good man. He had heard his mind as his beloved begged for death. The heart of the detective could not dispatch her so easily. In that same heart, strength beat so hard that it called to Leone.

The burnt creature pulled himself into a mud bank and began covering himself with mud and rocks, safely tucking himself away in an under-hang of tree roots, covered from the light that could kill him in the morning. There he would wait. Then he would find this detective.

Chapter Fifty

The Rescuers

Shana paced back and forth, cigarette in hand. Somehow Kyle had known Solange was in danger, she and Sijn sat waiting on him. Feelings of regret ran through her now. After all, they were dealing with vampires. Dereck had never harmed her and so far Kyle appeared to be trustworthy. Solange held the most concern for her, as she was a mad as a hatter and the writer remembered the jealousy between them over Dereck. Sijn sat here with her pregnant belly, carrying Dereck's child. They could only hope things worked out.

Sijn looked weary. Perhaps this ordeal stressed the mother-to-be too much, and Shana worried about that. This child remained the only living legacy of the man they had all loved. She swore the vampire woman's death before she would let her harm that child, if she lived through this.

"He's been gone too long," Sijn said.

"It's only been fifteen minutes," Shana told her. "Give him some more time."

"All this trouble to find her, I hope its not too late," the dark haired girl said.

"Me too," she agreed. Lighting another cigarette, which had to be the tenth one in fifteen minutes. "I need a drink."

With only a whisper, Kyle appeared in the room, and in his arms, an unconscious Solange shook violently. Blood covered her entire body in a splatter pattern. Two large stains appeared to be to injuries on her arm and her side, and there were blossoms of burnt red on her white skin and light dress. Soot built a film over the blood and what splattered-free skin remained. Ashes peppered her flaming red hair, which hung dull and lifeless with the filth that covered her. From her mouth a trail of blood, dried foam and something glowing went all the way down her neck to her bodice. Amounts of these still spewed from her mouth now in what Shana identified as vomiting. "Someone get me some soapy water and a washcloth," Kyle ordered with urgency. He laid her on his bed gently, softly talking to her in words Shana could barely hear.

Sijn went for the things the young vampire asked for. Getting closer to the bed she saw something strange about Solange. The stricken vampire's face had begun to shrivel. The once youthful, white face turned the color of aging parchment. Wrinkles sprang up all over and the mouth looked drawn and tight. Even her limbs had started to change, arms and legs shriveling. Horrified, the writer drew back. Nausea built up in her throat and she had to swallow hard to keep from vomiting. "What's wrong with her?"

"I think she's dying," Kyle said sadly, not letting go of the ever-aging hand.

"Can we do anything to stop it, to help her?" Shana asked, her voice frantic and cracking.

"How the hell should I know?" he asked angrily. "I've only been a vampire for two fucking weeks. It didn't come with a manual Shana."

At the sound of his voice, Solange started calling out, her voice little more than a whisper. "Dereck . . . I can hear you Dereck . . . help me...I know you've come for me." Her arms reached for Kyle. She thought he to be the one who couldn't help her. She thought him a man now dead. It broke her heart, knowing that she had promised that same dead man that she would take care of Solange. Looking at the dying woman, she realized she had failed him. The only thing he ever asked of her and she had failed. She began to weep.

"There's no time for crying now, Shana, we have to help her," Sijn said as she came back carrying a plastic basin full of steaming

288

water. She set it down on the other side of the bed and began wringing out a washcloth. "Dereck has helped her through us. We have to do whatever is necessary." Gently she began to wash Solange's face, removing the blood and soot from the wrinkled skin. Suddenly she pulled back. A strange look came over the girl's face and she said, "She needs blood."

"How do you know that?" Shana asked. Knowing that in her books, her vampires did indeed need blood to revive. However, real vampires had little resemblance to the characters in her books.

"Something told me in my mind," Sijn looked perplexed. "Who's gonna donate?"

"I don't think that would be wise," Kyle said. "In this condition, she could drain or kill either of you in minutes. It'll have to be me. Maybe my blood will help her." He lifted the withering body from the bed and pushed the lips against his neck. "Drink, Solange, drink," he pleaded. The only sound from her lips was a gurgling as more of the vile vomit rose in her throat. Softly he laid her back down. "She won't drink, I don't even think she knows we are here."

"Why don't you try to force her?" Shana suggested.

"Good idea, " Kyle agreed. He reached into his pocket and pulled out a small knife. Without a pause he ran it across is wrist and pressed it to her mouth. His thick blood flowed for a moment and then the wound healed up. He cut it again and pressed back to her mouth. More of the dark liquid squirted into her mouth. With his finger he took the edge of the cut and held it back to prevent the healing. The blood soon filled her mouth and at least some must have gone down her throat. She jerked and sputtered, the majority of the blood spilling out her mouth. Nothing happened. Kyle stopped.

"We are just gonna have to wait it out, I can't make her drink." He sounded defeated. "All we can do now is protect her and let her rest."

"I'll finish cleaning her up now. Kyle you go feed, you look like you need it. Shana, have a drink and sit down. I'll watch her for a while." Sijn ordered. Quickly she started cleaning the vampire again. While she did she noticed the woman's tongue lick her shriveled bloody lips.

"I don't think that's a good idea, Sijn," Shana told her. "Come away from her and let Kyle do it." Sijn moved away from the bed. "Wait, Kyle, you can feed from me, just don't take too much."

"Hope it won't make me drunk," he said.

"Just shut up and do it," Shana told him. She offered her neck to him willingly, hoping her trust was a wise thing. As the euphoria overtook her she thought she saw Solange move again.

CHAPTER FIFTY-ONE

Final Decision

Morris Sanford sat slumped at his desk. The last forty-eight hours had taken its toll on the detective. His shirt, sweat soaked, blood splattered, and scorched black in places, clung to him. He reeked of body odor, cigarettes, and burnt plastic. Going home to shower and change had not been possible for two days, and sleep had also been a luxury denied him. Sanford wore his jacket to cover the blood and hoped he smelled bad enough to keep everyone the hell away from him. Serial killers, explosions, vampires, and FBI tracking vampires, he had enough.

He looked down at his large hands where they trembled on his desk; for the first time in many years, Sanford was scared. Never before had he seen anything like last night. Oh sure, he had seen explosions before, watched people die before, but not like last night. The picture of that woman no, that creature, the anger literally glowing red in her eyes as she ripped Killian's head from his body. The blood had sprayed in a wide arc, but she drank none of it, had instead dropped the head and turned toward Sanford. As long as he lived he would see her face in his dreams, a beautiful but insane, blood dripping, fanged nightmare. Before Solange could take a step toward him, he had shot her, the blood blossoming into a red rose on her pale skin then starting heal as he watched.

Then the most miraculous thing happened. The vampire had knelt in front of him and asked him to kill her. He had shot in self-defense on many occasions but no way could he do an execution like that. For that's what he thought it would have been, an execution. Now those red eyes that stared back had turned a brilliant blue. Like a great ocean, they had sparkled, their wetness flooding over onto the blood streaked face. His heart reeled from the sudden emotion inflicted upon him by those eyes. Her pain was so evident. His pity so extreme he couldn't do it, or was there something besides the pity? Sanford didn't want to admit the want lingering in his heart. It must be some trick of the vampire, that makes you want them. Somehow she had known he wouldn't kill her if he wanted her. That had to be his answer.

"No, Detective, I assure you that Solange wanted to die," came a voice from nowhere.

Sanford literally jumped out of his chair with shock. He was alone, or so he had thought, in the office this evening. Looking around in sudden fear, his eyes settled on a man sitting in the chair across his desk. No sound had warned him of the vampire's presence. There he sat, looking like a nightmare vision, the skin on the thing's face charred, hair flowing strangely beautiful from a burnt scalp. When he talked or smiled it reminded Sanford of old leather. Despite his body's condition, he was dressed immaculately in a crushed velvet shirt of deep burgundy, the sleeves of which were full and lustrous, neatly cuffed at the wrists with shiny black cufflinks. The bottom fell down to his thighs, which were clad in skin-tight black leather. The guy looked like a rock star; that is, if he hadn't been burnt. "Noguchi?" Leone nodded. "You fucking people don't die do you?" Sanford exclaimed. "And don't come in here like that!"

With a small, painful smile, Leone said, "I didn't mean to frighten you Detective. And oh yes, we can die, but for some of us it takes quite a lot, indeed." He motioned his hand at Sanford and said, "Please, sit back down, I am not the type to kill, you are in no danger from me. In fact I am here to help you."

"Help me? How?" Sanford asked, curious as to how this creature could help him. He could barely take his eyes off that creased, black face and those glittering emerald eyes. "How could a creature like you possibly help me?" He felt himself almost sneer.

"What is it that you hold against me, Detective?" Leone asked, seeming so curious, when Sanford knew he probably had already read his mind.

"Well, let's start with your taste in women," Sanford told him.

The burnt man laughed out loud, surprising the detective. "Oh, you do amuse me, sir. My Angel has left quite an impression on you, Detective. I assure you, she hasn't always been as she is now. Like all people, we suffer, we enjoy, and life changes us, not always for the better. Such is the case with Solange." His face serious again, and his voice low, he asked, "But she is beautiful, is she not?" His knowing look, fixed on Sanford had told he had truly looked in the detective's mind.

"Yes, she is, but I have to admit, she scares the hell out of me," Sanford admitted. "I've never been one to be chickenshit, but I could have done some clucking last night."

"Which is why I'm here," Noguchi said as he steepled his fingers together and rested his charred chin upon them. "Something has to be done about her. It pains me to say it, but we may have to kill her. Before she knocked you down and fled the apartment, she had been ranting. Madness, my dear Detective, is a strange thing. One minute the beautiful girl you love so much rests her head on your chest, the next she is screaming and wailing about ungodly acts of revenge. Perhaps, with years of loving and constant supervision, she could once again be closer to the girl I loved. Perhaps not." He stopped, sighed, and closed his eyes. "She called me a coward for not killing her, hurled her pain and insults upon my already-broken heart. How could I? How could I stop that heart that my blood runs through, extinguish the light that kept me alive for centuries and still not go mad myself? Alas, the time has come for me to think of more than myself." Leone opened his eyes. "This is where you enter the picture, Detective."

"Me? You want me to kill her, don't you?" Sanford realized where the conversation was headed. "I can't do it, you think I won't chicken out a second time?"

"Together we can try," the vampire stated. "First thing you do is to fill out those papers from the FBI. After what you've seen, you will not go back to a normal lifestyle. You are too changed, too knowledgeable for that. Those people have the resources that can be used by us both. Besides, you like the writer woman." He smiled.

"Excuse me, but could you get the fuck out of my head?" He hated that. Noguchi had plucked Shana's face out of his brain. "Then, you can tell me what you will be doing?"

"I will be looking for my Angel," Leone told him.

"As I remember, she is not your angel anymore, someone else came along and picked her up." Sanford reminded him.

"He is unimportant, only her fledgling. I do not want to destroy him, but I will to stop her, if necessary," he told the detective. "I'm afraid that he and his mortal accomplices have bitten off more than they can chew. I can offer services to you that the agency can't provide. You have to help me help her. She wants death, yet can't do it herself. If that is truly what she wants, then I will give it to her. The one thing I ask of you is that if she does not want death, you let me take her somewhere safe. She'll be away from life, so no harm will come to anyone because of her. I can feed her and keep watch of her until she is well again or until I must kill her."

"Okay, you have a deal," Sanford said. "But I just want to ask, how did all this begin? Not just her, but you and others like you, how are you possible?"

The black-haired vampire simply looked at Sanford wearily and explained, "It is a long and tedious tale, Detective, parts of which I know not myself. I assure you at another time, I will tell you the things you want. The road that brought me to you is a long one, far too long to journey on this night. Besides I must feed." With that he stood up.

"Feed?" Sanford asked suspiciously.

"Yes, Detective, feed. I am a blood-drinker, never forget that, but I am not a killer. I take what I need and move to someone else, most never know they have been bitten," Leone assured him. "I must feed or I will look like this piece of charred steak for quite some time. How can I go to public places looking as this?" He smiled and he was gone.

Sanford sat there for a few moments, collecting his thoughts. Shana's face appeared in his mind again. Lying bitch that she was, he still wanted her. That would be first place he looked for Solange. He reached into his desk and pulled out a pen. It wouldn't take long to fill out the application and secrecy papers. It would take quite a while though for his nerves to settle down.

EPILOGUE

The road back home seemed longer than the road they had taken to Atlanta. Her heart was weary. Its blood pulsed with sadness and despair. Upon Shana's shoulders rested an immense gargoyle of burden. Everyone in the van slept while Mike drove. After all she'd been through the last several days, no sleep would come to her. Her fingers longed for the keyboard of her computer. Words and more words fought to erupt from her tired soul. The only healing tonic she knew, were these words. For now she had to settle for Jack Daniels.

In the back of the van two immense trunks rested side by side. Only the people in this van knew their contents. In one, a sleeping Solange hopefully healed in her rest. Kyle lay in the other, forever forsaking his Atlanta home. Black garment bags had been wrapped around them to further protect them. To watch Kyle lay Solange in the bag and then the trunk left her feeling quite chilled. It was like watching a funeral. To watch him put himself in the trunk had been even worse.

Now all rode in quiet. The sun bright overhead led them back home. In her lap, Shana held an edition of Dereck's diary. She would read all that there was of him, no matter how long it took. This particular book held the first meeting ever of Dereck and Solange. Sadly she couldn't put it down. She could almost hear his accented voice as she read.

"This very evening I stood on the balcony of someone's Malibu house, overlooking the ocean. Just one of many parties, I can't even remember whose party it was. It feels that as time drags by, they become so loathsomely boring. If not for the much needed blood, I would have no need to attend at all.

A lovely girl with long blonde hair had followed me about all evening. She came outside to try to entice me back inside. Even her beauty could not bring me from the melancholy I felt this evening. Though surrounded by so many, I longed for someone like myself to share the long night of immortality with. All of the other creatures of the night that I see night after night hold no interest to me any longer. It was then that I saw her, auburn hair flowing in the wind behind her. Tears ran down her face and blood down her dress as she ran for the ocean.

Quickly I jumped over the wooden railing and into the sand. My body was propelling me over the dunes with supernatural speed. I reached her just as she was thigh deep in the cold waves of the ocean. I grabbed her shoulders and pulled her to me. She fought me with such passion and strength, I knew she could not be young. An old vampire had surely made her, her blood sounded loudly in my head. Images of drowning and being ripped apart by creatures of the water filled her mind. I told her, "That would be no way for a creature such as us to die." I held her all the tighter.

"I can't do this anymore!" she had cried. Her voice was ridden with true despair. At one time or another all vampires feel this way. For most it passes for some it never does. My heart ached as she spoke to me. She finally gave in and rested her head upon my chest sobbing. I wrapped my arms even further around her, trying my best to soothe her.

She was so beautiful; even though she was wet, crying and covered with blood apparently not her own. Her waist slim, her breasts full and soft, and her face like a porcelain doll. I bent my head and kissed her cheeks and forehead. All the while talking to her like a child awakened in the night by frightful dreams. She clung to me all the harder.

"What is your name, beautiful one?" I asked softly.

"Solange," she told me hesitantly. "You're not going to hurt me." It had been a statement not a question. She peered at me with eyes such a blue that would only be found in the clearest sea. In her mind I saw her thoughts. She found me familiar. There was something about her that felt the same to me.

I lead her out of the water and upon the white sand. "How is it that you are so alone?" I asked her.

Solange turned her sorrow filled eyes to me and my heart was hers from that moment forward. I knew as I looked into those azure depths that I could never willingly leave her. "I've been alone for two hundreds years," she said sadly. "Two hundred years of death and loneliness."

"It does not have to be so, luv," I told her. "What of your maker? Why has he left you in such a state?"

"He is dead," she sighed. "He's been dead since the night I became a vampire." Images in her head became clear as a movie screen. In there I saw her maker and knew him as my own father in immortality. She saw my mind at that same moment. The same blood flowed in both our veins. "You knew Leone?"

"Yes, luv, and loved him as you did," I felt the tears spring from my own eyes. "He was so old and powerful. Are you sure he's dead?"

"I saw it with my own eyes, he died saving me," she cried and rested her head back on my chest. I knew this to be the heart of her suffering. I held her tight and cried with her.

"You will not be alone again, Angel luv," I told her. I promise."

Shana stopped reading. She couldn't bear to read anymore, it was just too sad. Her gaze went to the back of the van. Tears welled up in her eyes behind her dark glasses. She sat staring at the trunks, as they sped down the road to her home. She thought, I promise too, Solange. For Dereck I promise. Mike gave her a strange look as the tears made paths down her cheeks. He didn't say anything. She was glad of that.

Karen Diaz lives in Charlotte, NC, where she works as a tattoo artist. Under the name of Elmo she is a nationally known artist and stand up comedienne. Her artwork has been displayed in galleries in New York, Atlanta and all over the Southeast. She has painted portraits for many celebrities and rock bands such as L.A. Guns.

LaVergne, TN USA
23 May 2010
183562LV00004B/3/P